The Luck of the
Lonely Sea

Other Books by Patrick O'Hara:

THE RED SAILOR
GOD CAME ON FRIDAY

The Luck of the Lonely Sea

PATRICK O'HARA

DAVID McKAY COMPANY, INC.

NEW YORK

THE LUCK OF THE LONELY SEA

FIRST AMERICAN EDITION, 1966

The Luck of the
Lonely Sea

OUTSIDE it was hot and the sun was going down.

They were sitting at a table in the bar. The girl sat watching him very carefully. It was some time now since he had said anything.

'You want I get you another beer?' she asked, after a time, still carefully watching his face.

The man went on looking at the table.

She waited a little. 'I must go now,' she said, rising from the table. 'You get another drink. You will feel better.' Very quickly she put the tightly folded money into the pocket of his shirt.

'Don't worry about me,' he told her, but looking at her this time.

'Please,' she said, stopping him taking the money from his pocket. 'All this will go away.'

This time he did not say anything, and then she was gone out through the beaded doorway to the street.

The beer was warm now and he drank it off quickly then lit one of the cheap Chinese cigarettes.

'—Karl.'

He turned in his chair and saw the old man beckon to him. Then the young man, whose name was Karl Schepke, and who was tall and wide and had a sunburned face, ran the long, ragged blond hair back onto his neck and rose and crossed the floor of the bar to the counter.

'What is it?'

'These gentlemen,' Tsung said, indicating two Chinese deck sailors along the counter with a grave nod of his head. 'They have just told me that Tu Chin came ashore today with a broken leg. He was on the *Sungari*.'

Karl Schepke rubbed a hand across his stubbled jaw. 'That's one of Ling's boats.'

'You will go and see him?' the old man asked.

7

Karl Schepke looked back at him. 'Maybe.'

'One can always try. There is nothing to lose with trying.'

'Ask what they drink,' Schepke said, taking the tightly folded money from his pocket.

The two Chinese deck sailors had a beer, and Schepke had a beer along with them. The beer was freshly from the ice-box and the condensation beaded quickly on the tall glasses.

Some of the bar-girls had come in while they were talking and now the old man went out to the floor to take the orders from the tables.

'Hallo.' She was smiling.

'She's out,' Schepke said.

'I know,' the girl said, then still smiling, hitched the scarlet cheongsam about her hips and sat up onto one of the high stools. 'What you going drink with me?'

'You go ahead,' Karl Schepke told her.

'Oh, why you not drink with me?' she pouted. 'Hsiu-ju like you very much. Hsiu-ju much good-looking than Shuang-shuang.'

Karl Schepke did not say anything.

'Hey,' Hsiu-ju persisted. 'What the matter you not happy tonight? Come on. You smile, heh?'

The old man came back along the counter, his waxed moustaches drooping below his chin.

'Two beers,' Hsiu-ju told him, putting her money on the counter.

The old man brought two small Tiger beers from the ice-box and poured them smoothly into the glasses.

Schepke, not saying anything, pushed his money across the counter.

'No. I buy,' Hsiu-ju said.

The old man shrugged, smiling apologetically to Schepke. Then taking the girl's money, said: 'You seem very happy tonight, Hsiu-ju.'

'Hsiu-ju always plenty happy,' she told him with a swift uplifting of her chin. 'Only maybe I am more happy tonight because good business. Plenty American dollar. Three Matson sailors

8

come my house last night.' She was very proud about the three sailors.

The old man politely grinned his wide grin and rapidly bobbed his head in acknowledgement of this particular feat.

Then suddenly Hsiu-ju smilingly raised her glass to Schepke. '*Gottverdammmt!*'

'Sure,' Schepke said, and they drank a little of the ice-cold beer.

'I speak good German, yes?'

'You could go a long way,' Schepke said.

Hsiu-jut sat upright, tilting her head slightly, her hands on her hips, her thighs bared where the cheongsam fell away. 'Sure, sure. Hsiu-ju go plenty far, heh,' she said, smiling and very sure of herself and proud of the three sailors.

Karl Schepke was looking far into his beer.

'Oh, why you not be happy?' Hsiu-ju asked, suddenly herself again.

He lit another of the Chinese cigarettes.

Hsiu-ju sat close and put both hands around his arm. 'You come my house, heh?'

'A half-bottle,' Schepke told the old man and counted the money onto the counter.

'Where you go now?' Hsiu-ju asked, watching him.

'Upstairs.'

'You go drink yourself?'

'That way I appreciate it more.'

'No. You come with me. You have best time.' She climbed down from the high stool with a great deal of movement.

Schepke took the bottle from the old man and did not say anything.

'Please,' Hsiu-ju said, her lips wetly shiny. 'I give you everything like you never know before.'

'No thank you,' Schepke said. 'I have more than my share of everything as it is.'

She went with him toward the doorway at the back of the bar, her hands still around his arm. 'Please. Please, you stay.'

9

Schepke stopped and removed her hands from his arm. 'I told you,' he said.

She watched him pass through the beaded curtain and start upstairs. 'Humph! Goddam squareheads!' she said and turned back toward the tables.

UPSTAIRS, Karl Schepke sat on the edge of the high bed and uncorked the bottle.

Slowly, very slowly, the little man was drowning. Karl Schepke could feel the little man begin to struggle. It would take time though. But everything took time, no matter what it was. And the little man was worried now. It was beginning to swill around his chest.

Then sitting on the edge of the high bed in the darkness, Karl Schepke drank another long one from the bottle.

The window of the small square room overlooked the narrow street and from where he sat he looked directly out across the roof-tops on the other side of the street and it was dark above the roof-tops and with the moon somewhere down beyond the buildings so that the darkness of the sky was lighted by it, while the buildings remained deeply shadowed on the nearside so that the neon signs of the many bars burned very brightly in the darkness.

And then he drank another long one from the bottle, and waited. It was very dark out across the street and with the traffic very quiet as yet so that little noise carried in through the open window. Then he lit another cigarette while he waited, the match flaring briefly in the mirror of the dressing-table. And suddenly he stood up and went across to the window and pulled the paper blind down against the evening. Now it was very dark in the small square room and he lay his full length on the high bed, and waited.

It was very quiet in the darkness of the room and the sound of voices and music carried up faintly from the bar. But even in the darkness he was unable to shut everything out. And upstairs the little man was still struggling. These days it was taking the little man longer and longer to get it over with. And the bottle was almost empty now. The little man no one could win over. He did not need any one of the bright boys to help him work that out.

So he emptied the bottle and waited.

SHE saw the lights of the bar of the Hotel Aichau. It was late in the evening and she felt bad now after having been around most of the regular hotels and bars up in the city. The Hotel Aichau, standing on the Upper Coast Road, was the last place she was going to try before going home.

There were only two Europeans and the barman in the bar when she entered. As she crossed to the counter she walked so the tight low-cut cheongsam opened wide with the movement of her hips.

The barman watched her all the way, then watched her sit herself up onto one of the high stools.

'A Jack Rose,' she told him in English, her chin held high, looking past him at the glittering array of bottles and mirrors.

The two Europeans were sitting at a table against the far wall. They were talking very earnestly and had their Panama hats on the shelf under the table.

Then as she waited, the barman politely set the Jack Rose on the counter and took the two single dollar notes and rang them into the register. There was no change.

The barman went back to polishing glasses, then looked down at her. Although she was very angry she did not say anything, and the barman smiled. The barman was balding, and was tall and heavy, and he had seen all this many times before.

Suddenly the girl heard a movement over the back of the bar and she looked into the mirror on the other side of the counter.

'They are leaving now,' the barman said.

She turned and saw the two Europeans going out through the swing-doors, neither of them looking back.

'It is very quiet tonight,' the barman went on, polishing a glass, but watching her now, seeing the low-cut cheongsam and the smoothness of her skin.

She did not look at him.

'There will be nothing tonight now.' He had stopped polishing the glass and had set it with the others.

She finished the Jack Rose and stood down from the stool.

He was leaning on the counter, looking at all of her now. 'There is nothing in the Roads,' he said.

She turned quickly for the door.

'Wait—'

She stopped, turning slightly, but not looking at him.

'I have a room upstairs.'

She did not move.

'Fifteen dollars,' he said, his voice changed.

'—Thirty,' she said very quietly, still not turning, still not looking at him.

'Twenty. Nothing more.'

She did not say anything, just waited, feeling herself beginning to tremble now.

'You want another drink? You can have another drink.'

And this night it was quiet in the city.

THE old man was asleep in the narrow room at the end of the bar. It was not a loud noise, and if he had not known himself he would have passed it over and gone back to sleep. But now he was an old man and he no longer slept well in the night, and he rose and silently felt his way to the door.

He was at the far end of the counter, tall and darkly shadowed against the greyness of the far wall.

'Karl,' the old man said softly.

'I'm sorry,' Schepke said. 'I didn't want to wake you.'

'It is nothing,' the old man told him, and his eyes accustomed to the darkness of the bar, he saw the dull gleam of sweat on Schepke's chest and shoulders in the pale light filtering through the wooden shutters over the street windows.

'I couldn't sleep,' Schepke said very quietly. 'I thought maybe another drink would help.'

'I know how it is my son,' the old man said, finding his way along the narrow passage behind the counter. 'We will both have a drink. You are not the only one who finds sleep difficult these nights.' He stopped, finding the bottles and the upturned glasses. The brandy he poured for himself, setting the large Dutch gin close on the counter to where Schepke stood.

It was very quiet in the bar, and the night was quiet, and there was no sound of traffic passing now in the street.

'Go on,' urged the old man, edging the gin toward Schepke. 'It comes in this manner to all people at some time. There are few lucky ones, my son. I have known this thing more than once. True, my troubles are not as they were. But for a man to live with himself is not achieved overnight. It is such a great pity that things can never be quite as we wish, but neither can they remain the other way too long. But we have a duty to others as well as to ourselves. As with Shuang-shuang. You are her main reason for life. At this time you have begun to despise both yourself and her because of something outside of yourselves. I do not believe such a thing can ever be held against any man in the circumstances. Shuang-shuang's way of life is that she must give. It is no fault of yours that she has chosen to give to you. Take that away from her and she has nothing. Such a thing is not to be held against you. There are many more wicked things in the world than that. Think of all this that you give to her. But when the time comes, you must go. But go in such a manner you do not unfairly hurt her. At the same time let her see that it must be done. You should not have this one way too long.' He stopped talking and it was quiet again in the bar, and then he slowly sipped the brandy, feeling it go its burn-warming way into his chest.

Then: 'Come, drink, my son,' he said, and saw Schepke slowly raise the glass, not looking at him, to his mouth. He waited now until Schepke set the glass down. 'I am sorry to have talked so much,' he said. 'Forgive me.'

'No,' Schepke said quietly. 'There is nothing like that.'

'Then I think you should go back to bed now. Try to forget the thinking. Take this with you,' he said, offering the bottle of Dutch gin. 'At this time it may help to ease the way of things.'

Schepke hesitated, looking at the bottle, then took it. 'Thank you,' he said, and turned toward the doorway to the stairs.

It was very quiet now and the bar, lit only by the pale light filtering through the wooden shutters over the street windows, was gloomy and the air heavy with stale cigarette smoke and the drying of the swabbed floor. The old man felt it was now time for some light and he lit a candle from the drawer and stood a while in the quietness of the bar.

And this night it was quiet in the city.

THE old man, with the early morning Chinese newspapers spread out flat on the counter before him, looked up as she came through the beaded curtain.

'He has not been down yet?'

The old man shook his head, then watched her go quickly upstairs.

The stairway was narrow and dark and heavy with the scent of smouldering joss-sticks. The room was already hot and lit by the sun through a yellow paper blind. He lay asleep on the high bed, still wearing the crumpled cotton trousers, the long, ragged blond hair fallen across his forehead. She stood looking at him a moment, feeling her heart quicken, then she reached her hand up high behind her back and brought the zip all the way down and brought the shoulders of the green cheongsam down over her arms and rolled it quickly off over her hips to the floor.

He came instantly awake with the sudden movement of the bed under her weight, and started to sit up and she put both arms around his neck, holding him to her.

'Karl. Please, Karl.'

He put his arm up between them and pushed her away and sat up, cupping his hand over his eyes against the brilliant light of the sun through the yellow paper blind.

'Please, Karl,' she said again, very softly, her mouth against his cheek.

He took her hands from him and held them. He was still waking and the night was still with him. Everything revolved sluggishly inside of his head and he could feel her breasts warm and softly touching his back.

'Karl,' she said, her mouth still against his cheek.

'The time,' he said. 'What time is it?'

'It is early yet. Come back to bed.'

'What time is it?' he asked again.

'You must go somewhere?' she asked.

'I have to see a man. In the city.' He had not looked at her yet.

'It is something important?'

'Maybe I will go to work,' he said, then reached the crumpled packet of Chinese cigarettes from the floor and lit one. With the smoke came the waxy taste of the match. It had been a long night and now it was a bad morning.

'You go to see him later. Please.'

This time when the bed moved he stood up.

'Please,' she said, pleading.

'I told you I have to go,' he said, running his hair back onto his neck and taking his shirt from the corner of the dressing-table mirror.

'Karl. Listen to me. Please,' she said. 'I love you.'

He went on buttoning his shirt.

She swung her legs over the side of the high bed and her foot touched one of the bottles. Clasping her hands between her thighs, she watched him tuck the shirt inside the crumpled cotton trousers.

'I have to go now,' he said, when he was ready.

'No,' she said, standing up close to him, reaching her arms around his neck and bringing herself to her toes. 'Tell me you love me. Tell me you love me just a little.' She was looking at him with wide, shining eyes that hinted tears.

'You know,' he told her.

She put her head against his chest. 'Tell me,' she said, her voice a whisper.

'I love you,' he told her.

'Hold me tight.'

He held her tightly.

'You tell me truly?'

He looked down at her head.

'You really love me?' she questioned.

'I told you,' he said.

She lifted her face. 'Kiss me.'

He touched his mouth lightly to her forehead.

'My mouth. Kiss my mouth.'

He kissed her mouth and she held her arms tightly around his neck so that he had to hold her away to breathe.

'Come back to bed. Please.'

'I have to see this man,' he told her.

'Please.'

'I told him this morning,' he said.

'True?' she asked, running her fingers lightly along his shoulders.

He nodded without saying anything.

'All right,' she said. 'I believe you.'

'When I get back,' he said from the doorway.

16

'Kiss me again.'

He kissed her and left her standing in the doorway, smooth and round and wide-hipped, and with the room lit by the sun through a yellow paper blind.

THE offices of the Lu Jen Coastwise Trading Company were down in the city by the park. The park was very green and had many fine trees, and a cathedral, and all along the park the buildings stood up very clean and white in the hard summer sunlight. And through the trees Karl Schepke could see the sunlight far out on the blue ocean. The Roads were very quiet and the breeze came in very gently and cleanly smelling of the blue ocean.

He crossed the busy, black-oiled roadway and climbed the stairs. There were two white-suited clerks in the front office.

'Mr. Ling,' he said.

'You have an appointment?' the one wearing the spectacles asked.

'Tell him Schepke is outside.'

'Oh,' the boy said, smiling. He was a very smart boy with oiled-down hair.

'You just tell him, that's all you do,' Schepke said.

The boy went on smiling. 'I am sorry,' he said, shrugging lightly, 'but if you do not have an—'

'You heard me,' Schepke said, looming suddenly across the desk.

The smile went very quickly.

'All right,' Schepke said and started for the door at the rear of the office.

'No,' the boy said, quickly onto his feet and getting between Schepke and the door. '—I will tell Mr. Ling. Please wait.'

The other clerk sat at his desk and looked at the wall. The sunlight came in very brightly through the tall window. From up there Karl Schepke could see the flat blue ocean far out beyond the Roads.

'Mr. Schepke,' Mr. Ling said from the doorway to his office. Mr. Ling was short and balding and smooth-faced.

Schepke followed him into the office. Inside it was cool and quiet and the sunlight did not come in through the window.

'Well what is it I can do for you?' Mr. Ling asked, sitting into the big chair behind his desk.

'I heard Tu Chin broke a leg,' Schepke said.

'Then you heard correctly, Mr. Schepke.'

'You told me any time you wanted somebody.'

Mr. Ling smiled. 'I thought you were working out at the rubber factory.'

'That was a long time ago.'

Mr. Ling sat looking at him across the desk. 'You seem to have had a bad night.'

'All the nights are bad,' Schepke said, helping himself to the cigarettes on the desk.

'So you heard about Tu Chin,' Mr. Ling said lightly.

'You said the next time you wanted somebody,' Schepke again reminded him.

Mr. Ling looked disappointed. 'I am afraid I must also keep others in mind,' he said.

'Who?' Schepke said, watching his face very carefully.

'Unfortunately, I have just engaged Hsu Yung-chien. Just this morning.'

'That was him ran the *Tsingtao* on Hopei Reef,' Schepke said, still carefully watching Mr. Ling.

Mr. Ling shrugged. '—But yourself,' he said, cautiously.

'You know all that,' Schepke said, the bitterness showing in his voice. 'That was three years ago. The *Tsingtao* was last winter.'

Mr. Ling spread his hands palm uppermost before him. 'I am sorry,' he said. '—Perhaps next time.'

Schepke grabbed him suddenly by the lapels of his suit and lifted him bodily from the big chair. 'You said this time! *This* time! You hear me?'

'Let me go!' Mr. Ling shouted.

Schepke rammed him hard against the wall, at the same time hearing the office door flung open.

'The police!' Mr. Ling shouted.

Schepke rammed him hard against the wall again, then dropped him to the floor, not looking at him and going quickly out through the front office, past the clerks, the spectacled one talking fast into the telephone.

Outside on the street, he turned back along the roadway by the park and after a little way, turned into the bar of the Sun Hat Restaurant. It was a very smart bar, big and air-cooled, with most of the people inside drinking quietly before going in to lunch.

'Hey you! A big Dutchman!' he called to the barman.

'I say. Do you mind?' the man on his right said, moving his lady's glass from before Schepke.

'You!' Schepke called to the barman, at the same time ignoring the man's remark.

'Isn't that simply horrid, Charles?' the lady on the right with the flower-decked hat, said.

'Shut your mouth,' Schepke told her.

The lady's eyes widened with disbelief, while at the same time Charles discreetly coughed. Charles had the Englishman's long, stiff upper-lip.

Schepke stood away from the counter, big and tall and looming.

Charles looked to his lady.

'What about that Dutchman?' Schepke called to the barman.

The barman looked all the way through him, then Schepke caught his white jacket and lifted him half across the counter. 'What do you think I am?' he shouted into his face.

'Manager say—'

Schepke threw him suddenly and he hit the wall of glass shelves and mirrors, bringing down a shower of bottles and glassware.

The lady with the flower-decked hat screamed. Then Charles started to say something and Schepke hit him full on the mouth.

Charles was extremely surprised with the suddenness of every-thing. Then Schepke stepped over him toward the swing-doors and met the policemen following Mr. Ling's spectacled clerk. The first of them came through the doors with his truncheon drawn and Schepke ducked the swing and grabbed him by the front of his tunic and he went all the way across the bar and hit the wall of glass shelves and mirrors. Now the bar was filled with shouts and screams and all the lights along the back of the bar had gone out. The next three policemen came together and Schepke went down along with two of them in a welter of flying truncheons.

There was still plenty of shouting and people running around and the Englishman was on his back with his lady leaning over him holding her hat to her head with both hands and saying: 'Charles! Charles! Oh, my poor darling, Charles!'

And all the while Karl Schepke lay face-down by the doors on the blood-soaked carpet.

THE driver saw him come up from the jetty and stand looking along the front.

'You want to go shoreside, sir?' he called, drawing into the kerb.

'I might,' the man told him. 'I'm looking for somebody.'

'This is a big place,' the driver told him, grinning.

'I'm looking for a German sailor,' the man told him. 'His name is Schepke. Karl Schepke. He was on the beach.'

The driver shook his head. 'Maybe Ho You knows him. Ho You knows most sailors ever on the beach.'

'All right then,' the man said. 'Take me to Ho You.'

The roads were very busy along the front and the taxi moved slowly in the traffic. It was oppressively hot now in the after-noon and the man sat silently in the back of the slowly moving taxi and watched the traffic go past and the park was very green and the cathedral so white in the hard sunlight.

Ho You's bar was on the dock. When he came in through the open doorway he heard the talking of the people at the tables falter. On the epaulettes of the old-fashioned uniform he wore were the gold bars of a German Sea Kapitän. What caused the people to stare was not the fact that he was a German Sea Kapitän, but there was a certain strangeness about him, in his grey sunken face, in his manner, part of him; and it was not an easy thing to place this strangeness, and it was in all of him, even in the taut way he held himself as he walked.

Ho You watched him approach the counter, thinking he had never seen one in whom death walked so boldly. Then he stopped at the counter and leaned both arms carefully on the polished wood. Ho You felt the eyes go all the way through him, eyes that were sunk deeply in the face in the shadow of the gold-embroidered cap.

'Yes, Captain?'

'A beer,' the Kapitän told him in English.

Ho You brought a bottle from the ice-box and poured the cold, pale beer into a tall glass.

'I hear you know many people along the front.'

'Some,' Ho You answered.

'You know a German on the beach called Schepke? Karl Schepke.'

Ho You carefully considered it for a moment, then looked beyond the Kapitän. 'Yu Sung.'

A young barefoot Chinese rose from a table on the floor and came across to them. Ho You spoke to him, the Chinese glancing curiously at the Kapitän before replying.

'What does he say?'

'He says that if it is the blond one of the fire you seek then he believes he works at the Wang Teh rubber factory and lives at the bar of Old Tsung.'

'He's the one,' the Kapitän said. 'How do I find this place?'

'It is on the east side. Some way from the front. Tell taxi to take you to the Gateway Bar.'

'Thank you,' the Kapitän said, then took his change from the counter and gave the barefoot Chinese two dollars.

Standing at the counter, they watched him walk tautly out into the hard afternoon sunlight, and when he had gone, Ho You moved the untouched beer along the counter. Yu Sung looked at it then at Ho You, then turned back to his table.

It was early yet and the old man was eating when the Kapitän came in through the beaded doorway.

'Mr. Tsung?' the Kapitän asked in English.

The old man politely set his bowl aside and nodded.

'I came to see Herr Schepke.'

'But I am afraid this is not possible,' the old man said.

'I was told he was here.'

'It was something that happened this morning,' explained the old man. 'Now he is in jail. This time there is not even bail.'

'Would they consider allowing me to see him?'

'One cannot be certain as to what our police will allow and to what they will not allow. But they would not allow me to see him. However, with such an impressive uniform as yours, perhaps. They have him at the Central Police Station.'

'My thanks.'

'One moment.'

The Kapitän stopped in the doorway.

'You have come to help?'

'If that is possible,' the Kapitän answered him.

'I have had this feeling that the time was not far off,' the old man said, smiling. 'It is such a great pity that so early in life a little rain must fall.'

22

THE Kapitän found the Enquiry Room at the end of a long, yellow distempered corridor. Inside were two male typists and the Duty Inspector.

'You wish to see someone?' the Inspector asked.

'I believe you have a Karl Schepke in detention. I wish to know what might be done to free him.'

The Inspector smiled. 'I am afraid I do not think that possible,' he said.

'It is very important.'

'Then perhaps you should see the Superintendent,' the Inspector said, and crossed to a door at the far side of the room and knocked, and went inside.

The Kapitän waited, looking around the high room. The room was bare of any decoration except for rows of Wanted circulars pasted the length of one wall. The slightly empty-looking faces were mostly those of Malays and Chinese wanted for crimes ranging from bag-snatching to hatchet murder.

'Mr. Cheng will see you now,' the Inspector said from the doorway at the far side of the room.

Mr. Cheng was a small man with such a paunch that as he sat behind the heavy desk it appeared to rest on his knees.

'Please sit down, ah—' he paused, smiling.

'Kapitän Otto Emmermann,' the Kapitän told him.

'Well, Captain Emmermann, my Inspector informs me that you wish to talk with someone about Mr. Schepke.'

'I came a long way to see him. May I ask how long he is likely to be here?'

Mr. Cheng smiled. 'Tomorrow morning he goes to court. Then, undoubtedly, he will be going out to Changi. You know, Captain, it isn't the first time Mr. Schepke has been in jail.'

'And this time?'

'He has a fine knack of making trouble on a grand scale. You might say he is a sort of one-man riot-squad. A most successful one at that. A man of great determination and thoroughness is our Mr. Schepke. This time I think six months, if he is lucky.'

'I see,' the Kapitän said disappointedly.

'You would care to smoke?' Mr. Cheng asked, offering his cigar-box.

'Thank you. But not those.'

Mr. Cheng drew deeply on his cigar. 'May I ask why Mr. Schepke interests you so much?' he asked.

'I want him as First Officer,' Emmermann told him.

Mr. Cheng leaned his elbows forward onto the desk. 'I suppose you have heard about his previous trouble?'

'I know about the *Ilse Backenkölher* if that is what you mean. But as you know, every story has two sides. I happen to know Schepke extremely well.'

'And you wish to engage him as your First Officer?' Mr. Cheng asked, showing his interest now.

'If it is at all possible,' Emmermann answered him.

'When does your ship sail?'

'Tomorrow,' Emmermann told him. 'Probably late afternoon.'

Mr. Cheng sat back into the chair again, drawing deeply on his cigar.

'You know, this is interesting indeed, Captain,' he said, finally. 'I now begin to see the possibility of ridding myself of Mr. Schepke for some time to come.' He sat forward again, pressing one of the buttons on the intercommunication on his desk. 'Yes, Captain. Who knows but that we may very well arrive at a satisfactory arrangement yet.'

MOVING his chair to the far side of the room, behind the door, Emmermann took a leather cigar-case from the breast pocket of his high-collared tunic and carefully lit a thin black cheroot.

Schepke came in with the Inspector, his face drawn and pale beneath the dark sunburn, a large taped-down gauze pad across the left side of his forehead.

Emmermann followed him carefully with his eyes. It was three years since the loss of the *Ilse Backenkölher*. Schepke had not changed very much. No, Emmermann thought, maybe the changes are inside. Sometimes the greatest changes were those that occurred inside a man. Physically, men like Schepke never changed much whatever they went through.

Now Schepke stood at the desk with his back to Emmermann.

'How is the head?' Mr. Cheng asked.

'All right,' Schepke said.

'I am just wondering what I am going to do about you,' Mr. Cheng said, sitting back in his chair. 'This time you could go to jail for a long time. You know that.'

Schepke looked back at him but did not say anything.

'However,' Mr. Cheng went on, 'perhaps this time I have thought of something that may do us both some good.'

Now Schepke was suddenly curious.

'Ah,' Mr. Cheng said, smiling. 'I thought that might interest you. Now,' he said, leaning forward onto the desk, 'how would the prospect of a long voyage appeal to you?'

Schepke went on looking at him.

'Yes, or no?'

'I don't know what you mean,' Schepke said.

Mr. Cheng looked past him. 'Captain.'

Schepke turned and saw Emmermann for the first time. 'Good Christ!' he said. 'You! What are you doing here?'

'It's been a long time,' Emmermann said, joining them.

'You've been ill,' Schepke said, still speaking English.

'That's of no importance. What about you?'

'I'm all right.'

'Do you want to ship out?' Emmermann asked, watching his face.

Schepke glanced at Mr. Cheng.

'The Captain expects an answer,' Mr. Cheng told him. 'It is either that or Changi.'

'I lost my First Officer at Colombo,' Emmermann said. 'I sailed short-handed to keep it open for you.'

'Is there trouble on board?'

'Not exactly,' Emmermann said. 'But I want somebody I know.'

Schepke glanced at the badge on Emmermann's cap. 'That's Oesten-Liebe, isn't it?' he said.

'Much can happen in four years,' Emmermann replied, smiling thinly.

'You don't have to explain that to me.'

'Well?' Mr. Cheng said, leaning his elbows forward onto the desk.

Schepke rubbed a hand across the stubble on his jaw. 'It's all right with me,' he said. 'How do I get out of here?'

Mr. Cheng smiled. 'Now you do me a greater service than yourself,' he said.

'And the Limey?' Schepke asked.

'I will tell him we shot you at sunrise. That would please any Englishman,' Mr. Cheng said, smiling. 'Inspector. You better go with them. Take a car. All right, Captain?'

'Many thanks indeed,' Emmermann said, stiffly inclining his head.

'In the circumstances it has been a pleasure to have done business. And, Schepke,' Mr. Cheng went on. 'Should you be unfortunate enough to find yourself on the beach again, make certain it is someone else's beach. Understand?'

THE old man was wiping down the tables when they came in.

'Is she upstairs?' Schepke asked.

'She left a little while after you this morning. I do not think she knows anything about this.' And he glanced again at the Inspector. 'Everything is well?' he asked.

'I came back to pack.'

The old man watched them go on upstairs.

It was late in the afternoon /now and the sunlight no longer came in through the window. The Inspector sat on the edge of the dressing-table while Schepke brought a bamboo and reed-made suitcase from under the bed then went to the wardrobe.

'What sort of ship is she?' he asked, bringing the few clothes to the bed.

'Old,' Emmermann said, turning away from the open window. 'She's old and a coal-burner.'

Schepke looked at him across the room.

'Four years is a long time,' Emmermann said.

'Where are we bound?'

'Shanghai.'

Schepke turned back to the bed and opened the suitcase. Inside was a carefully folded khaki uniform and a white, high-peaked cap.

'You better put that on,' Emmermann told him. 'It will seem less odd when you go on board.'

Schepke laid the uniform out onto the bed. The cloth was mildewed and the Kapitän's gold bars on the epaulettes were green and silvered with dampness.

'What about these?' he asked, indicating the bars.

'Leave them,' Emmermann said.

Schepke turned back to the suitcase and brought out a large linen-backed envelope, and Emmermann and the Inspector watched him look carefully through the contents before returning everything to the suitcase.

Schepke saw them and smiled. 'At least I never was stateless,' he said.

'Who was the girl you talked with the old man about?' Emmermann casually asked.

'Just a girl,' Schepke said, and began to dress.

When they came downstairs the old man was waiting for them. 'You have time for a last drink?' he asked.

Schepke glanced at Emmermann, and he nodded.

'And you, Inspector?'

'I see no reason why not,' the Inspector said, smiling.

'Gin?' the old man asked. They nodded, and the old man poured their drinks.

Then: 'May Tien How watch over you, my son,' he said, raising his glass to Schepke.

They all drank, and then Schepke saw the old man was looking past him across the bar. She was watching them from just inside the doorway, a little bewildered by this sudden appearance of uniforms.

Then as she came toward them Schepke set his glass on the counter.

'You—you are leaving?' she said very quietly, her voice catching in her throat.

'I'm going back to sea,' he said simply. And he saw her lip begin to tremble, and he wished he had not stopped now for the drink; wished he had gone on out and had not seen her. 'It's only for a time,' he said, feeling awkward with the company.

'You are going a long way?' she asked, her voice sounding very small.

'Only Shanghai,' he told her.

'—No,' she said, her voice changing. 'You stay with me. You not go to Shanghai.'

'I'll be back,' he said. 'You see.'

She moved her head very slowly, her mouth tightening and the tears beginning to show in her eyes.

'I'll come back,' he said looking at her, avoiding her eyes.

Emmermann and the Inspector stood silently against the counter. Then the Inspector saw Emmermann glance at the clock on the far wall.

Schepke saw Emmermann, finished his drink, say something to the old man, then walk to the doorway.

'I have to go now,' he said to the girl, not looking at her, then picking up his suitcase. Then looking at her: 'Do you want to come down to the front?'

She moved her head very slowly, not saying anything.

He glanced from Emmermann to the old man and saw him silently motion with his head toward the doorway.

Then the Inspector cleared his throat and set his glass on the counter.

'Good night,' he said to the old man, and turned and walked past Schepke and the girl without looking at them. And Emmermann followed him on out to the car.

Schepke looked at the girl and suddenly she broke down and put her head against his chest.

'It won't be for long,' he said. 'Don't cry.'

'I never see you again. You will never come back,' she said against his chest.

He lifted her face. The tears ran wetly down her cheeks. She was crying silently now. Then he stooped and kissed her lightly on the forehead, then nodding to the old man, he walked out to the doorway.

'Goodbye, Shuang-shuang,' he said from the doorway.

She did not say anything, and she did not look at him.

They were both in the car when he came out. When he climbed in the Inspector started the motor and pulled out into the early evening traffic. The sun had gone now but the afterglow was still in the sky in the west and the clear tropical darkness was coming swiftly in off the vast South China Sea. Lights had come on in the shops and tea-houses, and in the windows of the restaurants and bars, and nearer the front, neon lights climbed colourfully up the tall buildings overlooking the Roads.

'She took it very badly,' Emmermann said after a time.

'She was a good girl,' Schepke said. 'There was nothing else.'

'And on her part?'

'It had got too complicated. I suppose they all get things complicated in the end. Even a whore.'

'All women threaten complications,' Emmermann said. 'A stumbling-block in the way of destiny.'

'Your own?' Schepke asked.

'I'm afraid not,' Emmermann said, smiling thinly. 'But he was obviously somebody who knew what he was talking about.'

They rode the rest of the way down to the front in silence,

Schepke looking out from the side window and feeling strange in the uniform again after such a long time.

The park was quiet and empty when they passed it and the trees stood out in dark shadowy masses against the glow of street lights on the west side where the road swung away toward the uptown godowns and warehouses.

When the Inspector stopped the car they said goodbye to him and went down the long flight of concrete steps to the hire boat jetty. The Inspector had been very polite and had shaken hands with them and had wished them a good voyage, and now as they stood on the jetty looking out across the Roads the sky was cool and clear and with stars faintly showing, high up, and in tight masses. The water was flat and reflecting the darkening sky and below the steps were the hire motor boats and sampans with carbide lamps hung under their canopies and the bright white flame reflecting on the water wrinkled by their closely-packed hulls.

'There she is.'

Schepke saw her lying way out in the Roads beyond the Outer Shoal Beacon, almost on the Port Limits. She was not quite so large as he had expected, but was low in the water and squat and blunt-bowed. A long yellowish haze of smoke hung between her and the shore and made the outline of her upper deck difficult to gauge.

'What's she called?' Schepke asked, lapsing for the first time into German.

'*Gertrud Lüth*. We're out from Wilhelmshafen with grain and heavy machinery.'

'She's old, all right,' Schepke said.

'And her heart's almost gone. Come on.'

They were standing now in the cockpit of the motor boat, Schepke leaning both arms on the brass rail along the after end of the canopy, feeling the warm breeze set up by the way of the boat now they were clear of the wall. Away to the south-east a heavy black mass of cloud sat low on the horizon, blanketing out the slow-climbing moon. A fast Custom launch passed ahead of them and when their bows hit her wash into the air, even the ocean was hot. The air, too, was heavy and smelling of the ocean and drying weed, and with it, was the acrid, damp-burning smell of the fires of the *Gertrud Lüth*.

Schepke lit a cigarette and watched her take shape. Her bows were straight and blunt and she was wide-bellied and with a high, old-fashioned counter stern. Then suddenly her deck-lights came on and he saw her heavy deck-cargo of yellow-painted machinery.

'She's well down.'

'Yes,' Emmermann said, neither of them looking at the other.

They were passing the Outer Shoal Beacon now and Schepke saw she had a wide-winged bridge, wooden-slatted around forward and wings, and with a row of narrow windows. All her superstructure was amidships, giving her a solid, almost top-heavy appearance. High on the fantail was a single, lighted deck-house, and her masts, like the funnel, stood up vertical and bare against the night. The funnel appeared to be painted a dark blue and was salt-encrusted and with a black Germanic cross high up on a rust-streaked white band. Karl Schepke, seeing all of her now, experienced a sudden strange sense of foreboding. A vast, uneasy air of doom seemed to hang over her. He had felt something very close to it when seeing Emmermann for the first time back at the police station.

'Something wrong?'

Schepke glanced at him in the pale glow of the cockpit light. 'I don't know,' he said.

'Perhaps you've been ashore too long.'

Schepke looked back out across the bows.

The Chinese boatman raised his head above the end of the canopy, and standing, moving with the slight movement of the boat, his hand on the throttle, stared silently ahead at the darkly-shadowed ship.

'The ladder is on the starboard side,' Emmermann told him in English.

The boatman never looked at him but sat back at the wheel to watch her through the windscreen.

It was dark now. It had gotten dark very quickly and the

moon was still hidden. They were close in, and even with her so low in the water, the dark walls loomed above them. The warm night air was thick with the fumes of her fires and as they passed around under her stern Schepke glanced overhead and saw her name in white, rust-eaten letters: GERTRUD LÜTH—HAMBURG. As they started up the long ladder Schepke was actually conscious of the uneasy feeling growing in the pit of his stomach, and looking below him, he could see the motor boat now pulling ahead into the darkness beyond the squat bows. They stepped into the alleyway under the boatdeck just aft of the overhanging wing of the bridge. Away to the south-east the ocean was dark and hidden under the great mass of black cloud. Beneath them the deck vibrated with the steady hum of machinery and the warm night air hung heavily with the choky smell of oil and grease. And suddenly a loud burst of hammering broke the quietness of the evening and carried out across the flat black ocean from the fantail. From either end of the alleyway he could see the wells laden with yellow-painted earth-movers and bull-dozers, all thickly greased and reflecting dully under the pale glow of deck-lights and scoop-shaped floods on the derrick plat-forms up near the mastheads.

'This way.'

Schepke took a last look along the alleyway then followed Emmermann in through the screen door to the starboard passage then forward to the midship stairway to the accommodation deck up aft and below the bridge. The air was close and heavy with the shipboard smell of a badly ventilated vessel in tropical waters.

'Evening, Herr Kapitän.'

Schepke stopped behind Emmermann on the stairway.

'Good evening, Dorsch. How is everything?'

'Fine, Kapitän.'

Emmermann turned now to Schepke. 'This is Second Engineer Dorsch,' he said.

Schepke nodded. Dorsch wiped some grease from the back of his hand and stared curiously from the bars on Schepke's epaul-ettes to the taped-down gauze pad on his forehead. Dorsch was bareheaded and had a long narrow face and thinning fair hair.

'This is the new First Officer,' Emmermann told him. 'Schepke has been out here for some time.'

'Pleased to meet you,' Dorsch said.

'Are they still in the messroom?' Emmermann asked him.

'Most of them.'

'Then I think we better go meet them.'

Dorsch watched them go past then went on down the stairway. They were sitting talking over coffee when they entered. Emmermann put his cap under his arm and crossed to the end of the table, everyone looking from him to Schepke as he set his suitcase against the bulkhead and hung his cap just inside the doorway.

'I thought you would like to meet our new First Officer,' Emmermann said, finally. 'Herr Schepke takes over duties as from tonight. Any questions?'

No one said anything, then the broad, heavy-featured one stood up and backed his chair away.

'Yes, Müller?'

Müller went on past them and out into the passage without looking at anyone.

'Good to have you on board, Herr Schepke.' He was wearing a suit of clean white overalls and he was built large and solid.

'Thank you,' Schepke said, taking the offered hand.

'This is Chief Engineer Hechler,' Emmermann said, then turned to the others. 'This is Third Officer Wilamowitz. This, Radio Officer Altmeyer. And Third Engineer Frauenheim.'

'Please sit down,' Hechler said.

'Go ahead,' Emmermann said. 'You'll have to excuse me now. I'll see you later. Hechler, you show him to Rösing's cabin.'

Hechler nodded.

'There's no hurry about anything tomorow,' Emmermann said, talking now to Schepke. 'Take time and have a good look around. Müller will take her alongside the coaling-berth.'

They watched him go out, his cap under his arm and carrying himself very tautly. And when he had gone, and the Chinese mess boy had brought fresh coffee, Frauenheim, with a slight nod, rose and left.

'Coffee?' Hechler asked.

'Thank you,' Schepke said, glancing around the messroom. The deckhead was low and panelled, and the bulkheads panelled with the same age-and-smoke-darkened oak, and even with all the lights burning the room remained dark and gloomy. And Schepke remembered all the inside of the ship was panelled with the same darkened oak, all the way from the starboard inboard passage upward.

'You have that feeling as well?' Hechler asked, watching him.

'What do you mean?'

'Like being in your own coffin with the lid down.'

'That's not such a bad way to put it,' Schepke agreed.

Wilamowitz was watching them from across the table. Wilamowitz had a grave, nervous face and looked to be in his early thirties.

'You've been out here long?' he asked suddenly.

Schepke looked across the table at him. 'About three years,' he said, indifferently.

Wilamowitz glanced at Schepke's cap with its giant spread eagle badge green and silvered with dampness. 'Isn't that the Backenkölher Line?'

'That's right,' Schepke told him.

'And you were Kapitän?'

Schepke looked at him across the table but did not say anything.

'There's a big difference between this and the Backenkölher Line,' Wilamowitz said.

'—I'll show you your cabin now if you want,' Hechler said.

'Thank you,' Schepke said, rising. 'Good night, Herr Wilamowitz. Altmeyer.'

'Good night,' Altmeyer said, smiling.

The cabin was the same darkly panelled oak and the only furniture was an old-fashioned writing-desk and a wardrobe with a heavy, sun-faded mirror set into its door. In the after outboard corner, opposite the bunk, was a porcelain wash-basin set into the angle of the bulkheads. The cabin air was stale and musty and Hechler, watching him, nodded toward the ventilating channel on the deckhead. 'They hadn't heard about air-conditioning when they built this one.'

Schepke smiled, looking out at the lighted boatdeck from the open scuttle. The sun-bleached decking shone under the lighting and he noticed the blistered and flaking paintwork of Number One lifeboat.

'I take it Müller is Second Officer.'

'That's right,' Hechler said. 'Personally I don't care for him. He's made a lot of trouble one way and another since coming on board.'

'How long has he been with you?'

'Just over a year.'

'And you?'

'I came with Emmermann. Wilamowitz was last to join. He's been with us the last three trips.'

'You don't seem to have a very high opinion of them.'

'I don't,' Hechler said from the doorway. 'But I'll leave you to form your own. If you want anything get hold of Kuang. He's the mess boy.'

'Thank you.'

'Not at all. Good night.'

SCHEPKE was wakened by the heavy vibrating rumble of the cables as the anchors came home. The cabin was very brightly lit by the reflection of the sun through the open scuttle from the sun-bleached decking. The air was cooler now, and before washing, he carefully removed the taped-down pad from his forehead. The long jagged cut was darkly bruised and held together by a neat row of black cat-gut stitching. Then as he dressed the whole ship shook and rattled with the violent pounding of the engines as they gathered way astern, the bows swinging slowly shoreward. From the scuttle, and beyond the bows of Number One lifeboat, he could see the water blindingly bright from the sunlight on it, and the buildings all along the front showed white and coolly-shadowed where the sun did not yet reach. Above the roof-tops the trees showed very green and fresh-looking, and the air from the ocean smelled clean and of the early morning.

He came out from the starboard alleyway onto the forward well as the engines were rung ahead. The air was cool but there was no breeze and the sea-birds were working the water close to the shore. They were headed in now, the Outer Shoal Beacon well away to port and the city spread all out on the starboard side. The city was quiet yet and there was very little traffic moving on the front. He stopped and looked carefully at the deck-cargo. Everything on the forward well was moored down around Number One and Two hatches, a bulldozer either side of the deck just forward of the bridge, then two high-cabined earth-movers, one either side and abaft the foremast, then finally another of the giant earth-movers athwartships below the forepeak. Everything was moored down by chains stoppered to massive eye-bolts bedded into the deck below the bulwarks. Then around and above each of the machines was a network of steel hawsers lashed to deck-cleats and bitts. Then as he stood looking around him noting everything as it was he realized that he had never before seen a ship so grossly overloaded. Everything about her was old and run-down, and she stood up gaunt and gloomy-looking in the hard early morning sunlight.

He was standing below the forepeak now as she slid slowly through the water, the city slipping silently past on the starboard side. Glancing aft, he saw Emmermann and Müller along with the quartermaster and lascar telegraphsman through the open windows of the bridge. Above him on the forepeak Wilamowitz and Dorsch were standing with the lascar cable-party, long trailers of steam drifting across the guard-rails from the capstan valves, and far out on the ocean the water was very blue and close to the sky.

'Good morning, Herr Schepke.'

He glanced up and saw Wilamowitz. 'How are you?'

36

'Fine. Just fine,' Wilamowitz said.

Dorsch, leaning on the rails, nodded. 'What do you think of her in daylight?' he said down into the well.

'They must have built her a long time ago,' Schepke admitted.

'Before even the sailing ships,' Dorsch said, grinning.

Schepke smiled with him, then nodded toward the lascar seamen. 'How many of them are on board?' he asked.

'All except us and the quartermasters,' Wilamowitz said, then spat out across the rails. 'Pigs! That's what they are, Herr Schepke. Pigs!'

'Oh, they get the job done,' Dorsch said, still leaning on the rails. 'Besides, they're less expensive than a home crew.'

The ship was swinging around now, tightly to starboard. Looking shoreward, Schepke saw the high steel framework and conveyor belts of the coaling-wharf. They were going to come in on the port side. They were still swinging, the berthing party strung out along the wharf. They came in slowly, the first of the lines snaking out toward the forepeak. Then Schepke suddenly saw the Chinese berthing master appear some way up the wharf furiously waving a pair of red hand-flags and shouting at the Chinese already hauling in on the manilas.

'What the hell's wrong now?' Wilamowitz asked.

'What is it?' Müller shouted from the bridge in English.

'No coal! Everything cancel!' shouted the berthing master through his hands as he ran toward them. 'Finish! *Kaput!*'

Wilamowitz immediately stopped the manila from being paid out any further, the berthing party standing dumbly with the line and the manila almost in the dock.

The gap was closing fast as the ship caught in the flood surging in under the pilings.

'Keep it going!' Schepke yelled at Dorsch and the lascars.

The ship ground against the pilings of the wharf, the catamarans groaning under the vast pressure exerted between the pilings and the black, rusted hull. Then one of them broke with an exploding of timbers that echoed all along the dock and front.

'What the hell are you doing?' Emmermann shouted ashore.

'No coal! Finish! *Kaput!*' shouted the berthing master.

'Go to hell!' Emmermann told him. 'Get those manilas on! Fast!'

The berthing master looked helplessly around him, then began shouting at the berthing party to get the manilas in.

Schepke gave the order to Dorsch to winch in as the bows began their swing away under the impact, the flood still holding her some.

They came in slowly this time, Wilamowitz still flustered with the rapidity of everything.

'What does he mean, cancelled?' Schepke said, looking to Dorsch.

Dorsch shrugged. 'All I know is we radioed the order to the agents three days ago. But there's always trouble of some kind.'

Emmermann was first ashore. They waited on the forepeak and saw him go on up the wharf toward the offices on the dock.

'Come on,' Dorsch said. 'We might as well have some coffee. This looks as though it's going to be another long wait.'

Müller and Frauenheim were already in the messroom when they came in. Frauenheim was a little, dried-up man with a curious white face.

'What was all that about, Franz?' Wilamowitz asked.

Müller went on stirring his coffee.

Wilamowitz took the chair alongside of him. 'You think the old man will be long, Franz?' he asked, not so sure of himself this time.

Again Müller ignored him. Then without moving his head he looked across the table at Schepke. 'Somebody better pour the First Officer's coffee. He's waiting.'

Schepke looked evenly back into the heavy, beard-stubbled face, but did not say anything.

'I hear you were with the Backenkölher Line,' Müller went on, staring at Schepke with small, wide-apart eyes.

Schepke glanced along the table. Wilamowitz had his chin down, staring into his coffee.

'If you've got something on your mind why don't you come right out with it?' he said across the table.

Müller drew deeply on his cigarette, then smiled and looked away.

The silence was heavy and uncomfortable. But now Karl Schepke quietly drank his coffee, thinking. So this is the one, he was thinking. There's always got to be the one. But Hechler. I guess Hechler's the one here you count on, old turtle-head. This Wilamowitz only fills the uniform. There's always one you can't count on for anything. But just you watch the big one, old turtle-head. This big one is the one, he was thinking.

'Well what do we do now, buy firewood?' Müller was talking toward the doorway.

Hechler ignored him, then took his chair at the table.

'What happens now?' Schepke asked.

'Maybe somebody should tell our First Officer he's with Oesten-Liebe.' Müller had gotten to his feet.

'Emmermann will have to go and argue with the agents when he gets back,' Hechler said. 'There's always something.'

'You've still got time to change your mind,' Müller said as he went out.

'Take no notice,' Hechler said.

Just then Altmeyer came in. He was in his early twenties and wore his hair cropped short.

'What are you so happy about?' Hechler asked. 'You won't get ashore.'

'Who wants to go ashore here?' the boy asked. 'I'll wait for Shanghai.'

'Listen to him,' Hechler said. 'Our boy's a budding Communist.'

'Don't listen to him, Herr Schepke. They wouldn't let him ashore in Shanghai, anyway.'

'Balls,' Hechler said. 'I just don't want to take anything home with me.'

'—Hechler!' It was Emmermann. 'You better come ashore with me. Bring your coal account books.'

'They really cancelled the order?' Hechler asked, unbelieving.

'We have to go up and see them. Karl, Müller will have to go ashore now. Don't let anybody persuade you to move her out. We don't move anywhere until we've been coaled.'

Forward in the bridge, Schepke watched all three of them go ashore. The coolness of the early morning had gone now and the sunlight came in very brightly through the dropped down windows. There was nothing to see of the city from the coaling wharf except warehouses and godowns along the dock. Out in the Roads it was still quiet and only the sunlight reflected blindingly bright on the flat blue ocean.

'—Karl.'

Schepke turned from the wheel. 'Rollmann!'

Rollmann came in from the doorway. 'How are you, Karl?'

Schepke took his hand.

'I only heard a few minutes ago that you were on board,' Rollmann went on. 'I was ashore last night. I met Emmermann on his way into town. He just told me.'

'It's been a long time, Horst.'

'It must be about eight years. It was on the *Amerika*.'

'How do you come to be on board this?' Schepke asked.

'You know how these things happen,' Rollmann said, glancing out into the well. 'I—I heard about the *Ilse Backenkölher*. Still, let's not talk about that.' His voice changed again. 'It's good to see you again. I wouldn't have believed that kid at Eckernförde would grow to this.'

'That was a long time ago, too,' Schepke said.

'Yes. Those days were not so happy,' Rollmann agreed.

'And these?'

Rollmann shrugged.

'How long have you been on board?' Schepke asked.

'I came with Otto. I came off the *Shaykh Saadi* to join him.'

'He's not the same man, Horst.'

'I know. I don't think the time is far away now.'

'He never mentioned anything.'

'You know him, Karl. But yourself. You've been ashore here since the fire?'

Schepke nodded. A large Japanese freighter was headed slowly into Keppel Harbour from the east, one of those high-snouted goal-posters with a green hull and her company name in white below her midship superstructure.

'What about this lot?' Schepke asked.

Rollmann laid an arm on the wheel. 'You really need me to tell you?'

'What about Müller?'

'He won't care much for you coming on board. When Rösing went down with peritonitis he expected to take over as First. However, Otto never made the move. I'm glad now. But the engineers are all right. Hechler's one of the best. Dorsch, too. I knew him as long ago as Eckernförde. He was with Dekker on the U 711 when taken prisoner.

'There doesn't seem much to choose from on deck,' Schepke said.

'I think you'll manage,' Rollmann told him, '—now I'll have to go. If you ever want me, my cabin's in the port inboard passage.'

'I'll remember that,' Schepke said, and watched him go out down the bridge stairway.

When Rollmann had gone he went back to the windows. The Jap had come to anchor, her cable party busy on the forepeak, her stern already swinging with the tide. Then further out, beyond the Outer Shoal Beacon, the ocean was flat and blue and the sunlight hard and sudden to his eyes.

It was almost noon when he saw the taxi come along the dock. He met Emmermann at the head of the main stairway.

'Everything all right?'

'No trouble at all,' Schepke told him.

'Good. Hechler's gone to arrange the coaling now.' While he spoke he dabbed the sweat from his face with a folded handkerchief. 'We didn't do as well ashore as I had hoped. We'll have to be careful. Things are getting worse than ever they were. You'll have to do all this, too, some day. This is the only way back for you.'

Schepke eased his cap back off his forehead.

'You don't seem very enthusiastic,' Emmermann said.

Schepke took a long quiet breath, feeling those eyes looking all the way through him.

'You get back where you ought to be,' Emmermann went on. 'I know it's going to be difficult but throw it away now and it's for good. Besides, I never imagined you would give up easily.'

'I never said anything about giving up,' Schepke said quietly.

'Then when we're through coaling take her out and anchor beyond the beacon.'

'Anything else?'

'Watch for Müller. He'll most probably be drunk when he gets back. I've never been completely aware of just how his mind works. Be careful of him.'

'Rollmann mentioned it.'

'Yes. I forgot to tell you he was on board. You can depend on him and Hechler. I was going—' he bit the words off suddenly, holding himself in under the ribs with his left hand and wiping the fresh outburst of sweat from his face with the handkerchief.

'You better let me help you to your cabin,' Schepke said, taking him under the arm.

'It's nothing. I'll be all right—just take her out when we've coaled.' He turned and went slowly, wearily toward his cabin, Schepke watching him from the head of the main stairway.

THE *Gertrud Lüth* was lying out at anchor almost on the Port Limits. It was very hot now in the mid-afternoon and a heat haze had closed down across the ocean to the south-east. The city, stretched out to port, lay white and hot in the hard sunlight. About four hundred metres off the port bow a Custom launch was at anchor with an English navy frogman going in over the side watched by his diving crew, one of them sitting on the canopy with a shotgun.

'It's hot down below there this afternoon, Herr Schepke.'

Schepke leaned off the rails of the flying bridge to see Altmeyer come out on deck. 'It's like this most of the summer,' he said. 'Even at night it never really gets cool.'

Altmeyer was looking off toward the launch. 'What are they doing?'

'They're searching for opium. When the smugglers come in on the big ships they dump it across the wall.'

'Into the harbour?' the boy asked, slightly puzzled.

'They're cork-packed waterproof packages weighted down with specially treated cord attached to weights. After a while the sea water working on the cord brings the packages back to the top to be picked up.'

'I guess they've got it all worked out,' the boy said, impressed.

'It's big money,' Schepke said.

'What about the one with the gun?'

'Sharks. Sometimes they come right in to the beach.'

Now the frogman came up empty-handed again, the diving crew hauling him inboard, his black rubber suit streaming water and brightly reflecting the sunlight.

'There's another boat coming out,' the boy said.

The boat was passing the Outer Shoal Beacon. Schepke could see Müller standing in the open cockpit looking toward the ship.

'We loaded some beer before we came out,' the boy said. 'Do you want to come below for one?'

'Not just now,' Schepke told him. 'I'll be down later.'

The boy grinned and Schepke watched him go down through the hatchway to the bridge. The Custom launch had finished for the day and was now swinging away, headed inshore, her twin screws kicking up a brilliant white wake from the flat blue water. Leaning on the rails, he watched her head in almost directly toward Assembly House and the Government Offices. Then, while he watched, the hire motor boat that had brought Müller out pulled around the bows and headed in behind the fast-moving Custom launch.

He was still leaning on the canvas screen rails when he saw Müller climb out on deck.

'What's this, Schepke? Homesick?'

Schepke looked back toward the city.

'What's wrong? Don't you care for the old sea-cow?' Müller went on drunkenly. 'But then you're one of those top sailors like Emmermann and Hechler. Isn't that right, Schepke?'

Schepke looked back across the Roads as a big Swedish freighter came slowly out from Keppel Harbour, the three gold crowns on her raked funnel glinting in the hard sunlight.

Müller looked past him to the freighter. 'I guess that's more in your line,' he said. 'How about it?'

Schepke leaned slowly off the rails. 'What is it, Müller? You want trouble now?'

Müller looked at him a moment, then changed his mind and turned abruptly and climbed into the hatchway.

Coming down from the bridge he ran into Wilamowitz.

'Where the hell are you going?' he snarled.

Wilamowitz stood aside, looking at him.

'I suppose you're going to see him,' Müller went on.

'I was only going to the bridge,' Wilamowitz said very quietly.

'Anybody would think this was one of those cracks of the Amerika-Lloyd Line, not a floating junk-yard! Next thing everybody will be calling each other "Mister" and those niggers down aft wearing collars and ties!'

Wilamowitz watched him go aft along the cabin deck.

'Something wrong?'

He turned to see Schepke in the bridge doorway. 'No. No, nothing's wrong,' he said.

'What about Müller?'

'No. No, it's just the ship. It's the heat.'

'There's nothing anybody can do about this ship, Wilamowitz.'

'What about Emmermann? He could do something.'

'It's the line,' Schepke said. 'Emmermann's nothing to do with it.'

Wilamowitz used his sleeve to wipe the sweat from his face. 'If I could get off her now without getting in trouble, I would. I've had a bad feeling about this trip ever since we left home.'

Schepke came on down the bridge stairway. 'Don't worry

about it,' he said. 'How about one of those beers I heard that we had?'

Wilamowitz sighed. 'All right.'

They started aft, Wilamowitz slim and nervous and Schepke big and blond and thinking all of it over as they went aft to the messroom.

Hechler and Altmeyer were sitting at the table when they entered.

'What's wrong with you, Willy?' Hechler asked. 'You've got a face as long as a week without breakfast.'

'I was thinking how good it will be when we're home,' Wilamowitz said sullenly.

'Good Christ. We're not even there yet and you're thinking about going home.'

Altmeyer sat quietly at the table and looked from one to the other while Schepke went through to the galley for the tins of lager.

'We could have done with more coal,' Wilamowitz said. 'It's a long way to Shanghai.'

Schepke brought a chair from the bulkhead and sat down opposite Altmeyer.

'So it's the coal that's worrying you, Willy,' Hechler said.

'I suppose you're happy with what Emmermann got?'

Hechler shrugged. 'Economics,' he said. 'When you're as old as I am and been on as many ships, you'll know all about economics. Son, the world goes around on economics.'

Altmeyer watched them talking and Schepke rose and looked out from the open scuttle. The ocean was empty and a humid breeze coming in off the flat blue water.

'How about you?' Hechler said over his shoulder. 'You worried?'

'What have I to worry about?' Schepke asked.

'Well I'm glad I'm not completely on my own. I've got Dorsch to do all the worrying below. He's a great worrier is Dorsch. But don't you worry, too, Willy. She got us out here, didn't she?'

Schepke sat back at the table. Altmeyer took the Chinese Good

45

Morning towel from around his neck and wiped the sweat from his face.

'That's what's bothering everybody,' Hechler said, watching him. 'The heat. But listen. If you think this is hot you should have been on the *Erik Godt*. Three years between the Bahamas and the Windward Passage in the Gulf of Mexico. Christ, that was hot.'

A sudden shuddering tremor passed through the ship, the steady hum of the generators growing with it as the deckhead lights brightened a little.

Hechler finished his drink and got up. 'You think I'm joking but when I came home from the Gulf I weighed half what I do now.'

Altmeyer laughed.

'What's so funny? You think I was always like this?' he stopped, grinning with the boy. 'Well I'll have to go now. That's main engines rung on.'

Schepke glanced at the big old-fashioned clock on the forward bulkhead. The hands showed ten minutes to six o'clock.

'I better get out on the forepeak,' Wilamowitz said, rising from the table.

Schepke finished his drink. The lager had warmed and the room smelled strongly of Hechler's cheroot.

'Had the latest weather report?'

'An hour ago,' Altmeyer told him. 'It's good for the next two days, anyway. The only place it's bad is off the southern coast of Japan.'

Schepke stopped in the doorway and put his cap on. 'Let's hope it stays that way,' he said.

Quartermasters Pulst and Roth were on the bridge along with Emmermann. Schepke went on out to the port wing. When he looked back his eyes met Emmermann's and he nodded slightly before signalling the forepeak. From the windows he could see Wilamowitz, Dorsch, and Rollmann up there with the cable party. Then suddenly the heavy metallic clatter of the capstans broke the quiet of the early evening and long trailers of steam carried back across the rails as they hove in the swivel.

It was 18.00 hours dead when the U flag went up on the weather anchor.

'Start engines,' Emmermann said.

'Start engines, sir,' repeated Pulst as he rang it onto the telegraph.

The whole ship trembled and shuddered before the sound and motion gradually settled into a steady pounding rhythm.

"Midships.'

'Wheel amidships, sir,' repeated Roth.

Out on the forepeak the A flag went up.

'Slow ahead.'

'Slow ahead, sir,' repeated Pulst.

Again the ship shuddered and vibrated beneath their feet before the sound and motion settled into a steady thump-thump-thump, and she began to take on way, slowly at first, her vertical stem barely creeping through the water; and then from up there in the port wing Schepke saw the lightly wrinkled water begin to slide past. Then Pulst reached for the siren lanyard and a sudden, crashing blast of noise and steam echoed out across the Roads as the *Gertrud Lüth* headed out toward the ocean.

'Half ahead,' Emmermann said.

'Half ahead, sir,' repeated Pulst as he again rang it onto the telegraph.

Now there was the steady hiss and froth of water running back along the weed-grown hull. Looking out from the after windows Schepke saw the city sprawled out astern, very quiet in the early evening and the sun shining brightly on the white buildings and the trees showing very green above the lower part of the city and out along the Upper East Coast Road toward the prison and airfield. Then the city was well astern and he found himself thinking about the Gateway and the old man and what the girl might be doing. Maybe, he was thinking, he should have stayed after all. Maybe he should have stayed with her and thought about nothing except how lucky he was. No one ever really knew how lucky he was at the time of it happening. You always thought about how lucky you were in the past.

Sure, he thought. Maybe I should have stayed. This could

be plenty more complicated than her now she's the past. I guess you've picked yourself a good one this time, old turtle-head. It's got that old complicated feeling, all right. But you're not one of the bright boys, old turtle-head. There's nothing you do now but stop the thinking and sit it out. But I guess you've picked a good one this time, old turtle-head. Old turtle-head.

Out on the forepeak the cable party were busy securing the anchors and cables. Emmermann stood with both hands gripping tightly on the brass rail fixed under the windows and running the length of the bridge, his eyes hooded under the peak of his cap, the faded, old-fashioned uniform buttoned close to his neck.

Schepke walked back along the wing and stood amidships. Away from the shore the breeze made cat's paws on the flat open water. It was not really much of a breeze and it would fall with darkness.

'Full ahead,' Emmermann called across the bridge.

'Full ahead, sir,' repeated Pulst.

Schepke crossed to the rail, lit a cigarette, and watched the sky to the east pale as the sun went down. After a while a lascar from the watch on deck came up and relieved Pulst on the telegraph, Roth remaining to complete the dog watches. To the east, out on the horizon, the ocean had greyed and trailings of thin high cloud had spread across the sky. Now the *Gertrud Lüth* was driving out into the darkening South China Sea, the water flat and, occasionally, small shoals of flying fish rising from under the bows to flit a few metres before diving back into the ocean.

'Karl,' Emmermann said quietly. 'You can go now.'

Schepke looked at him, his face that dirty grey under the gold-braided cap with its glittering eagle and anchors.

'There's nothing else?'

'Not at the moment,' Emmermann told him, and turned back to the rail as Schepke left. It was a fine clear evening and the falling breeze coming in through the open windows smelled cleanly of the ocean.

When Müller came onto the bridge after supper, night had come down and the moon shone large and white low on the

48

horizon. There was no breeze now and the sound of the water running back along the weed-grown hull carried up from the darkness beyond the walls. Away to the south-east the moonlight rode gently on the flat black ocean while the high trailings of cloud were building and now lit silvery white far above the moon. The rest of the sky was clear where there was no cloud, and stars shone. There were many stars this night and it was quiet and peaceful out beyond the walls of the *Gertrud Lüth*.

EMMERMANN shut the door of his cabin and drew the faded curtains on the two open scuttles. The cabin was large and panelled with the same darkened oak as the rest of the ship. Right forward, by the bulkhead, was a massive desk and shelves of books. Then Emmermann, standing by the bunk, slowly unbuttoned the high neck of his tunic then took his cap off and set it carefully on the blue cover. It was hot and humid in the cabin and he sighed deeply, cupping the palm of his hand over his eyes, then running his hand back over his high bald head. The breeze set up by the passage of the ship set the curtains over the open scuttles moving and the sound of the water rushing back along the hull carried in loud and close-sounding. Then suddenly the cabin swung violently around, and feeling himself falling, he grabbed the edge of the bunk and pulled himself across it. The pain was all through him and he lay biting hard on his teeth, clutching his stomach with both hands, sweat streaming down his face and neck. After a while, when feeling he could make it, he pulled himself to his feet and reached the cabinet over the wash-basin. He found the bottle and swallowed straight from the mouth, the bitter fluid numbing his throat as it went down. It would take time. Everything now was time. It was a thing there was so little of.

He was sitting at the desk when someone knocked on the door.

'Who is it?' he asked, carefully raising himself up into the chair and sitting back.

'Sam, sir,' the voice the other side of the door said.

'All right.'

A moon-faced Chinese came in walking very flat-footedly and carrying a tray. He was a round, heavy little man and carried his shoulders in a manner that made him appear to lean over backward.

'Supper, Captain,' he said, smiling, his bald head gleaming in the light.

Emmermann motioned him away.

'But Captain not eat two days now,' Sam said concernedly. 'Captain must eat.'

'Later, Sam.'

'I cook special,' Sam persisted. 'Captain must eat.'

'All right, put it down,' Emmermann told him.

Sam set the tray on the heavy table out in the middle of the cabin.

'Tell Schepke I want to see him.'

'Yes, Captain. Remember, must eat. Sam cook special.'

Emmermann sat quietly in the big chair when Sam had left. It was very quiet in the cabin and only the sound of the ocean carried in through the curtained scuttles. There was hardly any movement of the ship, only occasionally, she would rise in the long, low, easy lift of the ocean. The pain had begun to deaden itself now, although it was still there, cold and hard-feeling. He had thought about it a great deal lately, but somehow he never quite imagined it would get this way toward the end. He had always been able to see the end clearly, but it was always difficult to imagine anything truly in the physical sense until it actually happened. The worst part was having to take it all and wait. The waiting took such a long time. In the early days when he had thought about it, he had thought about it so very quickly. It was difficult for someone to think of something bad that he wanted no part of and to do the thinking slowly and carefully. People only thought about that side of it very quickly, if they thought about it at all. It had never been possible to think how

50

it would really be until now that he waited. It took such a long time, the waiting.

Outside, someone knocked on the door.

'Come in.'

It was Schepke.

'Sit down,' Emmermann said, watching him. There was a certain formidableness about Schepke. Always one had the impression he was looming over one in some way other than physically.

'How do you find her?' he asked, finally.

'There may be worse,' Schepke said. 'Although I have never seen one.'

'You've not changed,' Emmermann said. 'As for the *Ilse Backenkölher*, I care nothing about her. She's of no consequence whatever. Understand?'

'I'm grateful.'

'No. It is myself who is grateful. You weren't exactly in the position to refuse me. But tell me something, why do you think I'm on board such a ship?'

'It's no business of mine,' Schepke said.

'Nevertheless, I think you had better know,' Emmermann said, his eyes searching Schepke's wide sunburned face. 'You must already know I am ill. They all know. But you know how it is with Oesten-Liebe. They only put together the required crew, and then not always. No questions asked either way. You may have seen that by now. Of course, you can depend on Hechler, Rollmann, and the other engineers. They have their own reasons for being on board. But apart from Rollmann none of them know anything about you.'

'It's possible some of them may have already guessed about the *Ilse*,' Schepke said.

'Forget about her. You were only the scapegoat. If they guess anything, then let them guess. You can take care of yourself.' He reached down and brought a bottle of brandy and glasses from a drawer of the desk. 'Help yourself.'

He watched Schepke pour a drink. Then Schepke looked at him evenly across the desk. 'How bad are you, Otto?'

51

'It's now just a matter of waiting,' Emmermann said quietly. 'That's the difficult part.'

Schepke was thinking very carefully about it, Emmermann watching him.

'Perhaps you're thinking I should be ashore in some hospital listening to them tell me how soon I'll be well again.'

'I wasn't thinking that,' Schepke told him. 'But can nothing be done?'

'Nothing except cut you away a little at a time,' Emmermann said deprecatingly. 'But that's of no importance. What you're here for is to take command when the time arrives. It's up to you then.'

'Wouldn't it be better if you went ashore?'

Emmermann shook his head. I thought about all that. Just you do what you can afterward.' Then remaining seated in the big chair, he reached his hand out. Schepke took it, standing there big and blond, towering above the desk.

'Put the fan on as you go out.'

Schepke found the switch by the door. The long, wooden-bladed fan suspended from the deckhead wheeled slowly then gathered speed.

'Good night.'

'Good night, Karl.'

Now he was alone he was conscious of the shipboard noise, and the travelling sound of the fan, and the long low, easy lift of the ship, and above all the steady rush of the water out there in the darkness beyond the walls. Crossing to one of the scuttles he drew back the curtain, feeling the humid breeze set up by the way of the ship on his face; and out there the ocean was black and silent and with many stars showing in the sky where there was no cloud, and the moon having risen, shone large and white, the moonlight riding gently on the black wrinkled ocean away to the south-east. It was a fine night. There had been many fine nights. The days, too. There had been many fine days. But somehow it was the nights he remembered most clearly. He turned away from the open scuttle and put the lights out. Much of the worry had gone now with the finding of Schepke. Schepke had

52

not changed much, though perhaps there was a certain degree of bitterness. But with time and luck he would be all right.

Now he lay on the bunk in the darkness and watched the moonlight come in brightly between the open curtains over the scuttle. The small patch of moonlight moved gently on the far bulkhead with the movement of the ship as she rose in the long, easy lift of the ocean.

And it was a fine night and he was very sure about Schepke.

SCHEPKE came awake with Sam leaning over him.

'What is it?' he asked, sitting up, shielding his eyes against the light streaming in through the open doorway from the passage.

'No find Captain,' Sam said.

'What do you mean?'

'Look everywhere. No find.' Sam spoke so his jowls shook. 'He not sleep in cabin last night.'

'Have you been to the bridge?'

'Sure. I tell bridge. He not been to bridge either!'

'All right, I'll see to it,' Schepke told him, and as he dressed he pulled the curtain back from the open scuttle. The ocean was that hard, brittle blue of the early morning and the sky streamered with the rays of the rising sun. Glancing at his wrist watch he saw it was just after six o'clock.

Taking his cap from behind the door, he went on up to the bridge. The whole sky to the east was lit by the rising sun. He saw Wilamowitz in the starboard wing.

'Seen Emmermann?'

'No,' Wilamowitz told him. 'Sam was here asking the same thing.'

Schepke turned and went back down to the big cabin. The bunk was made up but there was a hollow where Emmermann had lain. He turned and went out and down to Rollmann's cabin. The bosun was shaving.

'Horst. You seen Otto?'

Rollmann looked surprised. '—Not since last night. He was pacing the starboard side alleyway just before I turned in. That was about midnight.'

'Sam can't find him. I've been in his cabin and he's not there. His bunk hasn't been slept in either.'

'Well he should be around somewhere,' Rollmann said slowly.

'Get the watch on deck to look through the ship just in case.'

'Right away,' Rollmann said, wiping the lather from his face.

Schepke went on aft to the port engine-room hatch. The sudden blast of humid air brought the sweat out in a rush as he went down the ladder to the catwalk. After the calm and quiet of the deck the heat and noise was tremendous.

Hechler was waiting for him on the footplate, his overalls open to the waist, sweat gleaming on his face and chest.

'What can I do for you?' he shouted, his hand cupped to his mouth.

'Seen Emmermann?'

'What would he be doing down here?'

'Nobody has seen him,' Schepke said, shouting against the tremendous pound and whine of the engines.

'I haven't seen him since early last night,' Hechler shouted.

Schepke slapped him on the shoulder and started up the ladder. As he came out onto the after well he saw Rollmann and two seamen above him on the boatdeck.

'Any luck?' he shouted.

'Nothing.' Rollmann came on down the ladder, the lascars following. 'There's nothing up there. That leaves the forepeak.'

'I'll be on the bridge,' Schepke told him, going around Number Three hatch to the starboard side, leaving Rollmann and the lascars going forward. He had that empty, lonely feeling now. He had wakened with it and now it began to grow. He looked across the wall. There was a cool breeze off the empty ocean. The blue of the ocean was deepening now as the sun rose. The water had roughened a little during the night and the ship had taken on some easy movement.

Wilamowitz was on the bridge with Roth and a lascar from the watch on deck. The sun had risen clear of the horizon and seemed to hang hesitantly above the ocean, huge and orange and blinding.

'What's happening?' he asked as he watched Schepke go to one of the forward windows.

'When did you last see him?'

'—Before supper,' Wilamowitz said, thinking.

Schepke saw Rollmann come out from the forepeak tunnel.

'Nothing there!' Rollmann shouted through his hands.

Schepke turned back below. Sam was in the galley.

'Listen,' Schepke told him. 'When did you last see the Kapitän?'

'Last night,' Sam said, his eyes wide. 'I take him supper. Cook special. This morning I take his coffee and nobody there.'

Rollmann came along the passage. 'Not a thing,' he told Schepke. 'We've been all through the ship.'

'You better go over it again. Make sure all the lockers are gone into.' He said it with little enthusiasm, then turned and went back again to the big cabin and put on the lights.

This time he saw the envelope against the cigar-box on the desk. Inside was a single sheet of paper. In the small neat hand, he read:

> *Sorry it had to be this way. The waiting was the difficult part. I hope you can forgive me.*
> *God be with you.*
>   *Emmermann.*

Müller and Dorsch were coming up the main stairway when he closed the door.

'What the hell's this about Emmermann?' Müller demanded.

'Is it true he's missing?' Dorsch asked.

'I'll see you in the messroom,' Schepke told them, going aft to Altmeyer's cabin.

The boy woke when he put the light on.

'Better get dressed,' he said. 'I want you to radio Singapore. I'll be in the messroom.'

Müller and Dorsch were waiting for him.

'What's going on, Schepke?' Müller demanded angrily.

Schepke ignored him as Rollmann came in followed by Altmeyer pulling on his tunic.

'There's no sign of him anywhere,' Rollmann said.

'I know. Tell Wilamowitz and the Chief I want them.'

'Do you want me to send that message now, Herr Schepke?' Altmeyer asked.

'What message?' Müller shouted at the boy.

'You'll find out soon enough,' Schepke told him, his voice oddly cold.

'You wanted me?' Wilamowitz asked as he came in.

'Sit down.'

In a little while Rollmann came back with Hechler.

'What's going on?' Hechler asked, seeing them all there.

'Emmermann went overboard during the night. I just found this in his cabin.' Schepke held the letter for them to see.

'Went overboard,' Wilamowitz said.

'What's in there?' Müller asked.

Again Schepke ignored him. 'Altmeyer. Send the following to our agents. *Emmermann missing, presumed lost overboard during the early hours of morning. First Officer Schepke assumed command. Ship continuing to destination.* Got that?'

'Yes, sir.'

'All right. Get it away.'

'Wait a minute!' Müller shouted. 'Before you send anything I want to see that letter. I'm not taking Schepke's word for anything.'

'Get that message away now, Altmeyer,' Schepke said evenly. 'As for you, Müller. You don't demand anything. I make the decisions from now on.'

Müller fought to keep control of himself, his hands clenched so tightly the knuckles stood out white and bloodless. Then when it seemed he was about to say something, he turned abruptly and left.

The messroom remained quiet. Schepke put the letter into the breast pocket of his tunic.

'I'll see you when Dorsch relieves me,' Hechler said. Wilamowitz went out along with him.

'I suppose we might as well have breakfast,' Dorsch said quietly. 'How about you, Herr Schepke?'

Schepke nodded. Dorsch would be all right. Müller was the one. Wilamowitz did not count one way or the other.

'Message sent and acknowledged, sir,' Altmeyer said coming in. 'I also got the weather report.'

Schepke took the report and read it through.

'You don't mind if I ask something?' Dorsch said.

'What is it?' Schepke asked.

'Would it be any good turning the ship around?'

'It happened during the night,' Schepke said quietly. 'That's a lot of ocean.'

'That's what I thought,' Dorsch said.

Kuang was bringing the breakfasts as Sam passed the plates through the hatchway.

'You won't be wanting me further at the moment, Herr Kapitän?' Rollmann said from the doorway.

'No, not now,' Schepke told him. '—But wait. Don't you eat here?'

'I like best to eat in my cabin,' Rollmann said.

'Just as you want. I'll see you later.'

'He's never eaten here since he came on board,' Dorsch said when Rollmann had gone.

'What about the seamen and quartermasters?' Schepke asked him.

'The quartermasters get theirs from Sam and the lascars take care of themselves. When the wind's astern you can smell it all over the ship.'

Kuang brought the coffee while they ate. The breeze came in through the open scuttles and already it was getting warmer with the climbing of the sun. The ocean was running choppy in the breeze and the ship was moving with it. Far out on the ocean a heat haze was already forming and the light breeze from the south-east was warming rapidly in the early morning. It was very quiet out there and the ocean was empty except for the *Gertrud Lüth*, black and gaunt, driving northward into the South China Sea.

It was shortly after midday when Müller followed Schepke from the charthouse at the rear of the bridge and went below. It was hot now, the breeze fallen completely away and the vast and empty ocean again lying flat and listless. The heat haze that had earlier showed far out on the horizon had thickened and closed in until it now lay in a smoky yellow cloud across the face of the ocean. Under the haze the water appeared oily-thick and sluggish, the surface wash running lazily and noiselessly away from the hull, and astern, the propeller threshing the water up greenly white from the cool depths. A lone porpoise had joined them during the forenoon and now surfaced to dive beyond the starboard bow to suddenly reappear to port, only to heel over and smoothly dive again. Next time she broke the surface she was right ahead, rolling and diving, her snout held high and clear of the water as she lifted cleanly.

Dorsch had just finished eating when Müller came in.

'Kuang!' Müller called toward the hatchway before sitting down at the table across from Dorsch. 'Christ, it's hot up there.'

'You want to try it below,' Dorsch said, pouring his coffee as Kuang brought Müller his dinner from the galley.

'What do you think about Emmermann?' Müller asked as he started to eat.

Dorsch shrugged.

'We should have seen that letter,' Müller went on. 'We don't know about anything. All we've got is Schepke's word for it.'

'It doesn't bother me,' Dorsch said.

'Well it bothers me plenty. And Schepke, what's he doing

here? I don't trust him at all. With Emmermann gone I should be in command now. What do we know about Schepke?'

'He seems all right to me,' Dorsch said evenly.

'Don't tell me that. Listen, the Backenkölher Line hasn't ran out here for two or three years now. So what's he been doing? Tell me that.'

Dorsch had gotten to his feet and was looking at him from the doorway. 'Maybe you better ask him yourself,' he said.

Müller went back to eating. He ate alone now while the mess boy cleared Dorsch's place at the table.

Back in his cabin he unlocked the drawer of his writing-desk and brought out a bottle of whisky. It was hot in the cabin and the condensation had beaded and now ran from the bulkheads. Outside the open scuttle the sun-bleached decking shimmered in the hazy sunlight and the only stirring of the humid air was caused by the passage of the ship through the flat, sluggishly moving water.

Suddenly he heard talking outside in the passage and he crossed to the door. Sam had just closed the galley door and was talking to Kuang as they went aft to the boatdeck toward their cabin quarters on the fantail. Müller waited a few moments then stepped out into the passage and went quickly forward to the big cabin by the main stairway. There was no one about, and further forward, at the end of the passage, was the stairway to the bridge and the locked door of the Radio Office reached by passing between the outer edge of the bridge stairway and the starboard bulkhead.

Inside the big cabin he ran the snib home on the door and quickly moved to the desk. The drawers on the right held nothing but cargo papers, a number of letters from the owners, and some old Pilot Books and Almanacs. The first drawer on the other side produced nothing but new logs and amendments to various charts. He stood up slowly, glancing around the cabin, wiping the sweat from his face with the sleeve of his tunic. There was no safe on board and the only remaining drawers were those down the face of the bunk. He knelt back at the desk. As he opened the next drawer the sound of voices carried through the locked door from the passage. He stopped, his hand on the drawer. Then slowly the voices moved aft along the passage. Hurriedly he turned back to the drawer, the sweat running between his shoulders.

In the drawer were a number of personal letters and a photograph album. He brought the album out and shook it. There was nothing but photographs faded brown with age and sea-water dampness. One of the photographs that fell free was of a younger, smiling Emmermann in tight-fitting coat and high-peaked cap of a U-boat Commander of the German Navy. The photograph was dated: Eckernförde, 1944. Müller smiled thinly and pushed everything back into the drawer. In the last drawer all he found was a half-empty bottle of brandy and some glasses. He sat up, again glancing about the cabin, noting the three deep, brass-handled drawers down the face of the bunk.

He started to slide the drawer in and rise to his feet, and it jammed. He eased it back, then forward, and again it jammed. Now he pulled the drawer all the way out and got down on his hands and knees. He found it toppled forward across the runners. The folder had been flat against the back of the drawer space. Inside were cuttings of a Court of Enquiry and a book of notes made by Emmermann. Hurriedly he put everything back into the folder and buttoned it inside his tunic.

Passing the galley he saw Hechler breaking ice into a jug held over the sink.

'Hot below?'

Hechler looked out through the doorway at him. 'What do you sound so happy about?'

Müller smiled. 'We've got nothing to be happy about,' he said.

'What do you mean, we?' Hechler asked, filling the jug with water as he swished the ice around inside.

'There's Schepke?' Müller said, watching Hechler's face.

'What's he got to do with it?'

Müller shrugged. 'Well if you don't know, you don't know,' he said.

Hechler watched him go aft to his cabin. Then Altmeyer came

in from the boatdeck on his way to the Radio Office. 'Something wrong?' he asked, seeing Hechler's face.

'I don't know. But I've got the feeling we're going to know one way or the other before long.'

'Well I can't say I ever liked Müller, anyway,' Altmeyer said.

'You're not the only one,' Hechler told him, and started back to the engine-room with the iced water.

SCHEPKE was in the big cabin working at Emmermann's desk. Outside the haze had risen and the sun was going down.

Someone knocked on the door.

'Yes?'

Hechler came in. 'Wilamowitz told me you were here,' he said.

'Come on in.'

Hechler closed the door behind him.

'You wanted to see me about below?' Schepke asked.

'I thought you better know about just how we stood. I mean we're all right as long as we don't run into a big blow. Or at least as long as she comes astern,' he added drily.

'I don't know how they get away with it.'

'You don't know half,' Hechler said. 'Only start asking questions and you're finished. Nobody asks questions with Oesten-Liebe.'

'How is she below? Apart from coal.'

'We try to do what we can. But she hasn't had a major refit in eight years.'

'I just found that out,' Schepke said, indicating the papers spread out on the desk.

'We're overloaded as well,' Hechler reminded him. 'That deck-cargo is worth more than the ship herself.'

'A lot of people don't know there is any deck-cargo,' Schepke said meaningfully. 'I found out plenty just reading these through.'

Hechler stayed silent and Schepke began putting the papers together.

'You ought to be careful of Müller,' Hechler said, watching him.

Schepke put the papers back into the drawers. 'I don't want any trouble if it can be avoided,' he said. 'There's hardly enough crew to go around as it is.'

'I guess not.'

'If ever there was a ghost ship this is it.'

'You can count on us below,' Hechler said.

Schepke looked at him. 'I was already counting on you.' He stood up from the desk. He was tired and there was much to think about after seeing Emmermann's papers.

'You coming for supper?' Hechler asked.

They joined Altmeyer at the table, Hechler sitting alongside Schepke and Altmeyer sitting across the other side. It was getting quickly dark. A light breeze had come with darkness and now it wrinkled the face of the ocean. Kuang brought the supper. The only place not set was the one at the head of the table where Emmermann had sat when eating in the mess-room.

'Well is the food good enough for you, Herr Kapitän?'

Schepke and Hechler paid no attention, but Altmeyer looked across the table to the doorway. Müller was drunk.

'What's the matter with everybody?' he asked as he came in from the doorway. 'Maybe I have leprosy or something. Is that it?' He stood leaning forward, both hands on the end of the table, watching Schepke carefully, sullenly.

No one said anything.

Müller stood there breathing heavily, glowering at them as they went on eating.

'Well we all know who the new Kapitän's friends are,' he said loudly. 'Kapitän! Huh! —You know where he's been?'

Hechler looked up from his plate. Kuang was now watching with Sam from the other side of the hatchway.

'Well do you?' Müller shouted.

'Does it matter?' Hechler said quietly. 'We've all been somewhere at one time or another.'

'Not like him. Not him,' Müller shouted, jabbing a finger at Schepke. 'It was him burned the *Ilse Backenkölher!*—Isn't that right, Herr Kapitän?'

Schepke sat quietly at the table. Müller looked first at Altmeyer, then Hechler. 'Ask him! Go on, ask him!'

Hechler cleared his throat. 'I don't see it matters any,' he said quietly.

Müller started to say something then reached for him. Schepke caught his arm and Müller swung around and threw him against the outboard bulkhead, getting both hands to his throat. Schepke got his arms up inside of Müller's and forced his head back and Müller let go suddenly and tripped and they both went sprawling out into the passage. Schepke got up first and grabbed him to his feet and hit him twice, rapidly, his full weight behind the blows. Müller crashed backward through the door of Altmeyer's cabin and Schepke went after him, hitting him again, and he went down against the end of the bunk, started to get to his feet, then fell back. He lay where he was, glowering at Schepke, blood running from his mouth.

'Get up!'

Müller reached both hands to the end of the bunk and pulled himself to his feet.

'You're on the bridge at midnight,' Schepke said very quietly. 'Be there—sober.'

They were all in the passage.

'Are you all right?' Hechler asked when Müller had gone.

Schepke nodded.

'I knew there would be trouble,' Altmeyer said.

'Forget it,' Schepke told them. 'Go on back to supper.'

When they had gone he lit a cigarette and went out onto the boatdeck. It was dark and the moon shone brightly white above the horizon. Away to the east, towering, moon-silvered mountains of cloud had piled high up into the night sky. It was cooler now with a breeze that was coming with the night. A brief

63

flicker of lightning lit the sky momentarily far to the north-west. As he watched, it came again, a long, rolling, flickering of light playing on the underside of a low mass of cloud a vast distance to the north-west. The steady thump-thump-thump, of the engines beat up muffled and hollow-sounding into the quiet tropical night. He flicked the cigarette out over the wall and watched its arcing flight until it disappeared in the black, frothing water in the shadow of the hull. He was thinking, and he was thinking, maybe, this would be a trip he might not so easily forget. But he did not think too long about it, and he turned his back to the port rail, and for a long time watched the moon away to the south-east climb steadily from the horizon. The night was quiet and pleasantly cool with the coming of the breeze; and astern, on all the ocean, was only the lonely wake of the *Gertrud Lüth.*

KARL SCHEPKE woke a little before half-past three o'clock in the morning, and lying in the darkness he was suddenly conscious of the sound of rain drumming on the boatdeck. After dressing, he went out and aft along the passage to the screen door to the boatdeck. The breeze had grown some and now gusted, bringing the rain in sudden heavy squalls. The sky was heavy with low black cloud and he watched the rain falling through the after deck and derrick platform lights on the after masthead. There was always a certain loneliness about a ship in the rain in the night.

In the galley he filled a mug with coffee and took it with him to the bridge. It was still not time to take over the morning watch and he stood in the port wing and sipped the bitter black coffee and watched the rain blur the windows, disfiguring the glow of the deck-lights on the drop of the forepeak. The ship was beginning to move with the ocean now and she rose long, and slowly, and wearily.

WHEN Schepke took over the morning watch, Müller went below to his cabin. The dull throbbing ache in his head had gotten worse as the night had gone on and now he got the bottle and poured himself a drink. Sitting on the bunk in the darkness he lit a cigarette and listened to the rain drumming on the boat-deck. After a while he heard the middle watch engineer go aft to his cabin. He smoked part of another cigarette then got up and edged the door open. The ship had settled again after the changing of the watch, and after hesitating a moment, he moved quietly along the the passage toward Altmeyer's cabin.

SCHEPKE dropped the narrow window down and suddenly felt the humid breeze and cool rain on his face. The breeze had backed away steadily since midnight and was now blowing moderately from north-north-east. He closed the window again and went back to the charthouse. The previous night's weather report was on the glass-topped chart table. Everything was clear in the immediate vicinity and only marked by a light freshening wind. The only likely bad trouble was a large area of deepening low pressure centred about seven hundred miles due north of the Caroline Islands and reported as moving slowly north-westerly over the Marianne Sea. It would bear watching. It was a bad time of the year in the China Seas and everything bore careful

65

watching. However, the Marianne Sea was a long, long way away.

He checked it all lightly on the chart in pencil then went back to the bridge. He opened one of the windows again. It was black dark and the moon was now firmly obscured by heavy low cloud. A slight sea was running before the breeze and the *Gertrud Lüth* was butting her bows squarely into it. He leaned on the rail. Apart from himself there was only the quartermaster Bahr and an old grey-bearded lascar from the watch on deck. It was dark in the bridge and the frail light from the overhead compass bowl cast a weird glow on the faces. Below the bridge the deck and foremast derrick platform lights threw grotesque shadows on the heavy mass of earth-moving machinery lashed down across the forward well.

'Go and get us some more coffee,' he said to the lascar. The old man bowed slightly, then collected Schepke's mug from the charthouse. All the while Bahr peered steadily into the night, occasionally glancing overhead at the compass. Schepke went back to the charthouse and put the big light on over the table, first closing the door to the bridge. He looked carefully again at the large, pencil-lined chart, then satisfied with his entry over the distant Marianne Sea, he put the light out and went back to the bridge as the old man came in from below.

Standing by the open window sipping the coffee, he wondered how it would be when daylight came in; and knowing it would be grey and overcast but with the clouds blown out by the breeze so that no rain would come.

'Kapitän, sir,' Bahr said, setting his mug on the ledge of the window directly before the wheel. 'I thought I could smell something smouldering. Smoke of some sort.'

Schepke raised his head, his back to the open window. 'Sure?'

Bahr hesitated. 'Well maybe not,' he said, grinning sheepishly.

Schepke walked the length of the bridge, then went back into the charthouse. There was not the smell of smoke or burning anywhere. Back on the bridge he scanned the forward well and forepeak.

'How about you?' he asked the old man.

'Nothing, Kapitän.'

Schepke stood back at the window. Overhead the breeze made a low moaning sound in the wireless telegraphy aerials. It had stopped raining and the air was cool and humid after the rain. Looking at his wrist watch he saw it was almost five-thirty. In another hour it would be daylight. Then as he scanned the ocean through the night-glasses he picked up the lights of a ship off the port bow, the lights showing very faintly and low on the horizon. After a while he saw there was not much of her and she was probably one of the smaller Chinese freighters on the Singapore run. The sky had greyed a little with the false dawn when they finally passed her about ten kilometres away on the port side.

'Kapitän!' Bahr turned away from the wheel.

Schepke let the night-glasses drop to his chest. He could smell it plainly now himself, a sort of smouldering rubber smell. Quickly he found the switch for the bridge lights and put them on. Everything seemed in order. The old man was leaning from one of the windows scanning the forward well. Schepke tried the charthouse. The smell was very faint, then as he stepped back onto the bridge a terrific hollow-sounding explosion flung them all to the deck, the whole ship seeming to lift from the ocean. Schepke found himself lying in the charthouse doorway, the bridge in complete darkness.

'It's the Radio Office!' Bahr was shouting somewhere in the darkness.

Schepke felt his way to the doorway to the bridge stairway and found it jammed.

'Kapitän! The helm's not answering!'

'Take the after steering position!' Schepke shouted, splintering a panel of the door with his foot. Outside he was met by a wall of flame and thick, acrid smoke. Tightly shielding his face with both arms, he jumped. Hitting the cabin passage, he scrambled clear as Bahr and the old man quickly followed him through the wall of brilliant orange flame roaring out through the Radio Office doorway directly under the bridge.

Groping aft along the passage he tore the first of the extinguishers from the bulkhead and smashed the cap down. Nothing happened. He flung it away and went further aft, trying to remember exactly where the others had been. The next one was on the starboard bulkhead and, smashing the cap down, he felt it immediately kick back. He went forward again until he blundered into the stairway, then standing there, directed the stream of foam into the doorway. Someone pushed in alongside of him, throwing buckets of water or sand. Schepke saw nothing now in the smoke and as he braced himself against the stairway handrail a further shattering explosion sent fragments of glass and white-hot metal ricocheting along the passage. It had been Hechler alongside of him and now they were both lying in the passage. He had lost the extinguisher, but as he climbed to his feet someone thrust another in his hands. The air was as though someone had suddenly and unexpectedly thrown the door to a blast furnace open. And Hechler was again alongside of him throwing whatever it was that someone further aft passed to him.

Then someone else blundered into him. 'The hose! Here's the hose! I've thrown the master switch!'

It was Frauenheim.

Schepke pulled the heavy brass nozzle through under his arm. Frauenheim had gone again and now the canvas hose kicked into life as he opened the sea-water hydrant. This time Schepke got down close to the deck and directed the hose in low, gradually working around and upward, seeing nothing but smoke and flame through his tear-streaming eyes.

After a while the flames seemed to have come under control, although the smoke now increased, and lying on the deck with water and debris pouring back across the breakwater of the doorway, Schepke went on blindly directing the powerful stream of sea-water into the office. Suddenly there was the heavy sound of something falling and a great shower of orange sparks blew out into the passage. Schepke scrambled forward onto the blown out door and directed the jet upward and around the part where he guessed the deckhead had come down.

68

There was no longer any flame now and Hechler pushed in around the stairway and peered over his arm.

'Turn it off!' Schepke shouted back into the passage. The smoke and heat was still too fierce to allow them any closer to the gaping doorway but quickly Schepke crawled up the stairway to the bridge where the breeze coming in through several of the windows was swirling the smoke around and eddying it out through the doorway to the cabin passage below. That part of the deck from the doorway almost to the wheel showed as a gaping, smouldering hole, the flames eating smally at the stretch of after bulkhead on the starboard side.

'Bring the hose up!'

Frauenheim stumbled up the fire-eaten stairway with it, and lying inward from the head of the stairway, directed the jet along the deck.

The smoke was beginning to clear in the passage when Schepke came down and saw them all gathered by the messroom, smoke-grimed, and in various stages of undress.

'Wilamowitz,' he shouted, 'take the flying bridge— Altmeyer! Come here.'

Altmeyer pushed his way out from behind the others, his face dirty and shocked.

'What happened?' Schepke asked, his voice cold and precise.

'I, I don't know, sir. I didn't know anything until the explosion.'

'When were you last in there?'

'When I closed down. I closed down right after I got the weather report at ten o'clock. I—'

'Was anybody else in there?' Schepke demanded impatiently.

'Nobody, sir,' the boy said.

'What about the key?'

'It's on the keyboard in my cabin. All the office keys are kept there.'

'You better see if they're still there,' Schepke told him, then saw Hechler as he came aft from the main fuse box. 'What do you think?'

'Well the boy certainly had the main supply off at the box. Frauenheim saw that when he first opened it.'

Schepke looked at the office. The door had been blown out and the panelling on the deck and bulkheads was charred and burned through to the steel plate.

'It'll be a while before anybody can get in there,' he said. 'What about the steering motor?'

'Frauenheim's gone around to try and get in from the boatdeck door.'

'This won't affect the main steering engine?'

'No. No, nothing like that,' Hechler assured him. 'Once the chain gear is connected up to the bridge she'll be all right. This two motor fluid system was installed sometime during the war. At least that's what it says in the books. It's just a pity that it was one of the few things on board that worked well.'

'How long will it take to connect up?'

'Not long but we'll have to wait until things cool down.'

Schepke turned to see Frauenheim come in from the boat-deck.

'You won't get in there just now,' Frauenheim said, shaking his head. 'The motor's finished. That explosion blew the forward office bulkhead right across it.'

'There's no lighting on the bridge either,' Schepke said.

'I'll see what we can do,' Hechler told him.

'Sir.'

They turned to see Altmeyer.

'The key isn't there,' the boy said.

'Are you sure you took it with you when you closed down?' Schepke asked.

'Yes, sir. I put it on the keyboard.'

Hechler glanced momentarily into Schepke's face.

'How was everything when you locked up?' Schepke asked.

'Just as usual,' the boy said.

'Sure about that?'

The boy nodded, still shocked.

'All right. Keep this to yourself,' Schepke told him.

'The fire never got a hold below,' Rollman told them as he came up the main stairway.

'See what you can do about the bridge,' Schepke said. 'The deckhead went toward the end.' As he turned away he caught sight of Müller watching them from outside the galley. 'Who's on watch below?'

'Dorsch,' Hechler said. 'He'll manage until one of us gets below.'

'All right, I'll leave it to you. If anybody wants me I'll be on deck.'

The after steering position was high on the fantail, the huge wheel situated just forward of the lascar seamen's deckhouse.

'How's she answering?'

'She needs plenty of wheel,' Bahr told him. 'She's heavy in the head.'

Up forward Schepke saw Wilamowitz on the flying bridge. He went around the deckhouse and searched astern. The freighter they had passed had gone and all the ocean astern was grey and empty and rising with the growing breeze. Far under the overhanging stern the water threshed up white and foaming, surging and tossing in the undercurrents of the propeller stream. All the stern shook and rattled with the pounding of the propeller, the vibration growing until everything shuddered wildly, then easing again until there was only the great rattling sounds as though something was running loose on bare metal.

Going forward, he climbed the vertical ladder from the boat-deck onto the rear of the flying bridge. Wilamowitz stood leaning against the big brass-helmeted binnacle, staring out across the bows.

'Anything about?'

'Not a thing,' Wilamowitz said. 'That freighter was hull down when I came up.'

'We should meet something soon. We're on the regular lane.'

The breeze was buffeting their words, and all the sky was grey, and the ocean was grey and the waves beginning to crest and foam whitely on their backs as they ran before the breeze so that occasionally the bows would send a shower of spray gusting over the forepeak.

'You better go and have breakfast,' Schepke said.

'What about the fire? Any idea how it started?'

Schepke hung the glasses around his neck, ignoring him. Then when he had gone he tied a handkerchief around his nose and mouth to guard against the acrid fumes gusting down to swirl around the tall vertical funnel. Below him he could hear Rollman and all spare hands already at work on the bridge. Overhead the breeze now moaned continually in the wireless telegraphy aerials and funnel stays. Then below again, clouds of grey ash dust was blowing astern as the black gang hauled ashes and dumped them over the wall from the after well. Away to the south-east the clouds were dark and closed down over the ocean. To the north the sky was low but the clouds blown out so that no rain came. And he put the glasses to his eyes again and swept the bleak horizon, but only the grey rising ocean came with the growing breeze from the north-east.

KARL SCHEPKE went below when Wilamowitz returned again for the forenoon watch. Everything stank with the smell of smoke and burned wood and rubber. With the increasing movement of the ship the smoke-blackened water and debris swirled the length of the passage.

Hechler was waiting for him outside the galley.

'Frauenheim's working on the steering gear now. You should get back on the bridge soon. Rollmann's almost finished there. The big trouble is you'll be without lights from now on. There isn't a single cable not burned through.'

'I suppose that's everything, echo-sounding gear as well?'

Hechler nodded. They had walked the length of the passage and were standing outside the Radio Office. It was barely

72

recognizable. The forward bulkhead dividing the office from the steering motor compartment had been completely removed and all that remained of the wireless equipment was a burned-out, heat-distorted mass sagging from the main steel bulkheads.

'It won't be easy to find how this started,' Hechler said.

'No. You can think plenty but prove nothing.'

From inside the steering motor compartment came the sound of Frauenheim lapsing into a long, deep-rattling bout of coughing.

'How long has he been like that?' Schepke asked.

'Since he came on board. I suppose it's got worse lately.'

Schepke glanced around at the debris.

'What are you going to do now?' Hechler asked.

'Everything depends on the weather. If that and the steering gear hold good we'll stay on course, otherwise we'll make for Hong Kong or Manila.'

'Well I don't suppose anybody would want to go back anyway,' Hechler said. 'Put back to Singapore now and they'd have us all on the beach. I guess the only sure thing we can do is keep going in a forward direction.'

'What do you want done about the office?' Rollmann standing in the bridge doorway asked. 'We'll have to shore the deckhead up from in there.'

'Go ahead,' Schepke told him. 'Block the doorway up when you're through. Somebody's probably going to want to see that place.'

'We better get something to eat,' Hechler said, looking at his wrist watch.

Müller and Altmeyer were still at the table when they went in.

'That was some fire you had this morning,' Müller said, looking at Schepke. 'You're lucky the bridge didn't go up.'

Altmeyer glanced the length of the table without raising his head, then put his cup down and quietly got up.

Müller watched him, smiling. Then turned again to Schepke: 'Maybe you should lock him up before he sets the whole ship on fire.'

'Maybe I should lock somebody else up,' Schepke said, looking at him across the table.

Müller's head came up swiftly. 'What does that mean?'

'You heard what I said,' Schepke told him.

Müller came to his feet suddenly, angrily. 'Are you saying I had something to do with that fire?' He spat it out, his face drained white beneath the sunburn.

'You know what I said.' Schepke was very easy about it, carefully watching Müller all the time.

'I helped as much as anybody to put that fire out,' Müller said angrily, but keeping a tight hold on himself.

Schepke sat watching him, not saying anything this time.

Müller backed his chair. 'All right, Schepke,' he said coldly and sullenly. 'I just hope one day you go to hell with this hulk.'

They watched him take his cap and go on out. It was very quiet. Then Hechler saw Sam watching them through the hatchway from the galley.

'How about some more coffee, Sam?'

Sam passed the long-spouted pot through the hatchway to Kuang.

'Keep a good breakfast for Frauenheim and Dorsch,' Hechler said to the boy. 'They'll be late coming in.'

The boy nodded, gathering together Müller's dishes.

'I'd feel better if Müller weren't on board,' Hechler went on quietly.

'There's more important things to worry about at the moment,' Schepke said.

They finished their breakfast in silence, then Hechler left first, going forward to see Frauenheim.

Schepke finished his coffee then rose and took his cap down and went out into the passage. Rollmann was coming aft, carrying a fire-blackened can.

'We found this in the office.'

Schepke took the can. It smelled of burned paraffin and the rim was jagged where it had been cut by a can-opener.

'It was in under the receivers,' Rollmann said. 'I wouldn't

74

swear for sure but I thought I saw this same can in the galley a while back.'

'Sam!' Schepke called into the galley doorway.

Sam put his head out, wiping his hands on the oversize apron he wore.

Sam glanced to the deck space behind the fastened back door. 'Seen this before?'

'Where you find?' he asked, at the same time slightly puzzled.

'Never mind that,' Schepke told him. 'Is it yours?'

Sam nodded. 'I keep for lighting range,' he said. 'Somebody must take it away.'

'When did you last see it?'

Sam looked vacant. Then: 'Yesterday,' he said, smiling suddenly and sure about it. 'I light fires yesterday morning.'

'What about today? What did you light them with today?'

'No light fires today. Range go out only one time every week to clean.'

Schepke handed the can back to Rollmann. 'Put it in my cabin,' he told him, then went forward and knocked on Altmeyer's door. Altmeyer came quickly off the bunk.

'All right,' Schepke told him. 'Sit down. What about the key?'

'It's not here,' the boy said nervously. 'I looked everywhere. It's not in the cabin.'

'What about the door? You lock it nights?'

'No, sir. Not since I came on board.'

Schepke thoughtfully lit a cigarette.

'All right,' he said, finally. 'Forget about it. You might have to tell your story to somebody else later on. What I want you to do now is get us in touch with the first ship we sight.'

'You believe me about the key?'

'Forget about the key. Go on up to the flying bridge. You better take the Aldis. The searchlights are useless.'

'Yes, sir,' the boy said brightly.

'Tell Wilamowitz I'll be in my cabin if he wants me.'

'Yes, sir,' the boy said.

75

CAREFULLY, Schepke cut the neat row of cat-gut stitches from his forehead, and after washing the narrowly scabbed wound, he stretched out on the bunk. The smell of the fire had crept in everywhere. He lay with his hands behind his head, the damp, acrid smell of the fire filling the cabin. The movement of the ship had grown considerably since early morning and he lay there feeling the slow, heavy movement of the ship and thinking; and thinking, he suddenly sat up, swinging his legs off the bunk and going to the writing-desk against the after bulkhead.

Bringing the shelf down, he found the chart he wanted and unrolled it onto the shelf. Then lighting a cigarette, he stood back looking at the intricate mass of black spidery lines and figures. The ship's course was firmly imprinted on his mind, and in his mind he laid it off onto the chart and mentally worked out the area and course of the depression. If it held to its present course it would be well in toward Hong Kong before the *Gertrud Lüth* turned on the lap to Formosa. The most they would run into then was the rough backwater. Even that would want careful handling because from what they were already meeting it was blowing big in the north. If there had been any real surplus of coal he could have lain into the breeze for a couple of days and let the blow run herself out in the Gulf of Tong King. But there was no coal for that and there was no telling how long the blow might last either. On the other hand even a big wind could blow herself out in a couple of days. And there was plenty ocean out there. Looking at all that ocean a breeze did not seem much to worry about. But with a ship like the *Gertrud Lüth* there was plenty to worry about even on a fine day with the ocean like a millpond and the birds sitting on the water.

But I'll have to watch this breeze, he was thinking. There's no guessing the course a blow will take out here. It's a bad time of the year as well. Hell, any time of the year is a bad time when it comes to a ship like this. But I'll watch this breeze though, he was thinking. In the north with the breeze from the north the depression's to the east. If she backs or veers and drops she'll be all right. But if she veers and grows it might be safer getting out and walking. That's what the Man did. That's what they say, anyway. Hell, I would have liked to have seen that, he was thinking. I suppose there's people will believe anything some of those old fellows wrote. It's a pity there's none of those bright boys on this old cow if she gets a big blow up. It would be interesting to see a few believers at work in a big blow and praying for the whale to come along. That's the thinking, he was thinking. That, or screw it. Now it's getting like the old days. Maybe if I fed that bastard Müller to the fishes it would change the luck. But one thing sure now is this old cow is making port even if I have to hold her guts together with my bare hands. That's it, old turtle-head. If we're going to think let's think like that. Maybe it won't even come a blow after all. Maybe, he was thinking.

HECHLER was sitting at the writing-desk in his cabin when Schepke entered.

'I see the wind is still getting up.'

'So far,' Schepke said. 'How's everything below?'

'Nothing to complain about, yet. How bad do you suppose we'll get it?'

Schepke sat down on the edge of the bunk. 'Difficult to say. It could get a lot worse even with the main blow two or three hundred kilometres to the north. The wind's still veering so the blow's closing slightly. We could safely expect that for some time yet. Once she starts backing we'll know she's drawing away northward. What we want now is to meet something out from

Hong Kong or Shanghai, or on the way down from Japan. The only way we can keep check meantime is by watching the wind. And the way these blows change around out here we might be in it before we know what's happening.'

Hechler indicated the account books on the desk. 'All we've got is a day in hand.'

'That's what I came to see you about,' Schepke said.

'What happens if it gets really bad? You going to put back to Manila or make for Hong Kong?'

'At the moment I'd rather we made Shanghai,' Schepke said quietly.

'Well I'm with you in that,' Hechler said. 'Old man Oesten will put us all on the beach if we show up anywhere else asking for coal.'

'We could always be leaving it too late,' Schepke warned him.

'Maybe in some ways it would be better too late than the beach,' Hechler said, watching him. 'You can count Dorsch and Frauenheim on that.'

'All right,' Schepke said, rising, '—the one real thing that worries me is why we haven't met anything from the north. Unless maybe they're lying up waiting for the blow to pass. This breeze could veer all day today and tonight and the main blow still pass northward without it getting much worse.'

'Sure,' Hechler said. 'Let's see what happens. It's the chance we take.'

ALL that day Karl Schepke watched the growing breeze and when he went out on deck in the late afternoon darkness was already coming down and there was a strong wind blowing the white cresting ocean before it from the north-east. The wind was taking them on the starboard bow now and the ship was beginning to roll and yaw her head as the swell built up. The swell was still running short but with the gullies beginning to form deeper as the ocean gathered speed before the wind.

In the forward well he stopped several times and carefully inspected the mooring chains that ran through the enormous caterpillar tracks of the earth-moving machines. Everything was firmly secured, and on the way aft he paused to look again at the two smaller bulldozers that faced aft just forward of the bridge superstructure, their long, broad, concave blades locked into position in front of their blunt-nosed radiators.

Müller watched him enter the bridge then go to the charthouse. Following him inside, he handed over the watch while Bahr took the wheel from Pulst. Going on out to the starboard wing, Karl Schepke hung the night-glasses around his neck and watched Müller follow Pulst from the bridge, and thinking, feeling it in the pit of his stomach, that perhaps now the time was not so far away.

Putting the glasses to his eyes, he carefully scanned the fading horizon. All that showed was the grey rising ocean, the deeply forming gullies, the grey crests breaking suddenly and foaming; and now the ugly grey swell beginning its monotonous march before the growing wind. The air had cooled still further with the lengthening of the day but was still humid and oppressive, and pervading it was the inescapable damp smoky smell of the burned out Radio Office.

The bridge was strangely quiet without the steady hum of the steering motor and wireless generators on the deck below, and the sound of the ocean now carried in loudly from the night. Looking around the bridge in the near darkness, Schepke saw Rollmann had made a sound job of repairing the deck. All the windows along the front of the bridge, apart from those in in the wings, had been smashed with the fierce heat and these Rollmann had sealed with canvas and sacking. Then suddenly he felt the air being sucked past him, and turning, saw the deckhead hatch open to the flying bridge and Altmeyer climbing stiffly down the vertical ladder on the after bulkhead.

'I thought you'd gone below when the watch changed?'

Altmeyer set the heavy portable Aldis lamp and batteries

79

against the bulkhead and turned to Schepke. 'I, I forgot about the time, Herr Kapitän.'

Schepke looked at the small, smoke- and fume-grimed face under the tightly pulled down cap. 'How long have you been up there?'

'Since you told me this morning, sir.'

'You had anything to eat?'

'Well, sir. No. I—' the boy said, watching Schepke's face in the near darkness and not so sure any more and trying to put a trace of matter-of-factness into his voice.

'I think you better make up for it,' Schepke told him. 'And after this you better stay here in the bridge.'

'Yes, sir.'

'And Altmeyer. If we sight anything we'll try and inform you in plenty of time.'

Altmeyer managed to bring a smile to his face.

Now it was dark and the deck-lights in the forward well cast shadows through the wings of the bridge. The ship was carrying two points of starboard wheel to keep her on course but still her head yawed as it came heavily, slow to ride, through the lengthening swell. All the ocean was dark and the foaming crests marching white and ghostly through the thickening night.

While searching the darkness, Schepke heard someone climb the stairway. Rollmann came in carrying a brass carbide lamp in either hand.

'They're the best I can do just now,' he said. 'I'll get some hurricane lamps rigged later. The steaming lights are already replaced.'

'Any other lights not working?'

'Only the ones whose leads come up through here,' Rollmann said, hanging the hook of one of the lamps through a light channel on the deckhead behind Bahr, the brightly white carbide flame reflecting up onto the downward hanging face of the compass. Schepke took the other lamp and hung it from the guard around the low deckhead light above the chart table, Rollmann watching him from the doorway.

'Any idea how bad it might get?'

80

Schepke looked at him, wide and weatherbeaten, framed in the doorway in the fluttering light of the pitching lamp. 'I wish I knew, Horst. We don't want to take much with this cargo.'

Rollmann frowned, watching Schepke's face, deeply shadowed under the high-peaked cap. 'I ran the last hawser around the three big ones this afternoon.'

Schepke nodded. 'I was out there before I came up.'

'Well, I'll leave you to it,' Rollmann said. 'I'll be in my cabin if I'm not on deck.'

Schepke turned back to the ocean. With the lengthening of the swell the ship still had her head in the gullies when the following crests took her, throwing the bows away with a jarring boom, the crests continuing their shuddering run the length of the starboard side. And now as he watched, the crest of a swell took her just under the curving forepeak rail on the bows and she slowed, shuddering, unable to lift herself clear, the mighty upthrust of water barely forcing her upward, the high, ghostly cloud of spume and spin'drift flung into the night, dimming the foremast and derrick platform lights. Then suddenly she was lying steeply down on her head and starboard side again as she slid deeply into the succeeding gully, and for the first time Schepke felt the pounding race of the propeller as it was flung clear of the water.

'How is she?' he called to Bahr.

Bahr was heaving bodily on the wheel to starboard to keep the bows from swinging. 'She's taking a long time to answer!' he shouted.

'That one was bigger than the others,' Schepke told him. Then: 'Down ten!' he called.

'Down ten, sir!' repeated the old man in English, at the same time spinning the revolution wheel around, then getting the repeat from the engine-room.

Again Schepke looked into the night. The weather was worsening fast, the long, slow-moving crests of the swell beginning to break and blow in the wind. All of it was bad, and the wind still veering and the ocean shifting with it. He dropped the window down and the wind blasted past him. The bows went

81

deep in a gully and the stern swung around and down and slowly settled, then came wearily away again with the great upthrust of water mounting beneath her. But she did not come away quickly enough and ground to a staggering halt half up the steep slope, and then slowly she started to come away again and the long, slow-moving crest hit her, solidly, jarring her from stem to stern. The broken water roared inboard just aft of the forepeak on the starboard side. Then as her head lifted clear, the raging torrent rushed white and foaming against and through the enormous tracks of the earth-moving machines. Almost immediately her head fell away fast and steeply and the water began its return rush toward the forepeak. Leaning from the window Schepke felt the stern begin its run and now they were falling away beam on, the propeller racing wildly before going deep again. He grabbed the rail below the window and saw Bahr struggling with the wheel, pulling heavily on it with both hands hard around to starboard. Then he was looking back into the night, anxiously watching the great shadowy mass of machinery on the forward well. Nothing appeared to have shifted. She was going away again when the upthrust began to take hold, and at the same time he saw the oncoming crest almost level with the bridge. She began to come away fast, rolling slowly onto her port side, her bulwarks under water, and suddenly, the black wall of water avalanched onto her decks with a long, thunderous roar, the foaming crest heaving bodily inboard and settling slowly down over the machinery. He watched the cluster of decklights around the foot of the foremast disappear greenly into the blackness, only the tall driving cabins of the three earth-moving machines broken whitely up into the night.

He felt her settle beneath his feet, then slowly start to lift, shuddering hugely, the stern freeing itself first and the water roaring back across the bulwarks. As he watched he was conscious of Bahr running the wheel back freely amidships. Then suddenly her head lifted and the water broke and threshed and ripped through the mass of machinery on its way aft. His eyes searched the deck anxiously. But again nothing appeared to have shifted and he felt himself relax a little as the tension ebbed.

Then her head started to fall away again and he peered to starboard. The shape of the oncoming swell was not so menacing this time. The ocean was angling more on the starboard bow now but with the stern remaining on the slope behind them instead of falling away as it had done previously.

'Half ahead!' he shouted, still at the open window, noting that the decklights around the foot of the foremast had remained out. The only light now falling on the forward well was from the derrick platform and the four round-lights on the drop of the forepeak. While he watched he was conscious of the changing speed, the shipboard noise easing a little as it fell away.

'That was a big one, Herr Kapitän.' The sweat was gleaming on Bahr's face and neck in the light of the wildly pitching carbide lamp.

Schepke nodded. 'How's she answering now?'

'She's still taking her time.'

'It's the chain gear. All we do is hope the main steering motor holds out.'

'That's all we do—hope!' It was Hechler, standing just inside the doorway, his overalls soaked through and clinging to his enormous bulk. 'I've been watching the main motor the last twenty minutes and she's on her limit now.'

'Is there anything you can do?' Schepke asked.

'It's no special part,' Hechler said. 'It's all of her.'

'What if we hove-to?'

Hechler shook his head, wiping the salt water from his face and neck. 'It's age that's beating her. She was never meant for this.'

'How long do you give her?' Schepke asked, anxious now about the way things were going.

'I wouldn't like to say. Maybe five minutes, maybe five weeks. But the five weeks is probably my optimism.'

'It's going to get a lot worse.'

Hechler did not say anything, only watched Schepke's face in the gloom.

'It's gathered since darkness,' Schepke went on. 'It's blowing

Force Seven now and the barometer still falling. I'd say the main blow has altered course and now moving down north of the Philippines. That's why it's got as bad as quickly as this.'

'I suppose that rules Manila out,' Hechler said.

'I wouldn't like to try it. I think we should stay on our original course and try and outrun it. If it gets much worse I'll put the wind on our starboard quarter and try running her that way. Only I want the wind further in the east before turning. We have a fair chance of making Hong Kong then, but turning now and the blow catches up with us we're going to end up on the Viet Nam beach. We still wouldn't probably be able to make Saigon from here, and if we turned for Manila we'd likely run straight into her. Anyway, we'd have the wind blowing down on our port side.'

'Sure,' Hechler said, nodding his agreement. 'If she starts rolling she'll probably roll over and not come up again. But what if this blow doesn't pass astern?'

Schepke shrugged his long-sloped shoulders. 'It's a chance. I wouldn't like to say where she might blow yet. She could still pass ahead. All we can do now is wait.'

Just then Rollmann came in the doorway, his hair plastered to his forehead and his storm coat gleaming wetly in the white carbide light.

'I've just been down in the wells,' he said. 'Everything's still holding but any more like that last one and I don't promise anything.'

'What about below?' Schepke asked Hechler.

'We're all right so far.'

'It's come in bad since dark,' Rollmann said.

'She'll blow big,' Schepke told him.

'Typhoon?'

'We'll see,' Schepke said. 'If it is it's my guess she's headed down north of the Philippines. I'd say the wind should be out of the east by daylight and if it keeps veering she should pass astern.'

Hechler nodded toward the window. 'I don't give much for our chances if that lot out there comes adrift.'

Schepke grabbed the rail as the bows fell away sharply, the wind rising to a howl in the wireless telegraphy aerials.

'We'll put into Hong Kong,' he said, suddenly making up his mind. 'I'll head her into the east while we can then use the wind and sea as a drift when we turn. Alter course now and we'll either end up on the Viet Nam beach or else fighting it out in the Gulf of Tong King. Right now we don't have coal for either.'

'Whatever you say,' Hechler said.

Schepke turned to Rollmann. 'Keep a close watch on the wells. All right?'

Rollmann nodded. 'I'll move part of the watch into the fore-peak tunnel.'

As he left Schepke turned again to Hechler. 'Can you have somebody keep a check on the main motor?'

'I'll get one of the greasers up there. There's not much else I can do. I'll take another look at it on the way below.'

Now it was all decided. If the company did not like it he would be back on the beach. He had no longer been thinking about that side of it. The luck had been bad for a long time. For a time he had thought the luck would change again. But he did not think about it now and in the charthouse he laid off the new course north-east by east.

The movement of the ship was still growing as the swell built up steadily. From the starboard wing he saw the glow of light in the forepeak tunnel as part of the watch on deck moved into the cordage locker. Out beyond the ship the ocean was in blackness. Spume was blowing back in clouds across the fore-deck and the ship's head arcing away to port each time she met the swell, lunging heavily and clumsily into it.

'Starboard ten!'

'Starboard ten, sir!' Bahr shouted as he put the wheel over. 'Ten starboard wheel on, sir!'

She was slow to answer. Then as her head began to rise she came around wearily, breasting the oncoming swell outward and upward, the spray and spin'drift cascading in a falling, wind-driven cloud back across the deck to port. She came swiftly away then, the bows going deep in the succeeding gully.

He was standing close to Bahr now, watching the swinging compass bowl. "Midships!'

"Midships! Wheel amidships, sir!'

'Steady!'

'Steady zero-six-five, sir!'

'Steer zero-six-eight!'

The ocean was running in slightly on the port bow now, the ship finding it easier, her bows breasting the ocean apart as she steamed doggedly into it. Schepke reached for the engine-room telephone, spinning the handle and almost immediately hearing Hechler shouting above the high-powered whine and pound of the engines.

'I've just taken her around,' Schepke said. 'We should have it easier until at least late morning. By that time we should know how she's going to blow. Keep me in touch with things below.' As he hung the receiver back on its hook he saw Wilamowitz come in the doorway.

'What is it?'

Wilamowitz frowned. 'It's midnight.'

Schepke looked at his wrist watch. The evening had gone quickly and he had lost track of all time.

They went into the charthouse together, Schepke explaining the new course, then noting the barometer still falling. 'It should be into Force Eight when Müller takes over. If I'm not on the bridge when you go off, wake me when you come down.'

KARL SCHEPKE came instantly awake. It was dark in the cabin and the wind and ocean seeming strangely loud. He sat up, the ship pitching and rolling wildly with the solid motion of the swell.

He was pulling on his tunic when Wilamowitz burst in.

'Hechler's started the pumps! We're making water in Number One!'

Schepke jammed his cap down and brushed past him. 'Get Müller awake and on the bridge!' he called back.

He met Hechler on the main stairway, his face serious, and his overalls open to the waist and sweat gleaming on his face and chest.

'I think we've sprung a couple of plates in Number One. We're not shipping anything big yet but it can get bad any time.'

They hurried back down the stairway and out into the starboard alleyway. Part of the way along the alleyway the ship lunged and rolled and angry black water roared in across the bulwarks. Grabbing the housing rail, they hung on, chest deep in wildly swirling water. Slowly the ship began to right herself, the overhead deck-lights reflecting sickly green on the solid mass of water caught up in the alleyway. Then as the water began to sweep aft, they struggled out onto the forward well.

A group of black storm-coated seamen were already gathered around the hatch of Number One hold. The bows drove deep again, then flung high into the night, scattering the men around the hatch. Schepke grabbed at a hawser above him as a huge wall of spray hammered back across the well. Everywhere around him was the terrific creaking and groaning of chains and hawsers as they strained under the massive weight of machinery. Looking toward the bridge, he saw Wilamowitz duck his head from a window as the wall of spray cleared the flying bridge.

'Get her going!' he yelled through his cupped hands. He saw Wilamowitz look dumbly toward him, the face of the bridge lit by the weak glow of the derrick platform lights. Quickly he made a wide circling motion with his right hand. 'Get her going!' he yelled. This time Wilamowitz raised a hand in acknowledgement, and Schepke turned and staggered up the angled deck toward the hatch.

'Where's Rollmann?'

One of the seamen pointed into the blackness of the hold where they had already broken back the hatch covers. Schepke grabbed the top of the combing and swung himself into the blackness to find the ladder.

'Horst!' It was terrifically hot in the darkness and he stepped from the ladder to sink to his knees in grain.

'Over here!' Rollmann called, somewhere in the darkness.

Again the ship lunged and Schepke held to the ladder until she slowed, his legs sinking deeper in the grain. Then the bows hit solidly with a mighty hollow boom and creaking of plates and timbers, all the while water pouring through the partly-open hatch. Then as the ship slowly began to lift, he floundered into the darkness, feeling his way around the bulkheads without finding any trace of surface dampness, deafened most of the time by the tremendous scouring rush of water along the outside of the hull.

When he found the ladder again, Rollmann was waiting for him.

'There's nothing showing,' Rollmann shouted.

'I didn't expect it to. Better shore up Number Two bulkhead. Do what you can. It'll be difficult. There's—' Something landed heavily, sharply, on his shoulder, then leapt again. Beside him, Rollmann cursed and blundered into the ladder.

'What is it?' Schepke shouted.

'Something hit me across the face.'

'It's the rats. One of them didn't make the top. Come on.'

Hechler was waiting for them. 'Find anything?' he asked, shouting into the wind.

'Nothing.' Schepke told him. 'Rollmann's going to shore Number Two. You keep me—' They grabbed together at the track of one of the machines as the bows hit another long rolling swell inboard across the forepeak. '—Come on!' Schepke shouted, starting aft for the alleyway. 'Keep me in touch with the pumps. Let me know what water we're shipping.'

'You'll be on the bridge?' Hechler asked as they made the inboard passage.

Schepke nodded and hurried for the bridge.

Both Müller and Wilamowitz were watching the forward well from the windows.

'What are they doing with Number Two?' Wilamowitz asked.

'Rollmann's shoring the forward bulkhead,' Schepke told him.

'Somebody seems to have put a jinx on this trip,' Müller said as he ran the window up.

Schepke ignored him, taking a quick look through the spray-lashed windows and seeing the storm-coated seamen struggling through the mass of machinery with huge bulks of timber.

'I don't know how I manage to pick them,' Müller said disgustedly.

Schepke stood away from the windows. 'What's on your mind, Müller?'

'We should have turned for Manila hours ago,' Müller said, his voice sullen, and him glowering at Schepke in the light of the wildly pitching carbide lamp.

Schepke watched him carefully. 'A beam on run in this and she'd roll herself under,' he said quietly. 'We'll try for Hong Kong.'

'You'll never make it,' Müller said contemptuously.

'Well if we don't there's no chance that you will.' Schepke left him with it and went into the charthouse.

All he could do now was to keep their head into it until it was safe to turn her stern and make the run for Hong Kong. Then as he stood up from the table he heard one of the telephones buzz on the bridge.

He took it from Müller.

'Yes?'

'Hechler here. I wanted you to know that the pumps are coping easily. We're not shipping as much as we thought.'

'Good. From now on I'll be sleeping in the charthouse.' He hung the receiver back on its hook and turned to Müller. 'You're all right,' he said. 'There's no trumpets calling yet.'

Müller glared at him sullenly but remained silent.

Schepke looked at his wrist watch. It was almost four o'clock.

'You better turn in and get some sleep while you can,' he said to Wilamowitz, then turned to the charthouse, leaving Müller with the watch. The bunk was against the after bulkhead, under the overhanging chart and writing-shelf. Lying down fully dressed, he settled his shoulder against the side of the bunk, and went to sleep with the whitely bright flame of the carbide lamp swinging and widely arcing low over the glass-topped table.

WHEN daylight began to come in, the *Gertrud Lüth* was on course almost due east, her engines slow ahead and her forward hatches once more battened down. The early morning sky was hazed and close to the ocean, the swell running long and heavy and the wind now blowing east-by-south, whipping the crests of the swell into long clouding streamers across the bows. Karl Schepke stood in the starboard wing staring through the spray-lashed windows at the strangely lighted sky to the south-east. Below him, the ocean was now continually pouring across the foredeck in a solid grey-green mass.

He turned back to the charthouse. During the night they had drifted back across their original course, the wind failing to veer as much or as fast as he had hoped. From calculations he now made he expected the wind to reach its full intensity somewhere toward late afternoon or evening. By then it would have settled down into a full storm. If it grew bigger, then the *Gertrud Lüth* would need plenty of luck to steam out a typhoon.

But she's out there, he was thinking. She's out there and all lit up. You just saw her. Sure, he was thinking, you'll need plenty more luck than I ever had. But there's no good getting used to anything, even the misfortune. I guess we know it comes so many ways. Sure, when things turn bad, they turn bad all right, old bad luck turtle-head. You, you're not even one of the lousy bright boys. Not even one of the lousy bright boys.

He came back onto the bridge to find Altmeyer in the starboard wing with the glasses.

'You won't find anything out there,' he told the boy. 'If there's anything out there it's the other side of the storm pushing time until they get a clear run.'

As he spoke the bows fell sharply away and they grabbed the rail. All the forward deck disappeared under a long low wall of grey-green water, then slowly, shudderingly, the dark shape of the forepeak broke whitely through the wind-torn water. Schepke had the window down, watching the deck reappear. The machinery was acting as a series of breakwaters and each time the ocean came inboard it was suddenly and violently flung high into the wind in great white sheets as it raced aft with the lifting motion of the bows. Rollmann had made a sound job of the deck-cargo and everything was intact except for the overhead exhausts on the motor of the athwartships earth-mover below the forepeak. That was the only damage he could see without going on deck, that and most of the glass in the driving cabins.

'What's that light?' Altmeyer asked, pointing away to the south-east.

'That's the storm area!' Schepke shouted, slamming the window up. 'That's where the big blow comes from. The further south that light travels the easier a run we'll have.'

Altmeyer was watching him talking. 'How bad is it going to get?' he asked.

Schepke did not hear him. He was watching the oncoming swell, deciding now to make the run, not quite certain how further the wind would continue to veer and not wanting to leave it too long.

'Port fifteen!' he called, at the same time spinning the handle of the engine-room telephone.

The ship lunged heavily to starboard as she started the slow, gyrating swing to port.

'Engine-room. Dorsch speaking,' the voice the other end of the line shouted.

'Schepke here. Tell Hechler I want him on the bridge.' The bows were coming around now.

'Up twenty!' he called to the lascar on the telegraph.

91

When she came beam on she took a tremendous sea while labouring in a steep gully and rolled, solid grey-green water completely burying everything except the midship superstructure.

'Full ahead!' he yelled, hoping the extra power would pull her free.

The ship lay buried and motionless.

The high-peaked cap jammed tightly down over his head, Schepke held grimly to the rail as yet another sea rolled inboard, booming loud and hollow-sounding on the starboard side superstructure.

Then slowly, achingly, he felt her begin to roll herself upright under the tremendous pinning force of the ocean. Then, with water roaring from every part of her, she was thrust suddenly clear. Now, high in the water, she caught the full force of the wind and spin'drift. Her head began to move swiftly away to port again. Schepke waited, glancing around the bridge. Only Bahr was on his feet. Altmeyer and the old man had been thrown against the after bulkhead and were still lying on the deck, surprised and shaken. Grabbing the telegraph, he rang it all the way back then up to half ahead, at the same time glancing overhead at the compass bowl to see the ship's head winging away northward.

'Meet her!' he yelled, grabbing the wheel along with Bahr and fighting it back to starboard.

'Steer due North!'

'Steer due North, sir!' Bahr shouted as Schepke left him again for the window.

Now the wind and ocean were running in a few points abaft the starboard beam. With the change of course the ship had developed a pitch and roll movement, lying her port side well into the ocean. Then as a bigger sea caught her abaft the beam, sending her head down, Hechler burst through the doorway, only catching hold on the junction boxes in time to stop himself being thrown.

'Good Christ!' he shouted. 'I thought we were gone when you brought her around! What happened?'

'We caught a big one abeam,' Schepke shouted, and started

into the starboard wing, Hechler following him and then coming up against the spray-lashed after windows. Schepke dropped one of them down for the wind to almost blast them across the bridge.

'See that?' he shouted, pointing to the south-east. 'See it?' he asked, still pointing.

Hechler shielded his eyes.

Away to the south-east the sky was low and black but with an eerie yellow light showing through it in much the same way as happens with one of the big land storms blowing off Africa's Skeleton Coast.

Schepke slammed the window shut.

'That's a typhoon, all right,' Hechler said. 'Think she'll keep on going?'

'Come here,' Schepke told him, going into the charthouse.

Hechler leaned over the glass-topped table, the chart a mass of intricate pencil lines and figures.

'See that?' Schepke asked. 'See those wind notations? The wind's trailing way astern of the centre and varying.'

'Think she'll change direction?'

'It's possible. I started worrying about that this morning when I took over from Müller. He had it noted that the wind never rose beyond forty-six during the first part of the middle, and then later he has it noted as dropping to forty and forty-one. It's only these last three hours that it's built up again and remained roughly the same direction.'

'It's possible it could turn north again, isn't it?' Hechler asked, the anxiety showing in his voice.

'There's no telling where they turn,' Schepke told him. 'At the moment I'd say we're just inside the outer fringe of the storm area.' He leaned up from the table, looking squarely at Hechler. 'If that wireless had been working we'd have known just exactly what was out there.'

Hechler wiped the sleeve of his overalls across his face. 'I hope she keeps headed south,' he said quietly.

'Well she's changed course since she grew off the Carolines,' Schepke said pointedly.

'I thought they usually ended up on the China coast after coming out of the Pacific in a northerly direction.'

'She could end up on the China coast yet,' Schepke said. 'That's why I started the run. Even if she turns north again we might still outrun her. If I'd known she was coming up this fast I'd never have lain into the wind last night.'

'You can't blame yourself for that,' Hechler told him. 'How were you going to know what was coming? Müller and Wilamowitz didn't know, did they?'

'Maybe I was too long on the beach,' Schepke said.

'Like hell!' Hechler said. 'You did what you thought was right. It was the wireless that started our troubles.'

'If we hadn't lain-to last night we'd have had another ten or twelve hours start on our run.'

'What are you going to do now?'

'We'll keep her headed due north,' Schepke told him, turning back to the chart. 'That's what I wanted to see you about. I want you to ease her up to as fast as she can safely steam.'

'Due north?' Hechler came back.

'As she is,' Schepke said, leaning across the table. 'I don't want to put her stern-on yet. We haven't the fuel to go steaming across the Gulf.'

'All right,' Hechler said, shrugging his immense shoulders. 'Start easing her up gradually so we can keep a close check on the pumps.'

Wilamowitz was on the bridge when they came out from the charthouse.

'Where have you been?' Schepke asked.

'I—you didn't call me. I didn't know anything until we hit that big one. I came on—'

'All right,' Schepke told him, no longer interested. 'Go down and help Rollmann keep watch on the deck-cargo. Tell him we'll be increasing speed.'

Schepke watched him follow Hechler below, then went out to the starboard wing. The yellow hazed darkness now completely blanketed the horizon to the south-east, and the swell, breaking as it built, was whipped by the wind into flying clouds of spin'drift. For a long time Karl Schepke stared away to the south-east before turning back along the bridge.

HECHLER arrived on the bridge just before darkness came down. After a day-long watch amid the tremendous heat and noise of the engine-room he looked tired and his overalls sweat-streaked and oil-stained.

'The pumps still coping?' Schepke asked.

Hechler nodded. 'For the moment,' he said. 'I'm worried about the shaft now. Frauenheim's been shutting down practically every time our head takes the stern clear. She's been racing so badly I found myself waiting for a bracket to shake loose.'

'You want me to ease her down?' Schepke asked, carefully watching the Chief's face.

Hechler shrugged, not wishing to commit himself.

Schepke turned back to the window as the bows went deep, the decks completely submerging. Then as the stern began its run, the foredeck began its slow lift, the forward well turning into a welter of boiling white as water broke and raced aft, sheeting high over the machinery.

'Down twelve!'

The old, grey-bearded lascar on the telegraph repeated the order as he rang the revolutions down on the counter.

'What's the position now?' Hechler asked.

Schepke shook his head. 'It's been backing to the east since mid-afternoon. We're still inside. The wind's strengthening as well and the ocean beginning to shift. The blow's going to come in abeam if it doesn't make another change of course soon.'

'How about the others, do they know?'

'They'll know soon enough,' Schepke told him. 'If there's anything below you want done in a hurry you better get it done now. By midnight we're likely to be in it.'

'Isn't there anything else we can do?'

'If it overtakes us now then all we can do is lie into it.'

'What about the drift?' Hechler asked worriedly. 'Even if we come through we'll have a long way to make up. We'd be well in toward the Gulf.'

'Leave that to me,' Schepke told him. 'If she does come through I'll take her into Hong Kong even if we have to burn the decking.'

'All right,' Hechler said. 'I'll be below if you want me.'

Schepke turned to the window, dropping it down, screwing the eye-pieces of the night-glasses around and searching the darkness.

Nothing showed. He ran the window up and wiped the sea-water from the glasses. Seas were continually breaking inboard now along the entire length of the starboard side.

'Half ahead!' he told the lascar. He waited until he felt the speed drop then turned to Bahr. 'Still heavy?'

Bahr nodded, the sweat gleaming in the light of the carbide lamp as it ran from his naked back and shoulders.

Schepke turned to the outer windows. Everywhere was a mighty blackness out of which roared the growing seas breaking savagely inboard across the starboard side, the decks a welter of torn water boiling up white under the few remaining deck and derrick platform lights. With the further easing of speed the movement of the ship had grown more severe and now she was rolling her bulwarks under.

'Kapitän!'

He turned to see Altmeyer burst in from below, sea-water streaming from his storm coat.

'The port for'ad bulldozer's just broke her hawsers! Roll-mann's out there now!'

Schepke flung himself across the bridge as the ship rolled onto even keel. Below the bridge the black storm-coated seamen were struggling chest-deep in swirling water as they fought to secure the broken hawsers.

'Starboard twenty!' he yelled, momentarily looking at Bahr, the noise of the storm drowning Bahr's voice as he rammed the wheel hard around to starboard, leaning all his weight to it, fighting it around.

Her head came away swiftly as she slid into the oncoming gully, taking the sea with a thunderous impact high on the forepeak. The whole deck forward of the bridge disappeared completely.

'Slow ahead!' Schepke yelled, ducking his head inside so his words were not lost.

The following two seas caught her almost simultaneously. For a brief moment he thought she was going all the way, then somehow she gathered herself, shuddering, her engines pounding, the propeller racing wildly for a hold, and suddenly she came away, water burying her decks and breaking and beginning its savage rush aft into the alleyways, streaming solidly across the sheer walls.

It was a moment before he saw the seamen move out again from the alleyways. The bulldozer was still there.

'Altmeyer! Tell Rollmann to get up here as soon as everything's secure!' He had not moved from the window, the wind and spray blasting past him into the near-darkness of the bridge. '—Wait!' he called after the boy. 'Who's down there?'

'Wilamowitz and Müller, sir!'

Schepke turned back to the window. They were still at work on the hawsers, the bows still fighting slowly around into the seas.

'Steady!'

'Steady!—Steady on zero-seven-seven, sir!'

'Steer zero-seven-five!' Schepke ordered. 'Down twenty!'

On this new course there was far less water coming on board. Only when she ploughed her forepeak under did she ship anything big and then it would roar solidly inboard to thunder high into the night as it hit upon the earth-moving machines in a series of breakwaters, the broken, wind-blown water then hammered into the face of the bridge. Slamming the window shut he reached for the row of telephones.

'Engine-room. Hechler here.' Hechler's voice was almost lost

97

amid the terrific pounding and high-powered whine of the engines.

'Listen, Hans. One of the for'ad bulldozers just parted her hawsers. We'll ride it out from now on. There's no use trying to outrun this blow any more. She's overtaking us as it is. Let me know if there's any increase of water.' He slammed the receiver back on the hook and turned to the charthouse.

'You! Schepke!' Müller shouted as he burst in from below, water streaming from his uniform. 'Do you know what's out there?'

Schepke looked back at him across the sloping deck. 'If I had done as you wanted and ran for Manila we would have been in it before midday. She's probably changed course four or five times since she grew up off the Carolines.'

'We should have turned back to Singapore after the fire!' Müller countered angrily. 'There was no need to come on!'

'Get out!' Schepke said, his voice changed.

'—Don't tell me to get out!'

Schepke's fist caught him on the mouth, sending him against the after end of the bridge. He followed up immediately, dragging him upright and hitting him twice more, low in the belly, sending him sprawling out through the doorway.

Rollmann caught the rail and swung himself clear as he went past him. Then he saw Schepke looming above him, wide and grim-faced.

'Are you all right?' Schepke asked, seeing Rollmann and the blood and sea-water streaming down the side of his face from a wound high on his head.

Rollmann nodded. 'I'll have Sam look at it later. I just wanted you to know everything is secure again. It wouldn't have been so easy if it had been one of the big ones.'

'—I haven't finished, Schepke! I haven't finished!' Müller's voice rose almost to a scream. 'Hear me, Schepke?'

Schepke ignored him. 'Who's on deck?'

'Everybody,' Rollmann said.

'Make sure they keep a strict watch on the wells. It's going to get a lot worse toward midnight.'

'I'll see to it.' Rollmann started down the stairway, then stopped. 'I think we've lost a couple of men,' he said. 'Wilamowitz is checking now.'

'There's nothing we can do in this weather,' Schepke said quietly.

He watched Rollmann go down into the passage then turned back to the charthouse.

It had been bad all the way along. It had gone bad very suddenly a long time ago. He could look back and feel and see it all exactly as it had happened, and looking at it, he could not feel nor see where at any time it had begun to change again. When it went bad it went bad all the way and the luck did not at any time seem likely to change. But thinking was not going to help any now. All the thinking in the world was not going to help any. Neither is the praying. Only I wasn't praying, he was thinking. The praying belongs to the bright boys, eh, old turtle-head. There's no understanding that business, anyway. We don't want to get things more complicated than they are. And praying a hell of a thing to start complications with. They even had fourteen. Jesus Christs all at the same time and they've been trying to prove ever since that only thirteen of them were idiots. Well that's the bright boys for you, old turtle-head. The boys with the smart words and the all-seeing eye. What was it one of them said? —All things come alike to all. For him that is joined to all the living there is hope; for a living dog is better than a dead lion. Yes, that's what the dog said, he was thinking. Bright dogs or bright boys, they're all one. And how did he die, in his bed and the sun going down outside? That's the trouble with the bright boys, they all die easy. I only hope we have our share of bright boys because this time it isn't going to be so comfortable. On the other hand, maybe we can save them. I guess saving them would be worth it just to hear all the bright things they'd have to say about the saving afterward. Maybe even one of them will walk the water like the other fellow did when the heat was on. Well I guess that would be worth seeing all right, old turtle-head. Old turtle-head.

'Kapitän!'

He turned to the bridge to meet Wilamowitz. 'What is it?' he called from the doorway.

'There's two men unaccounted for! —They must have gone overboard!' He was very upset.

'I'm sorry,' Schepke said. 'They didn't live long out there.'

Wilamowitz watched him in the light of the wildly pitching lamp. 'But they went overboard,' he said, his voice flat and incredulous.

'You couldn't have done anything even if you'd seen them go.'

'But they're—'

'Forget it!' Schepke said sharply. 'We could be with them before long.'

Wilamowitz looked away.

'You better take over here,' Schepke went on. 'Bahr has the course. Wake me at eleven o'clock, or sooner if the wind gauge touches sixty-five.' He stepped back into the charthouse and closed the door, leaving Wilamowitz to the bridge.

KARL SCHEPKE came awake with the beginning of a violent downward rush followed immediately by a muffled-sounding explosion that lifted him from the bunk and threw him against the chart table. It had gone dark suddenly and he was on the deck with charts and books and instruments coming down around him. The first thing he was aware of was the acrid, penetrating fumes of spilled carbide as the lamp rolled and crashed about the deck somewhere to his right. Finding the top of the table, he pulled himself to his feet on the steeply angled deck, found the door, and wrenching it open was faintly surprised to see the lamp on the bridge still burning and Pulst hanging grimly to the wheel, watched by Wilamowitz and the lascar telegraphsman from where they had been thrown on the deck. Again the bows drove deep as they fell away into a gully and again came the thunderous impact as another huge sea swept inboard. Then while the bows were still weighted downward yet another sea exploded on the face of the bridge. All the forward windows and canvas-blocked windows went together and Schepke landed with Pulst somewhere at the rear of the bridge as glass and canvas and splintered wood and water burst in upon them. Everything went black and dark and wet at once. Schepke fought his way forward on the angled deck until his hand touched the wheel, and grasping it, hauled himself to his feet. The deck stayed strangely angled steeply away forward, spray and solid water ripping through the gaping window spaces. Then while holding blindly to the wheel something rolled heavily against his legs and he felt someone fight for a hold on the wheel as the bows held fast.

'She's going!' someone screamed into his face, and the following sea hit them and they were flung violently backward into the welter of water and debris. This time the door at the rear of the bridge burst outward under the impact and water fountained out across the stairway to the cabin deck. Schepke pulled himself onto his knees, seeing the lights below in the passage reflect greenly up through the flooding water. He remained crouching, fascinated by the greenly lit water. Then as the flood of water lessened and the angle of the deck beneath him eased slowly upward, he pushed himself to his feet and staggered forward. He could feel the bows gathering momentum now as they broke free of the weight of water.

It was all darkness out there and the bows coming up. He could feel the deck right itself beneath his feet, water and debris swirling out through the doorway to the passage below. Then he saw someone move between him and the light reflecting through the doorway.

'Pulst!' he shouted, waiting, '—Pulst!'

Wilamowitz was on his knees, dazedly shaking his head, spitting water. Schepke got him under the arms and dragged him toward the wheel. Out on the forward well water was roaring outboard across the bulwarks, the wind whipping the spray and spin'drift back into the face of the bridge, hammering it through the gaping window spaces.

The bows fell away again, easily, sluggishly, and with the swift falling away came the long tortured scream of rending metal. Again a sea thundered inboard across the forepeak. At that moment Pulst staggered out of the darkness and grabbed the wheel, automatically leaning it to starboard to bring the bows around. Schepke, holding Wilamowitz to his feet, turned his back to the hammering spray. Wilamowitz grabbed at his arm, trying to tear himself free.

'She's going!' he screamed. 'Let me go!'

Schepke swung the back of his fist into his face, dropping him to his knees. 'Shut up!' he yelled, and dragged him upright and hit him again. 'Listen! Get out on deck and see what's happened. Tell Rollmann I'll be right down.'

'But she's going! She's going!' he shouted fearfully.

'Shut up. She's not going anywhere.— Now get out there!'

'I can't! Nobody can go out there!' He had hold on the front of Schepke's tunic now.

Schepke forced him to the doorway. 'Get Rollmann and get out there! Hear me? —Get out there!' He threw Wilamowitz out through the doorway and saw him grab the rail, look numbly up at him, then back toward the main stairway.

Back on the bridge he found Pulst still at the wheel trying desperately to get their head around into the wind.

'Stay with her!' he yelled, and turned back to the stairway as the bows began their long agonizing lift upward. There was no sign in the darkness anywhere of the lascar telegraphsman.

The cabin deck passage was full of water and debris and the slamming of wildly swinging doors. Most of the lights had gone out and the main stairway was in complete darkness. By the time he reached the midship flat he was struggling through water that almost swirled him off his feet. He stopped, puzzled by the amount of water and where it was coming from with such force. But he could see nothing in the darkness and as he turned toward the port passage the bows suddenly flung upward and there was a loud vibrating rumble followed by a tremendous grating crash that slammed him against the bulkhead and sent timbers and panelling hurtling from the forward flat bulkhead. This time he saw the water burst in white and hissing from the great hole gouged cleanly through the plates of the bridge facing. The massive blade of the bulldozer had almost cut completely through into the flat.

He drew a deep breath and ducked into the water to come up the other side of the fallen timbers. Ahead of him in the passage was someone with a lantern, the flame flaring with the wind.

'Kapitän?' the voice the other side of the lantern said.

'Who's that?'

'Bahr. I was on my way to the bridge.'

'Go on up.' Schepke told him. 'Pulst's there himself. Keep her into the wind.' He heard Bahr shout something in reply to him that was lost as he stumbled out into the alleyway. The wind caught him immediately and spun him against the housing, the water surging through the alleyway waist-deep. He gathered his balance then hauled himself forward by the housing rail. The bows had gone deep and as they began their long upward climb a huge wall of water exploded into the night high above the fore-peak, ghostly phosphorescent and driven aft across the flying bridge by the wind. The ship jarred to a halt, shuddering under the impact, her propeller high in the air. He stopped, grabbing a firmer hold on the rail as the weight of water bore aft, sending a number of storm-coated seamen sprawling before it.

The water came in a solid white wall, burying the men as they fought for a hold. Then as it cleared, Schepke saw Wilamowitz ahead of him, his tunic almost torn from his back.

'Come on!' Rollmann was shouting somewhere ahead.

They started back toward the well and overhead another light came on, brilliantly lighting the foredeck. Glancing at the bridge, Schepke saw someone had roped an arc-light out through one of the window spaces. The port side bulldozer had disappeared completely, leaving nothing but a tangle of mooring cable and hawsers, the bulwarks shorn away flush with the decking. But now everyone was gathered around the starboard side bulldozer, trying to free the blade from the face of the bridge. At first

103

nothing happened, then as the bows started to fall away the shifting weight of the huge machine dragged the blade free. Schepke moved in behind the high, square radiator along with Wilamowitz. Somewhere to the rear he heard Rollmann shouting for the men to stand by ready to secure. The machine moved slowly at first then gathered speed with the increasing angle of the deck, and as it neared its original position, seamen ran the still interwoven cables out from the tracks to where others waited with stoppers and shackles.

With only the first of the shackles in place a heavy sea exploded with a tremendous roar onto the forepeak then stormed up high into the blackness above them. They were still working furiously as the bulldozer began to move again, only to fetch up slowly as the inboard cables took the strain. Then the wall of water crashed down into the well, heavy and white and roaring and Karl Schepke saw the men swept clear as the cables parted with cannon-like reports. The huge machine lurched aft, gathering speed with the weight of water and the angling deck. He threw himself inboard toward the combing of Number Two hatch, the wild confusion of water avalanching across the entire forward deck as the bows flung high. Then clearly, above the noise of the storm and the rumbling of skidding tracks, he heard the sudden paralysing scream cut short by the tremendous grating crash.

When the water cleared he rose to see Wilamowitz pinned against the face of the bridge, almost cut in half by the long concave blade. Then the ship heeled as she rose and the body swung grotesquely from the waist, the water foaming up around the legs stained darkly with blood.

Seamen were picking themselves up all around the deck.

'Come on!' Schepke shouted. 'Get around her! Get those crowbars through the tracks!—Come on! Move!'

The body came free with the blade.

'Keep her moving!' Schepke roared as the seamen levered crowbars and bulks of timber through the tracks as if to walk the huge machine back bodily.

As the bows began their long descent the bulldozer gathered

speed, moving swiftly now, colliding with the earth-mover moored ahead. Schepke glanced anxiously around for Rollmann but saw no sign of him. This time they had two of the cables shackled to eye-bolts when the next sea rolled ponderously inboard across the sunken forepeak, moving smoothly, unhurriedly, coming on wide and black then sheeting high and white, engulfing the foremost of the huge machines, the enveloping cloud of spray hammering the face of the bridge as water raced chest-high across the angling deck. Karl Schepke grabbed the track with both hands as his feet swept out from under him. Holding his breath, the water thundered over him. Beneath it all he felt the huge machine surge aft, then jerk up as the cables took the weight, straining, the rear end lifting clear of the steeply angled deck.

Most of the seamen had gained shelter of the alleyways.

'Get out here!' Schepke roared. 'Get the rest of those cables shackled down! Never mind the stoppers! Get the shackles on!'

The next sea rolled in smoothly across the forepeak and broke in the drop to the forward well, exploding into the night as it hit the athwartships earth-mover. The seamen were already on their way to the alleyways. Schepke saw Wilamowitz's body alongside the after winch, and gathering it under the arms, dragged it in through the screen door to the starboard passage. A number of seamen already in the passage were standing against the bulkheads well forward. Schepke laid Wilamowitz on the deck amongst the swirling water and debris then looked at the watching faces.

'Anybody see Rollmann?'

No one answered.

'What about you?' Schepke asked the tall one with the long moustaches.

The lascar glanced at the rapidly staining water swirling around Wilamowitz. 'I never saw him again after this one dies,' he said quietly.

'Anybody else see him?'

Again no one answered.

'All right,' he said to the tall one. 'You take charge of the deck for now. Go back and get the stoppers on. Then get that hawser adrift on the port side. You know where it is, where the bulldozer went through the bulwarks.'

The lascar nodded, his dark moustachioed face shadowed under his gleaming black sou'wester.

'Put that hawser on the starboard side bulldozer,' Schepke told him. 'I want that machine lashed down like it was part of the deck. Understand?'

The lascar nodded and moved out toward the screen door. The others remained where they were, glaring sullenly at Schepke.

'You heard me!' Schepke yelled. 'Get out there!' He grabbed the nearest seaman and hurled him out through the screen door. That started them moving and the others followed, their long frocked coats brushing Wilamowitz as they stepped over him lying there grey and broken in the stained water, his head lolling with the movement of the ship.

There was a heaviness about the fore part of the ship now and Schepke started for the bridge, then changed his mind and went went back out into the alleyway. Holding to the housing rail, he made his way to the after well. The deck-lights on the after end of the midship superstructure still burned and in the glow of them he saw the machinery still securely moored. The well was running high with dead water but the seas were not breaking solidly inboard that far aft, only occasionally, when they ran the walls as she lay head down, would the towering crests run inboard across the bulwarks to surge up in a wild welter across the fantail.

For a time he crouched over the massive tracks examining the links of cable by hand. Satisfied, he turned back toward the alleyway and stumbled and went down over something bulky buried in the water. Reaching out in the darkness he touched a face. It was impossible to know who it was but he got his hand into the collar of the storm coat and dragged the body in through the screen door.

It was Rollmann, his face grey and waxy and curiously doll-like. There was a lot of blood coming from him, and moving the frock of the coat aside, Schepke saw the startling white of the thigh bone where the left leg had been almost severed above the knee. He had lost a lot of blood lying out there on deck and all that held the leg together was several tendons. Quickly, Schepke rolled him onto his face, put his arm around him and lifted him onto his shoulder. Stepping over Wilamowitz, his foot caught the head and it lolled, the big and empty eyes staring at the over-head lights. Now the water swirling around him did not stain so badly.

Schepke felt his way up into the dimly lit cabin passage. Huddled together at the head of the stairway was Sam and the mess boy, both very frightened and wearing bulky life-jackets.

'Get back in the messroom.' Schepke told them, and waited for them to go on ahead.

He laid Rollmann on his back on the long polished mess table. The stump of his leg was still bleeding badly and the lower part of the leg had fallen at right-angles across the table. All the time the mess boy went on staring at the back of Sam's head.

'You,' Schepke told him. 'Get all the towels and hot water you can. —Sam. Get the galley scissors and first-aid kit. Hurry!'

When they came back he had Rollmann's storm coat off and he took the scissors and cut the leg of the trousers away. The thigh bone had splintered lengthwise but the stump was cleanly cut. Taking one of the towels he tore a strip off and put a tourniquet on above the stump. Sam had the kit set out along one side of the table and Schepke took an Omnopon and put the needle in high on the hip, Sam looking away from it all. Rollmann had not moved any but was now breathing through his clenched teeth so the inward breath made a long laboured hissing.

Kuang came in with an old range steamer.

'Put it on the deck and come here. Both of you.' Schepke stood off the table. 'Hold him until I come back. All right?'

'What if he wakes?' Sam asked anxiously.

'Put his hand in his mouth. He'll want something to bite on.'

In the darkness of the bridge he saw them outlined against the gaping window spaces.

'Bahr!'

They were both at the wheel.

'The engine-room was asking for you,' Pulst shouted, 'we're making water again.'

Schepke turned his head to the spray hammering in through the window spaces and counted the boxes then spun the handle.

'Engine-room.' Hechler's voice sounded very small and far-away.

'Schepke here,' Schepke shouted, bracing himself against the rail. 'How bad are we making water?'

'We're holding our own again now,' Hechler answered. 'The level's risen some but it isn't gaining further.'

'Do what you can,' Schepke told him. 'I've got Rollmann in the messroom. His leg's to come off.' He fumbled the telephone onto its hook without waiting a reply.

'Who else is up here?'

'Only Altmeyer,' Pulst answered, shouting over his shoulder as their head fell away.

'Altmeyer!' Schepke shouted into the darkness.

Suddenly, as if in answer, the bridge was brilliantly lit as an arc-light came on showing Altmeyer hanging grimly to the rail as he roped the bowl of the arc-light to a light channel on the forward bulkhead. The bridge was almost completely wrecked. Even the charthouse door had gone along with most of the fittings and panelling, and inside the charthouse everything was swilling around on the deck. Then Schepke saw the storm-coated bundle that had been swept into the starboard wing. He went out and turned it over. It was the lascar telegraphsman.

'How is he?' Bahr asked.

'His neck's broken.'

'Roth's gone as well. I saw him in the alleyway just before I met you. He went out with one of the seamen to give Rollmann a hand. When the water cleared they'd both gone.'

'Where's Müller?'

'He hasn't been up here.' Pulst told him.

Schepke turned to see Altmeyer finish roping the arc-light into position. 'What about you?'

Altmeyer shook his head. 'I haven't seen Müller since the port bulldozer first came adrift.'

'You've done a good job with the lights,' Schepke told him, still shouting above the noise of the storm. 'See if you can do something with those windows. There's plenty of canvas and timber lying around.' He turned again to the quartermasters. 'Keep her into the wind until I get back. And if she starts to go it's better to take it below than out there.'

He hurried below to the passage. Müller's door was locked.

'Müller! —Müller, you in there?' he shouted through the door.

There was no answer but in the dimly lit passage the light inside the cabin showed through the top vent in the door. He put his shoulder to it and the lock gave and he saw Müller on the bunk. The dead-light was down over the scuttle and an empty bottle rolled on the deck. He bent down over the dressing-table and there were three other bottles in the bottom drawer. One after the other he smashed them into the wash-basin, shattered glass and whisky showering the cabin. Going out, he slammed the door behind him.

Sam and the boy were still holding Rollmann on the table.

'How is he?'

Sam shook his head. 'He never wake once,' he said, not looking well with any of it.

The boy was white and had his mouth tightly shut.

The bleeding had stopped as much as it would and the immediate stump had drained white and cold-looking.

'Get the meat saw.'

Sam slowly raised his head.

'Get it!' Schepke told him.

Sam came back with the saw and Schepke sawed the bone off up high and began tying the arteries and veins, sweat streaming down his face and shoulders as he worked.

'Get those needles ready!'

Sam wiped the sweat from his face with his arm and reached for the cat-gut and needles.

'Where's Kuang?' Schepke asked when he was ready for the needles.

Sam nodded along the table and Schepke stood away and saw the boy lying on his face on the deck.

'Give me the needles.'

He started sewing, bringing the skin down and sewing over the stump, leaving wicks for drainage.

All the time Schepke sewed, Sam kept his head away. He had not looked at anything since he had brought the saw.

Schepke finished the sewing and wiped the sweat from his face with one of the towels. Rollmann looked very close to death. He had never moved and now he was breathing smally through his open mouth. Suddenly the ship shuddered under a deafening roar and Schepke grabbed him as he slithered across the table. Sam hit the after bulkhead and went down hard. Then as the ship began to right herself Schepke gathered Rollmann up and carried him forward to the big cabin. The cabin was cool and musty-smelling and he laid him on the high-sided bunk between the pillows.

When he went back to the messroom the boy was sitting up looking at Sam in one of the chairs.

Schepke lifted him to his feet. 'Go in the galley and make all the coffee and sandwiches you can.'

Kuang stared at him blankly.

'Hear what I said?'

This time the boy nodded.

'Once everything is ready you take them around the ship and make sure everybody has something to eat and drink. All right?'

Again the boy nodded. Schepke watched him go out to the galley, still wearing the bulky life-jacket and full of fear and the smell of death.

'You come with me,' he said to Sam.

Rollmann lay on the bunk exactly as he had left him, between the two pillows, the blankets folded back, and covered only by the sheet.

'See these?' Schepke asked, holding the Omnopons.

'Yes, sir,' Sam said, watching him break the plastic and tin-foil seal then take the cork plug from the needle.

'All you do now is put it in his hip and squeeze it empty. Got that?'

'Yes, sir,' Sam said nervously.

'All right. Now watch the clock. In another hour you give him the first one.'

Sam nodded, not looking at the needle. Schepke returned the plug and handed it to him. 'Do you know if Emmermann had a gun?'

'A big gun,' Sam said impressively.

'Where did he keep it?'

Sam stepped away from the drawers down the face of the bunk.

In the first drawer there was only clothes. Then Schepke found it in the next, under some winter clothing, big and bulky and wrapped in oiled flannel inside a length of yellow oil-cloth. It was one of those big ugly Mausers many of the U-boat Commanders had carried. There were two boxes of shells. He loaded the gun from one of the boxes then emptied the remaining shells into the pocket of his tunic. Sam watched him nervously. Sam had not been himself since he had brought the saw.

'Remember what I said,' Schepke told him. 'The first one in an hour.'

ALTMEYER had a number of the windows directly forward of the wheel covered over when Schepke arrived on the bridge.

Glancing at the compass dial he saw their head lying almost due east.

'The Chief was on the phone,' Pulst said. 'He's coming topside.'

Schepke nodded. 'You'll have coffee and something to eat soon,' he told them.

Hechler came in as he was talking.

'Are we still in one piece up here?'

'As far as we know,' Schepke told him. 'How's Number One?'

'The pumps are still holding but we're not making any head-way.' There were heavy lines of tiredness on Hechler's face. 'We're taking water almost everywhere now,' he went on. 'The main steering motor is still standing up to it. That's one good thing.'

'I'm worried about Rollmann,' Schepke told him. 'He lost a lot of blood before I found him. I've done all I can but I don't give much for his chances.'

'What about out there?' Hechler asked, glancing at the ocean.

'We'll know soon,' Schepke said. 'Send somebody up to the galley when you get back. Kuang's there now. I'll be here on the bridge.'

Hechler started to say something then turned to leave.

'Something wrong?'

Hechler hesitated. 'Well,' he said, 'there's a bit of water beginning to swill around down there and some of the black gang look jumpy with it.'

'Keep a good hold on them,' Schepke told him. 'Keep them busy. Tell Dorsch and Frauenheim the same. There's enough trouble up here without any below.'

'I'll do what I can,' Hechler said.

Schepke went into the charthouse, found the carbide lamp, and lit it. Then taking a fresh chart from the canister he trans-ferred the immediate workings from the old one before putting it away in the drawer. They were already well to the north-west of the Hong Kong lane and still drifting. In the past hour the storm had slightly veered again as it wavered in its path. Wedging himself against the table he watched the wind-gauge repeater on the deckhead. Once when the bows rose he saw the needle forced, trembling, to touch seventy-two miles per hour, and between gusts, never saw it drop below sixty-eight. Glancing at his wrist watch he saw it had stopped.

Shaking it, the hand moved a few seconds then stopped again. On the heavy brass clock above the writing-shelf he saw it was twenty minutes past four o'clock.

'That's all the windows blocked, sir.'

He looked up to see Altmeyer the other side of the table. 'You'll remember this one,' he said quietly.

The boy tried to smile.

'Never mind,' Schepke told him. 'You've done well tonight. You should have joined the deck instead of all that morse business.'

'Is it going to get much worse?'

Schepke brought a crumpled packet of cigarettes from his pocket and offered them. 'It's difficult to say,' he said.

Altmeyer lit the cigarettes. 'We'll be all right, won't we, sir?' he asked, unable to hide the anxiety in his voice.

Outside was the sudden booming sound of the ocean on the forepeak. Outside, in the darkness, the ocean, and the wind in the aerials.

'I'll tell you what,' Schepke said. 'There's still a couple of windows in the starboard wing. Take the glasses off the bunk and keep a look-out. That way the time goes.'

'Yes, sir,' Altmeyer said and this time the smile flickered momentarily across his mouth.

'Down fifteen!' Schepke called to the bridge.

'Down fifteen, sir!' Pulst shouted, spinning the revolution counter.

Bahr glanced around at the doorway as he held the wheel down.

'That should about hold our head from swinging!' Schepke shouted in way of explaining. 'With the water in her head she should hold herself into the wind!'

Finishing with the chart, he went out and down into the cabin passage. Sam was sitting on the deck, wedged into the corner where the outboard bulkhead met the face of the bunk, his head lolling with the movement of the ship, his eyes closed, still wearing the life-jacket, and sitting there very big and round in it. Rollmann had not moved but now the stump of his leg had bloodied through to the sheet.

'Sam.'

Sam came awake as though the end had come. 'Sorry! Sorry, Kapitän! No sleep! Only sleep one minute!'

113

'All right,' Schepke told him. 'How is he? Any movement?'

Sam looked sadly at Rollmann and shook his head.

'Remember what I said.'

Sam nodded so vigorously all of him shook beneath the bulky life-jacket.

Then out in the passage, Schepke looked in at Müller. He was still asleep, the cabin reeking of whisky and stale air.

'Müller!'

Müller groaned uneasily, shifting his head on the pillow.

Schepke pulled the door shut behind him and started back along the passage and the first one hit her, the impact slamming him against the bulkhead. The next one hit her almost immediately. All four or five of them followed swiftly upon one another. She took them while sitting flat in the water. They came in long and low and ponderously sweeping her under from stem to stern. He had almost reached the head of the stairway when the last one drove in across the buried forepeak and detonated low on the face of the bridge.

He picked himself up in the passage and started back up the stairway. The ship was still sitting flat, but deeply in the water. Everyone was on the deck and most of the windows gone again and water ripping through the gaping window spaces. As he crossed the bridge he dragged Altmeyer to his feet and took the glasses from around his neck. The ship was fast shedding water, the bows beginning their long laborious lift, the engines almost pounding themselves from their beds as the propeller fought for a hold.

Out beyond the window spaces the ocean was brilliantly lit by a blood red glow and overhead the sky was lit that sickly smoky yellow. It was as though suddenly the door of a vast blast furnace had been swung open. All the ocean before them was flat and blood red, and further out, spinning and threshing downward as a giant whirlpool might. The ship was out clear from the water, the machinery still on deck, although the forepeak rails had gone along with the main boom, leaving the two forward derricks standing up starkly naked just below the drop from the forepeak.

'What's happened? —What is it?' Altmeyer yelled, his voice almost hysterical.

'Jesus Christ!' Bahr shouted as he dragged himself to the window spaces.

'We're out of it! See that! We're out of it!' Pulst was shouting.

'Shut up!' Schepke yelled. —'We're inside. All the way inside.' Inside of the storm centre the ship was beginning to slew with the undercurrents, hanging in the head, her decks angled to the bows and carrying a list to port.

Schepke grabbed the engine-room telephone and spun the handle.

'What in hell's happening up there?'

'Never mind that,' Schepke shouted, recognizing Dorch's voice. 'In a few minutes we'll hit a wall of water. Get everybody away from all fires and machinery and hold on.' He slammed the receiver back on its hook and lifted the glasses onto the wild frenzy of advancing water.

''Midships!'

Bahr grabbed the wheel and spun it around. 'Wheel amidships!' he answered, his voice wavering and flat-sounding.

'Leave it! Everybody get below to the passage!' Schepke told them, dropping the glasses to his chest, seeing the wall coming on swiftly now, towering high above the bows, blood red and black in the gully and wildly white on the crest. Altmeyer had backed into the charthouse doorway, staring wide-eyed at the sight before him.

'Get below!' Schepke yelled, and grabbed him and hurled him bodily out through the bridge doorway.

Away to port he saw the wall break as the gathering weight of water overbalanced, exploding in a tremendous roar of upflung surf. Out ahead of the bows it still gathered itself, towering bridge-high, black-shadowed and reflecting the angry blood red light of the storm. The wall was continuing to break to port as it came on, the unnatural quiet of the storm centre broken now with the roar of advancing surf, wildly white, flung high into the scorching air.

115

If we're going to go, we'll go now, Karl Schepke thought as he watched it come on like a mountain with snow on its long ridge, black, carrying the eerie reflection of the storm light.

The air was suffocatingly hot and moving in sudden waves.

'Break! Break you bastard!'

It was coming on fast, closing the gap rapidly.

'—Break! Break!' he was yelling, the air filled with the thunderous roar of boiling surf, and above it now, the long loud wailing of the storm. Grasping the rail, he watched it, the glasses swinging on his chest on their strap, the high-peaked cap jammed close down over his ragged blond hair. Suddenly the ship hit the frenzy of underwater currents and the bows bucked violently, the wheel spinning freely with no one at the helm.

The great angry wall of water detonated close in under the bows, sending up clouds of surf and spray that momentarily lit the immediate darkness vividly white before engulfing the ship completely. Karl Schepke was flung clear across the bridge with the impact. Water roared through the window spaces, stunning him, pinning him against the after bulkhead. Suddenly amidst it all he was aware of everything lit strangely green, the brightness seeming far away, and then, still pinned against the bulkhead, he realized the arc-light was still burning; and somehow fascinated by it he saw it get brighter and brighter and suddenly the pounding force of water had almost gone and he pulled his knees up under him, and pushed, and came up out of the water.

A big wind was blowing through the window spaces, and then the bows rose steeply, slamming him against the bulkhead. The *Gertrud Lüth* was still afloat, and she would not go now. He felt it. She would not go now. He was very sure about it and he pushed his way through the water rapidly emptying into the cabin passage and saw that outside it was still strangely lit, the low cloud broken now by a pale clear light as with a false dawn in the tropics. They had come through the first onslaught of water and here in the semi-circle the ocean had changed momentum. Although still running tremendously high, the swell came on in great, slow-moving rollers. Only the swell did not break, nor did they follow close upon each other, but they came on slowly, wide apart, quietly coming on, no spume nor spin'drift in the wind, but oddly silent as though the low black sky strove to depress them smooth and even in their motion. Then as he brought the wheel over, hauling the head around into the wind, he was suddenly aware of something oddly wrong with the fore-deck. Then the bows sent a massive shower of spray into the night and in the ghostly whiteness he saw the foremast had snapped almost level with the forepeak. Taking a quick look around, he saw it wedged securely in athwart the face of the bridge, the button and broken foot overhanging the bulwarks. The pale clear light breaking the cloud ceiling had quickly faded, and using the glasses now, screwing the eye-pieces around until about two kilometres away he made out the whiteness of the area where the seas built up wildly again under the full force of the storm.

Leaving the wheel, he grabbed the engine-room telephone from its hook and spun the handle. On the other end the receiver was already off its hook and no one answering. He spun the handle again, and waited. Still no one answered. Letting the receiver drop, he staggered up the angling deck as the bows fell away. Below him on the stairway was Pulst, dazedly hanging to the rail as he waited for the momentum of the ship to slow.

'Stay with her!' Schepke yelled. 'She won't go now!'

Bahr was sitting in the passage by the main stairway vacantly staring at the water ripping across the top stair. Altmeyer was lying further aft.

'Are you all right?'

Altmeyer nodded and started to say something.

'Go on up to Pulst!' Schepke told him. 'Keep her into the wind!'

Bahr was already on his feet when Schepke went past him on his way below.

The midship flat was full of water and blackness. In the port passage some of the emergency lighting had come on and the screen door to the alleyway slammed on its hinges as the bows flung high. He was almost half way along the passage to the

117

port inboard engine-room hatch when the cover went up and they came fighting out onto the deck. The two lights were behind him now and the other one glowing dimly above the after screen door.

'Get back!' he called to them. 'Get below!'

There was a momentary lull in the shouting and then he saw someone move forward out of the gloom.

'—Get back! All of you get below!' he shouted, and saw someone in the passage clearly now against the light. Then as he moved forward he caught the brief glimpse of a rising shovel.

'Drop it!' he shouted, grabbing the heavy Mauser from his pocket. 'Go on, get back!'

The figure in the passage paused, then came on in a wild rush, the others following him, all of them shouting.

Schepke squeezed the trigger as he lifted the gun, aiming at the deckhead above them. Nothing happened and he felt his stomach knot and turn over as he fumbled the safety-catch. Then he got the gun up again and shot him high in the chest. The suddenness of the shot in the passage deafened him and he felt the shovel come off his shoulder and go into the darkness and water at his feet. Whoever it was he had shot he had gone down and taken someone else with him. It was all confusion now and he saw someone else move close to him and he fired without aiming at anything definite and there was the vicious stunning thwock of the heavy bullet in flesh almost before the shot and flame. This time he fired twice more over the heads and heard the high-pitched whine of bullets ricochet off the deckhead. Someone was down in rear, crying out loudly. Then he saw all of them flatten against the bulkheads in the sudden brilliance of light from the open hatchway as those still on the ladder dropped swiftly below.

'Back! —Go on, back!' he shouted, knowing they saw him outlined in the glow of the two lights further up the passage. 'Now get below! —One at a time!'

None of them made any attempt to get onto the ladder inside the hatchway.

'Move!' he shouted, holding the gun away from directly in

front of him so they might catch a gleam of light on the black steel.

Two of them moved together. He counted seven of them as they passed down through the open hatchway, seeing their faces black and frightened and the water and sweat gleaming on their arms and shoulders in the brilliantly upflung light.

There were two bodies in the water by his feet and he stepped carefully across them toward the hatch. Someone was sitting up against the screen door, groaning loudly and holding both hands to his thigh. He was one of the black gang, and he had a white sweat-rag around his neck and was sitting up in the water holding his thigh on the inside, rocking back and forth from the waist up with the pain. He had his head turned toward the forward end of the passage and Schepke saw the whites of his eyes move in the brightness beyond the mouth of the hatchway.

'You shoot me. You shoot me,' he was saying, his voice sounding very surprised.

Schepke went on down the ladder, not looking at him again.

'You shoot me,' he was saying down the ladder. He had just realized that he had been shot and he was very surprised about it.

Frauenheim and Dorsch were waiting for him when he came off the ladder from the catwalk. They had Hechler sitting up on the footplate holding the back of his head with both hands.

'What happened?'

'They panicked!' Dorsch said, shouting above the pounding of the engines. 'Mostly the black gang!'

'It was that first sea we took that started it,' Frauenheim shouted, the colour drained from his face. 'We were sitting right down on our stern end.'

'How's Hechler?'

'He's not hurt bad.' Dorsch shouted. 'Somebody must have hit him with something.' He was lying on the footplate and everybody fighting up the ladder when Frauenheim and myself came out of the tunnel. We were in there when it happened.'

'That's right,' Frauenheim shouted. 'They were all on the ladder except the oilers. The oilers weren't in it.'

Dorsch nodded. The black gang were gathered the other side

119

of the footplate watching them, their faces wet with sweat again and showing fear.

Schepke gestured at them with the gun. 'Back in the stokehold,' he told them. 'The first one to make trouble gets shot. —Now move!'

Dorsch had Hechler on his feet now. He was holding himself up on the big throttle and easing his head around gently on his shoulders.

'The black God Jesus Christing bastards!' he was shouting. 'The murdering nigger bastards!' Then he saw Schepke standing on the far side of the footplate with the big black Mauser in his hand. 'Go on!' he shouted. 'Shoot the bastards!'

Frauenheim suddenly burst out laughing, then slowly lapsed into a long rumbling bout of coughing.

'What the hell are you laughing at?' Hechler demanded.

'Are you all right?' Schepke asked.

'What do you think?' Hechler asked, still nursing his head.

'You sound all right.'

Hechler gave him a long baleful glare from under his brows then rubbed the back of his head again. 'If I find the bastard who hit me—' he said.

'There's two of them dead topside,' Schepke told him. 'There's another with a bullet in his leg.'

'Jesus Christ!' Dorsch said, involuntarily looking at the gun.

'Losing two is better than everybody going,' Schepke said, then looked at the black oily water and dead ashes swirling around the footplate. 'How are you making out with the water?' he asked.

'We'll manage,' Hechler told him. 'One and Two are holding. Number Three's not making anything much.'

Just then there was a terrific boom up forward and Schepke grabbed the ladder as the impact brought him to his knees. They were lying over to starboard, the sound of water raging on the hull above the pounding of the engines, then clearly, as the bows went deep, the grating race of the propeller carried loudly above all else as it was flung high into the night.

Frauenheim was first up and threw the throttle.

The ship's head was up out of the seas again, Schepke wondering fleetingly if the main steering motor had gone and the ship now swinging away out of control.

'See to the motor!' he shouted to Hechler as he went up the ladder.

The lascar was still sitting against the screen door, bent over his legs, holding his thigh with both hands.

'Don't move any!' Schepke told him, then turned and went over the two bodies in the water in the darkness.

When he reached the bridge stairway the ship caught a long rolling sea on her port beam. Up ahead of him he saw Altmeyer come out through the doorway in a rush then pull up on the stairway.

'Müller's taken the wheel!' he shouted.

Schepke went past him. Pulst and Bahr were standing back against the after bulkhead, the ship at that moment lying her starboard beam under as she rolled and dropped away broadside. Müller had the wheel hard around to starboard, spray hammering through the window spaces in the port wing. Schepke had just taken the gun from his pocket when Müller saw him. The ship heeled suddenly, lurching as she took the oncoming sea on her port beam. Schepke stumbled, and fighting to keep his balance, lost the gun. As he turned to look for it Müller threw himself across the bridge. They went rolling over in the water, clawing for a hold, the arc-light broken loose and rolling around close by them. Müller came out of the tangle on top of Schepke, finding his throat with both hands, choking him as he hammered his head back against the deck. Everything was red and roaring and lit brilliantly, and then Schepke got an arm up and found Müller's eye with his thumb. Heaving upward at the same time, he suddenly felt Müller's hands lose their grip as he went over backward. He was first on his feet and hit Müller as he rose, groping for a hold. At the same time he saw someone cross the bridge to the wheel as the bows flung high.

'Get her around!' he shouted. 'Get her head in the wind!'

And she rolled again and Müller brought him down, his hands again clawing for his throat. Schepke got his knee up between them and threw him off, and as he scrambled up, the ship, turning, came on to a big smooth-running sea and, riding it heavily, her head rose, angling the deck so swiftly he hit Müller before setting himself and they went out through the bridge doorway, Müller pinning his arms down in a bear-hug. Part of the way down the stairway the handrail snapped and they went over into the stairwell by the Radio Office. Schepke took the fall on his back, and as Müller rolled clear he saw him grab a fire-axe from under the stairway. He was on his knees when Müller swung it waist-high, the blade scoring the bulkhead just before it hit him low on the left side of his chest. He went down with it and saw Müller swing the axe up over his shoulder and then Altmeyer was above him on the stairway and crashed part of a brass rail squarely onto his head. Müller staggered, then crumpled over slowly, his eyes widening, still holding to the axe.

'The gun! Get the gun!' Schepke shouted to the boy. Altmeyer went on staring at Müller lying face-down in the stairwell. 'Find the gun!' Schepke shouted to his bending face. Altmeyer looked at him suddenly, then turned for the bridge.

All the left side of Schepke's chest was numb and his breathing difficult, and the blood was running freely through his fingers where he held himself. As he waited for Altmeyer a stab of pain gradually centred through the numbness and grew with every breath. Müller had not moved. His mouth was open against the deck and there was blood running from his scalp and down through the dirty stubble on the side of his jaw. If Schepke had the gun right then he would have shot him. Instead he unbuttoned his tunic and pulled the sweat shirt from his trousers. It was a long open gash, parted so he could see the white gleam of bone through the blood.

Altmeyer had still not returned with the gun and he got up slowly, holding the wound together with the flat of his hand, trying to breathe easily and lightly against the deep stabbing pain. He waited with his back against the bulkhead, his legs wide apart so as not to be taken off-balance if they hit a big one. The ship was not rolling so severely now and he could feel her with her head almost into the wind. Müller groaned and moved onto his side. Just then Altmeyer came down with the big black Mauser and Schepke took it and slipped the catch off and held it on Müller as he sat up. Altmeyer watched nervously, his face dirty and grey, deep circles under his eyes.

'Up, Müller! —Get up!'

Müller moved sullenly, the hate showing in his flat little eyes, mean-looking and surly and with blood clotting the stubble on his jaw.

'Move!' Schepke told him, motioning him aft along the passage, and one sudden move and he would have put a bullet between his shoulders.

'All right!' They had stopped outside the dry food store next the galley. It had a high clipped-down door with a grated vent.

'Open it,' he told Altmeyer. 'Go around back of me.'

There were packing-cases stacked up inside and Schepke put the heavy gun to Müller's back and he went inside, and Altmeyer quickly closed the door and pulled the clips down onto the stops.

Karl Schepke was thinking maybe he should have put a bullet in him after all. There was no one on board more mean than Müller and what made it worse was that he did not know the consequences of half he ever did. He was one of the bright boys who went through with things in a hurry and did not even think about them afterward.

'Is there anything else I can do?' Altmeyer asked, watching Schepke anxiously.

'You better go back on the bridge. See if they want anything.'

The ship took a big one, very suddenly, shuddering under it, her head falling away. Schepke hit the bulkhead, taking most of the blow on his shoulder, the impact driving the breath from him and the pain feeling as though it cut him through the middle.

The sweat ran coldly on his back as Altmeyer helped him to his feet.

'I'll manage. Go on up to the bridge.'

Altmeyer looked at him for a moment then started back along the passage.

Both Sam and the boy were in the big cabin.

'Get some hot water and bandaging,' Schepke told them. 'Hurry it!'

They went out, staring at the blood soaking Schepke's tunic and trousers. Schepke took the tunic off and eased down into the big leather chair at the desk. The pain had settled into a long, deep throbbing through the left side of his chest. Sitting there, he looked across at the bunk. Rollmann had not moved. Then Sam and the boy came back bringing towels and water and bandaging.

'Here on the desk,' Schepke told them. 'Tear one of those towels,' he told Sam.

Gritting his teeth, sweat streaming down his face and neck, he washed the wound then made a pad from part of the towel and put it over the wound. Then standing, he took the wide gauze bandage and began winding it around the lower part of his chest, running it firmly over the pad. Both Sam and the boy stood on the other side of the desk watching him, still wearing the bulky life-jackets.

'Here.' Schepke held his tunic to Sam. 'Did you give it to Rollmann?' he asked as Sam helped him on with his tunic.

Sam nodded. 'He wake up twice but go away again very quickly,' he said.

'If he wakes again tell him everything's fine. Understand?'

Sam nodded again while Kuang looked vacant.

'Don't open the store the other side of the galley,' Schepke told them from the doorway. 'Müller's there.'

Altmeyer had a number of the windows blocked again and the wind was blowing in cooler than at any time during the storm. Pulst and Bahr were still handling the wheel between them.

'Ship's head now lying one-one-five, sir,' Bahr called to him. 'There was a sudden change of wind direction this side.'

Schepke nodded. The pain was throbbing all the way through his chest now. Glancing overhead at the compass, he suddenly remembered the wounded lascar. 'Altmeyer. Go down aft in the port passage,' he said to him. 'One of the black gang's down there. Put him in the big cabin. And watch his leg, he's been shot.' Then looking to Pulst: 'The seamen should be sheltering somewhere on the starboard side. Get two of them up here. Get somebody you know can handle the wheel.'

He went into the charthouse and found the chart washed onto the deck. Spreading it out flat on the table, he began making rapid calculations as to their estimated position. He was working on the canvas-backed log when he heard Pulst come back with the seamen. Both of them were openly apprehensive about being topside and they carried most of what they owned in linen wrapped bundles.

'Put those in the charthouse,' Schepke told them. 'You don't need them,' he said clearly in English. 'The ship doesn't sink. Understand?'

The seamen looked at each other, their frightened black faces gleaming in the powerful light of the arc.

'Go on, put them away,' Schepke told them.

When they came out from the charthouse Altmeyer had arrived.

'Find him?' Schepke asked.

'There's, there's two bodies down there,' the boy said falteringly.

'What about the other one?'

'There's two holes high on the inside of his thigh,' the boy said, running his tongue around his mouth.

'Good. It'll save digging for the bullet,' Schepke said. 'Wash his leg then bandage it and ask Sam to get him some blankets. He better stay in the big cabin. —And when you've done that you better get some sleep yourself.'

'Yes, sir.' He was a good boy but tired and exhausted now and finding it difficult to accept what was happening.

'Give these two the wheel,' Schepke told Bahr. 'Go on,' he said to the seamen. 'All you do is keep her head where it is now on the compass.'

Bahr and Pulst waited, watching the lascars.

'You better turn in,' Schepke told them. 'Don't go below to your own cabins. One of you take mine and the other take Müller's.'

'Are you sure you can manage alone?' Bahr asked, watching Schepke standing stooped over.

Schepke dismissed them with a nod. Then: 'Wait!' he called after them. 'What about the dead one who was here?'

'I put him aft in the cabin passage,' Pulst said.

'All right,' Schepke told them.

When they had gone he wedged himself between the telegraph and the bulkhead, his back and shoulder toward one of the open windows. The pain seemed to have settled dully in the pit of his stomach, jarring upward on the nerve ends every time the bows fell away. Daylight was beginning to come in, slowly greying the horizon to the east. The foredeck looked strangely barren when she rose, shedding water, the forward well a tangle of rigging and aerials, the forepeak completely devastated, all the rails and vents forward of the break gone. Settling himself against the bulkhead, he watched daylight come in.

Toward mid-morning the *Gertrud Lüth* was lying her head roughly on one hundred and twenty-seven degrees, the whole ocean shifting with the wind. Karl Schepke felt cold and raw with weariness and all that kept him awake was the terrible grating pain working on the nerve ends somewhere deep in his stomach, the left side of his chest completely numb now and only hurting inside, the pain stabbing fiercely upward whenever the bows fell away.

He tried thinking himself out of it all, and he thought about the girl, but he could not focus any picture of her clearly, and after a time he gave up trying to see her and just stood there jammed between the telegraph and the bulkhead feeling only the pain and tiredness, and occasionally everything would swing spinningly around and he would close his eyes and there would be only the pain and the storm outside.

Some time later, Pulst came in with a jug of coffee and some mugs. He set everything into the charthouse and came out and took the wheel, gesturing the seamen in to the coffee.

Karl Schepke saw him look at him uncertainly, his eyes screwed up against the wind whipping the spray in through the gaping window spaces.

'Where's Bahr?'

'He's gone below for our storm-coats,' Pulst told him.

The two seamen had come back onto the bridge with their linen wrapped bundles.

'You can go below now,' Schepke told them. Then said to Pulst: 'Think you can manage for a time?'

Pulst nodded, watching the compass.

'Keep her shifting with the wind,' Schepke went on. 'I'll be in the charthouse.'

It was Hechler who awoke him. Karl Schepke opened his eyes and saw Hechler leaning over him, his face grey and heavy with fatigue. He eased himself upright and sat his legs over the side of the bunk. All his left side had stiffened but with the pain now subsided into a steady numbing ache.

'What time is it?'

'It's just gone three o'clock.'

'Who's out there now?' Schepke asked nodding toward the doorway.

'Altmeyer and two seamen at the moment. They made up three watches, using the seamen to steer.'

'How is everything below?'

'We're doing better than I thought we would,' Hechler said.

Schepke looked at the chart, then at the overhead compass repeater.

'As long as we can keep her head up we're all right,' he said. 'How long can you give us?'

'I'd say three days is about the limit, steaming as we are,' Hechler told him.

Schepke leaned over the chart, working rapidly with a pencil.

'How far are we from Hong Kong?' Hechler, watching him, asked.

'We can't make a move until this eases.' Schepke was watching his face now. 'How far can you stretch those three days?'

'You'd want plenty of luck,' Hechler said quietly.

'Maybe the luck's due,' Schepke said, again looking at the chart. 'We can start by stripping down everything that'll burn. Come on.'

Wilamowitz's body was still lying in the starboard passage, water and debris swilling around it.

'Most of them are in the machine shop,' Hechler said as they went aft past the quartermasters' cabins.

'What's in there?' Schepke asked stopping outside a steel door on the inboard bulkhead.

'That. That's a storeroom. It's not used much. There's another one on the port side.'

'They can put the dead there,' Schepke told him, before going on to the machine shop. All the seamen were there except those on watch.

'I want two for sewing canvas,' Schepke said when the talking stilled.

One of the seamen moved off the after bulkhead. 'I can sew, Kapitän,' he said. Schepke looked at him. He was old and stooped. 'Who else?'

Another of the seamen raised his hand.

'All right. Get the dead together and put them in the store-room next door. You can work there. The Chief will send fire-bars up for weighting them.' He paused, looking around the rest of the men, then saw the one he had put in charge of the deck. '—You!' he said. 'What's your name?'

'Hussef, sir,' the lascar said.

'Start stripping the ship of anything that will burn. Understand?'

The lascar, watching him intently, nodded, his long moustaches moving with his head.

'Start on the passages,' Schepke told him. 'Strip them of all wood and panelling. Cabins as well. And get that foremast in off the well. Send everything below to the boiler-room.' He turned and saw Hechler watching. 'Any good?' he asked.

'It'll help,' Hechler told him. 'I'll shut down on one of the boilers.'

'I'll leave it to you.' He turned out into the passage and met the two seamen carrying Wilamowitz aft. The body had stiffened and they carried it as they might have done a hatch-cover.

Sam was waiting for him in the cabin passage. 'The bo'sun is awake now, sir,' he said excitedly. 'I was to look for you.'

Schepke followed him into the big cabin. Rollmann was lying very quietly on the bunk, his eyes closed and seeming very close to death.

'Horst,' he said leaning over him.

Rollmann's eyes flickered open, then focused on him.

'Get some water,' Schepke called to the boy.

He took the glass and held it to Rollmann's lips and he sipped a little, then choked, coughing.

'Take it easy,' Schepke told him, setting the glass on the shelf over the bunk.

'—How are we?' Rollmann's voice was very faint.

'Fine. We're fine. You're going to be all right.'

'My leg. It hurts. It hurts all the way up into my back. —It's cold.'

'We'll soon be in Hong Kong,' Schepke told him quietly. 'Try and rest now.'

'Wilamowitz. —I thought I saw him get caught.' Rollmann's voice was getting further away now.

'He's all right. Try and rest some and don't worry. You're going to be fine.'

Rollmann's eyes were already closed and he was not moving even when he breathed. He was still in the state of shock. And he was asleep now.

By early next morning the seas had begun to lessen, the storm blowing herself further away to the north. A little while after midday Karl Schepke glanced overhead at the compass and saw their head had come around fifteen degrees since daylight had come in and was now bearing one-five-five. The ocean was grey again now and the seas coming on evenly spaced, their crests foaming and streaming in the wind. Watching them, he knew he must make the decision. With the weather broken the way it was there was a strong possibility that rain and fog would set in with the weakening of the wind.

He looked back along the wing to Bahr and the two lascars. 'Stand by to come about after the burials.'

'I'll take the wheel myself,' Bahr said.

Below in the cabin passage the air was thick with dust and smelling of freshly splintered wood and varnish. Beneath the panelling the bulkheads were coated with rust and grown over with fungus growths accumulated with years of sea-water dampness and darkness.

'Hussef!'

The tall moustachioed lascar came out from a group of seamen working abreast the galley.

'Bring four men with you.' Schepke went on down the main stairway, carefully holding to the rail, every step sending the pain jarring up inside his chest. Part of his left arm-pit and groin had swollen and he could feel something inside knotted up tightly.

The four canvas-wrapped bodies were laid out along the deck-space of the storeroom.

'Bring them out to the after well,' he told Hussef.

Out on deck the seamen set up two spare hatch-covers on the starboard side and laid the bodies onto them. With such a wind blowing there was little use for the flag. There was still a lot of water coming inboard and the ocean was running big and the water a dirty greyish yellow with large patches of brown and green weed brought up from the depths; and it was not a day for a burial.

Stepping close to the covers, Karl Schepke removed his cap. 'Man that is born of woman hath but a short time to live and is full of misery—' The wind was whipping his words away across the fantail. '—He cometh up, and is cut down, like a flower; he fleeth as it were a shadow and never continueth on one stay.' He was remembering it now, the ship wallowing deeply in the seas. '—Yet deliver us not into the pains of eternal death—suffer us not at this last hour—for any pains of death to fall from thee. —Forasmuch as it hath pleased Almighty God to take unto himself the souls of our brothers here departed. —We therefore commit their bodies to the deep.' He nodded to Hussef. The seamen slowly upended the hatch-covers and the bodies slid easily over the wall, entering the water together, going steeply into a gully.

'—Looking for the resurrection of the body when the sea shall give up her dead. Amen.' He pulled his cap down over his head and turned to Hussef. 'You better put these covers below with the rest of the wood.' He went on up to the bridge.

'Port fifteen!'

'Port fifteen, sir!' repeated Bahr. 'Fifteen port wheel on, sir!'

The ship took a time to answer, then began to come around gradually, butting into the seas, driving the spray and spin'drift back into the face of the bridge. In a gully she took a long curling sea across her starboard beam, heeling deeply, rolling, then shedding water as she came away.

'Up twenty!' Schepke shouted, watching the oncoming seas from the starboard wing. The seas were sweeping in just aft the beam now. She was coming around easily.

'"Midships!'

'"Midships! —Wheel amidships!' Bahr shouted. 'Course zero-four-four, sir!'

'Steady on zero-four-zero!' Schepke told him. '—Half ahead!'

'Half ahead, sir!' repeated the lascar ringing the telegraph over.

'Very good,' Schepke said. Then looking from the after window at the seas: 'Up ten.'

The seas were running in just forward of the quarter, setting the ship into a long dropping roll, her head falling away to port in the out-racing gullies. Dropping the wing window down,

Karl Schepke searched the seas away to the north-east and east with the glasses. There was nothing.

He was still out in the wing when Pulst and two seamen arrived to take over from Bahr.

'Bahr,' Schepke said, and brought the heavy black Mauser from his tunic pocket. 'Move Müller out from the galley storeroom to the one where the bodies were. If he gives any trouble, shoot him.'

Bahr looked uncomfortably at the big gun.

'You know how to use it, don't you?'

'Yes, Herr Kapitän.' Bahr weighed the gun in his hand.

'Tell Sam to put some food and bedding in before you move him. Get Hussef to go along with you. Don't take any chances.'

He could see Bahr did not want the job but with the pain the way it was he did not want to move around too much.

On the second night after altering course for Hong Kong, Karl Schepke was asleep in the charthouse. Altmeyer was on the bridge alone with two seamen. He was out on the starboard wing when he saw them.

'Lights! Lights, Herr Kapitän! —Lights off the starboard bow!'

Schepke was instantly awake and onto the bridge.

'How were they? Sharp? Distant?' Schepke was looking from the window in the direction the boy was pointing.

'It was a sort of glow! They came on slowly then faded!' Altmeyer was very excited.

Schepke searched the darkness off the starboard bow. Visibility had gotten steadily worse since midday and when darkness had come it had been down to less than five hundred metres. Now the darkness had a cotton-wool effect.

'Stop engines.'

132

When the engines died there was only the sound of the long heavy swell running in directly abeam, sending the ship into a wide drunken roll.

'Douse that arc!' Schepke shouted.

In the sudden darkness the greyness of the swell stood out clearly beyond the ship's side.

About twenty minutes had gone before Schepke suddenly picked up the glow of lights through the swirling fog abaft the beam. He did not need the glasses. The lights hung out in the fog like a great incandescent wall.

'What is it?' Hechler spoke close to his shoulder.

'It's a liner,' Schepke told him. '—Altmeyer! Get off a rocket!'

He turned back to the window, hearing Altmeyer hurry up the ladder to the flying bridge.

'Think she'll see us?' Hechler asked.

'She must have picked us up on radar by now. —Half ahead! —Starboard ten!'

The engines came on as a rocket exploded overhead of the bridge, lighting the darkness and fog with an eerie red glow. Now the rudder was answering the wheel and their head was coming around, bringing the wall of lights back onto the bows.

'Hold her on the lights,' Schepke ordered.

As the light of the first rocket faded, another burst, filling the night with the same eerie glow.

'She's not stopping,' Hechler said incredulously.

Schepke tore the screen from the window forward of the wheel. 'She must see us! She's one of those cruise liners!'

'What the hell are they doing?' Hechler shouted.

The fading rocket went out suddenly and they heard Altmeyer on the ladder.

'She's not stopping, Herr Kapitän!'

'Put up another!'

'She's travelling a good sixteen knots with all the bastards asleep!' Hechler shouted.

The rocket went off suddenly overhead, but the lights were already fading.

133

'They must have seen us on radar if nothing else,' Schepke said bitterly.

'It's like all these liners,' Hechler said disgustedly. 'Everybody on watch is busy below knocking some whore's arse off!'

It was very quiet on the bridge as the lights disappeared into the surrounding fog and darkness.

'Bring her back on zero-four-zero,' Schepke said, the disappointment and bitterness showing in his voice.

The bows began to swing back onto the original course, everybody silent again and Altmeyer climbing down from the flying bridge.

'—She didn't see us. She didn't even see us.'

'We did all we could,' Schepke told him.

'I never saw anything like that,' Hechler said and spat through the open window.

'Put the arc back on,' Schepke ordered.

'I hope the dumb bastards run aground on Malaya!' Hechler went on. '—Some luck we have!'

'Don't talk to me about luck,' Schepke said. '—What brought you up here, anyway?'

'We were having some trouble with a bearing. Nothing serious but I thought you should know. We're keeping a close watch on them now.'

'How are One and Two holds?'

'We got the water down some in Number One. And the main steering motor is still holding good. —Maybe we've had some luck after all.'

'Maybe,' Schepke said.

'We should manage to keep the water down now as long as the steam holds out. I give us about sixty hours at the outside.'

'It's close,' Schepke said.

'Where do you make us now?'

They went into the charthouse.

'I make us about here.' Schepke indicated their reckoned position on the chart with a pencil. 'That's the best I can do.' Then looking squarely at Hechler across the table: 'You could do with a couple of hours sleep, Hans.'

'It can wait,' Hechler said, Schepke following him out onto the bridge.

'I'll let you know if we sight anything,' Schepke told him, then went on out to the starboard wing. All his chest was cold and there was a sort of deep swirling motion inside. He stood leaning on the rail below the window, staring out at the foggy darkness. He felt bad about the liner. The liner had taken with it much of the new enthusiasm.

'Karl!'

Schepke turned to see Hechler motion him out to the stairway.

'What is it?'

'Smell anything?'

Schepke stopped and smelled the air in the passage. 'What do you make it?' he asked.

'I once encountered that same stench before,' Hechler said gravely. 'Try the big cabin.'

Schepke almost vomited the moment he opened the door. The cabin was empty except for Rollmann.

'See where Sam is,' he told Hechler.

Rollmann appeared to be in some sort of coma, his whole body tensed, his head forced back into the pillow and his jaws clamped tightly together. Schepke lifted the sheet back. The stench was overpowering. The flesh above the hip was already discoloured and the whole limb cold and swollen so it bulged across the top of the bandaging. Then he heard Hechler come back. Sam was standing outside the doorway with the cuff of his apron covering his nose and mouth.

'Gaseous gangrene,' Schepke said to Hechler, and saw him nod his silent agreement. 'What happened to the seaman?' he now asked Sam.

Sam moistened his mouth. 'Seaman say smell too bad he not stay. I move him Second Officer's cabin.'

'Why didn't you tell me about this before?'

Sam looked at the deck close to his feet.

'Get some bandages and cotton wool. —Hans. Will you see if there's any sulphanilamide in the box?'

When they came back Schepke had taken the bandages from

the stump. The lower part of the limb was completely black.

Hechler watched across his shoulder. 'It came on fast,' he said.

'There's not much anybody can do with that,' Schepke said.

'They wouldn't save that in hospital,' Hechler said, turning away.

Schepke put the powder on thickly, then padded the stump with cotton wool before bandaging. When it was over he went across and swilled his hands and face in the wash-basin.

'Karl,' Hechler said from the bunk.

Rollmann was awake.

'How do you feel?' Schepke asked quietly.

Rollmann's mouth moved, slowly, dryly. '—Cold. It's cold,' the mouth said, the eyes as dull and as blind as stone.

Schepke gathered the sheet and blankets gently up over Roll-mann's chest.

'Karl? —Karl?'

'I'm here,' Schepke said.

'I can't feel anything.' The mouth barely moved.

'I'll do what I can, Horst. You'll be in hospital soon.'

'—We're there?'

'Not quite yet,' Schepke told him, talking close to his face. 'Try and rest some. I'll see you're all right. I'll be here.'

Rollmann relaxed his head into the pillow, the eyelids closing over the unfocused eyes.

They went out into the passage.

'How long will it take?'

'It's difficulty to say,' Hechler said. 'The boy I knew went mad and tried to eat his fingers. They put him in a buckle-down stretcher and he was dead the next morning.'

KARL SCHEPKE was asleep in the charthouse when Sam woke him. Daylight had come in and it was raining heavily.

'What is it?' Schepke said, at the same time hearing the wind and the rain drumming loudly overhead on the flying bridge.

'Bo'sun crazy!' Sam was shouting. 'Much crazy!'

Schepke eased himself from the bunk, the pain shifting with him.

'He take all bandages off!' Sam went on excitedly. 'Go much crazy!'

The stench was vile in the big cabin. Rollmann was lying on his back staring at the deckhead, the stump uncovered and black and swollen.

'Close the door.'

Sam closed the door and remained outside. Schepke sat onto the edge of the bunk, breathing as lightly as possible, his stomach heaving emptily up into his tightly choked throat.

After a while Rollmann saw him.

'—Karl?'

'I'm here,' Schepke told him.

Rollmann closed his eyes and reached his hand out feebly to Schepke's tunic.

'What is it, Horst?'

Rollmann's eyes flickered slowly open again only to stare emptily at the face before him.

'—What's that, Karl?' Rollmann's hand touched the pocket of Schepke's tunic. '—It's a gun. Isn't it? —Karl, hear me?'

'No. There isn't any gun.' Shepke took his hand and laid it across his chest under the blankets.

'Tell me,' Rollmann said, the sweat beading on his face with the exertion of talking.

'I told you,' Schepke said. 'There isn't any gun.'

'—Shoot me. Shoot me, Karl.' He was talking now with his eyes closed.

'You have it wrong, Horst. You're going to be all right. You'll be fine once we get you to hospital.'

'Shoot me! Please shoot me!'

'Take it easy. Just lie still.'

'—I'm going to die. I know it, Karl.' Schepke had to listen

very closely to hear his voice now. He stood looking down at the gaunt and hollow face on the pillow. He did not want to think. He moistened his lips, feeling the big Mauser heavy and bulky against his hip inside of his tunic.

'—Karl.'

'I couldn't do it, Horst,' he said quietly.

'Please. Hear me, Karl?' The eyes had opened again and the sweat ran through the stubble on the gaunt cheeks to the pillow.

'—Give it to me, Karl. Please—'

'I couldn't. Not you.'

'Please.'

Schepke did not look at him.

'—Karl.'

Slowly, Schepke stood off the bunk and brought a chair to the bulkhead by Rollmann's head.

'I'm going out to the galley now, Horst.' He spoke very quietly, not looking at him, taking his tunic off at the same time and hanging it across the back of the chair. Rollmann had moved his head, watching him dully.

'You're a good boy, Karl. Otto knew.'

'I'm sorry, Horst.'

'—You did everything. I'm grateful.'

Karl Schepke stood looking down at him from the side of the bunk.

Rollmann moved his head slightly, looking toward the chair. 'Thank you.'

'No,' Schepke told him, momentarily taking his hand.

He went out along the bare passage to the galley. The seamen were working in the after cabins, carrying everything out onto the boatdeck. Sam looked up from the range as he entered. He lifted a mug from the rack and ran it full of coffee from the urn. There was a large tray of bacon frying and Sam was cutting up freshly baked loaves.

Schepke set the mug onto the range and felt the pocket of his trousers with his right hand. '—Any cigarettes, Sam?'

Sam passed him cigarettes from the shelf over the hatchway. Schepke lit one and stood back against the doorway with his coffee. The coffee was black and bitter, but it did not wash the taste of death from his mouth.

'We go Hong Kong now, Kapitän?' Sam asked.

'We'll make Hong Kong all right, Sam,' Schepke said, glad of Sam talking. 'Maybe tomorrow night or morning,' he said.

Sam started to say something then stopped with the sound of the shot from up forward.

The seamen were already gathered around the big cabin when Karl Schepke stepped from the galley.

'The bo'sun,' Hussef said. 'He just shoot himself!'

Schepke went in past them and took the gun.

'Help me,' he told Hussef as he took his tunic from the chair.

After he had the tunic on he put the big black Mauser back into the pocket, the tall lascar watching him without saying anything.

'Get the old man to sew him up. We'll bury him as soon as he's through. Karl Schepke had not looked at Rollmann again.

THEY buried Rollmann at midday. The fog swirled in thick and damp and the bows of the *Gertrud Lüth* were lost from the bridge. The rain fell heavily through the fog and the seas rolled in smoothly from out of the gloom. Karl Schepke held the same course and speed all that day and night, the look-outs calling to the bridge only when they were relieved. It seemed as though all the vast South China Sea was empty except for the seas rolling in smoothly from out of the rain and fog. During the night the rain partly eased, only to come again heavily with daylight. Karl Schepke had not left the bridge since Rollmann had been buried. Most of the long night he had stood alone in the starboard wing, staring emptily out at the rain and darkness, the pain inside of him now beginning to fever. The pain showed in his face, too, and he was coldly tired and dirty, and out beyond the window there was nothing but the rain and darkness.

Late in the afternoon he left Bahr on the bridge and went below and called Hussef to the boatdeck. Of the four lifeboats, Number Two, the after boat port side, and Number Three, the forward boat starboard side, were in such a hopeless condition they did not even hold the rain.

'Cut those down,' he told Hussef. 'Break them up and put them below with the rest of the stuff.' He turned again and examined the remaining two boats. 'See what you can do with these. They will be all we have if the end comes suddenly.'

They went back across to the port side. The ship was carrying a lot of water and she was running very wearily and sluggishly. The ocean was directly on the starboard quarter now and the list to port had increased during the night.

He turned back toward the passage, Hussef walking with him, the rain driving coldly into their faces.

'Make sure the look-outs keep a special watch after dark. We could be on the coast soon.'

'Yes, Kapitän.'

'Go ahead with the boats.'

When Schepke arrived on the bridge he found Altmeyer waiting to take over from Bahr.

'Are you all right?'

'Yes, sir,' the boy said, forcing a smile that did not hide his weariness.

They were out in the starboard wing, Schepke watching the wraiths of fog drifting across the foredeck, giving it a slightly ghostly appearance. All the while the rain beat down steadily, drumming on the flying bridge and running in the scuppers.

'How's everything up here?' It was Hechler, his overalls open to the waist and all of him filthy dirty and gleaming with sweat.

'All right. What about you?' Schepke asked.

'We've been having more trouble with bearings. And Dorsch was in the gland space all afternoon.'

'Do you want to shut down for a while?'

'Not now,' Hechler told him. 'Maybe we'll have to later.
—When do you expect to be on the coast?'

'If we go on as we are, and my calculations are right, I'd say
sometime after midnight. Two o'clock at the latest.'

Hechler pushed his cap back off his forehead. 'We're going to
run it close.'

'In this we could be on the coast before we saw it.'

'Maybe I better get back below. I'll call you if there's any
more trouble. I don't want to leave it to the last minute if we
have to shut down.'

When Hechler left he went back to the wing and dropped the
window down. The fog smelled clean and off the ocean. Then
he turned and saw the old lascar watching him.

'Go on down and get us some coffee,' he said, then went to
the charthouse and lit the carbide lamp and got down the *South
China Pilot*. If his calculations were too far out the *Gertrud Lüth*
might by-pass Hong Kong and strike the Pearl River Estuary or
the Macao coast. But in the circumstances that would be close
enough to have done reasonably well. If the fog cleared a little
he would pick up the lights that close in. He was looking at
the lights and beacons again in the *Pilot* and knowing that this
late the fog was not going to clear and he was not going to see
any of them, even from the beach. He closed the *Pilot* and left
it on the chart table. A sudden wave of nausea swept over him
as he turned to the bridge and he caught himself at the table,
the bile retching vilely up into his mouth.

'Sir?'

He turned to see Altmeyer in the doorway, the concern showing in his pallid, darkly shadowed face.

'What is it?' Schepke asked, not moving.

Altmeyer hesitated. 'I brought your coffee.'

'Put it on the table.'

The boy set the coffee on the table without looking at him
then turned to leave.

'Wait,' Schepke told him. '—Can you manage out there for a
couple of hours?'

'Yes, sir.'

'Keep a close watch and wake me the first time you see or hear anything. All right?'

'Yes, sir.'

When he was gone Schepke leaned back onto the table. There was still the lightness in his head and the pain all down his left side and in his arm and leg. He swilled the bile from his mouth and spat it onto the deck then drank some of the coffee, the rain drumming incessantly overhead on the flying bridge.

When he woke the bulkhead clock showed it to be a little after eleven. Pulling his cap down he went on out to the bridge. They were all there, Bahr, and Pulst, and the boy. They were getting close now and they knew it would go one way or the other, and whichever way it went it would come suddenly.

'Douse the arc,' Schepke told the boy. 'The rest of you take those screens down.

Now the rain and the thick damp darkness came in through the window spaces the length of the bridge. Karl Schepke stood amidships, smelling the fog, tasting it as it swirled in about him. The fog would remain all night.

'Pulst. Call Hechler and ask what steam he has.'

The only light in the bridge now was the reflection from the carbide lamp in the charthouse. Outside the rain was falling very heavily through the fog.

'The Chief says about six hours at the most, Herr Kapitän! He says we may have to stop anytime now because of trouble with one of the main bearings!'

Schepke cursed inwardly. 'Altmeyer! Go on inside and stand by the charthouse clock. Tell me when it's twenty-three-fifty.'

He waited in the darkness and let her run on in the swirling fog and driving rain, occasionally glancing overhead at the faintly luminous markings on the compass. All through him now was a cold, empty feeling and heavy sickness, and all the while the fog came in cold and damply to swirl around the bridge. Then after a while he saw that the fog was beginning to drift rather than hang thickly above the foredeck and he sensed a breeze lifting lightly now out of the east.

'Twenty-three-fifty, sir!'

'Good.' Schepke said into the darkness, the sound of the rain on the flying bridge overcoming the sounds of the ship and the ocean.

After a while he went out to the starboard wing. The fog came in very thickly and damply out there now that it had begun to move with the lifting breeze.

'Stop engines!'

He heard the telegraph rung over and the engines die, and then the ship was wallowing deeply in the smooth-running seas. Leaning from the window he listened for the fog-muffled thunder of the ocean breaking on the shore. But there was nothing. Nor did the fog carry with it the smell of the shore; the sharp rancid smell of rotting weed and slime thrown up by the ocean.

'Half ahead!'

He stayed in the wing and let her run, watching the stretch of fog and hidden ocean beyond the bows. Now the wind was moving the fog sufficiently for it to blanket instead of drifting in deep-swirling wraiths.

'Time!' he called to the charthouse.

'Twenty minutes past midnight, sir!'

'Slow ahead!' he called to Pulst.

Again he let her run, holding to the rail below the window as the motion of the ship increased, expecting at any time to see something loom suddenly out of the fog, not quite knowing what to expect, but knowing the coast to be treacherous except on places on the back of the island and in some of the deep-lying bays to the east of Tathong Light.

'Stop engines!'

'Stop engines, sir!' came Pulst's voice from the darkness.

In the following quiet he listened again for the sound of the ocean on the shore. Again there was nothing except the sound of the open ocean and the rain falling heavily through the fog. Now the fog was moving out of the east.

'Time!'

'Ten minutes to one o'clock, sir!' Altmeyer answered.

Karl Schepke crossed the bridge to the wheel. 'Half ahead! Starboard ten!' He watched the compass closely as Pulst brought the bows slowly around, butting into the steep, smooth-running seas, sending water high across the forepeak. 'Steer zero-six-five!'

Pulst met her as she came around, the ocean running in almost abeam on the starboard side.

'Course zero-six-five, sir!'

'Good,' Schepke said, then took the receiver from the engine-room telephone and spun the handle. It was Frauenheim who answered, his voice almost lost in the noise of the engine-room.

'Where's Hechler?'

'He's back in the tunnel with Dorsch,' Frauenheim told him. 'We're having plenty of trouble now.'

'What about steam?'

'Everything's on the plates. All stokeholds are empty.'

'Tell Hechler to call me when he has time. And send every spare man up on deck as soon as you're through with them. The rest of you stand by to come topside at the first order. If things happen too quickly I'll sound the alarm.' He slammed the receiver back on its hook and went on out to the port wing. 'Time!'

'One o'clock, sir!' Altmeyer called.

He stayed at the window, rain gusting in about him, streaming from his high-peaked cap. Then suddenly he stood off the rail, the smell of landfall carrying in the fog.

'Steer zero-one-zero!' He hurried amidships as Pulst steadied on the new course. 'Let Bahr have the wheel for a while. You call Hechler and tell him we've started the run in.'

The rain was beginning to carry with the freshening breeze and the fog thinning sufficiently to see a little way beyond the bows.

'Hechler's still in the tunnel, sir!' Pulst called. 'I told Frauenheim!'

'All right. Go on down to the forepeak and let me know if you pick up anything as we go in.'

The ship drove steadily into the fog, rain streaming from her scuppers. Then after a while Schepke rang the telegraph onto slow ahead himself. 'Time!'

'Half past two o'clock, sir!' Altmeyer called.

'Bridge! —Forepeak!' Pulst's voice came hollow and empty-sounding across the foredeck. 'All clear forward!'

'Engine-room's calling, sir!' Bahr shouted as the button light glowed and dimmed on the box.

'Bridge. Schepke here.'

'We're going to have to stop soon,' Hechler shouted above the pound and whine of the engines. 'We've got the hoses on the big end bearing and there's more trouble with a condenser.'

'Try and keep her going as long as possible. We're not far off shore now.'

'—I'll do what I can but I can't promise anything,' Hechler told him.

'Don't waste time getting out of there if things go wrong.' He hung the receiver back on its hook and turned to the window. Everything was dark and wet and smelling of the fog.

'Where do you make us, Herr Kapitän?' Bahr's voice was not hiding his anxiety.

'We should be somewhere close off the south-east of the Po Toi Group,' Schepke told him.

'—Bridge!' came Pulst's cry across the foredeck. 'Breakers sounding off the port bow!'

Schepke grabbed the wheel from Bahr. 'Tell Hussef prepare to abandon ship! Clear both lifeboats away ready for lowering! —Altmeyer! See there's rockets on the flying bridge!'

Now he could hear the fog-muffled boom of the ocean on the shore. He spun the wheel, lying the bows directly into the wind, the shore sounding broadside on to port. Then amidst it all he heard the buzz of a telephone and saw the button light glow on the engine-room box.

'Bridge.'

'We'll have to stop,' Hechler shouted.

'Don't touch a thing. We're almost on the shore. Get Dorsch on the forepeak.' He let the receiver fall, holding to the wheel, the sound of breakers loud now but seeing nothing except the fog and the rain. Then he saw Dorsch move in the darkness of the well as he hurried to the forepeak. The sound of the ocean breaking on the shore was growing, muffled and thunderous-

145

sounding through the fog. Then there was the sudden, quick heavy clatter on the forepeak as steam came on to the capstans. He could see a number of figures dimly moving around and a lot of shouting coming back across the well.

'—Bridge!' It was Dorsch. 'We've lost both anchors!'

Schepke cursed himself for not having checked the forepeak earlier, the anchors probably having gone days ago when the storm was at its height.

'Breakers on the port beam!' Pulst shouted.

The ship had entered a thin patch of fog and the long combing seas showed clearly as they exploded thunderously high and ghostly into the darkness.

He grabbed the telegraph handle and slammed it all the way up then back to slow astern, at the same time spinning the wheel full around to starboard, the stern beginning its slow swing away from the shore as the propeller bit into the water. Now the bows were drawing around, the rain blinding him as it drove through the gaping window spaces.

'I'll take it, sir!' Bahr shouted somewhere close to him.

'Hold her as she is!' he told him, then leaned from one of the windows to see a sudden stretch of blackness about three hundred metres away on the port bow.

'Hard a starboard!'

The ship began to make a tighter turn stern first into the wind and rain. Schepke slammed the telegraph straight over to slow ahead. A quick pounding shudder passed through the entire ship as she came suddenly ahead, her propeller momentarily fighting dead water.

'Keep her parallel to the shore!' he shouted to Bahr.

The stretch of darkness was on the starboard bow now, widening rapidly as they ran down on it. Then as they drew abeam he saw the long combing seas rolling smoothly in past the solid darkness of tall cliffs. He waited until they dropped astern, watching the darkness ahead.

'Starboard ten!' he shouted, and suddenly there was a high, sharp cracking report above the bridge and the darkness was lit by an eerie red glow. Then as the ship started to ease in under her helm they heard the fog-muffled thunder of seas breaking on a shore all in about them. Yet another rocket exploded overhead revealing an almost solid wall of fog and rain about three hundred metres ahead.

'The engines!' Bahr yelled. 'The engines are stopping!'

'Give me the wheel!' Karl Schepke threw him aside before the engines died beneath his feet. Then suddenly, ahead of them on the port bow, he saw a raging barrier of surf and seas breaking fiercely up along a range of out-flung rock. Immediately he flung the wheel full around to starboard in a desperate attempt to pull clear.

The port side was first to hit, somewhere back on the quarter. Hanging bodily to the wheel he felt the ship jolt sickeningly onto her stern, then lurch free again, swinging fast to starboard with the impact. This time the seas caught the port quarter, heeling her far over to port, caught in the seas rolling squarely in on the beam, the bows head on to the long range of rock. Then as she swung stern first the seas caught the bows, lifting her crabwise away, reeling her clear of any obstruction, the seas now taking her on the starboard beam and driving her on into the darkness.

She hit again almost immediately, a dull, rumbling explosion occurring simultaneously deep in her forward holds and exploding the hatch covers upward in a giant fountain of water and grain. But still she continued her slow, lurching, skidding motion that started somewhere aft, the bows gone deep now and slewing to port, lifting, bumping, then setting slowly down, the ship listing far to port now as she settled, steam suddenly exploding overhead of the bridge in a gigantic white roaring cloud.

Karl Schepke held desperately to the wheel, the deck sharply angled beneath his feet. Then the ship lurched violently again as a huge sea broke against all the length of her side. Water roared through the bridge from the starboard wing, tearing him from the wheel and slamming him against the port wing bulkhead.

Altmeyer, high on the flying bridge, found himself caught up against the port outboard screen. Before the water cleared he found the hatchway again and swung in and down only to lose his balance on the angled deck and go slithering, clawing for a hold, into the port wing. In the darkness and water he hit heavily against someone.

'Who is it? —Who's that?'

'It's me! Altmeyer!' the boy shouted, recognizing Bahr's voice.

'Give me a hand! It's Schepke!'

Altmeyer found Schepke as Bahr started dragging him up the steeply angled deck toward the bridge doorway.

The ship was in utter darkness and there was a lot of noise and confusion below them in the passage as seamen who had been sheltering there when she first struck fought their way out to the boatdeck.

'Come on. Let's get him below,' Bahr shouted.

Suddenly a light lit up the main stairway and they saw Hechler with a lantern.

'Hans!'

Hechler stopped, seeing them with Schepke. 'Take him into Emmermann's cabin. It hasn't been stripped.'

He held the lantern while they laid him into the bunk, all the while the seas thudding into the lower side of the exposed hull, breaking clear over the starboard side superstructure.

'How is he?'

'He's still unconscious,' Altmeyer said.

'What's happening?' Dorsch asked coming in from the passage.

'Schepke's hurt,' Bahr told him.

'Any idea where we are?' Hechler asked, holding the lantern toward Bahr and the boy.

'We didn't have a chance to see anything,' Bahr told him.

'Here,' Hechler gave the lantern to Altmeyer. 'Go up and see if you can find the chart. —Dorsch! See if there's any more lamps or lanterns in the machine shop.'

Hechler and Bahr waited in the darkness, hearing the confusion of noise and shouting as the ship was pounded by the seas.

'Think she'll start to break?' Bahr asked anxiously.

'I don't think so,' Hechler, shouting above the noise, told him. 'If she does it should be somewhere forward. The bulkhead went between One and Two holds the second time she hit. The way it happened I'd say we're lying on some sort of shoal or sandbank.'

'I think we're in a bay,' Bahr told him, trying to remember everything clearly. 'There looked like an island some way in. That's where we hit after the engines stopped.'

'I got the chart,' Altmeyer told them as he came in.

'Spread it on the bunk,' Hechler told him, taking the lantern.

Altmeyer spread the chart out across Schepke's legs, Hechler holding the lantern above their heads as they bent over it.

'Christ! It could be a thousand bays!' Hechler said. 'Look at them!' He jabbed a finger at the mass of bays and inlets and islands off the New Territories and China mainland.

'Wait!' Altmeyer said. 'There's an area marked off here between the Lammas and Crooked Islands.'

'There's still plenty of places we could be,' Hechler said, bending closer to the chart.

'What happens now?' Bahr asked.

'We'll wait for daylight,' Hechler told them. 'It's safer here than going out there into Christ knows what.'

Just then Dorsch came in carrying a lighted lantern and two more, and closely followed by Frauenheim and Pulst. 'Müller's broken out! We saw him go up to the bridge ahead of us!'

'Close the door!' Hechler shouted. 'Get that table unlocked and behind it!'

'—Where's Schepke?' Müller was already in the doorway with a lighted lantern.

'He isn't here,' Hechler told him, stepping in front of the bunk.

Müller struck him aside with his forearm. Holding the lantern higher, he saw Schepke lying unconscious on the bunk, his face grey and hollowed. Without warning he suddenly drove his fist savagely into Schepke's stomach. Hechler lunged, Müller swinging the lantern, catching him high on the forehead, dropping him to the deck. Then turning swiftly to Schepke he ran his hand over his tunic.

'Back! All of you!' he ordered, levelling the big Mauser. 'On your feet, Hechler!' Covering them with the gun, he glanced quickly at the chart. 'Where are we?' he asked, turning to them again.

'Find out yourself!' Hechler told him, bleeding from the wound on his forehead.

'—You! Altmeyer! You were with him!'

'I don't know,' the boy said. 'He was working on it himself.'

Keeping them covered, Müller glanced quickly at the chart again, then backed to the doorway. 'Stay here,' he told them. 'Don't anybody come out on deck!'

'Close the door,' Hechler ordered as soon as he had gone. 'Get that table behind it!'

Bahr and Altmeyer unlocked the table and barricaded the door with it. Hechler jammed two of the lanterns into the shelves on the forward bulkhead and lit them.

'Schepke's coming around,' Altmeyer called, leaning across the bunk.

Schepke opened his eyes again when Hechler touched his wide shoulder. 'Karl,' he said quietly.

Schepke shifted his head slightly on the pillow, his lips moving.

'What is it?' Hechler asked, leaning his face close to him.

'—The fog,' Schepke said, his voice very faint. 'The fog and that bearing.'

'Listen,' Hechler urged, 'do you know where we are?'

'—A bay,' Schepke said, closing his eyes, hearing the dull, steady boom of the seas as they rolled smoothly in out of the vast expanse of the South China Sea.

Hechler sensed him slipping away. 'What bay? What bay, Karl?'

'—We were almost through. Almost—' Schepke was having difficulty breathing now, '—almost Tolo. The channel,' he went on, his words very faint. 'That island. Further out.'

'What island?' Hechler asked, sweat beading together on his forehead with the blood. 'What island, Karl?'

'Chik Chau. Tap Mun Chau out there too. —Was the fog. The fog and the luck.'

Hechler leaned over the chart, the lantern held high. Karl

Schepke, his eyes closed, started talking. '—The head's out some-where to the channel. The villages should be marked. Should be in close to Mount Hallowes. —Was the fog and the luck.' This time his head sank back into the pillow.

'Think he'll be all right?' Frauenheim asked.

'He'll want help soon,' Hechler said. 'It's his insides.'

'We must be somewhere here,' Altmeyer said, his finger on the chart. 'Here's the islands he mentioned. And Tolo. It must have been Tolo Channel. We could be in here somewhere between Tolo Channel and the west side of Tap Mun Chau. Our head's almost due north. I checked it when I was on the bridge.'

'There's Mount Hallowes,' Frauenheim said. '—And there's villages marked.'

'We weren't so far off Tathong Point,' Hechler said. 'With any luck he would have made it.'

'It's getting light,' Altmeyer said looking to the scuttles.

They crowded around the scuttles, peering through the stream-ing glass at the ocean in the cold grey half-light of dawn.

'That must be Tap Mun Chau,' Hechler said, his face almost flat against the forward scuttle as he peered astern. Visibility had improved with the wind but it was still raining and gusting coldly grey across the long oily-smooth seas sweeping in from the ocean. Everything, including the barren island of Tap Mun Chau was bleak and cold-looking in the raw early light.

'There's a lot of commotion on the port side,' Bahr said. 'I think they're launching the lifeboat.'

'We should see the shore from there,' Altmeyer said.

Outside in the passage they met Sam and the mess boy, both of them wide-eyed with fear, wearing the life-jackets and begin-ning an outburst of Cantonese in excitement.

'Shut up!' Frauenheim said. '—Now what's happening!'

'Take lifeboat!' Sam said. 'No take us!'

'They've just launched the boat!' Altmeyer shouted from one of the port side cabins.

Hechler was first onto the boatdeck. Most of the black gang were sheltering in the lee of the housing. The *Gertrud Lüth* was lying beam on about five hundred metres from the shore, the high hills, and Mount Hallowes beyond, dark and ominous-looking, shrouded in fog and rain. There was no sign of a village but a large crowd of people were strung out along the pale sandy beach beyond reach of the thundering surf.

The lifeboat had covered about a hundred metres, the black storm-coated seamen pulling for the shore through the comparatively smooth water in the lee of the hugely listed ship. Then Hechler saw the ridge-like area just ahead of them where the surf reared up out of nowhere in a great spewing swell, paused, then took off in a mad foaming race for the shore about three hundred metres further on, finally hitting the beach with a thunderous roar that sent clouds of spray soaring high into the wind.

'They won't get through that!' Dorsch yelled.

The lifeboat, with Müller at the helm, suddenly lurched, the stern thrown high as they reached the point where the smooth rolling seas seemed to explode on some underwater shelf. It swung, pitched, then spun around out of control, the oars free of the men's grasp, and all the while the rain hissed on the ocean. Then the boat was thrown completely out of the water, coming down directly into the raging surf to be immediately gathered up and swept under with tremendous force and power.

'See that! —See it!' Frauenheim shouted.

'Can you see anybody!' Dorsch asked, searching the long stretch of raging surf.

On the shore they could see people crowding close to the water.

'There's somebody!' Frauenheim yelled, seeing the black head, then the body swept up and flung high in the water as it raced for the beach.

'There's some more!' Dorsch was pointing as more heads and bodies appeared darkly in the raging surf.

'You can bet Müller's there!' Hechler shouted. 'That bastard would never drown!'

The ship lurched suddenly under the impact of a sea exploding on the starboard side, showering the boatdeck with a ragged torrent of white water. Hechler lost his footing and clung to the rails as the water roared around him. Dorsch and Bahr grabbed him and hauled him back to the safety of the cabin passage, everybody else already there.

Hechler made the big cabin and sat into the chair behind the desk.

'Are you all right?' Dorsch asked.

'I won't forget this trip in a hurry,' Hechler told him, holding his knee.

'What will happen now?' Pulst asked.

'There should be help of some kind soon,' Frauenheim said.

'I'm glad I wasn't in that boat,' Bahr said.

'They're still searching the beach,' Altmeyer coming in, told them.

'You could make the beach and still be drowned,' Hechler said. 'I'll stay where I am.' He saw the two Chinese in their bulky life-jackets standing nervously in the doorway. 'You better stay here,' he told them. 'I never saw a drowned Chinaman yet.'

Just then the *Gertrud Lüth* took a large sea under her hull and she rose drunkenly, throwing everyone to the deck, buckled and torn plates grating on sand and shingle as she settled on a more even keel a little nearer the shore.

'She's breaking!' Pulst shouted, starting for the doorway along with the two Chinese.

Dorsch grabbed him as he went past, bringing him down into the doorway.

'She's breaking! —She's breaking!'

'Shut up!' Hechler yelled, bending over them, holding Pulst to the deck by his throat. 'She isn't breaking! She's come down off a sandbank!'

The ship had settled deeply this time, the seas now rolling effortlessly across her starboard bulwarks to break on board, clouds of spray soaring high into the wind.

Pulst stood slowly to his feet, glancing about the big cabin, then sitting down quietly with his back against the desk.

'Any idea about how many are still on board?' Hechler asked them.

153

'I counted twenty-two of us on deck just now,' Frauenheim said.

'Listen!' Altmeyer shouted.

It came again, the high whoop, whoop, whooping shriek of a ship's siren carrying in the wind. They crowded the two scuttles, and as the water momentarily cleared from the glass they saw the grey, tropical-painted destroyer rolling heavily in the smooth-running seas beyond Tap Mun Chau.

'I'll get the Aldis!' Altmeyer shouted excitedly.

Dorsch and Bahr crowded into the passage behind him. They found the Aldis lamp jammed in under the bunk in the chart-house and carried it onto the starboard wing. The destroyer had eased her rolling now as she came in under the lee of the hills on the northern and eastern shores, her port searchlight already stabbing into the cold grey rain.

'She's American!' Dorsch shouted, ducking a shower of spray sweeping through the window spaces.

'What's she saying?' Bahr asked.

Altmeyer ignored them, sighting the lamp through an open window and triggering the lens. On board the destroyer the searchlight settled into a series of long flashes as she acknow-ledged Altmeyer's signal.

'What's happening?' Bahr asked.

'I told them there's twenty-two on board and we can't make shore.'

'What's she say now?'

'Will — attempt — to — take — you — off. Stand — by — to — receive — boats,' Altmeyer read.

'I'll tell Hechler!' Dorsch shouted.

The destroyer had stopped, the ocean boiling white under her stern, her bows swinging toward the *Gertrud Lüth* as she edged around clear of the northernmost tip of Tap Mun Chau.

In the big cabin Hechler and Frauenheim were buckling Schepke into a canvas stretcher, Pulst and Dorsch watching from the spray-lashed scuttles.

'What's happening?' Hechler asked.

'They're streaming a motor boat and whaler,' Dorsch told him.

'We better get Schepke outside!'

'How are we going to get off?' Frauenheim asked.

'We better get Schepke outside.'

Dorsch, seeing the destroyer close off Tap Mun Chau, still paying the manila out as the boats drifted down toward the half-submerged bows of the *Gertrud Lüth*. 'Come on! Get the stretcher!'

Carrying Schepke between them they went out and down the main stairway, aft along the inboard port passage, then out into the alleyway and the seas and the spray-lashed forward well. Most of the seamen had already gathered in the forepeak tunnel.

The two boats were about fifty metres off the starboard bow and still drifting down, the manila running tautly away from the bows of the motor boat to the destroyer's iron deck.

Altmeyer and Bahr appeared on the forepeak as Hechler finished tying a heaving-line around the stretcher. The two boats were right ahead, the seamen tense and intent as the bows of the *Gertrud Lüth* loomed above them. Then the helmsman of the motor boat shouted in under the canopy and the water astern threshed white as she and the whaler fought ahead on the manila.

High on the forepeak Hechler shouted for the stretcher to be lowered. It went over the stem and down smoothly and swiftly, the helmsman edging the motor boat in close, two men forward of the canopy waiting ready to hook the stretcher on board. Suddenly a sea swept around the massive, rust-eaten bows and lifted the boat almost clear of the water, slewing her around in the trough, almost tearing the stretcher from the heaving-line, burying it in a mass of grey water. Quickly the helmsman dropped the boat astern and came up in the following sea, the two seamen hooking the stretcher onto the canopy and slashing the line free. Then as the boat came ahead in the trough she rammed the stem, almost overturning and sending splinters of wood into the helmsman's face. She drove off crabwise, the oncoming sea righting her, driving them clear, the helmsman fighting to keep the bows from swinging.

Hechler saw the two seamen lash the stretcher down forward, the men aft in the whaler ready with boat-hooks and lifebuoys.

'Go on!' Hechler yelled at the men around him. 'Jump! One at a time! —For Christsake jump!'

Bahr went first, leaping out and away from the stem, dropping as the sea swept past. On board the motor boat the men had a lifebuoy overboard on a line and ready with boat-hooks. Bahr surfaced so close to the motor-boat the two men had him first time across the gunwale.

Dorsch was next to go. They went over the side quickly, one at a time, waiting for the crests of the seas to pass then dropping onto their backs, some with life-jackets, others barefoot and wearing only their underwear, each dropping so he came up in the following sea, the men in the boats working frantically to haul them on board.

'What about you, Hans?' Frauenheim asked when most of the others had gone.

' Somebody has to stay.'

'I'll stay with you.'

'I'll stay as well,' Altmeyer told them.

'No! You go over!' Hechler told him, a great flurry of spray blinding them as a sea exploded onto the bows.

'You'll need somebody to work the lamp!' Altmeyer argued.

'All right!' Hechler turned to see Pulst make his leap, leaving Sam with his bulky life-jacket.

'Where's Kuang?' Hechler asked.

Sam pointed to the boats. They were crowded now, men jammed between the thwarts of the whaler, both boats precariously low in the water.

'You next!'

Sam looked at the seas.

'Go on, jump!' Hechler told him.

Sam looked at the seas again. Hechler put his foot in the small of his back and sent him sprawling out across the bows.

The destroyer was rolling hugely in the seas sweeping around the north end of Tap Mun Chau.

'They've got him!' Frauenheim shouted.

Hechler turned back to see one of the men in the motor boat shoot a green Very light into the wind. Almost immediately the manila came up tautly and the motor boat headed laboriously into the seas with her engine roaring full ahead.

'What happens now?' Altmeyer asked.

'We stay on board until the agents get somebody out,' Hechler told him. 'They should be able to reach us from the shore when this goes down.'

'We better see if we can find some dry bedding and move into Emmermann's cabin,' Frauenheim said.

They started back across the forward well, Mount Hallowes and the hills around almost lost in the cold driving rain.

'Hey!' Altmeyer called to them. 'There's somebody else on board! That stoker who was shot is still in Schepke's cabin!'

'Well it's too late now!' Hechler told him.

THE room was lit brightly green when Karl Schepke awoke. It was a long narrow room and he was in a smoothly-made bed with a dark cover that somehow had lost its original colour in this bright green light. He lay quietly and tried to think where he was and what all had happened, but with so many thoughts he could not think clearly of any one thing and he gave it up and concentrated on the room and realized the brightly green light was caused by the sunlight on the drawn curtains over the window a little to the right of the bed. And then the door the other side of the room opened and a doctor came in wearing a white coat.

'Good afternoon,' the doctor said, smiling. 'We expected you to wake. How do you feel?'

Karl Schepke watched him talk. He was an Englishman doctor, tall and quiet speaking.

'You do understand English?' the doctor spoke very carefully.

'Yes,' Schepke said. Then said: 'Where am I?'

'There is no need for alarm,' the doctor assured. 'You are doing very well. We are in the hospital on the Peak overlooking the city.'

Karl Schepke remembered the out-flung range of rock and the fog and the island as the ship swept away from it; and he saw all these things fleetingly.

'How was everybody? Was anybody—'

'Please,' the doctor said. 'We will talk about these things later. But everything is perfectly all right.'

'How long will I have to stay here?'

The doctor smiled. 'This is the first time you have been properly awake in the past nine days,' he said.

'—What!'

'It was an induced sleep,' the doctor assured, still smiling. 'You were exhausted and in a very bad condition internally. We had to operate as soon as you arrived. I think you could consider yourself extremely lucky indeed.'

'What happened?'

'Not at the moment.' The doctor still smiled. 'Now please try and rest. I will come back and see you later.'

Karl Schepke lay back and closed his eyes against the brightly green light. Outside of the window it was afternoon and bright and warm and the waters of the harbour far below were very blue against the hard angular whiteness of Kowloon's waterfront.

HECHLER and Dorsch were the first visitors. They arrived one afternoon wearing civilian suits and seeming very well in themselves.

'How are you, Karl?' Hechler asked as they came in.

'Fine. I'm fine,' Schepke, sitting up, told them. 'But you. You still look better than I feel.'

'Oh, we're all right,' Dorsch said, setting some packages down by the bed, on the floor.

'This is better quarters than we have,' Hechler said, looking about the room. 'We're at a place down on Jardines Bazaar. The Hotel Zetland. At night they let the back rooms to the whores working the front.'

'We brought your suitcase and cap,' Dorsch said. 'We had to leave them with the porter downstairs. Everything that was in your cabin is there.'

'Thank you,' Schepke told him. 'How did things go?'

Dorsch looked to Hechler.

'Not so badly,' Hechler said, shrugging his bulky shoulders.

'You'll never guess,' Dorsch said. '—There's a salvage crew working on her right now. They already have the deck-cargo ashore.'

'That's right,' Hechler said. 'There's also some talk that she's been sold to somebody local.'

'We should have made it,' Schepke said.

'You can't complain,' Hechler told him. 'You did everything you could. You did well enough to put her where you did.'

'Everybody says the same,' Dorsch said. 'Look at this.' He unfolded a newspaper from his pocket. It was a back copy of the *South China Morning Post* carrying the story of the grounding and with a photograph of the ship lying on even keel a little way out from the shore.

'Read it,' he urged. 'Even back home they know about it.'

'I heard about the boat,' Schepke said, ignoring the newspaper.

Again Dorsch looked to Hechler.

'Müller got out,' Hechler said. 'He took your gun and most of the seamen went with him.'

'We haven't seen him since the day after we came ashore,' Dorsch said quietly. 'The Consul fixed us up in different hotels. Only Altmeyer and the quartermasters are with us.'

'Frauenheim's in hospital,' Hechler said. 'He's in a place over the back of the island. He wasn't hurt or anything. Somebody just decided he should have some treatment and a rest.'

'And what's happening now?' Schepke asked.

'I don't think anything until after the Enquiry.'

'The Consul is going to get us home,' Dorsch said. 'He says there's no worry about that.'

'What about the Enquiry?'

'There's nothing definite yet,' Hechler said, and just then the door opened and one of the Chinese nurses came in.

'Yes?' Hechler asked, looking at her expectantly.

She looked at him, then at her wrist watch, then at Dorsch.

'I suppose that's it,' Hechler said.

'I'd like to know about Müller if you hear anything,' Schepke told them.

'Sure,' Hechler said. 'We'll see what we can find out. Look after yourself.'

The nurse followed them out and closed the door behind them and Karl Schepke heard them go on down the long corridor. And it was quiet with them gone and he lay on the smoothly-made bed, bright sunlight coming into the room and some birds making long melodious calling sounds outside of the window. He wondered what lay outside of the window, and he imagined flower-beds and trees and the sunlight streaming through the foliage. And it was all one long monotonous day, and all the days went that way.

Then the first morning he was allowed up it was raining, a thin rain that hung in the air, the clouds closed right down over the hospital up there on the Peak and outside of the window there were no flower-beds nor trees with sunlight streaming through the foliage, just the cold thin rain hanging in the grey cloud that swirled damply down around the slopes of the Peak and completely obscuring everything immediately outside of the window.

'Captain.' The doctor closed the door. 'A Mr. Erich von Pittkamer has called to see you. I believe he is your German Consul.'

'Thank you,' Schepke said from the chair by the window.

The doctor returned with von Pittkamer, then left them.

'Kapitän Schepke.' Von Pittkamer was tall and gaunt and wore a carefully trimmed grey beard. 'Please don't get up.' He reached

160

his hand out. He had long, cold and delicate hands. 'I brought your pay cheque with me, Kapitän. It was sent to me this morning by the agents.'

'Thank you,' Schepke said.

Von Pittkamer smiled. 'The doctor tells me you are doing well.'

'Yes. Everything's fine.'

'Good. You will be interested to know that the hearing of the Formal Enquiry commences on the twenty-third. Do you forsee any difficulties, Kapitän?'

'I don't think so. I think I did all I could.'

'Yes, I know. Tell me, were you aware that the *Gertrud Lüth* was under contract to the State?'

Schepke looked up at him. 'There was nothing to that effect in the ship's documents. However, I can't see that it makes any difference to me personally.'

'You will find that here in Hong Kong things will mostly be handled by the English.'

'I haven't heard from the Receiver of Wreck yet.'

'I should not worry about that. There will probably be a writ from him sometime in the next few days. He has already begun taking depositions.' Von Pittkamer had an old-fashioned air about him and now he withdrew a gold watch from the pocket of his waistcoat and clicked the cover open with his thumbnail. 'I am afraid I must go now, Kapitän. Please don't hesitate to let me know if you require anything. After the Enquiry we will see what can be done about getting you home.' Von Pittkamer politely inclined his head. 'Good-bye,' he said.

'Good-bye,' Schepke told him.

It was grey and gloomy outside and now the rain had begun to fall more heavily, falling against the window panes.

THE following day Hechler came with Dorsch and Altmeyer. They brought two bottles of gin with them and took turns drinking from the one water glass. All three had been drinking before coming up from the city and now Hechler looked a little blown and sad. Then the third time Karl Schepke passed him the glass he refused it.

'Go on,' Schepke urged. 'Drown him.'

Hechler looked questioningly at him.

'Forget it,' Schepke said.

'Drown who?' Altmeyer asked, smiling. 'Drown who, Herr Kapitän?'

Schepke looked at him. He was slightly drunk and perhaps somewhat proud in himself after the storm and he still had the bloom of someone who expected everything to be beautiful and exciting. He was a boy in whom disillusion had not yet set in.

'Never mind who,' Hechler said, then turned to Schepke. 'Did you know they brought her in? She's up in Taikoo.'

'It's the first I heard,' Schepke told them.

'I was down at the dock yesterday,' Dorsch said. 'One of the Limey surveyors told me she's been bought by a Chinese company.'

'Hell knows what they want a hulk like her for,' Hechler said. 'The best thing about her was the engines. Besides, she was almost gutted inside. The only inside woodwork left was the bridge and Emmermann's cabin, and the messroom. There was nothing else.'

'How about Frauenheim?'

'He's looking better than I ever saw him,' Altmeyer said. 'I saw him yesterday. He expects them to let him out before the Enquiry.'

'Listen, have you seen Müller?' Schepke asked. 'The Receiver of Wreck was here yesterday for a deposition and he said he hadn't been able to find him.'

'No, we haven't seen him, either,' Dorsch said. 'Maybe he's across in Kowloon.'

'I meant to ask von Pittkamer but I forgot,' Schepke said.

'What did you say about Müller in the deposition?' Hechler asked.

'I didn't say much about anything.'

162

Hechler looked disbelievingly at him.

'I have enough to think about without thinking about him,' Schepke said.

'I hate to think what would have happened if he had been in command,' Dorsch said.

'It still caught up with us,' Schepke reminded them. 'Maybe if we had ran for Manila we would have come through that too.'

Hechler shrugged. Dorsch finished the first bottle and put it along with the other into the bed locker. 'I suppose Madame Butterfly will be in soon,' he said.

'Yes,' Hechler said rising from the edge of the bed. 'Maybe we better leave now. All right with you, Karl?'

'Sure. I'll see you all before the Enquiry.' He went to the doorway with them and watched them go down the long corridor.

When they had gone he tidied the room and opened the window so that the curtains now moved with the breeze. Then in a little while the doctor came with one of the nurses.

'How is it?' Schepke asked lying on his right side on the bed.

'Very well,' the doctor told him. 'It's almost healed. We will keep the dressing dry now.'

'When can I leave?' Schepke turned onto his stomach as the nurse fixed a dressing in place.

'So you want to leave us,' the doctor said, watching. 'I suppose I could let you go if you promise to take proper care of yourself. What do you say?'

'You have my word, Doctor. Thank you.'

'You will have to come back and see us again.'

'Of course,' Schepke said, sitting up now as the nurse finished the bandaging.

'Then I will inform your Consul about your discharge tomorrow.'

'Would you ask him to send some clothes? I seem to have lost everything but my cap and underwear.'

'Your uniform is here, Captain,' the doctor said, smiling. You see, above all else we have a grand room service here. I am sure it will be almost as good as new.' He seemed almost too cheerful to be an Englishman doctor.

THEY drove down from the Peak into the city to just outside of the English Navy Dockyard, then right along Queen's Road East to downtown Wanchai. Karl Schepke sat and watched the pale yellow-painted buildings of the Navy Barrack glide past on the left. Then as they made a turn to the left, moving slowly now behind a tramcar, they passed the main gateway to the barrack and there were blue-suited, white-gaitered seamen on guard, rifles on their shoulders, standing either side of the gateway. Then the taxi swung out and drove smoothly past the tramcar on the outside and on down into Wanchai.

Karl Schepke, sitting in the back, watched the buildings go past as they drove down Hennessy Road.

'This will do.'

The driver pulled into the side of the roadway and Schepke looked back at the hotel. The stonework was freshly painted and a sign hung out front that said: Kwangtung Hotel.

He walked back carrying his suitcase. A small boy was sitting at a desk just inside of the doorway.

'Yes, sir,' he said bowing low, very impressed with the uniform.

'You have a room?' Schepke asked, setting the suitcase down by the desk.

'Yes, sir. Plenty room, sir,' the boy said and disappeared through a doorway behind the desk to arrive back almost immediately with an old man with a goatee beard.

The old man looked very carefully at the uniform. 'You are American?'

'No,' Schepke told him. 'German.'

'How long do you stay?'

Schepke shrugged. 'Maybe one month. Maybe longer.'

The old man smiled a mouthful of gold and pearl teeth and

swivelled the register around on the desk. 'Very good room,' he said, smiling. 'Kwangtung Hotel, Number One.' And the boy too was smiling.

The room was on the first floor, overlooking the street. It was a pleasant room with an adjoining bathroom and a telephone on the table by the bed. The boy gave him the key and he tipped him. Then he remembered the watch, and brought it from the suitcase. 'Do you know a good watchmaker?'

'You want mend watch?' the boy said, taking it and holding it to his ear.

'Do you know somebody?'

The boy nodded vigorously. 'Pancho know Number One watchmaker.'

'You have it mended then, Pancho,' Schepke told him as they went back downstairs, the boy still looking at the watch.

'Who is Shuang-shuang?' he asked, looking at the back of the case.

'She's a friend,' Schepke told him.

'She big friend give you watch like this,' Pancho said, smiling.

'Plenty big friend,' Schepke said as he went out into the street.

It was pleasant walking in the street with the traffic close by and the smells of the open-fronted shops and eating houses and the stalls on the pavements. There was no longer the harsh clinical smell of the hospital with him and he walked on down the street, under the buildings built out over the pavement, then turned left down Fleming Road. He was on the front, the water of the harbour hard and metallic-looking in the grey light of the late afternoon, and across the water a damp low haze hid most of Kowloon beyond the wharves and high go-downs and Tsim Sha Tsui clock tower above the Star Ferry Landing Stage. He turned right and walked along the front on Gloucester Road, a cold, damp breeze blowing up Lei U Mun Channel from the ocean and setting the hard, metallic-looking water slap slapping against the concrete and pilings of the front. The breeze smelled smoky and of the hills out along the channel; and coming in out of the channel was a big, buff-painted freighter.

Schepke watched her come in as he walked along the front.

She was a Dane with a deck-cargo of railway carriages and she was hardly moving now as she passed Hung Hom, her cable party gathered on the forepeak as she prepared to enter the Northern Fairway. The harbour was almost empty. The only other shipping across the harbour were two small freighters anchored off Jordan Road Ferry Pier. Back down the harbour, off Sheung Wan, on the Victoria side, was a passenger liner, her head swung around into the breeze blowing up the channel. She had all the new raked lines and a tripod mast and was wide and white and with the Tricolor blowing out in the breeze across her stern. Karl Schepke thought she was probably the *Cambodia* or the *Viet Nam*, but she was too far away in the haze to make clear her name.

When he stopped walking he was outside of a bar, and he went in without looking at the name. It was dimly lit and with music coming from somewhere overhead.

'Gin,' he told the barman, then took the drink to a table. The music appeared to come from somewhere in the darkened ceiling. There were some girls sitting at a table in the far corner, watching him, their features shadowy and indistinct in the gloom. Then one of them got up, all hips and legs, and came across.

'Hallo.'

Karl Schepke sipped the gin, tasting it carefully.

'You American?' she asked, trying to make up her own mind.

Karl Schepke lit a cigarette.

'You not ask a lady to sit?'

'I don't ask ladies anything,' Karl Schepke said quietly.

She raised her head still higher and looked at him, and still looking at him that way over her flat nose, she went back to her table.

Looking at them, Karl Schepke did not think very much of any of them.

Then when he finished his drink he got up and went across to the counter and had two more, and then went out into the evening. He went back along Gloucester Road. It was almost dark and the many lights and signs had come on and out across the water were the lights of Kowloon spread out flatly and hanging mistily in the haze that has a way of holding in banks just above the shore in the East in autumn.

He decided to eat and watched for an eating house as he went back along the front. Most of the shops were shuttered against the breeze and people out walking were hurrying against the raw dampness coming in off the water. Then as he walked he began to have the feeling that someone was watching him. How, he did not know, but he was sure now and, crossing O'Brien Road, he glanced around and there was no one near him and he could see nothing out in the darkness along the edge of the front. He went on across the roadway. There were fewer lights burning along that stretch of the front and the open shops were further apart, dark open doorways between them leading to high tenements overhead. Then he passed a U.S. Navy outfitter and went on, and the first shot blew a hole in the wall behind him, showering him with masonry. At the same time as he started to turn, someone caught him around the throat and lifted him bodily into a doorway, slamming him back against the wall then down onto the cold concrete of the floor. Then someone was lying heavily across his legs, and the next shot came so close he heard it pass above him in the darkness and go screaming off in a wild ricochet from somewhere at the rear of the passage. Then lying there, he was vaguely aware of the sound of someone running close by on the front. Suddenly the tremendous weight pinning his legs shifted and he scrambled into the doorway. Everyone on the front seemed to have disappeared with the sound of the first shot. Then he sat up and saw this man standing above him, looking out toward O'Brien Road. He was the largest man Karl Schepke had ever seen, and his face broad and wide cheekboned, and as impassive as though hewn from rock. Schepke started to say something then heard whistles blowing close by, and when he turned back he had gone, the only sounds those of someone of great weight moving lightly, swiftly into the enclosed darkness toward the rear of the passage.

Karl Schepke was still in the doorway when the first of the policemen arrived.

'You! What happened?' he demanded, waving his pistol in Schepke's face.

'I don't know,' Schepke told him quietly. 'Somebody shot at me.'

'Who shot at you?'

'If I knew I would tell you,' Schepke told him, his voice changing.

Then the second policeman jabbed his pistol into Schepke's stomach. 'You American? You shooting somebody?' he shouted.

'Put that away!' Schepke told him, and the crowd of Chinese that had swiftly gathered were very impressed with all the pistol brandishing.

'Back against the wall!' the taller of the two said, still with his pistol in Schepke's stomach.

Just then a police wagon pulled into the crowd and an Inspector of Police stepped smartly down from the running-board and pushed his way through to the pavement.

'What is it?' he asked, looking from the policemen to Schepke.

'Somebody shot at me,' Schepke told him.

'You weren't the one shooting?'

'If I had been shooting at myself I wouldn't have missed,' Schepke said coldly.

The Inspector looked at him a moment then nodded to the two policemen. Almost reluctantly they holstered their pistols then looked both ways along the front.

'Would you care to accompany me?' the Inspector asked, turning again to Schepke.

Karl Schepke sighed, then climbed into the wagon and the driver made a tight turn and drove a little way back along the front to the high-pillared Wanchai Police Station.

Inside, he waited with two Chinese policemen in the Enquiry Room while the Inspector disappeared along a stone corridor across the other side of the room. In a little while he returned with another Englishman, tall and heavy, and wearing civilian clothes.

'Inspector Hardy tells me you were involved in a shooting incident not far from here.'

'Inspector Hardy informs you correctly,' Schepke said coldly.

The Englishman smiled. 'Would you care to come this way?'

Schepke followed him down the corridor. The office was almost at the end.

'Please be seated,' the Englishman said, closing the door. 'Cigarette?'

'Thank you.' Schepke lit the cigarette and sat back, the Englishman not hiding his interest in his uniform.

'You wouldn't be from the *Gertrud Lüth*?' he asked tentatively.

'I am.'

The Englishman looked again at the silvered bars of Schepke's tunic. 'You're not Captain Schepke?' he said surprised.

'Correct again,' Schepke said.

'Well I'm very pleased to meet you, Captain,' the Englishman said, smiling. 'You see, I do read our newspapers. However, I thought you were in hospital.'

'I was discharged this afternoon. I'm now staying at the Kwangtung Hotel in Hennessy Road.'

'I know it,' the Englishman said. 'By the way, my name is Menzies. Superintendent Menzies.' He reached his hand out. Then: 'But returning to this shooting incident. Perhaps you would care to tell me what happened.'

'It was over very quickly,' Schepke told him. 'I was walking back along the front when the first shot hit the wall. Then almost before I could move somebody grabbed me into a doorway. We were on the floor when the next shot came. After that I heard somebody running, and that's all.'

'Can you think of anyone who would wish to shoot you?'

Karl Schepke shrugged. 'I just came from the hospital this afternoon.'

'You've made no enemies here before?'

'Perhaps somebody made a mistake,' Schepke offered. 'Last time I was in Hong Kong was with the *Ilse Backenkölher* three and a half years ago.'

'I doubt very much if anyone made a mistake,' Menzies said thoughtfully. 'Not with a man your size and wearing a uniform like that. We have our regular gunmen and hatchetmen but this is none of their work. No, I think whoever fired those shots intended them for you all right, Captain.'

Again Schepke shrugged.

'Think, Captain. Think carefully.'

'I have thought.'

Menzies leaned forward his hands on the desk. 'You mentioned someone grabbing you into a doorway. Hardy didn't mention this.'

'He was the biggest man I ever saw,' Schepke said.

Menzies immediately sat up off the desk. 'Tell me about him.'

Schepke looked at him across the desk, a little puzzled. 'Well he was big,' he said. 'And I think he was bald. Either that or he had his head shaved. I would know him anywhere. Anybody would. There can't be many people that big.'

'Is that him?' Menzies asked eagerly, opening a large manila folder onto the desk. There were three photographs on the first page, each with a number across the bottom.

'That's him,' Schepke said, seeing the same impassive, rock-hewn face.

'What happened to him?'

'I'm not sure. He disappeared somewhere inside the building.'

Menzies snatched up the telephone and spoke rapidly in Cantonese.

'Something wrong?' Schepke asked.

Menzies leaned onto the desk. 'Your friend escaped from Fort Stanley last night.'

'Well I have nothing against him,' Schepke said, smiling thinly.

'That is what surprises me. He'll kill a man as soon as look at him. He was due to hang the end of this month.' As he spoke the urgent clanging bell of a police wagon carried in from the front.

'A man his size shouldn't be difficult to find.'

Menzies smiled. 'Unfortunately he is. There are many people so afraid of him as to hide him and say nothing. He also knows every back street and alley in Victoria and Kowloon. Actually he is Japanese. At one time he was quite famous as a sumo wrestler and Karate specialist. He fled from Japan when sought for questioning for a killing way back in nineteen-fifty-six. We believe he arrived here about three years ago on the *Heiwa Maru*. —Can you remember which hand he used when he grabbed you into that doorway?'

Schepke considered it a moment. He had been brought in past him. 'The left, I think.'

Menzies nodded. 'The right hand is useless except for the first finger and thumb. The hand is used only as a weapon. Karate deformed and lethalized it many years ago. Last night he killed two warders with a single chop of that same hand. —I think you have a lot of luck, Captain.'

'Isn't it more probable that the shots were intended for him?' Schepke asked.

'No. No, no one shoots at Kamei except the police. And then they always miss.' Menzies smiled. 'What about your own crew?'

'The Second Officer, maybe. Müller. He could be worried about the Enquiry. —But I don't think he would attempt to shoot me in the street.'

'Do you think the Enquiry could go badly for him?'

'It's possible.'

'We could check him out.'

'If you can find him,' Schepke said. 'The others didn't have much success.'

'What others?' Menzies asked.

'The Chief Engineer and other officers. They're living at the Hotel Zetland. I believe it's somewhere down by Jardines Bazaar.'

'I know the place,' Menzies said, 'I'll see what we can do. I'll get in touch with you at your hotel.'

'Thank you,' Schepke said, rising. 'Good night, Super-intendent.' Then he stopped in the doorway. 'By the way, what was our friend's name?'

'Kamei,' Menzies said. 'Kinjayamen Kamei. But I don't think he will bother you further. If my guess is correct he's waiting the chance to slip across to the Kowloon side. He'll probably try the junks and sampans at Causeway Bay Shelter. Either that or Kennedy Town.'

'Good night,' Schepke said.

'Good night, Captain.'

Karl Schepke left the police station and walked back along Gloucester Road. There were three police wagons stopped where the shooting had been, their portable lights directed overhead at the roof-tops and the policemen up there searching the high flat roofs. And out across the harbour it was very dark and the haze hiding the lights of Tsim Sha Tsui clock tower.

Two evenings later Karl Schepke was in the small bar of the Kwangtung Hotel. It was almost midnight. Menzies had just left. They had talked about Kamei and the shooting, and Menzies had said he had not been able to find out a great deal about Müller.

'At the moment he's living at the White Bear with a Shanghai girl. She's one of those refugees turned whore and moved down from the shacks above Causeway Bay. We questioned him yesterday morning about the shooting and he said they had been across in Kowloon since early that afternoon and hadn't returned until late. The girl corroborated that. Then when we asked about a possible gun, he denied ever owning one.'

'Hechler swears he took the Mauser,' Schepke said.

'Well they went out later and we searched the room and there was no sign of any gun.'

'I never was sure about him,' Schepke said. 'But he's the only one I could name. He caused plenty of trouble on the way up.'

'Well, I'm sorry,' Menzies said, taking his hat from the counter. 'Perhaps you'll let me know if you come across anything yourself.'

Karl Schepke nodded. 'What about the Jap?' he then asked.
'Oh, him. He got away.'
After Menzies left he had another of the ice-cold Holsteins
then went upstairs to bed.

THE Formal Enquiry opened at the Central Law Courts on the
twenty-third at ten o'clock in the morning. It was a fine clear
morning with the sun out and the city looked clean and white,
and Karl Schepke walked uptown past the English Navy
Barrack in the warm sunlight to the courts. The hearing was
being held in one of the upstairs courts and when he was shown
inside he saw most of the crew already there. Altogether there
were between fifty and sixty people seated in the court. He saw
Hechler along with Frauenheim and Dorsch down near the floor
of the court and he went down and took a seat alongside
of them.

'Hello, Karl. How are you?' Hechler asked.

'Fine,' Schepke told him. Frauenheim was looking better than
at any time during the trip north. 'How's the chest?' Schepke
asked.

'Better than ever,' Frauenheim said, grinning. 'It was the rest
I wanted. Hans was driving us too hard.'

'Listen to that,' Hechler said. 'I looked after him like his
mother.'

Schepke glanced around the court, noting the various coun-
sels and representatives.

'Who's for the company?'

Hechler nodded along the front bench in the floor of the
court. 'The Limey with the spectacles,' he said. 'His name's
Ashman. They're mostly all bloody Limeys.'

While they were talking the chairman and his three assessors came in and took their seats overlooking the floor of the court. They were all Englishmen, wearing lounge suits, the chairman wearing thick-lensed spectacles. Most of the counsel for the interested parties were Englishmen too, and on the same bench was a tall, scholarly-looking German with a card before him that read: 'Translator'.

'Gentlemen,' the chairman said, pausing for the talking to stop. 'Gentlemen. This court meets here today to make a thorough investigation into the stranding of the German steamship *Gertrud Lüth*. It will be the duty of this Court to examine not only the circumstances, but to examine all factors relevant to that stranding. This investigation, therefore, covers the working state of the ship at the time she set out on voyage from Wilhelmshafen, her sea-worthiness, the condition of all machinery and workings relevant to her well-being, the nature of her cargo and the manner of its stowage, and the state of her fire-fighting equipment. This investigation will also cover the behaviour and conduct of those concerned in the running of the vessel to the extent that they may or may not have contributed to her subsequent stranding.

'It is also our sad business today to investigate all factors leading to the loss of life of several members of the crew, including her original Captain. I therefore remind you that this is a Formal Enquiry to determine the cause of stranding and, whilst I am anxious that all due respect be paid to the dead and that no undue advantage be taken of any man who, through death, is unable to testify, I wish to impress upon all gathered here today that we are to investigate the whole and complete business thoroughly and impartially.' He paused, gently clearing his throat. 'I now call upon Mr. Bernhard Hoffmann to open proceedings on behalf of the West German State Marine.'

Hoffmann had handled many of the more serious investigations on behalf of the State Marine, and now he rose, tall, balding, his notes carefully arranged on the bench before him.

'Mr. Learned Chairman. I wish to bring to your notice here at the outset that the German steamship *Gertrud Lüth*, owned by the Oesten-Liebe Steamship Company of Hamburg, was under contract to the West German State Marine to make a transportation of grain between the ports of Wilhelmshafen and Shanghai. She was *not* under any contract whatsoever to embark a deck-cargo of heavy machinery!' Hoffmann broke off as a murmur of surprise passed through the court. 'At no time until her subsequent stranding was the West German State Marine aware that the *Gertrud Lüth* had embarked any cargo other than that which she was contracted to do. However, we are now in receipt of certain documents that confirm additional cargo was previously arranged between the owners, Oesten-Liebe, and the Lehmann-Willenbrock Engineering Company of Frankfurt and Turin. This additional cargo consisted of five earth-moving machines and four bulldozers, and was embarked at the port of Naples. This resulted in the ship sailing grossly overloaded and in a most dangerous and unseaworthy condition. I also wish to point out here that there are certain discrepancies arising in details of the crew listed as sailing from Wilhelmshafen and as to the actual number now known to have been on board. For instance, there were nine crewmen short on deck alone. And a further seven short in the crew listed below decks. Also, since the stranding it has been discovered that code numbers on the lifeboats were not those listed as having been on board when the ship was granted a certificate of seaworthiness. Altogether it appears that the *Gertrud Lüth* was little more than an actual ghost ship. This is established evidence, Mr. Learned Chairman, and I give it here at the outset of this investigation so as to avoid possible delay at a later stage.' Hoffmann completely held the interest of the court, each and every face turned upon him, and Ashman visibly disturbed by this opening statement. 'Unfortunately,' Hoffmann went on, 'the man best suited to help us answer many of the questions arising from these subjects, Kapitän Otto Emmermann, is no longer with us. What we know, the facts we have already been able to establish, and here I speak for the West German State Marine, I put forward to you, Mr. Learned Chairman, as indisputable evidence. But perhaps much that occurred on board the ill-fated *Gertrud Lüth* shall never be truly known because it appears to be a policy of the owning company that no one person should know the full extent of any one thing other than that which effects his own particular station of ship. There are many things which have been attributing factors to the stranding of the *Gertrud Lüth* apart from those which may be classed as Acts of God outside the realm of man and which he has no control over whatsoever. One of the foremost was the position of fuel. It appears to be another policy of the owning company to have kept the ship so short of fuel as to have placed it in a most hazardous position in making any one leg of the voyage to the East. Radioed fuel orders were cut to such an extent that it is best said that the ship succeeded in reaching certain ports only because of the skill and ingenuity of Kapitän Emmermann and Chief Engineer Hechler.' Again Hoffmann paused, this time to sip a few mouthfuls of water from the glass before him. 'Now, at this early stage of the Enquiry I will take the rather unusual step, after knowing what evidence there already is, and after having seen depositions taken by the Receiver of Wreck, and say here and now that if it had not been for the praiseworthy seamanship of Kapitän Karl Schepke, I very much doubt indeed, in these circumstances, if the *Gertrud Lüth* would ever have been brought within sight of shore again!' Hoffmann glanced coldly around the floor of the court, then abruptly sat down.

For two or three minutes he sat there, the full effect of his opening statements hanging over the court and the silence broken only by an uneasy clearing of throats and the changing of positions. Karl Schepke glanced about him, seeing various members of the crew, some appearing strangely out of place in civilian clothes. Then he noticed Müller well to the rear of the court, tense and anxious-looking.

Hoffmann was on his feet again. ·

'Mr. Learned Chairman,' he began. 'I propose that in the prevailing circumstances we focus our main interest at this point in that part of the intended voyage between Singapore and Shanghai. And with this end in view, I call upon Karl Schepke.'

Schepke rose and crossed the floor of the court to the witness box. Again a low murmur of voices and the shifting of feet travelled lightly through the court as he took the stand and prepared to answer Hoffmann's questions.

'Name?' Hoffmann asked, the low murmur of conversation subsiding now as he opened the questioning.

'Karl Schepke.'

'Educated?'

'During the war. Nowhere in particular. I joined the Marine as a cadet in nineteen-forty-six. Mate's Certificate nineteen-fifty-two. Master's Certificate nineteen-fifty-six. First command nineteen-fifty-eight, the *Johanne Kjolbro* of the Backenkölher Line. Relinquished command through illness in Kobe, April, nineteen-sixty-one.'

'Excuse me, Kapitän,' Hoffmann interrupted. 'You appear to be extremely well versed in the procedure of such a Court as this. Would you care to explain?'

'I have faced such an Enquiry before,' Schepke said, his voice cold and clear.

'And what happened at that Enquiry, Kapitän?'

'I had my Master's Certificate suspended for two years.'

There was the sudden quiet sound of light movement in the court as certain people leaned involuntarily forward, their attention held by Shepke and Hoffmann.

'Please continue, Kapitän. And though the West German State Marine is already aware, it may be of interest to certain parties to mention the illness which caused you to relinquish command of the *Johanne Kjolbro* at Kobe.'

'It was an appendicitis,' Schepke answered. 'There was no other reason. Then in September of nineteen-sixty-one I sailed for Hamburg as First Officer of the *Ilse Backenkölher* after her own First Officer had come ashore.'

'Why did the First Officer of the *Ilse Backenkölher* come ashore at Kobe, Kapitän?'

'I believe he did not get along well with the Kapitän and Second Officer.'

'And you were quite happy to join her?'

'No. Not quite. But I wanted to get home and took the first opportunity that came along.'

177

'You were happy on board the *Ilse Backenkölher*?'

'Not exactly. I didn't agree with certain aspects of the running of the ship.'

'How long had you been on board before you formed these, what shall we say, opinions?'

'A matter of days. Before we made our first port of call, Hong Kong.'

'And what was it that happened in Singapore, Kapitän?' Hoffmann asked, glancing first at the Chairman, then around the court.

'She was burned out.'

'And you were held to blame?'

'Yes, sir,' Schepke answered evenly.

'And were you?'

'No, sir. But I am afraid that was not the opinion of the Court.'

'Thank you, Kapitän,' Hoffmann said. Then turning to the Chairman: 'Mr. Learned Chairman, I know part of my examination may at first appear to have no direct bearing on the present Enquiry but I think it only fair that the Court be made aware of Kapitän Schepke's past. At the same time, I wish it to be made clear that the West German State Marine is fully aware of this and in the case of the Enquiry into the loss of the *Ilse Backenkölher* we made a careful study of all evidence given and after sentence was passed we instructed him that there were excellent grounds for appeal. However, for reasons never made known to us, he refused to lodge one. Now the point which I wish to make clear is that although knowing the court's decision, the West German State Marine still retained a respect of his seamanship, and we do not wish to reflect on the past by holding his suspension against him in any way whatsoever. And when he made an application early last year for the return of his Master's Certificate, the West German State Marine made no objection.'

Then again Hoffmann turned to Karl Schepke.

'Now, Kapitän,' he said. 'Would you care to explain to the Court the reason which brought you on board the *Gertrud Lüth*?'

'The post of First Officer was offered me by Kapitän Emmermann. I believe Rösing, the original First Officer was taken ashore at Colombo.'

'In fact,' Hoffmann said, 'it would be correct to say that Kapitän Emmermann refused a replacement at Colombo and sailed for Singapore with the single intention of shipping you?'

Schepke hesitated momentarily. 'That may be,' he said.

'All right,' Hoffmann said. 'Did Kapitän Emmermann offer any reason as to why he particularly wished to sign you as First Officer of the *Gertrud Lüth*?'

'He seemed to think that I was, in his own personal estimation, the man for the post. He gave me the impression that he had little confidence in the deck officers already on board. Although he made it clear that he held the engineers in high regard.'

'Then it may be said that he had more faith in you, at that time on the beach, than he had in his own officers?'

'Perhaps,' Schepke said quietly.

'Of course, Emmermann knew you both as a man and as a seaman. Did he ever mention the *Ilse Backenkölher* to you prior to going on board the *Gertrud Lüth*?'

'I cannot remember exactly,' Schepke told him.

'Did he appear to believe that the destruction of the *Ilse Backenkölher* was caused through no fault of yours?'

'It's possible.'

'Would you care to tell the Court how you met Emmermann in the first instance?'

'It was during the war. My people had been killed in an Allied bombing raid and I ended up at Eckernförde where I worked as a mess boy in the U Boat officers mess. Emmermann was at that time in command of one of the boats. Rollmann, bo'sun of the *Gertrud Lüth*, was bo'sun of the same boat.' Schepke paused.

'Please go on, Kapitän,' Hoffmann urged. 'I know all these facts already but it may prove of great interest to the Court later in the proceedings when it comes to consider the decisions that will have to be made.'

'I knew Emmermann for almost three years. Then later in the

war when the order *Rainbow* was issued I sailed with him and a skeleton crew to scuttle his boat in the bay. Afterward we made our way through to Plon where the Donitz Guard Battalion was formed. We were eventually captured by the British and sent to prison camps where both Emmermann and Rollmann were court-martialled for scuttling the U boat.'

'And it was this same camp where you yourself was held prisoner for more than a year?'

'It was.'

'How old were you at that time, Kapitän?'

'About thirteen years old,' Schepke answered quietly.

'And how was it you eventually gained entrance to the Marine as a cadet?'

'Through the help of Emmermann who was still at that time serving his term of imprisonment.'

'Then when Emmermann was eventually released and restored to a Kapitän of Marine, you sailed with him. Is that correct?' Hoffmann asked, the court still quiet and without movement.

'Yes, I sailed with him,' Schepke said. 'He also helped me sit my Mate's and Master's Certificates.'

'Previous to meeting Emmermann in Singapore, when was the last time you met, Kapitän?'

'—Calcutta,' Schepke said, hesitating momentarily. 'We were on our way home. Emmermann was on the *Corrientes* and on voyage to Manila.'

'Emmermann was not with the Backenkölher Line then?' Hoffmann asked.

'He never was as far as I know. At the time of our meeting in Calcutta he was with the German-Orient-Asia Line.'

'Thank you, Kapitän,' Hoffmann said. 'Now I think we can move on to the time you joined the *Gertrud Lüth*. Perhaps you will tell the Court what your first impressions were of her. Such as was she in your own opinion seaworthy? Did you personally inspect such things as lifeboats and fire-fighting equipment? How did you regard the rest of the crew? Were her officers, in your opinion, competent?'

Schepke glanced around the floor of the court before going

on. 'You will understand,' he said, 'that in the short time I had on board before sailing I had no real opportunity to make a close inspection of the ship. However, my first impression was that she was grossly and dangerously overloaded. An off-hand inspection of her lifeboats revealed two of them entirely useless. Indeed, they could not even hold rainwater. The other two were in very bad condition although I thought it probable they would float if launched. The condition of the fire-fighting equipment was quite good. Hoses seemed to be intact and the fire-extinguishers I handled were full, although I found later that a number of them were without cartridges. As regards the deck crew I thought them fairly efficient, but short-handed. As far as the officers are concerned, I would rather not make any comment at this stage.'

'And what about Kapitän Emmermann?' Hoffmann asked, sorting through his notes.

Schepke hesitated a moment before going on. 'I think mentally he was as alert as ever, although possibly somewhat depressed. Physically, he was not the same man I had once known.'

'Then you regarded him as being in need of medical attention?' Hoffmann asked.

'I did,' Schepke said evenly. 'I believe he was suffering from some extreme form of illness.'

'Cancer, perhaps?' Hoffmann asked, and it was obvious to all that he knew a great deal about both Emmermann and Schepke.

'Possibly,' Schepke said.

'Can you say at that time what may have had an unsettling effect on the crew?'

'I think the morning we went alongside to coal and found our order had been cancelled.'

'And was there enough fuel on board at that time to complete the voyage to Shanghai?'

'The ship could not possibly have reached Shanghai.'

'Do you hold any opinion as to why the order was cancelled?'

'I think perhaps the owners cancelled most radioed orders and then had their agents haggle with Emmermann in an attempt to cut down expenditure to the lowest possible point.'

'And did Kapitän Emmermann go ashore that day after the order was cancelled?'

'He did. He went ashore to see the agents and we finally embarked enough coal to give us almost two days safety margin in case we ran into bad weather on the final run.'

'Were you happy with the situation?'

'I had confidence in Emmermann,' Schepke told him.

'Did you express any opinion on the situation?'

'No. I had been ashore for almost three years and I was glad of a berth on board any ship.'

'Yes,' Hoffmann said. 'I think the Court appreciates your point. —Now, according to your entry in the ship's log, Kapitän Emmermann was presumed lost overboard. This is so?'

'Yes, sir.'

'How do you think he came to be lost overboard during a perfectly calm and normal night at sea?'

'He left this behind,' Schepke said, producing a note from the breast pocket of his tunic. 'It has been damaged but it is still legible and can be seen to be in his own hand.'

Hoffmann took the note, read it, then passed it to the chairman.

'When you assumed command, did you find any resentment amongst the other officers?' Hoffmann went on.

'Some,' Schepke answered.

'Will you tell the Court how that resentment showed itself?'

'Well, Second Officer Müller didn't entirely agree with some of my decisions. However, his resentment was rather personal. I could understand his point in a way. There I was in command after having just come on board.'

'I see,' Hoffmann said. Then glancing at his notes: 'Now the question of this fire that destroyed the radio office. Have you any idea how it happened?'

'I believe that the fire was started on purpose.' Schepke said.

'Why do you think that? And for what possible reason?' Hoffmann prompted.

'Rollmann found a paraffin can in the office when shoring the bridge deck. The Chinese chef recognized it as having come from the galley. But I am unable to furnish any reason for somebody starting the fire unless—'

'Unless what? —Unless out of petty jealousy?' Hoffmann said. 'Is that what you were about to say, Kapitän?'

Karl Schepke looked back at him but did not say anything.

'As you wish,' Hoffmann told him. 'At this point you then proceeded to run into bad weather. Is that correct?'

'It is,' Schepke answered. 'It was nothing bad at first. It was a gradual worsening. I didn't believe we were standing into any imminent danger. The last weather report we had was to the effect that an area of deepening depression was moving north-westerly from the Carolines.'

'Did you not at that time consider altering course for Manila, or even returning to Singapore?'

'First of all let me say that returning to Singapore was out of the question as far as most people on board were concerned. Most of us were in no position to find it easy in finding another ship if dismissed by Oesten-Liebe. Putting back to Singapore would only have been a last consideration. Besides, I didn't think conditions at that time warranted such action. Nor did I think running for Manila necessary. You must remember that at this time we were unaware that we were standing into a typhoon, never mind know in which direction it was travelling. Then by the time we were standing into it we were already taking water in Number One hold to such a degree I thought it the best course to stand into it for the time being because in my own estimation the blow was continuing to veer southerly and I fully expected it to either blow out or else pass astern of us. That is why I at that time decided against making a run for Manila. If I altered course I would then be steaming right into its path. Instead I altered course and laid the ship into the wind and seas, prepared to resume our original course to Shanghai or Hong Kong depending on the fuel left after the blow passed. When the weather continued to deteriorate I decided to make for Hong Kong as soon as conditions allowed. That was the time part of our forward deck-cargo broke adrift. We lost Wila-mowitz at this time and had Rollmann seriously injured. There were also two others swept overboard, including Quartermaster Roth.'

'After Wilamowitz died that left yourself and Müller the only deck officers on board,' Hoffmann said. 'How did you arrange to work the ship between you?'

'It never came to that,' Schepke said quietly.

'What happened?' Hoffmann asked. 'Didn't you see Müller?'

'I believe he had gone to his cabin before the deck-cargo came adrift the second time.'

'Why was it he went to his cabin, Kapitän?'

'There was a difference of opinion.'

'He went to his cabin because of a difference of opinion?' Hoffmann said incredulously.

'More or less,' Schepke said. 'Although I didn't know at that time.'

'Just what was this difference of opinion?'

'He wanted to run for Manila. I was against it. I believed that to make such a run at that time would be to hazard the ship and her crew.'

'When next did you see Müller?'

'Just before I amputated Rollmann's left leg,' Schepke answered. 'He was in his cabin. Other than that I wish to make no further comment.'

'Then you were running the ship topside yourself at this time?' Hoffmann asked.

'Radio Officer Altmeyer more or less took over a sea watch. He and Quartermasters Pulst and Bahr were of great help.'

'And what happened to Müller?'

'I saw him again after we passed through the storm centre. I had been below to the engine-room. I gathered there was some sort of trouble below and when I reached the port inboard passage part of the black gang were already on deck after having knocked the Chief Engineer unconscious. I shot two of them when they came at me. Another was wounded in the thigh. Then after I got them back below I felt the ship alter course and when

I got back topside Altmeyer told me that Müller had taken the wheel and was turning back. I then ordered Müller off the wheel and below to his cabin.'

'And he went?' Hoffmann asked, carefully watching Schepke's face.

'He did,' Schepke said, his voice not changing any.

'According to certain depositions made to the Receiver of Wreck under oath, your last statement conflicts. Did in fact a brawl not ensue and did Müller not strike you with a fire-axe before being knocked unconscious by Altmeyer? And subsequently, was Müller not locked in the galley storeroom?'

'The bridge stairway handrail broke and I hurt myself in the fall,' Schepke said.

'I see.' Hoffmann glanced at his notes, not pursuing the matter. 'Kapitän, would you be kind enough to relate the circumstances under which Rollmann met his death?'

'Gaseous gangrene set in after amputation of his left leg. He then shot himself.'

'Could you, Kapitän, at that time, see any hope of preventing death by gangrene?'

'I am not a doctor,' Schepke said. 'But I would say none. The infection was critical. He was unconscious for long spells and suffering extreme pain.'

'This gun that he used to end his life. Could you tell the Court where he got it?'

'I was dressing his leg. He was conscious at the time. My tunic was across a chair by the bunk and he must have taken the gun when I went to the galley.'

'Then he knew you had a gun?'

'He did.'

Hoffmann turned back to his notes, a slight movement passing through the court as people moved in their seats.

'Now, Kapitän,' Hoffmann said, turning again to the witness box. 'I want you to forget these other matters for the time being and tell the Court honestly and truthfully if whether or not you feel you did everything in your power to bring the *Gertrud Lüth* to port.'

Schepke glanced momentarily around the court. 'I do,' he said simply.

'Thank you, Kapitän,' Hoffmann said, bowing to the chairman then sitting down.

Ashman rose immediately. 'Mr. Learned Chairman,' he said. 'I would like to ask your permission to cross-examine Captain Schepke and one or two of the statements he has just made.'

The chairman nodded his approval then sat back as Ashman crossed the floor of the court.

'Captain Schepke,' he said coldly. 'As Mr. Hoffmann has so kindly told us, you are—or *were* considered a highly competent seaman. Before joining the *Gertrud Lüth* you were, so to put it, on the beach for the better part of three years after the Enquiry into the loss of the *Ilse Backenkölher*. During the last year, after you had your Master's Certificate returned to you, did you at any time attempt to find a berth on board any other ship?'

'I did,' Schepke answered.

'And what was the result of your attempt, or attempts?'

'I failed.'

'Why did you fail, Captain?' Ashman asked with confidence. Karl Schepke shrugged.

Ashman smiled. 'Was it not simply because shipping companies and agents did not wish to take a risk with you?'

'I don't know,' Schepke answered, an edge coming into his voice as he straightened his shoulders.

Ashman turned to the chairman. 'Mr. Learned Chairman,' he said. 'I wish it to be known to the Court that at no time was the Oesten-Liebe Shipping Company aware that Kapitän Emmermann had engaged the services of Mr. Schepke as First Officer. Indeed, they were at all times under the assumption that Kapitän Emmermann had engaged a replacement Second Officer at Colombo and had promoted Mr. Müller to First Officer. Mr. Müller has been with the company some time and has proved himself an apt and suitable officer able to take full command if the situation arose. I therefore wish to make it quite clear that my clients were completely unaware that Mr. Schepke had taken

186

on the post of First Officer. Had they done so they would have refused to let the ship sail.'

'All right, Mr. Ashman. You have made your point,' the chairman said.

Ashman turned again to Schepke. 'Mr. Schepke. Perhaps you would care to explain why you refused to turn back to Singapore after Captain Emmermann disappeared? And later again why you did not turn back when the Radio Office was destroyed?'

Karl Schepke leaned forward on the rail of the box, looking directly at Ashman. 'Perhaps you are unaware that most of those on board the *Gertrud Lüth* were not in a position to make decisions that would jeopardize their own future. Almost all those on board were so for the simple reason that they were unable to find a berth with any other company. To have returned to Singapore would have meant instant dismissal. And I am certain that a man of your integrity and understanding can quite well see the problem. Furthermore, I am not on trial here for the condition of the ship and her unseaworthiness at the time of sailing from Singapore.'

Ashman was momentarily taken aback. '—Those are very serious allegations, Mr. Schepke. Among other things you are inferring that my clients are unscrupulous in their manner of recruiting officers and men for their ships.'

'You understand perfectly,' Schepke said, showing the first sign of anger. 'If your clients can defy State Marine Regulations, I don't see that recruiting unsuitable officers and crewmen would bother their conscience very much.' All the attention of the court was on Schepke now. 'As regards the question of the fire,' he went on quickly before Ashman could interrupt. 'I might just bring it to light that ships sailed the world for many years before wireless was invented and the last weather report we had in no way hinted that we were eventually to stand into a typhoon. Had I known that, of course, I should have immediately altered course for Manila. Then again I would have done the same when the weather worsened later had we not already been shipping water badly in Number One hold. But by then, and the ship in the condition she was, and with the wind rapidly veering, there was no alternative but to sit the blow out as it made to pass astern, and at the same time, between us and Manila. I trust I make myself perfectly clear?'

A great sigh of tension escaped the court as Schepke finished his sudden outburst. Ashman stared at his notes as if unaware of any of it, but all the same badly taken out of his stride. Then clearing his throat: 'Let us return to the question of the fire. You mention it being started deliberately. You even mention a certain paraffin can. Unfortunately, this can in question was never found. I wonder, if in fact, it ever existed and if it is not just something invented to cover your own incompetence in discovering the fire. After all, you were on watch on the bridge at that particular time.'

'That paraffin can existed,' Karl Schepke said evenly. 'I suggest you call the chef and ask him. He recognized it as having come from the galley.'

'Then indirectly you accuse the chef of starting the fire?' Ashman said smilingly.

'I do not!' Schepke shouted, the colour draining from his face. '—But I do believe somebody deliberately started that fire.'

'Then you can name someone?'

'—I make no comment.'

'As you wish, Mr. Schepke,' Ashman said smugly. 'But why did you fail to notice the fire when you were standing directly above it?'

'The action of the smouldering fire was so advanced in that enclosed compartment that by the time we were aware of its being, the compartment exploded. Try questioning those on the bridge with me at that time, Herr Ashman.'

Ashman coughed uncomfortably, then moved through his notes, unsure of exactly where to go on with his cross-examination.

'We, we now come to this murderous shooting incident that occurred in the—'

'I have already explained this!' Schepke broke in angrily.

'But you shot two defenceless men to death and wounded another! This was quite an heroic act, Mr. Schepke.'

188

'I say nothing more!'

'What about Rollmann?' Ashman countered. 'Just what were the real circumstances of this unfortunate man's death?'

'I have already explained that to the Court.'

'Mr. Schepke,' Ashman said. 'Don't you think it was being unduly careless to have left that gun within such easy reach of the deceased?'

'I accept the consequences of my own actions absolutely,' Schepke said, his voice cold and brittle. 'Every man has the right to make his own destruction.'

'Then Rollmann took his life while the balance of his mind was disturbed?' Ashman said. 'That appears to be what you mean, Mr. Schepke.'

'If that is how you choose to put it,' Schepke said. 'But thank God that more or less is only the opinion of the English. Yes, Rollmann asked me to shoot him. He was fully aware at that time that he was going to die. But instead of waiting for himself to rot, he chose to end it with a bullet. Rollmann's mind was at no time disturbed! You understand that?' The court had gone deathly quiet. Then Schepke went on again, looking coldly at Ashman. 'I only hope, Herr Ashman, that you never have the misfortune to suffer gangrene. In which case you might later suffer the humiliation of having one of your hypocritical countrymen classify you as having been mentally disturbed!' The words came cold and clear, brittle as ice, echoing in the high dreary courtroom. 'Furthermore, Herr Ashman, I take violent exception to you attempting to incriminate me wherever you think possible to do so. Your clients had broken every conceivable marine regulation before the *Gertrud Lüth* left European waters. She was in need of a long and thorough overhaul, her boats practically useless, short of experienced crew, and hazardously overloaded. I personally did all within my knowledge and experience to bring her safely to port, but failed. Herr Ashman, I am in no way ashamed of what happened during that voyage, and I wish to state openly to the Court that I have nothing to hide. Is that clear, Herr Ashman?'

Ashman was no longer looking at him. Then barely looking at

the chairman, said: 'No more questions, Mr. Learned Chairman.' His voice was subdued, and taking his notes, he crossed the floor of the court without looking at anyone.

'Is there anyone here who may wish to question the witness further?' the chairman asked. He waited, looking to the benches around the floor of the court. '—The witness may step down.'

Karl Schepke went back to his seat, a buzz of conversation sweeping the court along with the movement of feet and bodies as the tension was suddenly broken.

'Congratulations,' Hechler said. 'Our friend Hoffmann knows it all.'

Schepke nodded his agreement. 'I don't think it will last long,' he said. 'There's too much proof available of the state the ship was in for Ashman to disagree with much of it.' Then looking across the floor he saw the chairman glance at the clock then adjourn the court until afternoon.

'Two o'clock please, gentlemen,' the chairman said, rising, and the court rose with him, standing as he left with his three assessors.

Von Pittkamer was waiting outside in the high bare passage.

'May I offer my congratulations, Herr Kapitän.'

Karl Schepke nodded but did not say anything.

'What tactics do you think Herr Ashman will pursue next?' von Pittkamer asked as they walked downstairs.

'None, I should think,' Schepke told him. 'There should be very little hope for him.'

Von Pittkamer nodded that long serious face of his. 'I think you are right,' he said. 'At this pace the Enquiry itself should be lucky to last three days. But what about afterward? Have you given thought to that?'

'I think it better to wait until the time comes,' Schepke said.

'You can depend on me for any help necessary.'

'Thank you,' Schepke told him as they walked to the doorway. Von Pittkamer carried a cane and wore a severe grey suit and black Homburg. A number of the officers were waiting for them out on the steps.

'Good day,' von Pittkamer said to them, nodding that grave

and serious face of his, and looking long and old in the bright sunlight as he walked with his cane to the car.

'What did he say?' Dorsch asked.

'He'll do what he can to help later,' Schepke told them.

There were trees out in front of the Courts and the foliage was very green in the sunlight.

'Let's have a drink,' Hechler said.

They walked toward the front, the sunlight shining brightly on the new Star Ferry Concourse. There were many people hurrying toward the ferry from the city and it was pleasant walking in the sunlight after the coldness of the drab courtroom, and Karl Schepke was glad now that it was more or less over for him.

The buildings along the front were tall and solidly built, looking out across the harbour to Kowloon, the city sprawled out white and hot-looking under the hills of the New Territories, Big Hat Mountain rising solidly in the background.

They turned up a side street away from the front and there was a bar named The Viaduct.

Inside of the bar it was cool and modern and with a counter that went all the way along one wall to a glass partition where inside there were tables and people sitting at the tables eating.

They ordered San Miguel beers. The beers came very cold and collared high in the glasses.

'Worried?' Schepke said to Altmeyer.

Altmeyer started. '—A little,' he said. 'I've never been in court before.'

'Don't think about it. Just answer the questions as best you can.'

'That's right,' Hechler said. 'Hoffmann knows it all already. They're not after us. Apart from Ashman. That bastard would try to jail his own mother. We're just the victims of circumstance. That's what we are. Right, Karl?'

'That's as good as any,' Schepke said.

'Don't mind me asking,' Frauenheim broke in. 'I'm just curious to know why you let Müller off the hook.'

'That's right,' Dorsch said. 'You could have put him on the beach for a long time. He had it coming.'

'You heard about the *Ilse Backenkölher*,' Schepke said. 'That didn't help me any afterward. This time I want everything quiet. I don't want this Enquiry played up. Let Oesten-Liebe take it all. That way I can do myself good. But whatever way this goes it won't help me. It won't help any of us.' He left it at that and no one took it any further.

They had another beer then went in to eat.

When they came out to the bar again it was almost two o'clock. Karl Schepke stopped at the counter.

'Hadn't we better get back?' Hechler asked.

'You go ahead,' Schepke told him. 'They shouldn't want me again.'

Hechler and the others went on out and Karl Schepke bought a beer and took it to one of the tables. Sitting there he watched the people come and go in the bar. Then after a while he sat and looked into his beer and tried to think about the future.

'I thought you would have brightened after this morning.'

'Oh, it's you,' Schepke said, looking up to find Menzies standing by the table. 'Please sit down.'

The floorman came over. Schepke told him two beers.

'You were across there?'

'Yes. It was the first time I ever was to a shipping Enquiry. I thought it might be interesting.'

'And was it?' Schepke asked.

'It seems to me your company was at fault,' Menzies said.

'I'd rather it never happened,' Schepke told him. 'It was my first ship in three years.'

'You seem to have done all you could. Only your company's agent seemed to be against you.'

'Even so it won't be easy to find another berth. Shipping companies don't look for people just through with an Enquiry.'

'You might find something.'

'There's the waiting,' Schepke said. 'There's plenty of waiting on the beach. At least it'll be a change from Singapore.'

192

Menzies looked across the table at him. 'That's all you can do, wait?'

Schepke nodded, then sipped his beer. The beer was very cold and clean-tasting.

'But what are you doing here,' he asked, changing the subject.

Menzies smiled. 'Even policemen like an occasional beer,' he said, beckoning the floorman.

'Have you caught up with Kamei yet?'

'I'm afraid not,' Menzies said. 'We believe he's across in Kowloon.'

The floorman brought the beers. The bar and restaurant had emptied quite considerably.

'There are a few local companies you could try,' Menzies offered. 'Some of them run the China coast and to Indo-China and Viet Nam.'

'I suppose it would be worth a try,' Schepke said without any real enthusiasm.

'What about going home?'

'I would if I could feel certain of a ship. I'd go Second or Third with a decent line.'

'Well I hope you find something,' Menzies said, looking at his wrist watch. 'Are you going back to Court?'

'Is that where you're going?'

'Yes. But not your one. I want to see about a case I have coming up next week.'

They went out and started back toward the Courts. The air outside in the narrow street was dry and dusty and smelling of the fumes of the traffic. They walked back onto Connaught Road Central. One of the ferries had just left the landing stage. Karl Schepke watched it begin its crossing of the harbour. 'Have you any idea who bought the *Gertrud Lüth*?'

'I'm afraid not,' Menzies told him. 'I even made a few enquiries after reading that she'd been sold to an undisclosed party. I like to know most of what goes on as well.' He smiled.

As they walked, Karl Schepke looked back across the city and toward Mount Parker. 'It's changed quite a lot.'

'Yes,' Menzies agreed. 'With ground so expensive they build

upward now. It's amazing to see all this money spent when the New Territories revert to the Communists in another thirty years. The island won't exist without them.'

They had reached the Courts. Schepke looked back at the harbour.

'Are you going inside?' Menzies asked.

'No. I don't think they'll want me. Perhaps we can have another drink sometime.' He left Menzies going up the steps to the Courts and started back downtown toward Wanchai, past the almost empty English Navy Barrack, the afternoon sunlight shimmering off the black oiled roadway.

PANCHO was waiting for him.

'Your watch,' he said, grinning that broad grin.

Karl Schepke took the watch and held it to his ear. 'How much?'

'Eight dollar,' the boy said proudly.

Schepke handed him a ten dollar note. 'Anybody in the bar?'

'No, sir,' the boy told him, bringing two crumpled dollar notes from his pocket.

'Keep them.' Schepke went on into the bar. 'Give me a bottle of gin,' he said after the boy had put the lights on along the bar. 'Make sure it's Dutch.'

'Yes, sir.'

He took the bottle to a table in the far corner. It was cool in the bar and the lights shaded. Then out in the hallway someone rang the desk bell. He drank the first one slowly. It would be a long night. They were all long nights on the beach.

Someone came into the bar behind Pancho. They were both Chinese, well-dressed, wearing wide-brimmed hats, the one wearing the spectacles carrying a brief-case.

'Someone to see you,' Pancho said coming to the table, both Chinese following him, smiling.

'Good evening, Captain,' the one wearing the spectacles said, setting his brief-case carefully on the floor close to the table, then both of them taking off their hats, their hair shining and smoothed down close to their heads.

'You sure you have the right man?' Karl Schepke asked, not moving from the table.

'Yes, Captain. I am most certain. Please allow me to introduce ourselves. This is Mr. Sung,' he said, inclining his head to the other. Mr. Sung shook hands. Mr. Sung smelled of brilliantine and shaving lotion.

'My own name is Wang,' the spectacled one said. He, too, shook hands. They were both in their late forties.

'Sit down. Drink?' Schepke asked, moving the bottle across the table.

'No thank you,' Mr. Wang said, smiling.

'Thank you all the same,' Mr. Sung said. They both spoke good English.

Then Mr. Wang called something to the boy and he brought them two glasses with something in them that might have been cherry wine.

'What can I do for you?' Schepke asked, addressing them both.

'I believe you look for another ship, Captain,' Mr. Wang said.

Karl Schepke looked from one to the other. 'You know of one?' he asked, taking notice of them now.

Mr. Sung smiled.

'You can make plenty of money, Captain,' Mr. Wang said.

Schepke leaned his elbows on the table. 'Just what is all this?'

'We were in court this morning,' Mr. Sung said, smiling.

'I may not be cleared,' Schepke told him.

They both smiled knowingly, confidently.

'You make a joke, Captain,' Mr. Wang said.

Mr. Sung went on smiling. But Mr. Wang was the one who did the big business.

'I take it you quite well know the South China coast?' Mr.
Wang asked.

'You might say that,' Schepke said, nodding.

'All right. Then all you do is run the American and
Nationalist blockade.'

'Wait a minute,' Schepke told him. 'Even the Limeys get shot
doing that.'

'An occupational hazard, Captain,' Mr. Wang said, smiling.
Mr. Sung went on smiling wisely, nodding in agreement with his
big business associate. 'The pay is six thousand Hong Kong
dollars the month, Captain,' Mr. Wang went on. 'Reasonable,
you would say?'

Karl Schepke mentally translated the six thousand dollars.
'You could say that,' he said non-committally. 'What sort of
ship is she?'

They both smiled hugely this time.

'The *Gertrud Lüth*, Captain,' Mr. Wang said.

'Now it's your turn to joke,' Schepke told him.

'I assure you it is not a joke, Captain. —Money is no object,'
Mr. Wang went on.

'Correct,' Mr. Sung said.

'Well, Captain?' Mr. Wang asked, watching Schepke across
the table.

Karl Schepke was still a little unsure, of it all.

'You would make plenty of money, Captain,' Mr. Sung said.

'And maybe get shot as well,' Schepke told him.

They both smiled wisely again. They had finished the cherry
wine.

'What about a crew?' Schepke asked, his mind working now
on all that money after so long without any.

'The working crew would be Chinese, of course,' Mr. Wang
said. 'But we wish all deck and engineer officers to be European.'

'And where do you get the officers?'

'There are possibilities,' Mr. Wang assured him.

'Big possibilities,' Mr. Sung said. Mr. Sung was a very
polished gentleman.

'Well I can't give you an answer right now,' Schepke said.

'And I want to know more about what I'm getting into. I like to know just who is shooting at me for what.'

'Of course,' Mr. Wang said. 'We fully appreciate your concern.' He rose now, taking his brief-case, and put on his hat. Mr. Sung rose with him, then handed Schepke their business card. 'Please let us have an answer at your convenience,' he said. 'After which we will be delighted to furnish any details you wish to know.'

'Good night,' Captain,' Mr. Wang said.

'Good night,' Schepke said, walking across the bar with them. He watched them with Pancho as they went on down the hall.

'Plenty money,' Pancho said, impressed.

'You seen them before?'

'No,' the boy said. 'They plenty big money from Kowloon side.'

Karl Schepke looked at the card Mr. Sung had left, and read: The Mihsien Steamship Company. The address was across in Kowloon's Nathan Road.

Well that's something all right, old turtle-head, he was thinking. Six thousand dollars the month is a lot of money. Even for getting shot at.

KARL SCHEPKE was just getting up the morning of the third day of the Enquiry when there was a knock on the door and the boy showed in Hechler.

'I thought you'd have been up early today?' Hechler said, dropping his cap onto the bedside table.

'I didn't think much about it.'

'You don't sound very interested,' Hechler said, standing now in the doorway of the bathroom as Schepke washed.

'None of it's done me any good.' He had taken the dressing off the wound on his left side and Hechler looked at the thickly crusted scab and the thin straight line of the incision running around onto his back where the surgeons had opened him up.

'Been back to the hospital?'

Schepke finished drying his face and neck. 'It's healed except for the scab,' he said.

'Maybe you should let them look at it just the same.'

'To hell with them.'

'What's troubling you?'

'Forget it.'

Hechler followed him back into the room. 'We had a visit from Chinatown last night.'

Schepke stopped buttoning his shirt. 'Mr. Big Business?'

'They didn't say they'd been to see you.'

'They were here a couple of nights ago. They're looking for somebody to run the blockade on the China mainland.'

'So they told us,' Hechler said.

'What did you tell them?'

Hechler thoughtfully inclined his head. 'Well the money's good,' he said. 'If we have to wait around here on the beach for any time we could give it a try.'

'You know the ship?'

'They told us,' Hechler said. 'We went out to Taikoo after they left and took a look at her. They're doing a good job. One of the Limey surveyors told us she'd be out of dock next week.'

Schepke put his cap on and they went out and downstairs.

'What did you tell them?' Hechler wanted to know.

'I want to see what von Pittkamer can do first.'

'We said about the same.'

Schepke put his keys on the desk and they went out through the downstairs hall. Outside it was bright sunlight.

'Are you coming uptown now?' Hechler asked, looking at his watch. 'The summing up begins at ten.'

'You go ahead. I want to get a shave and haircut.' They walked up Hennessy Road in the bright morning sunlight to the junction with Queens Road East where Schepke left Hechler and crossed the roadway to a barber shop.

It was almost eleven o'clock when he came out. He did not

expect any judgement to be passed at the Enquiry until sometime in the afternoon and a little way on he saw the bar of the Gaylord Hotel already open and he went in and bought a beer. The beer was cold and the bar had that empty smoky feeling the morning after a busy night and the two barmen were behind the counter polishing glasses. The bar opened onto the hallway to the stairway upstairs and after a while two English Navy officers came in from upstairs and had a beer. Karl Schepke ordered another and then the girls came in after having put on new faces and combed up their hair. The girls were faded-looking after the night, and suddenly Schepke found himself thinking about Shuang-shuang and strangely enough finding difficulty in remembering her face.

I guess that's the great disappointment about Chinese whores, he was thinking, they all look the same, dressed or naked. Most of the time it's easier telling them apart when they're dressed. But Shuang-shuang was more pretty than most, though. Even naked she had what most of them don't know about. But even then she knew all about the European failing for forgetting Chinese faces and that's why she always wore the green cheongsam. Anybody wanting her asked for the girl in the green cheongsam. I guess it's strange how you can't remember the faces, though, he was thinking. To hell with them, he suddenly thought. You can't get anywhere thinking. Not even thinking about a Chinese whore in a green cheongsam. Come on you big gutless bastard, he was thinking. Thinking never did anybody any good.

He finished his beer and went out. He was feeling bad about the whole place already. All the beaches were the same. Once outside he walked on up to Central, past a dreary English Army Barrack, the English Navy Barrack on the opposite side of the roadway, and then on past the brick-walled dockyard.

When he arrived at the Courts people were already coming out down the steps. Among them he saw von Pittkamer. Von Pittkamer smiled when he saw him. 'Congratulations.'

'Yes?' Schepke said questioningly.

'You should have been in there today.'

'What happened?'

'Well it's not over yet but I certainly believe that the Oesten-Liebe Company will be out of business after this. The whole thing has been disastrous for them. But yourself, you have come out of it very well indeed.'

'What about the others?'

'Everybody did very well apart from Müller,' von Pittkamer went on. 'He was heavily fined and cautioned. I think it would have finished him altogether had you given evidence against him.'

'I didn't think it would have been over until this afternoon, or even tomorrow morning.'

'I saw it would finish quickly once the Court settled to business,' von Pittkamer said. 'But there is something else I had hoped to talk with you about. Perhaps you would accompany me to my office?'

'All right,' Schepke said. They walked to where the chauffeur stood by the car. Then as they turned and drove back past the court buildings they saw Hechler and the others come out into the sunlight. Hechler was talking with Dorsch and the others laughing amongst themselves. Then as the car swept around onto Connaught Road Central, Karl Schepke saw them all start down toward the New City Hall.

It was a short drive to the consular offices and they stopped close by to the Marine Department. Von Pittkamer's office was on the first floor. From the windows was a wide view of Kowloon lying white and hot-looking across the flat blue waters of the harbour. All the city shimmered in the sunlight, from Tsim Sha Tsui clock tower and the vehicular ferry to Yaumati Typhoon Shelter, and the ferry at Shum Shui Po, and on westward to Cheung Sha Wan and the Immigration and Quarantine Anchorage on the south side of Stonecutters Island; and all of it shimmering in the hard afternoon sunlight.

'A drink?' von Pittkamer asked.

Schepke turned from the window. 'Thank you,' he said. 'A gin, please.'

Von Pittkamer handed him his drink then sat carefully into the chair behind the desk. 'Please sit down,' he said. 'I am sorry to have inconvenienced you by bringing you here but it is difficult to talk about certain things outside.'

'I understand,' Schepke said.

Von Pittkamer set his drink on the desk. 'I think I may have some news that will interest you,' he said. 'However, I do not wish you to build hopes.'

Schepke sat forward on his chair, watching von Pittkamer's face.

'The *Heinrich Winter* is due in here sometime tomorrow from Yokohama,' von Pittkamer went on. 'We had a message from her last night saying she was putting in to Taipeh with her Second Officer. He had suffered a coronary attack earlier in the evening and was in immediate need of medical attention. I take it they now wish a replacement. What would you say?'

'Whose is she?'

'Kleinschmidt and Merten,' von Pittkamer told him, sitting forward to the desk. 'I could cable her offices suggesting you as replacement.'

'That's kind of you,' Schepke said. 'But if this fails is there any chance of something local?'

'There is always that possibility. However, the difficulty there is that most vessels operating from Hong Kong are British owned and manned by Chinese crew, apart from officers who come out under contract from England.'

'There is one other thing,' Schepke said. 'This company who bought the *Gertrud Lüth*. I had an offer from them to run the blockade on Red China.'

'That is entirely up to you,' von Pittkamer said slowly. 'I should think they would pay well.' He smiled. 'I do not believe there is all that much danger in it really. After all, it is only occasionally that such an incident as a ship being machine-gunned or shelled really happens. It all, of course, results from the Americans and Chinese Nationalists opposing certain cargo being shipped into Red China. But there are many people at it, even the British.'

'Do you know this Mihsien Steamship Company?'

'I am afraid not. It is my guess that they have just set up business. Under that name, anyway.'

'There must be money behind them,' Schepke said.

'They are probably financed by Peking,' von Pittkamer said. 'Peking has money in a number of Hong Kong companies. If I were you I should think very carefully before arriving at any decision.'

'I'll do that,' Schepke said, finishing his drink and rising. 'Thank you for everything.'

'It is my pleasure,' von Pittkamer said. 'I will get a cable off now and at the same time see if whether or not the *Heinrich Winter* can ship the other officers and men home.'

'I'll tell them. Thank you again.'

'Good-bye. I will see that you are informed as soon as the ship arrives.'

Karl Schepke went downstairs and out onto the street and walked around to The Viaduct Bar.

THE *Heinrich Winter* docked late in the afternoon of the next day. Karl Schepke, sitting in the bar of the Kwangtung Hotel, received a message from a member of the Consulate to come uptown immediately. In turn, he called Hechler at the Hotel Zetland.

'Yes. We saw her come in,' Hechler said.

'You better stop for me on the way up,' Schepke told him.

'Right away,' Hechler said, and hung up.

Karl Schepke went back to the table and finished his drink.

'You go away now, maybe?' The boy was watching him from behind the counter.

'Maybe,' Schepke said. 'It depends.' He got his cap and went out to the doorway.

Hechler, Dorsch, and Frauenheim were in the taxi.

'The others went on ahead with Bahr and Pulst,' Hechler told him as he climbed in the back. They were all excited with the thought of a sudden and unexpected home-going. Then as the taxi swung around onto Connaught Road Central, clearing the Star Ferry Concourse, they saw the *Heinrich Winter* lying out at A11 buoy on the other side of the Central Fairway. She was one of the new turbine ships, a heavy freighter, her decks crowded with derricks.

The others were already in the waiting-room when they arrived. An official let them in and then led Schepke upstairs to von Pittkamer's office.

Both of them rose to meet him.

'Herr Schepke,' von Pittkamer said coming from behind his desk. 'This is Kapitän Mohr of the *Heinrich Winter*.'

'Pleased to meet you, Herr Kapitän,' Schepke said.

'My pleasure,' Mohr said politely. 'Herr von Pittkamer has just told me of the outcome of the Enquiry. My congratulations.' Mohr was an elderly man dressed in immaculate starched whites.

'Please sit down,' von Pittkamer said.

There was something about von Pittkamer's voice that caused Schepke to look at him again. 'Well?' he said, then looking at Mohr.

'I am afraid it is not the news we expected,' von Pittkamer said, sadly. 'The company is flying a replacement to meet the ship at Singapore. I am sorry.'

'I am sorry, too,' Schepke said bitterly.

'Had the cable not come through I would gladly have taken you on board,' Mohr said.

'Thank you,' Schepke told him, then turned to von Pittkamer. 'May I see the cable?'

'It is not important,' von Pittkamer said, shrugging it off lightly.

'Please.'

'As you wish.' Von Pittkamer handed him the cable form. It was addressed to von Pittkamer and all it read was:

Under no condition ship Schepke. Replacement being flown to meet ship at Singapore.

Jochen Merten.

'What about the others? Are they going home?'

'I can take you all as far as Singapore,' Mohr told him. 'Beyond that I can't make any promise. We don't know our next exact port of call until we reach there.'

'You better ask what they want to do,' Schepke said turning to von Pittkamer. He was bitter about the whole business.

Von Pittkamer spoke into the telephone and minutes later Hechler and the others were shown in and introduced to Mohr. Hechler looked across to the window to Schepke, but he made no sign whatever.

'I am afraid things have not quite worked out as we expected,' von Pittkamer told them. 'However, Kapitän Mohr says he will take you all as far as Singapore. Other than that he can promise nothing.'

They were all disappointed now.

'What about you, Karl?' Hechler asked.

'I'll stay,' Schepke told him. 'It's all the same to me.'

'When else is anything due in?' Dorsch asked von Pittkamer.

'As far as I know there will be nothing for some weeks.'

'It's going to be a long wait,' Frauenheim said.

'The waiting's part of the beach,' Schepke said. A lot had gone suddenly from him and he was standing by the window when he said it, looking absently out across the flat blue water toward Kowloon.

'What are we going to do in Singapore?' Hechler asked.

'I just told you,' Schepke said. 'On the beach you wait no matter where you are.' Then without saying anything further he turned abruptly and went out, the old bitterness back in him again.

HE read the list of company offices on the wall outside Tai Po Buildings and saw the offices were on the second floor.

There was a girl at the desk in the outer office.

'I want to see Mr. Wang,' he told her.

'He is expecting you?' the girl asked politely.

'He knows me.'

She buzzed the intercom and spoke Cantonese into the receiver, and Mr. Wang came out almost immediately, smiling. He was very confident, Mr. Wang.

'Come right this way, Captain,' he said expansively.

The office was beautifully furnished in European style.

'You would care for a drink?' he asked, going to a long glass-fronted cocktail cabinet. 'I have some specially imported Schiedam.'

'Thank you,' Schepke told him, glancing around the office. 'This must be a prospering business.'

Mr. Wang smiled, handing him the Schiedam. 'I cannot complain, Captain,' he said. 'The *Gertrud Lüth*, however, is our first ship.'

'Does that mean she's Communist owned now?'

Mr. Wang brought his brows together but did not say anything.

'Don't worry,' Schepke told him. 'It's not important to me one way or the other.'

'No. The *Gertrud Lüth* is not owned by the Communists,' Mr. Wang said, the smile back on his smoothly shaven face. However, I do a great deal of business with them —And why not?'

'Sure. Why not?' Schepke said.

'Of course, I do not break any rules. But their money is as good as that of anyone else. I am sure you appreciate that, Captain.'

'As I said, I'm not worried one way or the other.' Schepke told him. 'I just came to take the job you offered.'

'Splendid!' Mr. Wang said, smiling. 'Splendid, Captain.'

'When does she come out of dock?'

'Sunday, I now believe. However, it will be the major part of a week at least before she is ready for sea.' All the while he talked he sorted through a mass of papers on the desk. 'I have already been making enquiries about crew,' he went on.

'So I heard.'

'Then you think your friends will be equally as interested?'

'If they don't ship out to Singapore.'

Mr. Wang rubbed his chin thoughtfully. 'There are certain alternatives,' he said, finally. 'Although I would prefer European officers. Perhaps I should contact your friends again as soon as possible.'

'That's up to you,' Schepke told him. 'I've made up my mind.'

'I appreciate that very much, Captain. I have your word?'

'I just told you,' Schepke said, rising and setting his empty glass on the shelf of the cocktail cabinet. The window overlooked the street. There was a large hotel directly opposite and a white-suited and turbaned Sikh on duty outside on the steps. A great deal of traffic moved in the roadway and the bright sunlight glinted on the cellulose and windows.

'One thing about this Chinese crew,' he said from the window. 'They'll have to be able to understand English. Or most of them will.'

'It is possible we can arrange that. There are many good seamen in Hong Kong and Kowloon who have sailed on English ships.'

'I'm sure there are.'

'I think perhaps we should go into these arrangements afterward. At the same time I have already made out contracts for any officer joining us. They are the usual sort of thing,' Mr. Wang hastened to assure. 'But what I think I should do at the moment is accompany you back to Victoria and see your friends before they decide anything.'

'I don't think you need bother,' Schepke said from the window. 'I think they're on their way here now.'

Mr. Wang hurriedly joined him at the window. Hechler, Dorsch, and Frauenheim and Altmeyer, and the two quarter-masters were all hurrying along the pavement on the other side of the street.

'Well,' Schepke said, 'it looks as though everything's on your side. All you want now are the First, Second, and Third deck officers.'

'I do not expect that to present so great a difficulty, Captain,' Mr. Wang said, smiling. There was not much that worried Mr. Wang for long. Mr. Wang and Peking were big business.

THE evening before going on board ship, Karl Schepke was in his room when Pancho knocked on the door and informed him that there was someone downstairs who wished to see him.

Müller was sitting at the corner table. Apart from him the bar was empty. He was sitting at the table without a drink, wearing a dirty white shirt and without a coat.

'What do you want?'

Müller hesitated, moistening his lips. It was some time since he had washed and there was a heavy, dirty stubble on his face.

'I was to see Mr. Wang,' he said, looking at Schepke from under his brows.

'So?'

'I heard he wanted a crew. He said he couldn't use me unless you said it was all right.' He went on fast now. 'Give me a chance, Schepke. I've eight thousand dollars to pay. You know that. I can't get off the island until it's paid. I can't even get a shore job.'

'You're nothing but trouble,' Schepke said, looking at him coldly.

'Give me a chance! You're the only one I can ask!'

'Sit down,' Schepke told him. Schepke sat down along with him and beckoned Pancho over.

'You've been on the beach. You know what it is.' Müller was leaning across the table, pleading.

Schepke ignored him. Then Pancho brought the bottle and one glass.

'Bring another glass,' he told him.

'How would you have felt?' Müller went on. 'I was with

Emmermann a long time. I knew he was going to die. That's why I stayed with the ship. It was my chance.'

'I don't want to hear it,' Schepke told him.

Pancho set the other glass on the table and filled them.

'Thanks,' Müller said, and drank most of the gin over in one swallow.

Karl Schepke sat watching him, saying nothing, but thinking all this over and wishing he had never set eyes on him again.

'I'm sorry about that fight,' Müller said, pleadingly. 'I'm sorry. —Hear me?'

'I hear you,' Schepke told him. '—What about this other time?'

'I don't know what you're talking about.'

'The shooting on the front,' Schepke said evenly, watching Müller's face all the time.

'I didn't know anything about that until the police called,' Müller said, leaning across the table. 'Honest to Christ, I didn't know anything about it. Believe me.'

'What did Wang say?'

'He told me he couldn't use me unless you said it was all right. He said he would have to use Chink officers. He says he's even having trouble getting any of the local Chinks interested in sailing the mainland.'

Karl Schepke watched him across the table. Any Chinese on board he wanted them on deck. He had sailed before with Chinese on the bridge and this time he did not want any of them unless he could help it.

'Does Wang know you're here now?'

'He told me to come right over. He said for you to call him tonight.'

Karl Schepke did not like any of it.

'I won't give any trouble,' Müller went on. 'I give you my word. I'm a good seaman. You know that.'

'I don't know anything,' Schepke told him.

'This time you can count on me. I won't give any trouble. You know how it is on the beach.'

'You haven't got your feet wet yet.'

'Give me a chance!'

'What did you do with the gun?' Schepke asked him.

'—Gun?' Müller said, surprised.

'The one you took from me.'

'I lost it when the boat overturned. I didn't have it when I came ashore.'

Karl Schepke finished his drink and rose from the table.

'What are you going to do?' Müller asked anxiously.

'Wang can tell you tomorrow one way or the other.'

'You've got to give me a chance, Schepke. Please.'

'I don't have to give you anything,' Schepke told him, and went out and upstairs, leaving him still sitting at the table.

MÜLLER joined the *Gertrud Lüth* the afternoon she came in from her sea trials. Now, two days later they were lying at B6 buoy just off Kennedy Town and West Point, busy loading flour and bran from a steady stream of junks and barges. Karl Schepke had paced the bridge all afternoon waiting for the two Chinese deck officers Mr. Wang had promised, and now as the sun started to go down out across the Pearl River Estuary he got one of the junkmen to send out a hire motor boat.

Mr. Wang was sitting at his desk.

'Well you'll have to find somebody,' Schepke told him. 'Nobody takes a ship out without officers.'

'But I signed Cheng,' Mr. Wang said. 'I told him to go out to the ship this afternoon. He knows the coast and the Yangtze well. Maybe he is on board now.'

'What about the Third and the bo'sun?' Schepke argued.

'It is most difficult, Captain. I explained it to you. You have taken Müller in preference already. No one wants to go China-side any more. They are afraid the Communists will keep them. The Communists never keep anyone. But you understand how it is, they are simple-minded.'

'That's nothing to me,' Schepke told him. 'All I know is you promised me two deck officers and neither of them has turned up.'

'Something must have gone wrong,' Mr. Wang said. 'They must have been delayed.'

'Just where the hell are they coming from?' Schepke asked. 'You can cross the harbour for twenty cents.'

'I have no idea what happened,' Mr. Wang told him. 'I am only surmising.'

'All right,' Schepke said resignedly. 'If this Cheng's on board when I get back I'll take her out. But you better have somebody waiting when we get back.'

'I promise,' Mr. Wang said, brightening considerably. 'You have my word. It may be possible I can get the Third Officer and bo'sun of the *Tsung Kow* when she arrives from Manila. She should be here tomorrow or the day after.'

'Just make sure they're here when I get back,' Schepke told him from the doorway.

'Of course. Have a pleasant voyage, Captain.'

Karl Schepke went out and downstairs. It was dark now and all the street lights had come on and there were great sheets of lights, and coloured lights in the shop windows and in the windows of the bars and hotels. He turned and walked away from Prince Edward Road, back along Nathan Road toward Shan Tung Street. Crossing the busy roadway there was a sudden harsh clanging of police bells and two police cars turned sharply in behind him and went roaring on down toward the Mongkok Ferry, their bells hammering the night air apart. Then when he crossed Canton Road the cars were coming back from the way of the ferry, their tyres screaming as they took the tight left-hand turn into Canton Road.

When he reached the ferry landing stage a sudden fierce burst of shooting carried back across the black water from where Argyle Street ran out to Tai Kok Tsui. A great number of people had already crowded onto the front, all of them gazing intently out across the black water toward the breakwater running out from the west end of Argyle Street toward the breakwater of Yaumati Typhoon Anchorage. Not taking much interest, Schepke went down the steps and waved a hire motor boat in. The boat came alongside with a young barefooted boy up in the bows with a boathook.

'B Six buoy,' Schepke told the old man at the helm.

The old man nodded his shaven head and swung the boat out into the fairway toward the breakwater and its entrance lights. Inside of the anchorage they pulled up past a vehicular ferry just left on the trip to Hong Kong. Then as they drew ahead another scattered burst of shooting occurred somewhere on the lighted roadway above their starboard side.

'What's happening?' Schepke asked the old man in English.

'Police,' the old man said. 'Police always shoot. Always shoot wrong man. Police no good.' He shook his head sadly and spat across the gunwale.

Looking back at the ferry, Karl Schepke saw her decks lined with people looking out toward Argyle Street. Whatever was the cause of the shooting was happening on the arm of the wall making the north part of the entrance to the anchorage. Then as they closed on the entrance he saw a police car draw up suddenly and the policemen get out onto the concrete wall and start shooting into the darkness of the open harbour on the other side. They came out past the entrance lights and it was suddenly very dark out there after the brightness of the street and breakwater lights. The shooting had stopped now and the policemen had scattered back onto the roadway.

Once outside in the harbour the old man slowed the boat and all three of them were looking back across the stern when something suddenly broke up out of the water close to the starboard side and a pair of massive arms reached across the gunwale, the boat then tipping far over as the rest of the body swung itself drippingly in over the side.

'Kamei!' Schepke said, recognizing the gigantic hulk of a man kneeling exhaustedly now on the floor of the cockpit.

'Are you all right?' he said again into the cockpit.

The huge Jap looked up at him.

'You remember me?' Schepke asked him in English.

'I remember,' Kamei said, moving his huge shaven head, then looking back toward the lights of Argyle Street.

'Are you hit?'

'—Police!' He spat contemptuously on the floor of the cockpit.

The sudden ear-shattering blast of the siren deafened them and Karl Schepke turned to see the lights of the vehicular ferry crowding the black starless sky as it loomed above them. Turning, he dived in past Kamei, found the throttle, and slammed it wide open. The sudden roar of the petrol engine filled the cockpit and he could feel the boat start to pull slowly, then quickly away as the ponderous steel bows of the ferry seemed almost to fall upon the stern. Then reaching his feet he tore the old man's hand free from the helm and headed the boat out at a sharp angle from the hull of the ferry, all the time aware of someone high above them yelling through a hailer.

As they pulled away Kamei moved back into the stern and sat down, the shifting of his tremendous weight seeming almost to sit the whole boat on her stern.

'Here!' Schepke called to the old man in English. 'Look after the engine. I'll take the helm.'

The old man, with a last glance across the stern, turned in under the canopy, taking the boy with him. Schepke, standing in the stern, glanced down at the massive head and shoulders of Kamei beside him in the darkness.

'Police come now,' Kamei said quietly, all the while looking out across the stern.

Schepke took another look toward Kowloon. A cluster of lights showed on the outer side of the Yaumati Typhoon Anchorage where two motor boats had just rounded the breakwater.

'Cut the running lights!' he called into the canopy.

The lights above the canopy went out, leaving the boat in darkness. Even as it was, Karl Schepke did not believe the police could see them out there in the darkness with nothing to silhouette them. On the water there was too much darkness and all the lights of Victoria and the Peak were strung out above them. The police would have to guess which way they had gone, even allowing for the fact that they knew Kamei was on board.

'They don't see us,' he said into the darkness.

'No,' Kamei said. 'We get a good start.'

'That night somebody shot at me,' Schepke said straight ahead.

'Did you see who it was?'

'It happen very quickly,' Kamei said. 'There was no time to see.'

'You speak good English.'

Kamei was looking out across the stern again.

They were coming in toward the first of the buoys now and Schepke took the boat between B18 and 19, then passed A17 on their port side as he put them across the Northern Fairway. There was a big Dane lying at A12, one of the Maersk boats, her decks ablaze with lights as she off-loaded, her bows pointed directly up harbour toward the Tsim Sha Tsui clock tower and Blackhead Point. He put the boat close in under the Dane's high bows, under her cables, then around onto her starboard side. There was a swarm of junks and barges all along the length of her starboard side and Schepke made a straight run past them, cutting diagonally westward across the Central Fairway.

Now he made out a heavy freighter, high-walled, lying at B12 buoy, and he headed their bows in on the port bow and ran closely down her side, the deck high above them, the machinery turning over dully inside of her and no one about on deck as he swung their bows closely in around her stern, momentarily seeing in big white letters high above them on her counter: *Kyoto Maru—Kobe*. Once around the Jap he saw one of the local cargo boats of the Port Arthur and Gulf of Pohai run at B10. She, too, he rounded on the stern, and came around seeing the *Gertrud Lüth* darkly silhouetted against the lights of the Shek Tong Sui and Sai Ying Poon districts of Victoria.

'Stop engine!' he called into the canopy.

It was some moments before the engine silenced, and then almost immediately he saw the launch.

'Full astern!'

213

The old man threw the throttle astern and Schepke hurriedly took them back into the darkness of the cargo boat's stern.

'All right!' he called, standing up tall now, watching the police launch kick a bow wave up across her head as she raced up the Southern Fairway, her searchlight stabbing the darkness off her port beam as she roared up the harbour. Kamei looked back at Schepke from where he crouched by the canopy, watching the launch. Schepke watched her until she passed between the lights of the Conduit Bar up on the east side of West Point.

'Start her up,' he called to the old man. 'Take it easy.'

They edged carefully out from under the stern and Schepke headed them slowly in on the *Gertrud Lüth*. While they came in on the port ladder he could feel Kamei watching him closely.

'What do you want to do now?'

Kamei glanced back across the harbour toward Kowloon, then shrugged his massive shoulders.

'Here!' Schepke called to the old man, letting go the helm as the boy up forward hooked onto the grating of the ladder, the black-shadowed walls of the *Gertrud Lüth* rising sheer above them.

'Do you want to go on board?'

Kamei seemed momentarily undecided, almost as if he was unable to realize what was being offered. 'Where do you go?'

'Shanghai,' Schepke told him. 'We sail as soon as we board her.'

'I go with you,' Kamei announced suddenly, standing up tall and wide, almost filling the cockpit.

'What about them?' Schepke asked, looking at the old man and the boy.

'They will say nothing,' Kamei said, and brought his right hand down on the roof of the canopy with such force that all of the boat shuddered under the impact. Then looking at the old man he spoke a rapid stream of Cantonese, the old man and the boy with their backs flat against the canopy.

'What did you tell them?'

'I tell them they speak and my friends cut their throats and throw them in the harbour.'

Karl Schepke motioned him onto the ladder then brought some money from his tunic pocket and pushed it down the front of the old man's shirt.

As they climbed the ladder the old man already had the boat away from the ship's side and angling her in across the bows toward the lights of Victoria.

'Are you sure about them?'

Kamei looked back at him on the ladder. 'They will say nothing,' he said. He was very sure about it.

As they came up into the alleyway Schepke saw Hechler suddenly stand up off the housing and turn gaping at them.

'It's all right. He's a friend of mine.'

'Well you can certainly pick your friends, boy,' Hechler said, looking carefully at the Jap.

'Something is wrong?' Kamei asked Schepke in English.

'No. This is the Chief Engineer. There's nothing wrong.' And in the lighting of the alleyway he was aware for the first time that Kamei wore nothing but some sort of sleeveless shirt and a pair of floppy trousers.

'You haven't seen us come on board,' he said looking at Hechler again. 'There may be some trouble before we get clear.'

'That's fine with me,' Hechler told him, glancing off-handedly at Kamei.

'Did the Second come on board?'

Hechler nodded. 'About an hour ago. And Altmeyer's just got back from the Marine.'

'Good. We'll slip in about fifteen minutes,' Schepke told him, then motioned Kamei to follow him up to the cabin deck.

'You'll be all right here,' he told him, unlocking the door of his cabin. 'I'll come back once we're clear of the harbour. Don't leave here no matter what happens.' He pulled the door shut and went aft to the messroom. Altmeyer was just leaving.

'Find this Cheng and tell him to get the ladders inboard and have the cable party on the forepeak.'

'Right away, sir.'

'—Wait!' he said, suddenly remembering what Wang had said about the new Third. 'When you've seen Cheng ask

215

the signal tower when the *Tsung Kow* gets in.'

'Are we slipping now?'

He turned and saw Müller rising from the long table. 'Yes. You better go on up to the bridge. Don't wait for me.'

Müller took his cap and went out and Schepke turned to see Sam watching him through the galley hatchway.

'You eat now, Kapitän?'

'Later, Sam. —Are you sure you and the boy still want to sail?'

Sam smiled hugely. 'Chinese have old proverb,' he said. 'Lightning never strike same tree twice.'

'I hope you're right,' Schepke told him, and turned and went aft to Hechler's cabin. Going swiftly through the drawers of the dressing-table he found an old pair of overalls.

Kamei was already on his feet when he opened the door.

'It's only me,' Schepke told him, giving him the overalls. 'Listen, is it true you were bo'sun on a Jap?'

Kamei nodded, a little unsure of himself in the surroundings.

'Do you think you could work this ship?'

'I think so,' Kamei said slowly.

'All right. From now on you're bo'sun. See what you can do.'

Suddenly the cabin light flickered and the deck vibrated as the engines turned slowly over.

'—Why is it you do this?' Kamei asked as Schepke turned to leave.

'I owe you something, remember?' Schepke said simply, and closed the door behind him.

As he went along the strangely bare, white-enamelled passage to the bridge he heard the jangle of telegraph bells and felt the deck shudder as the engines threshed astern through the silent black water of the harbour.

The bridge was in darkness, lit only by the reflection of the shaded deck and derrick lights. Bahr was on the wheel and Pulst standing by the telegraph. Bahr had starboard wheel on and Schepke watched the foremast and bows begin their swing. framed against the lights of Central Victoria.

"Midships,' he called.

"Midships. Wheel amidships, sir,' Bahr replied.

'Buoy showing clearly on the port bow,' Müller called from the wing.

'Slow ahead,' Schepke ordered, dropping one of the windows down, feeling all the smells of the city and the harbour and the cool night air damply on his face. The ship nosed slowly out into the Southern Fairway, the lights of Victoria strung out brightly all along her starboard side.

'Port five.'

'Port five. Five port wheel on, sir.'

Schepke saw Altmeyer come in accompanied by Cheng wearing a white uniform and cap. He was a short man with a cap that was too big for him.

'That message, sir,' Altmeyer reported. 'The *Tsung Kow* sailed yesterday afternoon for Saigon.'

'All right,' Schepke told him. 'Stand by the starboard searchlight. Make: *S.S. Gertrud Lüth outward bound for Shanghai.*'

'Yes, sir.' Altmeyer went up the ladder and out through the hatchway to the flying bridge.

"Midships,' Schepke said, leaning from the window again, seeing the Marine Signal Station on Connaught Road Central coming up on the starboard side, thousands of brilliantly coloured lights of the city scoring the silent black water.

'Wheel amidships, sir.'

He could hear Altmeyer now on the searchlight, the signal tower light blinking an acknowledgement. Ahead of them he could see an English man-of-war, lit up, lying at Number Three buoy directly off *Tamar* dock jetty.

'Port ten.'

'Port ten,' repeated Bahr. 'Ten port wheel on, sir.'

'A One buoy showing clearly off the port bow,' Müller called along the bridge as the bows edged gently in toward Kowloon, Tsim Sha Tsui clock tower showing high and dark above the many lights of the Star Ferry Pier.

"Midships,' Schepke called, noting that Cheng was watching

it all very closely. He had a feeling about Mr. Cheng already and he could not even see him properly in the gloom of the bridge.

"Midships,' Bahr replied. 'Wheel amidships, sir.'

'Starboard five.'

'Starboard five. Five starboard wheel on, sir.'

No. 1 and A29 buoys showed clearly off the starboard bow now as they passed the clock tower. There was no sign of any police boats and Karl Schepke guessed they were probably working between Kowloon and Stonecutters Island.

"Midships.'

"Midships. Wheel amidships, sir.'

The *Gertrud Lüth* was directly off Blackhead Point now, Kowloon Signal Station showing clearly to eastward of it. Away to starboard was the mass of lights that was Causeway Bay, and on the port side he could see Cust Rock light and the lights of Kowloon Docks, and further eastward was the string of lighted buoys in the prohibited area off the end of Kai Tak aircraft runway.

'Starboard five.'

'Starboard five. Five starboard wheel on, sir.'

They were out past North Point now, the string of runway lights on the port beam.

"Midships,' he called, hearing Altmeyer come down into the bridge.

They were coming in to Lei U Mun Pass now, the lights showing clear and bright on the opposing headlands. They passed slowly and smoothly between them, Junk Bay now on the port beam, Sai Wan on the starboard bow, Cape Collinson light showing very brightly still further ahead.

'Starboard five,' he called, putting the port hand turning buoy on the starboard beam.

"Midships.'

"Midships. Wheel amidships, sir.'

They were directly off Cape Collinson light, Pottinger Peak showing dark and high-humped in the background.

'Half ahead.'

'Half ahead, sir,' repeated Pulst as he rang the engines on.

Tathong Channel was clear ahead. The blanket of cloud had broken and now the moonlight showed on the flat black water. To starboard Big Wave Bay swept away toward Mount Collinson and Karl Schepke watched the car headlights sweeping along the shore road toward the cluster of lights that was Shek O Wan.

'Full ahead.'

'Full ahead, sir,' repeated Pulst.

Karl Schepke felt the deck come truly alive now and the sound of the flat black water as it hissed and rushed along the hull as the *Gertrud Lüth* slammed on down the channel and around Tathong Light to the ocean. Outside, he set course eastward, putting the Nine Pin group of islands on the port beam and Cape D'Aguilar directly astern as he cleared Hong Kong. Outside of the high hills enclosing the harbour it was a fine night with the moon showing brightly and the moonlight riding the flat black ocean, a light breeze blowing in from the south-east and the wake of the *Gertrud Lüth* boiling up coral white in the brilliant Pacific moonlight.

KARL SCHEPKE brought them up the Whangpoo River, past the forts at Woosung, the river cold and grey-looking in the early light and long drifting wraiths of mist lying across the flat water. There was a large number of junks and sampans about on the river, their immense oblong sails of straw-matting hanging limply in the damp mist and their black-coated crews working the oars in pairs, standing upright, walking the two paces forward then back.

'Pilot boat coming up on the port side,' Müller called from the wing.

'Slow ahead,' Schepke told Pulst, then joined Müller in the

wing. Kamei had the Jacob's ladder over the side and as the boat came on in they saw the blue uniformed pilot on the gunwale ready to jump.

Cheng brought him directly to the bridge. The pilot was a slim young man with a neatly-pressed uniform, two silver rings on his sleeve and the one star on his cap.

'Pleased to meet you, Captain,' he said, smiling. 'Pilot Officer Tien Han.' He bowed stiffly.

'She's all yours,' Schepke told him.

The pilot brought the *Gertrud Lüth* the rest of the way up the river, using the Southern Fairway, past some local cargo boats and river steamers tied up at the starboard hand buoys, and on to the Chang Ka Pang Wharf. Across the river, in the now rising mist, Karl Schepke saw the famous Shanghai Bund with its huge blocks of offices and banks and hotel buildings. A fast grey launch with the number MR9 on her hull was coming in fast from across the river, clipping the cold grey water high in the morning air.

'With my compliments, Captain.'

Schepke turned as the pilot saluted. 'Thank you,' he said. 'May I offer you a drink?'

The pilot considered it a moment then bowed his acceptance. Behind him Müller shrugged.

'See everything's secured,' Schepke told him, then followed the pilot below.

He brought a bottle of whisky from his cabin and opened it in the messroom.

'Good health to you, Captain,' the pilot said.

'And to you,' Schepke told him as someone knocked on the open door.

With Cheng was a smart-looking Chinese wearing a grey European style suit.

'Major Pao,' Cheng said.

Major Pao came in past him, smiling, his hand out. He was an extremely efficient-looking Chinese.

'Major,' Schepke said, slightly puzzled.

'Please do not be alarmed, Captain,' the Major said. 'I am

220

here to see that you have everything you require. You might say Chinese Public Relations.' He smiled.

Karl Schepke shrugged. 'A drink?'

Major Pao glanced at the bottle. 'Thank you, Captain.'

They all had another drink and then the pilot left.

'When were you expecting to sail again, Captain?' the Major asked.

'I was told a turn round of two days.'

'Oh, that is such great pity. You see, I am afraid there will be an unavoidable delay. Our main shipment of canned goods has not arrived from Hankow yet. Unfortunately the steamer was holed in a collision last night and her cargo will now have to be transferred. However, Hong Kong has already been informed.'

'Then I suppose it's all right with me,' Schepke told him.

'While you are here we may perhaps arrange for you to come ashore and visit our beautiful city,' Major Pao said, smiling.

'I would rather see the ship off-loaded.'

'Your ship will be off-loaded by midday tomorrow, Captain,' he said, still smiling, obviously pleased with himself. 'In the China of today we do not have the wastage of man hours as before. When one man completes his task another takes over. Everything is for the advancement of the Chinese people.'

Karl Schepke noticed Hechler listening in the open doorway.

'Ah,' the Major said, following Schepke's gaze. 'I take it this is your Engineer.' He shook hands with Hechler, then Hechler set his account books on the table.

'These are your coal and water accounts?' the Major asked. Hechler glanced from him to Schepke. 'I have already made arrangements for the water barges to come out,' the Major went on. 'They should be here in the early afternoon. The coaling wharf is immediately astern. Please pass your orders to the Bund Signal Station and proceed to coal any time you wish. —Now,' he said, looking at his wrist watch, 'I am afraid I must take leave of your hospitality. Please excuse me, gentlemen. Perhaps I shall call for you tomorrow, Captain?' He bowed immaculately from the waist.

Karl Schepke went to the doorway with him.

'Please do not put yourself to any trouble, Captain. I shall find my own way. Thank you. And remember, should you require anything just ask for Major Pao.' He left smiling, very confident and sure of himself.

'Good Christ,' Hechler said, 'we haven't had service like this in years.'

'It seems they work all night as well,' Schepke said. 'Everything is for the advancement of the Chinese people.'

'I never heard it put that way before,' Hechler said, smiling. 'Do you think they get paid for it?'

Karl Schepke shrugged.

'What was he, some sort of undercover man?'

'I think we're going to find out soon enough,' Schepke told him. 'You better get Altmeyer to send in your orders.' He left Hechler going over his accounts and went down into the forward well. Kamei already had the hatches broken open, and now he stood up as he saw Schepke cross the well; standing there bare-footed and wearing the sleeveless shirt and Hechler's overalls tied around his waist.

'I just wondered if you had thought about what you want to do,' Schepke asked him.

'Which port do we call next?' Kamei asked.

'Taipeh.'

'Formosa?' Kamei said, puzzled. 'But the Nationalists never touch Communist cargo.'

'They won't know it,' Schepke told him. 'It's tinned goods labelled and packed as in Hong Kong and with an American Import Licence covering them. The rest of the cargo is raw cotton. It goes back to Hong Kong. Everything's been officially cleared.'

'You have thought of it all, Captain,' Kamei said, grinning.

'Not me. The owners do the thinking. All I'm in this for is the money.'

'Well,' Kamei said, thinking. 'Maybe it is better I go shoreside on Formosa. They find me here they probably shoot first and ask questions later.'

'You'll have to get some clothes before leaving. You should

be able to get something ashore. Come up to my cabin when you're through and I'll have some money ready.'

'They are not all as you are.'

'It's nothing,' Schepke said. 'What about the seamen? How do they shape?'

'Some are good. As good as most ships,' Kamei told him, then looked thoughtfully at the deck.

'Something wrong?'

'Maybe it is nothing,' Kamei said looking at him again. 'I just think three of them have one time been Navy sailors. They are much better than the other men. Much smarter. Know more. Understand, Captain?'

'That's probable,' Schepke said. 'There are thousands of seamen in Hong Kong. They might have been on board one of those Limey transports or tankers.'

'I still have this feeling about them,' Kamei said. 'But maybe it is nothing.'

MAJOR PAO arrived on board early next afternoon when the off-loading had been completed. They were already alongside the coaling wharf and up ahead on Chang Ka Pang Wharf coolies were arranging huge bales of raw cotton ready to be loaded when the *Gertrud Lüth* put back alongside.

They were in the messroom.

'But I insist, Captain,' Major Pao said. 'You must come ashore. Surely your officers are capable of taking care of the ship for such a short time.'

Karl Schepke looked from Major Pao to Müller.

'I can manage,' Müller said.

'You see, Captain.'

'All right,' Schepke told him, then turned again to Müller. 'You know what to do when they're through coaling.'

They were in the launch. It was a very warm day and the sun was shining brightly on the city as they came in to the landing stage.

'Impressive, don't you think, Captain?' Major Pao said.

'It's impressive,' Schepke agreed without enthusiasm.

'Is there one place you especially wish to visit?' the Major asked now they were on the Bund.

'It's all the same to me,' Schepke told him, and he was not thinking about visiting any place in particular.

They started toward the northern end of the Bund. The only true Chinese structure in sight was the enormous gateway of red and gold lacquer that marked the entrance to Nanking Road.

'Do you see that building, Captain?' the Major asked, pointing ahead of them at perhaps the tallest of the skyscrapers. 'That was once a famous hotel for the most prominent of capitalists. Now we have made it an apartment building called Shanghai Mansions. The ground floor is a general store. One is able to acquire the very best of Chinese goods there.'

Karl Schepke had been looking about him at the buildings and the people, and he never had expected anything to have changed so much.

'Do you wish to visit Shanghai Mansions, Captain?' the Major was asking.

'I'm not thinking of buying anything,' Schepke told him.

'You just wish to enjoy the city then?'

He nodded. He had not seen anything he might enjoy yet. In almost all the doorways were glass-framed portraits of Mao Tse-Tung that were probably put out at daylight and taken in just before the premises closed.

'Would the Captain wish to visit the People's Park?' the Major asked with great politeness.

'What about Blood Alley?' Schepke asked suddenly. 'We could get drunk.'

'But I thought you had not been here before, Captain?' the Major said, surprised.

'It's some time ago.'

'Then there is no longer any Blood Alley, Captain. We cleaned all that up. There are no such places anywhere in China.'

'All right,' Schepke said. 'No Blood Alley but what about a beer?'

Major Pao coughed lightly. 'I am afraid there is no call for beer in the New China, and what little there is very probably does not appeal to a Western.'

'What about the U.B. and the E.W.O.?' Schepke countered. 'We brought cargoes in for them when they were the biggest breweries in the Far East.'

'The E.W.O. is now a highly successful bean sauce factory,' the Major said with much refinement.

'Isn't that amazing,' Schepke said solemnly. 'Bean sauce. How do you feel the morning after getting drunk on bean sauce?'

'I do not believe you understand, Captain,' the Major said seriously. 'Bean sauce is not an alcoholic beverage.'

'Really?' Schepke said. 'We've made an alcoholic beverage from potatoes for years.'

'Then we will have a drink,' the Major said stiffly.

The building they entered had at one time undoubtedly been one of the most luxurious hotels in the city, although now most of the decoration had gone and an air of austerity taken over in its place.

'This must have been some place,' Schepke said as they went in through the entrance hall.

'You use the past tense, Captain,' the Major said, showing slight annoyance for the first time.

'Well what is it now?'

'It is the headquarters of the Union of Seamen amongst other things. This way, please.'

They entered what had once been a long and magnificent bar. Almost all the counter and shelves were empty and at the far end of the bar were some tables and a number of severely dressed men and women sitting at them drinking tea. All of them stared curiously at Schepke until the Major turned his attention to them and they immediately showed great and sudden interest in their green tea and flat colourless biscuits.

Then the Major spoke to the white overalled woman behind the counter and she brought two small bottles from under the counter and opened and poured them into glasses. The contents of the bottles were the colour of weak tea.

'Kampei, kampei,' the Major said and drank a little of the beer.

Karl Schepke regarded it as a weak edition of a poor English lemonade.

'Is this the best we have?' he asked.

The Major straightened his shoulders. 'I believe our Captain is a pleasurable man. You must please see that the people of New China have no interest in the drinking of beer and the sleeping with whores.'

'Every man should have his own choice,' Schepke said. 'Or does that not apply in New China?'

'We find better and more worthwhile things to do,' the Major said, smiling blandly.

'Perhaps that's because Uncle's watching you,' Schepke told him, nodding at the huge portrait of Mao Tse-Tung on the back wall.

'Uncle?' the Major said.

'I thought that was him.' Karl Schepke looked again at the heavy, unsmiling face within the gilt frame.

'That is our chairman,' the Major said reverently. 'He is the chairman of the committee that governs our New China.'

'And everybody listens to him?'

'Of course. He is for the advancement of the Chinese people.'

'Providing you all think the same.'

'I assure you, Captain, the people of the New China are all of one mind.'

'There's got to be an individual somewhere,' Schepke argued. 'What do you do when he comes along—make him a Minister, too, or shoot him?'

'You must realize that rebels are never welcome,' the Major said, unimpressed, remaining aloofly authoritative.

'You can finish this if you want,' Schepke told him, pushing his drink along the counter and starting for the hallway.

226

'Where do you go now?' the Major asked, catching up with him.

'To see what you might have that you don't know about.'

There was a boy outside on the steps when they left. He wore a dirty work suit. Both his legs were off and he ran after Schepke on his stumps, holding out a tin mug. Karl Schepke put his hand in his pocket but the Major caught the boy by the shoulder and hit him full in the mouth with his clenched fist, sending him sprawling on his back. Then standing with his foot on the boy's chest he glanced both ways along the Bund and waved down a green army truck. The two soldiers climbed down and bundled the boy into the cabin between them.

'What are they going to do with him?' Schepke asked as the truck moved off.

Major Pao shrugged. 'It is not for you to distress yourself,' he said. 'You must realize the China of today is no longer the China of Pearl Buck.'

'What about his legs?'

Again Major Pao shrugged, then began walking, obviously deciding the matter closed.

They walked without talking. Some way further on Karl Schepke turned down a long narrow street running away from the Bund.

'There is nothing here but small shops,' Major Pao told him. 'We should go on.'

Somewhere ahead Schepke could hear the sounds of music. The building was on the other side of the street.

'What did I tell you,' he said. 'There's a place you didn't know about.'

'It is a private club, Captain. No one is allowed inside who is not a member.'

'Not even allies, Major?'

Major Pao seemed genuinely embarrassed. 'Very well,' he said, finally.

They went in through the hallway to one of the downstairs rooms. A number of army officers and girls were sitting at the tables, and the talking faltered as they entered and crossed to the small bar in the corner. Overhead of the bar was a loudspeaker connected to an unseen gramophone, and now the Major stood uncomfortably at the bar while Karl Schepke could feel the eyes of the people at the tables on his back.

'What will it be, Major?'

The Major spoke quietly to the barman and he brought out and poured another of the pale beers.

'I'll have a gin,' Schepke told the barman.

The barman poured the gin and set the glass on the counter. It was English gin.

'Your health, Major.'

Major Pao did not say anything but merely sipped the beer and looked extremely ill at ease.

Karl Schepke glanced around the room, the officers turning their attention to their drinks. Altogether there were about ten officers and six girls in the room. Two of the girls were White Russian, and all of them wore low-cut cheongsams so the cleavage of their breasts showed. The two White Russian girls were extremely pretty, with long eyelashes, smooth tawny skin and long honey-coloured hair falling to their shoulders.

Then as he turned back to his drink he saw one of the officers get up and leave, his cap still on the table.

'This is a fine place, Major.'

Major Pao seemed not to have heard him. Then an elderly thick-set man wearing a civilian suit came into the doorway behind the officer who had just returned, and nodded almost imperceptibly across the room.

'Excuse me,' Major Pao said.

'Of course.' Karl Schepke watched him follow the other man into a separate room across the hallway. As soon as the door was closed he finished his drink and walked unconcernedly out of the bar and out onto the street.

He walked swiftly along the street and turned into the first alleyway he came to. After about a quarter of an hour's walking he came out suddenly by what he remembered to be the old English racecourse, the grandstand enclosed now and made into some sort of reading room or library and a number of Chinese sitting behind the glass. He went into the public garden and found a seat under the acacia trees. Then sitting there, he lit a cigarette, and lighting it, was suddenly aware of someone watching him from under the shadow of trees further along the path. He was an old man with a goatee beard, wearing a small black tasselled cap and a long black Chinese coat buttoned to the shoulder. Karl Schepke glanced casually both ways along the path, seeing no one else about. Looking back to the old man again, their eyes met. The old man smiled nervously then came out from under the trees. Karl Schepke watched him all the way.

Halting by the seat, the old man looked back along the path.

'Is there something I can do?' Schepke asked him carefully in English. The old man moistened his lips. His beard was grey and wispy and he had black unblinking eyes. Then he looked at Schepke's uniform again. 'You are American?' he asked, speaking quietly in English then peering furtively back at the trees.

'No. German,' Schepke told him.

'I thought perhaps you were American,' the old man said. 'It is now many years since I have seen an American. It was the uniform,' he explained.

'I know.' Schepke said smiling. 'Is there something I can do for you?'

'It was only to talk,' the old man said.

'You can sit a while?'

The old man sat nervously down on the edge of the seat, after first looking again to the trees. There were many trees and birds singing amongst the foliage. It was quiet in the park and there was no one about.

'You are from a ship?' the old man asked after a few moments.

'Yes. From across the river.'

'You have been to China before?'

'Some years ago,' Schepke said. 'Before what it is today.'

'Ah,' the old man said, 'today it is the New China.'

'So I have been told,' Schepke said, careful now about this old man.

Then the old man looked at him closely, there on the seat

under the acacia trees. 'I am afraid this is no longer our China. The days of happiness have gone forever. No longer does one belong to himself. Man should always have the right to live as he chooses. Now, today, man's rights have gone with his happiness. It is a sad New China.'

'You must have seen it all,' Schepke said quietly, still not sure of himself with this old man in the long black coat.

And the old man moved his head gently. 'In seventy years one sees many things,' he said, his wispy beard moving with his words. 'A remembrance of things past is not always happy. There is much sadness in life. There are many things, that if a man could, he would not wish to remember.'

'What is it that you do?' Schepke asked him, puzzled.

'—Now, nothing,' the old man said. 'In Free China I was a painter. But in these times it is easily forgotten that a man can fulfil only that which is intended in him. Man cannot do with justice that which is ordered when there is no feeling in him to inspire such a doing. I can only paint that which I truly feel. Now there is nothing.'

'You have always lived here in Shanghai?'

'No,' the old man said, and for the first time, smiling faintly. 'An honest painter could not tolerate to live in such a place. It is only lately that I came here. Most of my life I lived in a village far up the Great. It was a place called Witches' Mountain Gorge. The village was five hundred feet up a sheer limestone cliff. It was a very beautiful village with wonderful memories.' The old man's eyes had gone back now to the past. 'I lived there with my two sons and daughter. Then one day the first of the soldiers came. They called themselves the People's Liberation Army. First they took the headman's house and imprisoned the people indiscriminately. My sons attempted to flee the river one night but were caught and held as political prisoners. How the matter became political I have never yet found a suitable explanation, except perhaps that one of different ideals and opinions from those in power at once become enemies of the State. However, soon the rearguard of soldiers arrived and set up a People's Court in the square and the first batch of prisoners were brought out and crowded together until they filled the square and the soldier judge stood up on a table and proclaimed the death sentence. Then the soldiers shot them and left the bodies where they fell. When there were too many dead in the square the soldiers roped the other prisoners together and beat them with their rifle butts to the edge of the cliff then clubbed them over the side into the river. Many were old men who did not know what they had done. Some were Nationalist soldiers who had been brought to the village when they had been caught or surrendered, many of them wounded, and they sang as they died. Many of the others were only boys and they wept. All night it went on and in the morning it was said by others lower on the river that the water ran red with blood, and months afterward there were corpses rotting all along the banks in the hot summer sun. Even the birds would not come afterward.

'There is a flower here in China called the Buddha's Hand. It grows out of the water on long stalks bearing great pink flowers, shaped like a man's hand raised in supplication. From the centre of the flower comes a soft, pervasive incense. Now, ever since there has been a great abundance of these flowers along that part of the river where they had not been known to grow before.' When he had finished it was as if a great weight had loosed itself from him.

Then he turned and saw Schepke still looking at him, and he smiled. It was a fragile smile that passed across his lips as a light wind might.

'You must forgive an old man and his past,' he said softly.

'Your daughter,' Schepke said. 'You never mentioned your daughter.'

The old man's face saddened again. 'I still have her. But she is no longer happy. I am afraid the disillusionment set in the night her brothers died.'

'I can imagine,' Schepke said.

'It was two years before she went on with her work. She was studying to be an actress. She had come home from Peking when the troubles began, and after having achieved some degree of success. Then when things had regained some form of order my

231

daughter and I were commanded to appear before the Arts Union in Peking. My daughter went back to the theatre and I was sent to Yunnan Province to assist in compiling a Cultural Legacy of the Nahsi People. Mostly it was the copying of Nahsi murals. Interesting work for students or young artists but not for an old man who all his life had painted crickets and grasshoppers. But I am afraid the State was not interested in a Cultural Survey of Insects. It is a pity that they are ignorant of the fact that before one begins painting one must have heart, hand and mind in the tip of the brush. For an old man it was not a difficult decision to make when declining the task. However, at that time I was unaware that my daughter was arriving at the same decision. I was imprisoned for two years at Kaifeng for subversive action against the State. It was only lately that I was sent here to Shanghai. My daughter arrived about a year ago and was directed to work as a clerk at the Union of Engineers.'

'Then they no longer allow her to be an actress?'

The old man moved his head sadly, averting his eyes. 'She cannot allow herself to do as the State orders. To her all is contrived, false, and without true expression.'

'Is there nothing you can do?' Schepke asked.

'How does one escape from the State?' the old man said, allowing himself to smile. 'Freedom has gone from China for good.'

'Would it not be easier to comply?' Schepke said. 'With such odds there seems little an old man and his daughter can do.'

The old man smiled again, sadly. 'In this life one must do what he believes true and right. He must stand or fall by himself. I am sure that talking with you, seeing you, you have found this yourself.'

He was a strange-looking old man, this man on the seat under the acacia trees, with the wispy beard, the tight-fitting cap, and the long black coat.

Then Karl Schepke noticed two students come along the path, both of them carrying books, and when he turned back the old man left abruptly, hurrying along the path that led towards the street. Karl Schepke went after him, but when he came out

232

through the gateway the old man was crossing the roadway, hurrying. He started to call after him, then stopped himself as a car drove swiftly into the kerb alongside of him.

'A friend of yours, Captain?'

He was looking at Major Pao. 'I went for a walk in the park and got lost. I was going to ask the way to the Bund.' He did not look toward the old man as he spoke. He hoped now that he was away and that the Major would not know him.

'Perhaps I can help,' Major Pao said, and spoke to the driver who promptly got out and opened the rear door.

They made a tight turn and drove back the way of the Bund, Karl Schepke sitting alongside Major Pao in the back.

'I wish to offer my apologies for that incident earlier on, Major,' Schepke said as they left the park behind.

'It was of no consequence, Captain,' Major Pao said, smiling, obviously wishing everything forgotten.

The driver turned the car onto the Bund and they drove south along the front. The blue was beginning to fade in the sky now and the Whangpoo looked cold and brittle as the sun began to go down beyond the city. Across the river the *Gertrud Lüth* was back at Chang Ka Pang Wharf.

'What was it the old man said, Captain?' Major Pao asked suddenly.

'Old man?' Schepke said.

'It does not matter,' Major Pao said, smiling his dismissal of the subject.

'There was no old man talked to me.'

'Yes,' Major Pao said, smiling. 'You have told me.'

The car had stopped by the landing stage. Karl Schepke climbed out onto the front. There was a cool breeze coming in from the river.

'I am afraid I cannot accompany you to your ship, Captain. There are some matters that require my immediate attention on shore. Until the next time.'

'Good-bye, Major.' Karl Schepke turned and walked down the steps to the launch. The Major's car had already moved away.

They started back across the river. There was a freshening breeze from the south-east and the waters were choppy. Looking back at the city, the setting sun appeared to be suspended just above the rooftops along the Bund. The *Gertrud Lüth* lay directly ahead, the red sunlight reflecting brightly on her starboard wing windows and heavy glass scuttles along the cabin deck. Even in the sunlight, and under new coats of black and white paint, the *Gertrud Lüth* remained her old self, heavy and squat and ugly.

He took one last look back across the river as they neared the wharf, remembering the old man. He had been a tired, sincere old man who had begun to feel the burden of life weigh heavily. He was a troubled old man. But there were other things to think about other than troubled old men. China was probably full of troubled old men who would remain so until they went to wherever it was that troubled old men went.

No, he was thinking, to hell with China. You leave China to take care of herself, old turtle-head. You have enough troubles of your own without thinking about the yellow stuff. Just keep things simple, old turtle-head. Hell, he was thinking, what are you worrying about an old man for?

IT was almost midnight when the last of the bales of raw cotton were put below. Then the lights began to go out along the wharf as the ponderous-looking trucks moved out up the wharf with the dock coolies packed in behind the high sides. It was quiet now except for the sound of the river and the shipboard noises. Karl Schepke stood looking down from the bridge, watching Kamei supervise the temporary covering of the forward hatches. Sometime during the afternoon he had found time to fit himself out with a mandarin type jacket and work trousers. He was a massively-built man, exceptionally swift and light in all his movements despite his weight and size. And there was his curiously deformed right hand, his last three fingers permanently clenched, almost as though they grew directly into the palm.

Then as Karl Schepke turned to leave, Cheng came up onto the bridge, his white tunic unbuttoned at the neck and his hair carefully smoothed back over his skull.

'Good evening, Captain,' he said as he crossed the bridge. 'Is there any news yet of the cargo from Hankow?'

'There was a signal. It should be here sometime during the early morning.'

'Then with good fortune we should be clear by midday.'

Karl Schepke saw him smiling in the glow of the deck and derrick lights as he leaned on the open window. 'What were you doing before you came on board?'

Cheng turned politely from the open window. 'I was on the Saigon run,' he said. 'That and Manila. Nothing as exciting as you, Captain.'

'Do you know the Yangtze?' Schepke asked him, watching his face in the gloom.

'Only as far as Nanking,' Cheng said, smiling. 'My father was a junkman at Kiang Yin. I was born on the Great. We moved to Hong Kong in nineteen-forty-nine.'

Karl Schepke lit a cigarette, the match flaring in the gloom.

'You enjoyed your visit ashore yesterday?' Cheng asked matter-of-factly.

'I'm afraid Shanghai is not a sailor's city any longer.' He stopped, then decided to go on. 'However, it doesn't matter very much. My only concern is the money. I can always go ashore in Hong Kong. One thing I'll say for the English, they haven't forbidden the making of beer.'

Cheng smiled with him. 'I appreciate your point, Captain. Politics are of no interest to me either.'

Karl Schepke looked at his wrist watch. 'I'm afraid you'll have to excuse me,' he said. 'I had almost forgotten supper.'

When he left, Cheng glanced back at the foredeck to see the hatches covered by tarpaulins and the deck deserted. Quickly he went out into the port wing. All the windows were down and he peered both ways along the wharf then picked out the darker patch that was the gateway to the godown directly opposite the bridge.

'Müller! Müller!' he said, dropping his voice, calling gently to the boatdeck. Then looking from the after windows he saw Müller toss a heaving-line out across the side onto the wharf, the dark shadowy figures of the two Chinese close with him as they leaned across the rail peering into the gloom beyond the ship's high wall. Swiftly now, Cheng struck a match, held it for a moment, then arced it out through the wing window. The answering light wavered far below and then Cheng saw Müller signal the three Chinese.

The line came in smoothly with Müller keeping watch on whatever was below. Then the line came up swiftly, Müller grasping something and lifting it inboard across the rail.

'Schepke is in the messroom,' Cheng said below. 'Hurry.'

He went quickly to the stairway. There was no one below in the passage. The messroom and galley doors were open but Müller did not have to pass them. Then he saw Müller appear at the after screen doorway, and he nodded, and Müller came in quickly and went into his cabin, carefully carrying the black leather knapsack by the shoulder straps.

SHORTLY after midday the *Gertrud Lüth* dropped quietly down the Whangpoo to the Yangtze.

It came on to rain heavily during the night and when they came in to Taipeh the morning sky was grey and low and the rain falling in the southerly wind. Two American destroyers and a Nationalist gunboat were lying at the midstream harbour buoys as the *Gertrud Lüth* swung her bows in toward the dock, the city grey and drab-looking in the steadily falling rain. The pilot cutter met her as she cleared the harbour buoys and apart from a small British merchantman the inner harbour was occupied only by a large American transport ship, grey and deserted-looking in the cold wet morning.

The Nationalist pilot brought them in to the wharf directly ahead of the transport and they tied up opposite a long line of corrugated iron sheds, the high sliding doors already open and gangs of storm-coated Chinese waiting alongside a stream of lifting trucks. It was an open, miserable harbour, and with guardhouses spaced at intervals along the wharves and the army sentries sheltering inside with their rifles.

On the forward well Kamei was already having One and Two hatches broken open and preparing to off-load.

'There's somebody coming on board now,' Müller called from the port wing.

Karl Schepke collected the brief-case from the charthouse and hurried below to the foredeck. Two blue raincoated Chinese and an American army officer were waiting for him in the alleyway.

'Good day, Captain,' the American said, saluting. 'I am Captain Anders, Chief Port Security Officer.'

'Pleased to meet you, Herr Kapitän,' Schepke said. The two Chinese remained silent, one of them carrying a heavy brief-case.

'May we see the papers, Captain?' the American asked.

Schepke handed him the manifest and Certificates of Import.

'With your permission,' the American said, turning to the open hatches.

Karl Schepke led the way across the foredeck. The rain was cold and falling heavily in the wind. They all climbed down into Number Two hold, the packing cases loaded in above the huge bales of raw cotton. The American at once began checking the case numbers against the manifest, then against a list of his own.

'I believe you've just come down from Shanghai,' the American remarked as he worked.

'We left yesterday,' Schepke told him.

'May I ask what you have below these cases?'

'Cotton. It's all cotton,' Schepke said, seeing Kamei towering above the hatch combing on deck, watching them carefully.

'It must have given you a great deal of unnecessary work to rearrange your cargo. It would have been easier to call here before going up-river.'

'The cargo for Shanghai was in bulk,' Schepke explained. 'We carried it aft. Besides, I was ordered to call there first.'

'And the cargo?'

'It was fertilizer.'

The taller of the two Chinese said something to the American and he nodded in agreement.

'Something wrong?' Schepke asked.

'The Lieutenant says they would have wanted the cargo now to give them time to distribute it for the spring planting.' Then he handed Schepke back the manifest. 'These seem perfectly all right,' he said politely. 'Can you open one of the cases?'

Karl Schepke called to Kamei for a bale hook then prised the lid from the nearest case.

The American brought one of the tins out and examined its raised code number against another list, then passed it to the taller of the two Chinese. He in turn nodded then returned the tin to the case.

'Everything checks, Captain,' the American said. 'You can start to off-load as soon as you wish. There's no cargo to embark here so you may yet be able to sail on the night tide.'

'Thank you,' Schepke said.

They went back across the foredeck to the port alleyway.

'There is just one other thing, Captain,' the American said, pausing at the brow. 'I'm afraid no one will be allowed ashore while you're here. It's a port regulation.'

'I understand,' Schepke said, returning the salute. He watched the three of them go down the brow in the falling rain.

'Makes you wonder whose side you'd be on in another war.'

He turned to see Hechler grinning broadly.

'You know, the more yellow stuff I see the less I like it,' Hechler went on. 'If they found out about this cargo, shooting would be the last thing they would do. Besides, something tells me we're being underpaid.'

'I'm beginning to think that myself,' Schepke told him.

'The first opportunity that comes along, I'm off here,' Hechler said, serious now.

'We're victims of circumstance, Hans,' Schepke said lightly.

'Well I don't want to be a victim too long. I don't trust this yellow stuff at all.'

'Come on,' Schepke told him. 'Let's have a drink.'

And the cold rain swept across the city in the southerly wind, and the city grey and bleak-looking in the early morning.

IT was dark now and still raining, the scattered lights of the city weak and cold-looking in the thinly blown rain. Out on the foredeck Kamei had the crew battening down the hatches as the last of the coolies went ashore. Karl Schepke, leaning on the wheel, watched the work go on below him from the rain-blurred windows. During the afternoon another American transport had come in from Stateside and was tied up ahead, her decks jammed with an assortment of trucks and jeeps. Now, in the darkness, he looked out ahead at the great black hulk of the *Fort Somerville*'s stern, her deck and masthead lights casting a yellow glow across the wharf, the cobbles and crane rails wetly reflecting the lights in the falling rain. The wharf was deserted and not even the sentries showed themselves outside of the guardhouses.

He leaned up off the wheel as Müller came in shaking the rain from his storm-coat.

'Those are all the hatches battened down and the ship secured for sea,' he reported, putting the light on in the charthouse and hanging his coat behind the door. 'What time do we sail?'

'High water's at twenty-three-sixteen. We'll slip right after. I've told Hechler. I'm going down to eat now then turn in for a while. Call me at ten-thirty.'

'Is there anything else you want doing?'

'No. Everything's ready.' Schepke started to leave.

239

'You're—' Müller began to say something then stopped.

'What is it?'

'You're pleased with the way I've handled things so far?'

Karl Schepke looked back at him evenly in the light from the charthouse. 'You've done all right,' he said, and went on below.

Altmeyer was waiting for him. 'I've just got the weather and clearance papers, sir.'

Schepke took them from him and saw him still waiting. 'What is it?'

'There was two of them followed me to the signal tower when I went to collect these.'

'Soldiers?'

Altmeyer nodded. 'Yes, sir. I wondered if something was wrong.'

'I don't think so,' Schepke told him. 'A state of war exists here. They still shell this island from the mainland.' He went on aft to the messroom.

'Still raining, Captain?' Cheng asked.

Schepke nodded and started on his supper as soon as Kuang brought it.

'I don't think the weather will settle until after the North-East Monsoon is out,' Cheng said, after a while. 'That will not come until April. There will be a great deal of bad weather yet.'

Schepke nodded politely and went on eating.

After a time Cheng rose and collected his cap. 'I think I will get some sleep before we sail,' he said.

'We'll be slipping about twenty-three-thirty,' Schepke told him.

When he was through eating Kuang brought a fresh pot of coffee and set it on the table.

'Put it in my cabin,' Schepke told him, and got his cap and went onto the the boatdeck. Just before midday the army had put a double sentry box at the foot of the brow and the sentries had carefully inspected the papers and identity cards of everyone who had gone on board. They were still there, a portable light strung out across the roof of the box and lighting the brow. He turned back into the passage now and went below. Kamei was in the port alleyway, looking out across the wharf at the city.

240

'I think you better stay on board,' Schepke told him. 'There seems little chance of getting ashore here. Anyway, it looks as bad, if not worse, than the Communist side.'

Kamei looked below at the wharf.

'If you went over the wall they would shoot you before you were halfway across the dock,' Schepke went on. 'Even if you made it a man your size would be noticed as somebody strange. You don't even have any papers.'

'You think it is safe to return to Hong Kong?' Kamei asked.

'What else is there? You'll have to stay below while we're in harbour. The biggest worry is the crew when they go ashore.'

'They will not talk,' Kamei said, smiling, the smile showing only about his mouth. 'But you?'

'I've had worries ever since I can remember,' Schepke said.

'I am humbly grateful,' Kamei said.

'Forget it. Stand by ready to slip after twenty-three-hundred.'

He left Kamei still in the alleyway and went up to his cabin.

Kuang had left the coffee on the shelf over the bunk. He was thinking about Hechler now and what Wang would do about another engineer. If Hechler went, Dorsch and Frauenheim would probably go with him. And after having made the first trip he was not anxious about remaining too long on board himself.

He finished the coffee and lay out on the bunk.

The only thing he could say for the *Gertrud Lüth* was that she was better than the beach. And the money. In six months he could move down to Manila. Manila was a regular port of call and after time had stilled any talk of the *Gertrud Lüth* it might be possible to ship out without too much trouble. Yes, Manila would be all right, he was thinking. Manila would be fine. He went to sleep thinking about Manila.

MÜLLER was waiting for Cheng on the bridge.

'He's just finished eating now.'

Müller moved across to the doorway. From there he could see most of the way along the passage.

'You're sure you've changed your mind about the one astern?'

'She was empty,' Cheng told him. 'We will take the *Fort Somerville*. The other was merely waiting for engine spares from Okinawa.'

Müller looked back at him in the gloom of the bridge. He did not feel confident about any of it. Then thoughtfully, he rubbed his thumbnail across the stubble on his jaw.

'What are you thinking about this time?' Cheng asked.

Müller raised his eyes. 'I wouldn't like to see anything go wrong.'

'There is nothing to go wrong,' Cheng told him, disapproval showing plainly in his voice.

'He's just gone aft to the boatdeck,' Müller said, his attention turned to the passage below.

'You are certain he said he was going to sleep after supper?'

'He told me to call him at ten-thirty.' Müller's eyes had not left the passage. Then in a few moments he saw Schepke come in and go below on the main stairway.

'What's happening?' Cheng asked.

'He's gone below somewhere.'

Cheng said something aloud to himself then went to the window. Müller lit a cigarette and waited quietly by the doorway, and in a little while he saw Schepke come back up top and go in and shut his cabin door. 'He's in his cabin.'

'We will give him a few minutes,' Cheng said, checking the luminous dial of his wrist watch. 'We have almost two hours yet.'

242

It was cold and dark and with the rain blowing thinly in from across the city. Müller, firmly holding the knapsack by the shoulder straps, slowly descended into the gloom of the after well from the boatdeck. All about him the rain ran from the superstructure, running in the scuppers and swilling across the deck with the low, slow lift of the incoming swell.

'Müller!'

He recognized Cheng's hushed voice calling from the gloom just forward of the deck-lights high on the break of the fantail. Making his way carefully around the combing of Number Three hatch he came upon the three storm-coated figures crouched in the lee of the port bulwarks.

Cheng took the knapsack and very carefully brought out the six limpets from their wadding and set them onto the deck. Next he took the canvas folder of firing watches from his storm-coat and expertly clipped them to the firing mechanisms.

'Are you sure they're timed properly?' Müller asked as Cheng put the limpets back into their wadding in the knapsack.

Cheng ignored him, giving the knapsack to the flat-faced one called Tah Gu Tze. The crewman settled the knapsack squarely onto his shoulders after taking off his storm-coat then looked to Cheng.

Müller raised his head and peered across the dripping bulwarks. The brow was forward of them at the waist, the rear of the double sentry box toward them and no one about.

'All right,' he said, and saw Cheng glance hurriedly at the fantail and boatdeck. There was no one about and he nodded to the other crewmen and they swiftly dropped the lightly weighted nylon ladder across the wall, the inboard end already secured to a deck cleat.

'Work carefully,' Cheng told the one with the knapsack. 'Make certain everything is set as it should. Be as quick as possible, but remember, below the waterline.'

Müller saw the man raise his head, glance quickly out toward the sentry box then roll smoothly over the bulwarks onto the ladder, the soles of his slipper type shoes wetly catching the glow of the deck-lights as he went over. Glancing nervously overhead at the boatdeck, Müller settled to watch the taut jerking inboard end of the nylon ladder as the man descended the sheer wall. Then suddenly the ladder leapt on the bulwarks and went slack and they knew Tah Gu Tze had reached the catamarans and gone in underneath on the pilings of the wharf.

CLOSE to midnight the *Gertrud Lüth* slipped quietly out into the darkness of the Formosa Straits. The wind was still southerly, the rain blowing coldly with it, setting up a long loping sea that set the ship rolling sluggishly as she bore on into the night, sending shoals of spray up on the port side to be whipped across her decks by the cross-wind. There was always a fair amount of shipping using the Straits, both bound for southern and northern China and north to Japan, and for some time Karl Schepke had been watching the low rolling lights of a northbound ship off the starboard bow.

Dropping the night-glasses onto his chest he reached for the engine-room telephone and spun the handle.

'Engine-room!' came Hechler's reply amid the high-powered pound and whine of the engines.

'Schepke here. We've got a warship on our starboard bow. I think we should step speed up and get to hell off this part of the coast.'

'That's fine with me,' Hechler replied. 'After all the work that's been put out on her down here it might be interesting to see just how she stands up to things.'

'Full ahead,' Schepke called to the Chinese on the telegraph as he replaced the receiver.

'Full ahead, sir.'

'Up twenty.'

'Up twenty, sir,' the Chinese repeated as he rang the revolutions onto the counter.

Karl Schepke felt the ship surge ahead. Moments later he saw the searchlight of the low rolling warship beam out across the ocean.

Her Majesty's Brittanic Warship Cockade *requests recognition.*

He read the message as it came, Bahr watching him from the wheel. Then raising the night-glasses he searched the darkness out beyond the bows.

'She's signalling again, sir,' Bahr called.

Schepke turned and saw the warship had begun a repeat of the previous signal.

The *Gertrud Lüth* bore unheedingly into the night, the warship slipping rapidly astern.

'Herr Kapitän!' Altmeyer said as he entered the bridge. 'There's a Limey warship somewhere close by calling us for recognition.'

'She's astern now. Ignore her.'

'Yes, sir,' Altmeyer said, relaxing. 'I had just switched on to listen to the traffic and she almost deafened me.'

'That's all right,' Schepke told him. 'She's got nothing to do with us. To hell with these Limeys.'

About an hour later he picked up two more sets of lights, one of them away on the port bow and the other right ahead. The rain was beginning to ease now and he smoked and paced the bridge and watched the lights ahead gradually take shape as the *Gertrud Lüth* overhauled them. Whoever they were they had course set and headed toward Hong Kong. The air in the bridge was heavy and stale with cigarette smoke and he dropped one of the port wing windows down and felt the cold clean air suck in past him. The rain was very fine now, hanging in the wind as it began to ease. By daylight he felt the wind would be gone.

Glancing at his wrist watch he saw it was almost time for the morning watch to take over. Running the window up, he crossed to the engine-room telephone.

'Want to shut her down?'

'I'd rather you kept her going as she is,' Hechler said. 'I'd like to see how she holds together. I want Frauenheim to sound the wells, say at daylight?'

'I'm going off now. Suit yourself.'

Cheng was waiting for him.

'She's all yours,' Schepke told him as they went to the chart-house. 'Keep her as she is. Hechler wants to see how she runs. All the same you might have to ease her before daylight as the wind's easing fast and when she falls away we can run into fog.'

'Very good, Captain,' Cheng said, smiling politely.

'Call me when it starts to get light.'

'Good night, Captain.'

Karl Schepke went out without replying. There was something about Cheng that bothered him, something that was too smooth.

KARL SCHEPKE woke with Altmeyer leaning across the bunk calling him.

'Something wrong?' he asked, sitting up.

'I'm not sure, sir,' Altmeyer said. 'It's coming across without making very much sense.'

'Go on,' Schepke told him, already dressing.

'Well I couldn't get to sleep so I went along to the office. I had the radio on intermediate and suddenly I heard a number of people talking about us. It was all Chinese stuff and all I could make out was our name. Then just now I heard Taipeh send out a General requesting all south and northbound shipping in the Straits to report if they had seen us.'

'Did you tell anybody else about this?' Schepke asked as they went forward to the Radio Office.

'I came straight to you, sir,' Altmeyer said, closing the door then sitting into the swivel chair and fitting the headphones.

Karl Schepke glanced at the bulkhead clock and saw it showed a little after five o'clock.

'—There!' Altmeyer said, suddenly, swivelling the left headphone. 'That's Taipeh now.'

Schepke heard the metallic, static-disturbed voice of an English-speaking operator at Taipeh requesting all shipping to report in on sighting the southbound *Gertrud Lüth*.

'Keep listening,' he told the boy and went out hurriedly to see Hechler's broad back as he went aft. 'Hans!'

Hechler waited for him.

'There's an alert out for us. I just heard Taipeh send out a General.'

'What in hell's that for?' Hechler asked, puzzled.

'You know as much as I do,' Schepke told him. 'I told Altmeyer to keep listening.'

'What are you going to do?'

'I think we should keep going. I've got a feeling we're involved in something we don't know anything about.'

'I'll have a cup of coffee then go back below and keep Frauenheim company,' Hechler said, pausing outside of the galley. 'They did a good job at Taikoo,' he went on. 'I don't think you need worry about the ship any.'

Karl Schepke went on up to the bridge.

'Something is wrong, Captain?' Cheng asked, surprised at seeing him.

'I don't know,' Schepke said evenly.

'I am not sure I understand, Captain.'

'Never mind. Just go down to the main box and slip all the deck, derrick, and alleyway lights. Then get Müller up here.'

From the window he watched the lights go out, and now everything was dark except for the navigation lights and the lights in the inboard passages and cabins.

'Kapitän, sir,' Altmeyer said as he came onto the bridge.

'There's a lot of coded stuff coming across on high frequency. I'm afraid there's none of it any good to me.'

'All right,' Schepke told him. 'Keep listening,' He went into the charthouse and leaned across the glass-topped table, noting all the Formosa ports that could harbour warships, American or Nationalist. Unknowingly, by running the *Gertrud Lüth* full out they had made better time through the Straits than normally anything but a fast freighter would have made and he presumed it just possible that anyone searching for them would not allow for so much headway.

Well I guess the luck's maybe changed after all, old turtle-head, he was thinking. Maybe. And maybe it wasn't the yellow stuff that built the Great Wall. Maybe.

And outside it was still dark in the Straits and the morning had not yet begun to come in.

LEAVING the main switch box, Cheng knocked lightly on the door of the Radio Office.

Altmeyer turned to see him come in and pushed the head-phones forward off his ears.

'There is some sort of trouble?' Cheng asked.

'It's Taipeh,' the boy told him. 'They put out a General for us.'

'Then it is something serious?'

Altmeyer shrugged. 'Even the Kapitän doesn't know yet,' he said.

Cheng nodded thoughtfully then went out and hurried aft.

Müller was asleep.

'Müller! Wake up!'

Müller sleepily focused his eyes.

'Wake up!' Cheng told him. 'Something is wrong. Taipeh has sent out an alert for us.'

Müller came swiftly off the bunk, wide awake. 'Nothing was supposed to happen until morning!'

'Keep your voice down!' Cheng hissed. 'One of the timing mechanisms must have proved faulty.'

'They were bound to suspect us in any case,' Müller argued. 'The whole thing was stupid.'

'You are not being paid to criticize!' Cheng hissed, the contempt showing in his words. 'We are paid only to obey instructions. It has just been unfortunate. There is much espionage going on all the time and these charges exploding at the precise time could have been set by someone on shore. A dockworker, maybe. We have men everywhere. No one can prove anything, not even if we are stopped.'

Müller sighed deeply. 'I still don't like it,' he said, pulling on his tunic.

'Not even the money?' Cheng said contemptuously.

Müller stared back at him for a brief moment, then went on buttoning his tunic.

It had begun to rain again. There was no wind now and the rain fell hissing on the darkness of the ocean. After Cheng had gone below Karl Schepke picked up the blur of approaching lights on the starboard bow and now he watched them as they came on through the heavily falling rain, arcing with the movement of the ocean. She was a large freighter probably bound north for Japan. He went on out to the port wing and put the glasses astern. There was no sign of the lights of the two ships they had passed earlier in the morning. Then as he turned back amidships Cheng and Müller came in from below.

'Get me the register.' He saw Cheng move as he put the glasses on the freighter again. She was taking shape now, big and solid, her lights showing high in the darkness.

Dropping the glasses onto his chest he took the heavy register from Cheng and stood under the pale glow of light from the compass bowl, running his finger down the lists of ship names.

'Get Altmeyer up here.'

The lights were closing to pass on the starboard side. Almost immediately a searchlight flashed out across the intervening darkness, the rain falling brilliantly through the flashing beam.

Karl Schepke watched it, reading it as it came:

Bad night. Visibility poor further south. T.S. Kroonstad, *bound Yokohama.*

He turned as Cheng came in with Altmeyer hastily pulling on his storm coat.

'Make:

'*Many thanks.* S.S. Zanoni Maru, *bound Saigon.*'

He crossed to the starboard wing now and watched the large Dutchman draw abeam, at the same time hearing the metallic clatter and seeing the sudden brilliance of light reflect on the ocean as Altmeyer hammered out the signal. The Dutchman steamed steadily on through the heavily falling rain, acknowledging the signal as she slipped rapidly astern.

Then Altmeyer came in off the flying bridge and fastened the hatch down, rain streaming from his storm-coat.

'Fine,' Schepke told him. 'Heard anything else?'

'The British warship *Cockade* reported in on intermediate that she had passed an unidentified merchantman proceeding south at one-fourteen. There's still some coded stuff on high frequency but I can't make out if it's shipping or shore stations. Our R/D is rigged only for low and intermediate.'

'May I ask what is happening, Captain?' Cheng interrupted.

Schepke looked first at him, then at Müller. 'I thought somebody on board might be able to tell me,' he said.

'Tell you what?' Müller said.

'Carry on, Altmeyer,' Schepke said, dismissing the boy, and at the same time ignoring Müller. 'Cheng. You organize some extra look-outs. It's going to be light soon and I think we're going to find somebody very intent on finding us. I just hope this rain and low cloud ceiling holds.'

'We're going to run?' Müller asked.

'Don't tell me you're really one of the bright boys after all,' Schepke said. 'What do you suggest we do, go back?'

'Well I mean what the hell's happening?'

'If I knew I would tell you,' Schepke said, watching him. 'But whatever it is they won't be wanting to hang medals on us.'

'I think the Captain is right,' Cheng interrupted. 'It is better to keep going. We all know how politically involved even the smallest incident can become in these waters.'

Karl Schepke did not say anything. But he was thinking, and he was thinking, if this old sea-cow ever reaches Hong Kong and I ever set foot on board her again, you, Mr. Chinaman, are going to take a lot of watching.

HE was in the messroom when he heard someone shouting on the boatdeck. Kicking the chair from under him, he went out at a run. Kamei and two of the Chinese look-outs were on the port side, all three of them staring intently at the mass of low cloud on the port quarter.

'Aeroplane,' Kamei said. 'It is very low.'

Karl Schepke already heard it, the cloud-muffled drone of her motors growing to a roar as she seemed to pass directly overhead.

'She has not seen us,' Kamei said.

'Not visibly,' Schepke told him. 'But she'll have us on radar. She sounds like a slow coastal patrol, probably a flying-boat.'

The sound of the motors had eased now as the aeroplane passed widely away to starboard, in the direction of the mist-shrouded mainland. Karl Schepke looked out toward the ocean.

251

The rain had eased again and visibility had opened to ten or eleven hundred metres. Then looking back toward the mainland he saw the mist and the heavy fog-bank further in.

'Get all hands off the deck,' he told Kamei as he turned for the bridge.

'Did you see it?' Müller asked as he came in from below.

'Starboard ten!' Schepke shouted, ignoring him, dropping one of the forward windows down as the low hammering roar of motors passed wide ahead of the bows as they began their swing shoreward.

'She's still there!' Müller shouted.

Schepke glanced at the Chinese on the wheel. 'She's coming in for a closer look,' he said. 'Take us into that fog-bank and get back on course. Don't slacken speed any.'

Müller immediately began shouting fresh orders to the two Chinese and the ship angled sharply in toward the fog-bank.

Then Karl Schepke heard her low down, coming on, the roar of her motors growing steadily louder. And suddenly she was low and dark, her white float belly seeming to hang just clear of the grey ocean as she came in on the port quarter. She seemed to take a long time, her two wing engines throttled right back and hammering the sky apart. He knew she could not possibly miss seeing the name boldly across the stern. Then suddenly her port wing dipped slightly as she banked, aiming her nose at the bridge. He glimpsed momentarily the identification marks on the underside of the wings and then found himself watching the red and yellow tracer shells seeming to float gently out from her nose then curve slowly in toward him. Then quite abruptly her belly lifted and he went down flat on the deck as she barely cleared the foremast, the terrific hammering of her engines drowning the clatter of her guns as she went over.

The deck around him was littered with glass from the smashed windows of the wing and he raised his head and saw the forward bulkhead just below the window rail a mass of splintered wood. Everyone was flat on the deck, Müller with his head toward him listening to the receding roar of the motors. The two Chinese were flat on their faces, their arms across their heads.

'Is everybody all right?' Schepke asked, rising.

Müller nodded and rose to his feet as Schepke steadied the wheel. They were coming in fast toward the fog-bank, everyone now watching nervously from the forward windows. Then they heard the mounting roar of the motors as the flying-boat swung around somewhere close by.

'Get ready!' Schepke shouted. 'Müller! Tell Altmeyer to radio Hong Kong! Tell him we're being attacked by a Nationalist flying-boat!'

He turned to see her come down through the cloud almost directly in line with the bows. The pilot had misjudged their position slightly and almost at once he started to pull up without levelling out.

Glass showered in upon him as he threw himself to the deck, the whole ship vibrating under him as the motors reached their mighty crescendo as the flying-boat flashed up over the bridge.

Karl Schepke was already pulling the wheel around to port, bringing their head away from the land now that they were inside the fog-bank, visibility sharply decreased to about one hundred metres.

'Take the wheel!' he told the nearest of the two Chinese.

'Here she comes again!' Müller shouted as he came in from below.

This time the roar of her motors seemed everywhere in the fog and then suddenly grew loud and passed somewhere close astern.

'She won't see us in this,' Schepke said. 'Get back on course and we'll stay inside until dark.' He was already on his way below.

Cheng was in the passage.

'What the hell are you smiling about?' Schepke snarled. 'If I thought you knew anything about this I'd throw you over the wall!'

'What would I know about anything?' Cheng protested.

Schepke ignored him and pushed past on his way to the boat-deck.

The decking and two lifeboats, and the port wing of the bridge were heavily holed and splintered. Then, glancing overhead, he saw the cannon shells had hammered great holes in the funnel casing and snapped a number of stays.

'We are lucky there is the fog.'

He turned to see Kamei. They could still hear the cloud and fog-muffled motors as the flying-boat circled steadily somewhere above them.

'Did you see anything wrong back at Taipeh?' Schepke said to him.

Kamei slowly moved his massive shaven head. 'Nothing,' he said. 'I do not understand this at all.'

'You're not the only one,' Shepke said.

'You think we will get clear now?'

'We're too far south to get stopped unless they've got a warship in the area. If nothing else happens before dark we should be all right. After dark, I'll take her out from the coast and run without lights.'

'It will be dangerous now,' Kamei said, looking astern at the Straits. 'Next time they see us they will shoot. The only time we go through the Straits now is when dark.'

'I'd like to know what happened back there,' Schepke said. 'From now on you keep a close watch on everybody. If you see or hear anything suspicious, tell me. Understand?'

'I understand,' Kamei said, and he was looking back toward the fog-shrouded Straits.

KARL SCHEPKE brought the *Gertrud Lüth* slowly around Tsim Sha Tsiu and docked her at the bottom of Kowloon's Navy Street. Before they were through tying up an excited crowd of dockworkers had gathered to gape at the gunned superstructure. Schepke looked out toward the Star Ferry Pier and there was a

British freighter of the Prince Line tied up at the wharf, a crowd gathered on her forward well and looking down across the empty dock between the two wharves.

'It looks as though the news got out ahead of us,' Schepke said, turning to Müller.

'There's no sign of Wang.'

'Take care of her,' Schepke told him and went below to the cabin deck.

Hechler was leaving his cabin, dressed, and putting on his cap.

'In a hurry, Hans?'

Hechler nodded. 'I'm going across to see von Pittkamer.'

'Let me know how you get on.'

'Sure,' Hechler said.

Karl Schepke went into his cabin and ran some water into the bowl and washed. The ship was quiet except for the hum of the generators, and after dressing, he went aft to the messroom. Frauenheim, Cheng, and Altmeyer were sitting at the long table, sunlight slanting in through the open scuttles and a warm breeze coming in off the harbour.

'Anybody staying on board tonight?'

'I can stay,' Cheng said.

'Then you better arrange for off-loading in case I'm late in getting back.'

'You will be ashore all night?'

'Maybe. And don't use Kamei tomorrow. I don't want him on deck.'

When he went below Kamei was lying on his bunk.

'Stay here tomorrow,' he told him. 'It's better you're not seen on deck while we're in harbour.'

'I understand,' Kamei said.

Karl Schepke carefully lit a cigarette. 'Do you know where I can buy a gun?'

Kamei, looking at him, nodded. 'Go to Flower Market Road. Go to the lantern shop. Ask for Chu Wei. Tell him Kamei sent you. He will get you a gun.'

255

HE had come without announcement, past the girl at the desk in the outer office, throwing his cap on the divan.

Mr. Wang rose nervously.

'All right,' Schepke told him angrily, his hands flat on the polished top of the desk, leaning his face close to Mr. Wang's. 'Now you can tell me what happened at Taipeh!'

Mr. Wang dabbed nervously at his forehead with a silk handkerchief. 'I am afraid I am not at all certain of what you mean, Captain,' he said.

'What do you think I am?' Schepke demanded, then heard the door behind him open.

'I am sorry if I have interrupted you, gentlemen.'

'Oh, no. No.' Mr. Wang said, smiling his relief, lifting his head toward the newcomer, his heavy-rimmed spectacles catching the light so there momentarily appeared no eyes in his face. Then smilingly, he returned to Schepke. 'This is Mr. Saito.'

Mr. Saito was an old man. He held his hat in his hand and leaned both hands on a cane.

'So?' Schepke said, looking from one to the other.

'Mr. Saito is our managing director,' Mr. Wang said with some reverence.

'Isn't that wonderful?' Schepke said.

Mr. Saito smiled amusedly.

'I still want to know what happened at Taipeh,' Schepke said to Mr. Wang.

'Perhaps I can offer some explanation,' Mr. Saito politely interrupted.

'Are you in this, too?' Schepke said, not thinking very much of either of them.

Mr. Saito sat delicately down on the divan. 'Captain,' he said quietly. 'I assure you that I have made the strongest possible protest direct to the Generalissimo himself. It was made just as soon as it was known as to exactly what had transpired at Taipeh.'

'And what did transpire?' Schepke asked, tired of all the polite evasion.

'Unfortunately an explosion occurred on board the *Fort Somerville* shortly after you had put to sea. I believe her engine-room was severely damaged and a number of her crew killed. Naturally, they assumed it was an act of espionage, and as you had been berthed alongside of her they turned their suspicions on you, Captain. You see, it also appeared to them that you had fled from the scene once you left harbour. You were reported to be moving at full speed through the Straits and ignoring all contact with other shipping. I personally do not know your reasons for such haste, but I am sure that you see their point, Captain. Also, you had just come down from Shanghai.'

Karl Schepke considered it carefully. 'And what happens now?' he asked.

Mr. Saito smiled. 'An official note of apology was handed to us this afternoon shortly before you docked. I also complained on the grounds that such an act would never have been perpetrated by any sane person or persons. No one in his proper mind would have done such a thing that would so obviously bring suspicion upon himself so swiftly. I suggested to them that if this were proved to be an act of espionage it might very well have been carried out by someone on shore to coincide with your sailing so that any suspicion would naturally fall upon you. I pointed out also that all but one of the officers of the *Gertrud Lüth* were German, men of the utmost integrity and for any number of reasons could not possibly hold any grudge with the Nationalist Government of Formosa.'

'And they apologized?'

'Immediately,' Mr. Saito said, smiling. 'They apologized with the utmost regret for their ill-concluded actions and make an offer for all needful compensation.' Mr. Saito talked very impressively.

'A drink, gentlemen?' Mr. Wang asked, again smiling and confident.

Karl Schepke was looking at Mr. Saito. Mr. Saito seemed to have all the answers to hand.

'I trust you are in a far happier frame of mind now, Captain.'

Karl Schepke shrugged, admitting nothing. Mr. Wang handed the drinks around, remembering the Schiedam.

'Is there anything else I can help with?' Mr. Saito asked.

'There's this Major Pao in Shanghai,' Schepke told him. 'He seems to be some sort of intelligence man. I don't want him around if it's possible. Outside of sailing the *Gertrud Lüth* I don't want to get involved with anything else. China can go to hell for all I care. My only interest in this is the money.'

'Precisely, Captain. I understand you completely,' Mr. Saito said. 'The money is all that matters to any of us. We are entirely free agents. We do this simply for what we can achieve for ourselves. But quite frankly, Captain, you need have no fear of Red China. They are as much interested in the well-being of the *Gertrud Lüth* as any of us. No, I would not worry about Major Pao, Captain. I am certain they have no wish to upset you in any way. However, I am prepared to institute certain discreet inquiries as to just what it is that Major Pao represents. This I will most certainly do if it were to give you peace of mind.'

'All right,' let's see what happens next time we call,' Schepke said. 'If there's any trouble I'll let you know. I just don't want to find myself involved in anything I know nothing about.'

'Of course, Captain.' Mr. Saito said. 'I think precisely as you do.'

'There is one other thing. —Just who owns the *Gertrud Lüth*?'

Mr. Saito smiled, Mr. Wang, sitting at the desk, ventured nothing.

'The *Gertrud Lüth* is owned by myself and certain associates,' Mr. Saito said. 'However, when we purchased the ship we found we required rather more money than at first thought, and as we had already decided how we were to trade it did not prove too difficult to interest the party which was to benefit most from our being.' He paused, looking at Schepke, then added, 'Beyond that there is no political pressure whatsoever.'

'Then don't you think it unwise to trade directly with Formosa?' Schepke asked. 'They're going to find out sometime.'

Mr. Wang, watching them, gently nodded.

'I am in complete agreement with you, Captain,' Mr. Saito said. 'Indeed we have already arrived at this very conclusion. You have my personal assurance that the *Gertrud Lüth* will not call again at any Nationalist sea port. I trust this is to your entire satisfaction, Captain Schepke?'

'For the moment,' Schepke told him, and in the circumstances prevailing there was nothing else he could say. 'I just want it made clear that I've no wish to get involved with anything outside of running the ship.'

'Of course. I, too, wish it no other way, Captain.'

'Just so long as we understand each other.'

Mr. Wang stood up and came around from behind his desk. 'I think you will be interested to know, Captain, that I now have a Third Officer and bosun for you.'

'That's another thing,' Schepke said, turning his attention to Mr. Wang. 'You told me the Third was arriving on the *Tsung Kow*. Yet she'd just sailed from here.'

'Ah,' Mr. Wang said, smiling disarmingly. 'That was a slight mistake on my part. You see, I had just previously completed some business with the *Tsung Kow* and I should have said the *Hai Tsung*. Anyway, they are both here and I can have them on board tomorrow. Or even tonight,' he hastened to add, still smiling.

'If they're Chinese I don't want them on board,' Schepke told him. 'Anyway, I have a bosun. As for the Third, I'll have his watches stood between us. You can split his pay with the others.'

'But, Captain,' Mr. Wang said. 'I have made the arrangements.'

'Let the Captain do as he wishes,' Mr. Saito interrupted. 'Knowing how he has already handled the ship I have no argument.'

'Thank you,' Schepke told him. 'Now let's get down to business. I want to know what's happening next.'

'Well we would appreciate a quick turn around,' Mr. Saito said. 'We have an urgent cargo of light machinery on hand for Chingkiang. There is a quantity of flour to go with it. There is no need to go to a buoy. Everything is stored this side. At the same time you can make arrangements with your Engineer to ship all the coal you require for the complete trip. It is not easy to coal at Chingkiang as everything has to be hauled by rail from either Shanghai or Nanking.'

'What about the damage?'

'That can be attended to while you load. By the way,' Mr. Saito went on, 'the return cargo is wool. Very expensive wool. Not that China can afford to part with it but in this case it is of more value sold abroad. Most of it you will find has come down from Mongolia, Tibet, and Shansi. A great part of it will ultimately find its way to the more exclusive and expensive carpet mills of America.'

'I can see we have a far-reaching effect,' Schepke said.

'It is all money in the bank,' Mr. Saito said, rising now, smiling. 'Now, gentlemen, if there are no more difficulties I wish to be excused. I have a rather urgent business appointment soon. Good night, Captain. Mr. Wang.' He placed his hat delicately on his white head and bowed politely before leaving.

'Is there anything else I can do for you, Captain?' Mr. Wang asked, his old confidence returned.

'No thank you,' Schepke told him, finding his cap.

'Good night to you, Captain,' Mr. Wang called after him.

Karl Schepke walked downstairs into the growing darkness. There was no sign of Mr. Saito. The street lights and the lights of the traffic were coming on, bright only in the shadows of the tall buildings enclosing the roadway, the clear, high-clouded sky still coppery bright with the setting of the sun far out beyond Hainan.

Then he lit a cigarette and turned and walked northward in search of the lantern shop in Flower Market Road.

THE *Gertrud Lüth* had entered the mighty mouth of the Yangtze at daybreak, had embarked two river pilots from a cutter that put out from directly under the massive guns at Woosung, then proceeded up-river, ploughing her high blunt bows through the fast-running waters and leaving a swirling wake of mist straggling around her high stern. Nothing moved in the early morning except the yellowish waters of the river. Away to port was the vast rolling south bank, the opposite shore flatter, swampier, shrouded in the heavy mist that rainbowed with the rising of the sun.

Karl Schepke had remained on the bridge with the two pilots all the way up the river, and now in the last hour of the first watch, dropping speed, they came through Silver Island Pass where the river narrowed and ran like a mill-race between the cliffs, the light of the full moon lighting the waters and the shore so the temples on the island and on the high black perpendicular cliff on the south shore stood out in silvered detail. Then strung out in a long straggling mass were the lights of Chingkiang in the near distance, and beyond, deeply shadowed and etched in moonlight was a terrifically tall and graceful pagoda.

The *Gertrud Lüth* anchored directly off the Chingkiang front and before the cable-party had come down from the forepeak Karl Schepke saw the lights of a cutter headed out from shore, her bows angled upstream against the fast-running river as it surged toward Silver Island Pass.

'Pilot ship comes,' explained the pilot whose name was Sun Mo Long and who had previously announced himself to be Old Sun from Wanhsien.

Schepke saw Kamei had already begun lowering the port side ladder, and as he turned again toward Chingkiang saw the boat, having headed in directly toward the port ladder, being swept broadside on downstream by the current.

'Boatman know less than one turtle,' Old Sun said, then showing his long stained teeth, laughing heartily with the younger pilot who spoke no English but of whom Old Sun had authoritatively referred to as Young Cho Yik Tong from Yellow Cat Gorge.

Now the boatman having got the bows around again, the cutter was fighting upstream toward the ladder, her engine at maximum thrust.

'She comes now,' Old Sun said. 'Many good nights, Captain.'

'And to you,' Schepke said, watching them descend the long ladder, at the same time seeing the bowman in the cutter reach and hook onto the brass rail stanchion.

There was no light out as yet on the ladder and in the gloom he saw someone step onto the grating and come up past the two pilots.

'Good evening, Captain. Pleasant voyage?'

'What do you want?'

'Come now, Captain,' Major Pao said, smiling. 'Is this how you greet old friends?'

'Since when were you an old friend?' Schepke asked, his voice not changing any.

Major Pao put his head back and laughed. Then, smiling: 'I hear you were unfortunately involved in some trouble with the Nationalists on your return voyage.'

'Bad news travels fast,' Schepke said. 'What do you want, the papers?'

'If you please, Captain.'

Karl Schepke handed over the ship's papers and manifest in the messroom.

'Thank you,' Major Pao said, taking the papers. 'I am very much afraid that you will have to discharge and embark your cargo out here on the river. Unfortunately we had a large fire three nights ago and a great deal of damage was caused to the China Merchants Wharf. It will be some weeks before the larger shipping using the river can dock again. However, we have already had some larger lighters sent down from Nanking and they will be out here at daylight. I trust this meets with your approval?'

'I get paid just the same, Major.'

'Well I am afraid I must go now,' Major Pao said, fastening his brief-case. 'If I do not board that cutter soon it may well be on the other side of the Pass.'

Karl Schepke walked with him to the ladder. It was a fine moonlit night and there was a cool breeze off the river that smelled both of the waters and of the evening dew on the land.

'Good night, Captain.'

'Good night,' Schepke told him.

'By the way. We have three bars in town. Try the one on the bund of the Concession. I will tell them to expect you.'

He went on down to the cutter. Schepke, leaning on the bulwark capping, watched the cutter angle back across the river, its engine sound carrying loudly across the water.

'Our friend again?' Hechler asked as he joined him in the alleyway.

Schepke went on looking out across the water at the lights of Chingkiang. The lights stretched quite a way down the darkness of the river.

'Is something bothering you?' Hechler asked, striking a match, shielding the flame in the palm of his hand as he lit a cheroot.

'I was thinking how it is that some people enter your life and suddenly they are always there even when they are gone.'

'Do you mean him?' Hechler asked, looking at the lights of the cutter.

'It's not only him,' Schepke said.

'Maybe you've been out here too long, Karl. Too long away from your own people.'

'None of them are my people. No matter whose people they are. I take care of myself.'

'You'll feel different once you're home again. You've had a long run of bad luck. You've had more bad luck than most people have in a lifetime.'

It was a sweet, cool breeze off the river; and Karl Schepke did not say anything.

Hechler drew on his cheroot, watching Schepke's deeply shadowed face. 'Von Pittkamer promised to get us on board the first homebound ship that calls. With any luck we might hear something when we get back.'

'Don't talk to me about luck,' Schepke told him. 'I don't remember any of it.'

'Come on,' Hechler said. 'Let's go up and get a drink. It's one of those nights.'

It was the third day in the river now, a little after midday. The river was wide and yellow and hurrying into Silver Island Pass, sweeping around Ta Sha and on down toward Tan-tu Reach then widening toward Rose Island before curving down to Kiang Yin.

From the bridge, in the steeply risen sun, Karl Schepke watched the cumbersome burlap-wrapped bales of wool swing slowly inboard across the forward well, the red marked bales of long tasselled Tibetan wool going down into Number One hatch under Kamei's watchful eye. Then across the river he saw two more lighters putting out from Chingkiang's sprawling front and he stubbed his cigarette out and went below.

Altmeyer and Cheng were already at the table.

'I'll eat now, Kuang,' he told the boy.

'When do you expect us to be ready to sail, Captain,' Cheng asked across the table.

'About midnight,' Schepke told him. 'Müller already has Three and Four holds battened down.'

'Are you going ashore for the papers yourself, Herr Kapitän?' Altmeyer asked.

Schepke looked at him across the table. 'If you're that anxious to get ashore you can come with me.'

'Who's that?' Müller asked as he came in. 'Who's going ashore?'

264

'The Kapitän and I,' Altmeyer told him.

'I could do with a beer,' Müller said, sitting at the table. 'I heard that there's a couple of places ashore where you can get a drink.'

'That's what Pao said,' Schepke said.

'Do you think I could go along with you?' Müller asked. 'Three and Four are battened down ready for sea. Once One and Two are ready there's only the water-boat to come.'

'How is it with you?' Schepke asked, looking to Cheng.

'By all means. I can manage perfectly.'

'All right,' Schepke said. 'We can go together. I've to call at the Concession, anyway. The bar's along there somewhere.'

'Thank you,' Müller said.

Karl Schepke nodded across the table. The warm breeze was coming in through the open scuttles from the river, bringing the continuous noise of the winches with it.

THEY went ashore in one of the lighters, standing on the open deck, the sun shining brightly above the town and a humid breeze blowing down-river and bringing the drying smell of the banks with it.

'The Concession. How do we find the Concession?' Schepke asked one of the boatmen as they came in to one of the small wharfs.

The boatman pointed ahead at a street opening directly off the front.

'How far?'

The boatman nodded, grinned, and tried to look wise all at the same time.

'Come on,' Schepke told the others, and they started across the front, everyone stopping to look curiously after them as they entered the long narrow street leading up into the town.

'I don't think they ever saw a European before,' Altmeyer said as they walked.

'There's not been many European ships upstream that had their crews allowed ashore,' Schepke said. 'At least not since the Liberation. That's fifteen years ago, or close to it.'

'Who were they liberated from?'

'You don't know?'

Altmeyer shook his head.

'Themselves. That's who they were liberated from, themselves.'

'I never heard anything about that,' Altmeyer said.

'Neither did they until it happened.'

The street appeared endless, full of dingy open-fronted shops, the goods, mostly dishes of rice, vegetables, and curious-looking fish were set out on long wooden trestles on the narrow clay pavements. Many of the walls of the shops and houses were cracked and worn bare to the stonework with the wind and rain, and all along the narrow street the people paused to stare at the three men in the strange uniforms. There was no motor traffic, but a great many soldiers were about, most of them appearing to have come from the north, having the wide-cheekboned faces of the Mongols, all of them wearing baggy greenish uniforms, their legs tightly putteed above their canvas boots and wearing long-peaked caps with the red star on a white background.

Then as the three of them came up the street they saw a high-wheeled military ambulance drawn up close to the pavement. Two medical orderlies came out of a house wearing masks and carrying a blanket-covered stretcher, followed closely by two weeping women in high-collared black coats. Only the head of the man on the stretcher was visible, his face pale, the colour of burnt wax, the eyes sunk deeply in the shaven head. Altmeyer looked from the stretcher to Schepke. Karl Schepke went on walking.

Quite suddenly they came to a broad canal, crossed a heavy wooden bridge, and found all was comparatively quiet after the long narrow street. They had come up out of the lower section of the town around the front and ahead of them was the broad, almost deserted bund of the old Chingkiang Concession with its rows of trees and its one wide pavement.

'Which way?' Müller asked, and the high-wheeled ambulance drove across the bridge past them, then turned fast down the bund toward the old walled city, the wheels raising twin clouds of red dust, the medical orderlies staring out from the open windscreen, still wearing their white masks and only their eyes showing. Then as they crossed the bund, the fine powdery red dust rising under their feet, they met two officers of the Chinese People's Liberation Army coming down the steps outside of a white plaster-work building.

'Excuse us,' Schepke said. 'Can you tell me where I will find Major Pao?'

Both the officers smiled pleasantly.

'Major Pao is at the Customs House,' the taller of the two said, at the same time indicating an old building next door that had a crumbling plaster wall around it.

'And the bar?' Müller asked.

'Of course,' the officer said, still smiling. 'The officers' bar. See?' He pointed out a low stone walled building further along the bund.

'Thank you,' Schepke told him.

They both bowed slightly, saluted, then turned in the direction of the bridge.

'You both go ahead,' Schepke said. 'I'll see you after I get the clearance papers.' He left them and went in through the gateway to the Customs House.

There was a soldier on duty at the desk in the hallway. He was young and impressionable and smartly rose and bowed.

'Major Pao,' Schepke told him. 'I think he expects me.'

The soldier lifted the metal receiver of the desk telephone, pressed the buzzer, then spoke Mandarin rapidly into the mouthpiece.

'How wonderful that you could come ashore, Captain,' the Major said, standing in the doorway across the hall, smiling, wearing a smartly-pressed, well-fitting uniform. 'In another hour I was preparing to leave for the ship myself.'

'I thought the walk might do some good,' Schepke said. The Major stood politely aside to allow him into the room. Inside the room was a large desk and rows of steel filing cabinets ranged along the walls.

'May I ask what time you intend to sail, Captain?'

'About midnight. I'll want the water-boat first.'

'Ah,' the Major said. 'Let me just go and check on the question of water. I believe we were having difficulty of some kind with waterboats this morning.'

He went out leaving the door open.

Karl Schepke crossed behind the desk and looked out from the open french windows. Down below were the gardens, bare but freshly dug, and the dry stone paths, and the cherry trees, and beyond the low plaster-work wall was the bund and the river where it swept in, the sunlight lighting the yellow muddy waters. To the right was a low wooden jetty, the water around it packed tightly with junks and sampans. Further out were anchored a number of larger junks with huge, fiercely staring eyes painted above the heavy bows. Away to the left was the canal, broad and gloomy with the sunlight on its still muddy yellow water. Then as he watched, a platoon of soldiers marched in from the town, bayonets gleaming dully in the sunlight, their marching feet raising the powdery red dust in clouds to hang in the still air. Shortly after they passed came another ambulance, again the red dust billowing up from under its high wheels.

'I am afraid we are having some trouble in the town.' The Major was beside him. 'We are treating everyone at the military hospitals,' he went on, then indicating Schepke to a chair. 'Now, the matter of a water-boat,' he said. 'One is under repair and the other went out to one of the gunboats below the Pass this morning and so far has been unable to return because of engine trouble. Unfortunately our other boat is at Nanking meantime so I hope you can bring your ship in to the north end of China Merchants Wharf. I am told it will be possible to have the required hoses rigged directly to the storage tanks. And I humbly apologize for any inconvenience.'

'I think we can manage.'

'Good. Now here are all your required papers.' He moved a cardboard folder across the desk, at the same time setting out the various receipts. 'For your signature,' he explained, handing Schepke his pen.

Karl Schepke signed the receipts and handed them back.

'You also have instructions there for all shipping proceeding down-river,' the Major said. 'The most important of these is that you display a red light above a green on both sides so that shore installations know you are proceeding with permission. Anyone not following these instructions is liable to be stopped or fired upon without warning. And, of course,' he said, smiling. 'We do not wish to cause you any unnecessary trouble.'

'Of course,' Schepke said.

'And now that our business has been attended to may I offer you a drink?' the Major said, at the same time leaning behind him to slide open the door of a locker to reveal an array of bottles and glasses inside on the shelves. 'I believe it is gin, Captain,' he said, bringing out and setting on the desk two glasses and a bottle of Bols. 'It seems almost as though we catered for you,' he said, smiling.

As they drank, a sudden loud wailing was drowned by an accompaniment of shouts and laughter that carried up along the bund.

'What's happening?' Schepke asked.

'It is not really important,' Major Pao said. 'It is some political prisoners we have.'

Karl Schepke finished his drink, rose, and picked up the folder of ship's papers.

'You are leaving already?' Major Pao asked.

'I'll have to see about bringing the ship alongside,' Schepke told him.

Major Pao rose from the desk and went toward the door. 'I am extremely sorry that time has not allowed me to visit you again. Perhaps next time.'

'Yes,' Schepke said. 'Good-bye, Major.'

'Pleasant voyage, Captain.'

Karl Schepke left the Major in the hallway and went on down

the steps and out onto the bund. The first thing he noticed was that the tall iron gates at the entrance to the bund had been closed and were now guarded by soldiers. Out beyond the jetty people had gathered on the decks of the junks and sampans, staring curiously ashore toward the far end of the bund. Down there the soldiers had gathered in two separate groups outside of a tall building next to the one that had been explained as being the officers' bar.

He started toward them and there was a lot of laughter and shouting among the soldiers but from the way they were gathered it was impossible for him to see what was happening. Then as he neared the bar a hushed silence fell on the soldiers and someone among them began reading aloud in a high formal voice. Stopping outside of the high red-roofed building next to the bar, he saw most of the windows were occupied by army officers and civilians. Then someone shouted again and the soldiers laughed. He went on toward the bar and joined two waiters on the steps. The soldiers had moved into a wide semicircle to reveal two shaven-headed Chinese kneeling in the powdery dust. Both were naked to the waist and had their hands tied behind their backs. Two soldiers stood directly in front of them, holding the men's queues, stretching their necks. Before Schepke fully realized what was happening the executioner stepped forward and measured, then raised the two-handed sword. The head severed and rolled in the dust with the one stroke, the corpse remaining kneeling for a moment before pitching slowly forward, blood spouting from the ugly stump of neck. A loud burst of applause came from the soldiers, and the executioner, smiling widely, stepped across the corpse at his feet, aimed the sword, carefully measuring the distance, then slowly raised it again. The kneeling man remained as he was, unmoving, his eyes opened wide, staring at the blood-spattered powdery dust before him. Karl Schepke turned quickly in through the doorway past the gaping waiters, and as he entered the bar another burst of applause carried in loudly from the bund.

The few people in the bar were gathered around the two windows. Then he saw Müller's back toward him but there was no sign of Altmeyer. As he took a seat at one of the tables Müller came across.

'Were you out there?' he asked. 'Christ, I never saw anything like that.'

'Where's Altmeyer?'

Müller glanced about the bar. 'He was here a few minutes ago.'

Just then they saw him come in from across the hall. He looked pale and he sat down at the table and the two waiters came in from the doorway.

'What do you want?' Schepke asked.

'I'll have whisky,' Müller said, then turned to the waiter. 'One gin and two whiskies.'

'Not for me,' Altmeyer interrupted. 'Nothing for me.'

'One gin and one whisky,' Müller told the waiter.

'I'll have to go back on board after this,' Schepke told them. 'We'll have to come alongside for water.'

'I'll go with you,' Altmeyer said. 'I don't want to stay here.'

Schepke paid the waiter when he came back with the drinks.

'Is it all right if I stay a while?' Müller asked.

'If you want,' Schepke told him. 'Join us at the north end of the China Merchants Wharf. And don't get drunk.'

Müller watched them leave, and after they had gone he rose and went across to the counter. The barman waited for him to sit down. The barman was old and thin and had a deeply wrinkled face.

'The same,' Müller told him, setting his empty glass on the counter.

The two floor waiters were standing together by the windows and the only other person in the bar now was a stout, middle-aged officer with his face in a large newspaper. Then the barman carefully set the drink on the counter and glanced first at the officer, then at the two floor waiters.

'Your ship,' he asked, careful to keep his voice low. 'She is the big one in the river?'

'That's right,' Müller told him. 'What do you want?'

'You sail tonight?'

'For Hong Kong,' Müller said, watching him.

The barman glanced nervously about the bar. 'She is not Communist?' he asked, sweat beginning to show on his brow.

'No. Now what do you want?'

'One must be careful.' The old man swabbed the counter, not looking at Müller while he spoke. Then: 'You wish to make money?' he asked.

'How much?' Müller asked, leaning his elbows onto the counter.

'It is not for me,' the old man explained. 'In a few minutes I finish here. Leave quietly after me.'

'Give me another whisky,' Müller told him, raising his voice again.

When the old man poured the drink he took it to the table nearest the open doorway.

After a while the relief barman came in and the old man changed his coat and came out from behind the counter. Müller let him leave then finished his drink and walked quietly out onto the bund. There were very few people about now and out on the front the headless bodies hung from meat hooks driven into a crude scaffolding. Then he saw the barman a little way down the bund toward the town gateway. He went after him and then the old man turned into an alleyway alongside one of the buildings. It was a high, narrow alleyway running back somewhere from the bund. The old man was already some way ahead and after a few minutes he dropped back and waited to take Müller by the arm and guide him down a narrow opening between buildings.

They came out at the rear of a low, reed-thatched house. There were a number of trees directly behind the house and an area of long grass and weeds growing wild.

'Stay here,' the old man whispered. He started carefully through the grass and weeds toward the house and Müller watched him gain cover of the trees. The buildings they had passed between seemed to be some sort of storehouses, and the surrounding buildings were so high they cut the sunlight off so that everything smelled of dampness and decay. A cold hollow feeling and spread through his stomach and he silently cursed himself for being so foolish as to have come. Then suddenly he heard the sound of feet moving out in the alleyway and he froze, his heart beating loudly up into his throat. At that moment the barman rose from the long grass and beckoned him. Quickly he bent low in the grass and weeds and moved toward the trees.

'It is safe here,' the barman told him. 'No one comes to this place.'

'I heard somebody in the alleyway,' Müller said, the sweat beaded on his forehead and jaw.

The barman glanced back the way they had come then peered toward the rear of the house. All that showed of the house was a narrow window and a rough board door. Then as they watched, they saw the door open and an old man with a beard and long black coat come out and glance casually at the overgrown area of grass and weeds that had once been the garden. After a few moments he returned again to the house, leaving the door slightly open.

'Come,' the barman said, rising swiftly to his feet.

It was dark inside the house and smelling heavily of decay and paraffin fumes.

'You are from the foreign ship?' a voice quietly questioned in the darkness.

'What's all this about?' Müller demanded nervously. The barman was as nervous as Müller now and broke into a hurried stream of Mandarin.

'What's going on?' Müller asked in English.

A match was struck suddenly in the darkness and the old man in the long black coat held the flame to a small paraffin lamp. 'Please,' he said, turning to Müller. 'There is no danger.'

Again the barman spoke and this time the old man brought a bundle of notes from the folds of his coat, and the barman grabbed them and ducked hurriedly out through the doorway.

'Wait!' Müller shouted as he disappeared into the long grass and weeds.

The old man laid his hand on his arm. 'Please,' he said. 'You are safe with me. The soldiers do not come until after darkness.'

'I'll leave now!' Müller said angrily.

'Please,' the old man said, and he was holding an old brown leather bag open at the mouth so the money showed.

'That's American,' Müller said, the anger suddenly gone, putting his hand into the bag and examining some of the money in the light of the lamp. The bills were very old, slightly mildewed, and tightly bound with red silk.

'It is yours if you can help,' the old man said.

'What do you want me to do?' Müller asked, still nervous, but again looking at the open bag.

The old man drew him further into the passage and closed the door. At the far end of the passage was the main room of the house, sparsely furnished and lit by another paraffin lamp. There was one small window at the front of the house and Müller saw out into a courtyard that was cobbled and had a small well close to the house.

'No one will come yet,' the old man assured him. 'I would not have brought you here had there been danger.'

'Hurry up and say what you have to,' Müller told him.

'Now that you are here I hardly know where to begin.'

'How much money have you?' Müller asked, still nervous, the sweat prickling his face and scalp.

'There is a little more than six thousand dollars,' the old man told him. 'I have managed to keep it hidden one way and another since the Liberation.'

'How come that it's American?'

'Many years ago an American used to come to my village from Shanghai to buy my paintings. That time ago it was very much money. Perhaps it has since lost some value but it may still be worth something.'

'What do you want me to do?' Müller was anxious now, glancing out at the courtyard.

'Before Wei-mu left he told me you go next to Hong Kong.'

'Tonight,' Müller said, watching the courtyard.

'It is possible you could take someone?'

'What?' Müller said, unbelieving. 'Did you see what happened on the front today?'

274

'I did not see it, but I know,' the old man answered sadly. 'It happens everywhere in China today.'

Müller drew a deep breath. 'How would you get on board?'

'You could not help with that?' the old man asked.

'Let me see the money again.' He took the bag from the old man and examined a number of the bundles of notes close to the lamp. They were almost all in large bills, many of them partially discoloured and some mildewed. It was a great deal of money. If he could get the old man to Hong Kong he could then ship out for home and still have most of it with him when he arrived. Then he remembered about Schepke having to bring the ship alongside to water.

'What is it you think now?' the old man asked, carefully watching Müller's face in the light of the paraffin lamp. He did not fully trust this man but after tomorrow there would not be another time.

'Can you get to the front without being seen?'

'We could try. There is nothing left to lose.'

'*We?*' Müller said.

'My daughter,' the old explained. 'It is her I wish you to take. She was brought here from Shanghai this morning. Tomorrow we leave for the penal colony north of the river.'

'Where is she now?'

'At the moment she is asleep.'

'I don't know,' Müller told him. 'I don't know what I might be getting into.'

'But you will take her? Please?'

'—I do not go anywhere without my father.' They turned to see her standing in the light just inside the room from the passage.

Müller ran his eyes over the long coat she wore that however loose did not quite hide her figure.

Now she crossed the room to her father and took his arm in hers, holding herself very proudly. Müller watched her while she spoke with her father. Twice she looked at him, her voice rising gently, then her father pleading again. Outside daylight was failing. Müller looked back at them. She had high cheekbones and dark, long-lashed eyes. Her hair was black and tied above her head and reflecting the light of the paraffin lamp.

'What's happening now?'

The old man shrugged helplessly.

'I go only if my father goes,' the girl said, determinedly.

'That's not a lot of money for you both,' Müller told her.

'It is all that we have.'

Müller looked from her to her father. 'All right,' he said. 'If I can get you on board you can both come. But I want some of that money first even for the attempt.'

'Here.' The old man reached the bag out to him. 'Take what you require.'

Müller widened the mouth of the bag and brought out two bundles of notes and put them in his tunic pocket. 'Remember,' he said. 'There are no promises. If I get you on board you're on your own. You never saw me before.'

'Thank you,' the old man said, gratefully.

'The first thing you do is make your own way to the wharf. I don't want to be with you if you're caught.'

'We understand,' the old man said. 'We will leave after the soldiers have been.' He went to the window and looked out to the courtyard. 'They will come soon to make the curfew check. You must wait in the garden. You will be in no danger there. Come, I will show you where to hide. When the soldiers have been we will leave for the river.'

MÜLLER, lying in the damp grass, watched it get dark. It was cool now with the darkness and the dew was falling, and after a time he heard the sound of marching feet beyond the house, a shouted order, and the slam of rifle butts on the cobbles. After a few minutes there came the shouting of further orders and he

276

listened with bated breath to the sound of marching feet as they faded again into the cool night. It was quiet now in the garden except for the buzz of cicadas and the flickering glitter of fireflies up around the trees.

Out in the darkness a bolt moved on the door and the old man came slowly and carefully through the grass and weeds.

'We are ready,' he said very softly in the darkness. 'The soldiers will not come again until morning.' As he spoke the girl took shape beside him, wearing some sort of dark cloak with a wide hood turned up over her head.

'We will go the way you came,' the old man said. 'We will keep a safe distance behind you and if we are stopped you know nothing.'

'You have the money?' Müller asked.

'It is here,' the old man answered, patting his coat. The girl was standing close to him and Müller sensed she carried some sort of small bundle beneath her cloak. Then he turned abruptly and started through the garden. It was very dark in the shadow of the buildings and no stars showed in the sky.

The bund was in near darkness, and the only lights showing were those in the windows of the buildings and the scattered riding lights and carbide lamps on the junks and sampans along by the jetty. He hurried now, his footsteps sounding very quiet in the damp powdery dust of the bund, and as he turned onto the bridge over the canal he paused momentarily and glanced back through the wide gateway. There was no sign of the girl and her father, nothing but the shadowy outlines of the trees and the lighted windows of the buildings high above them. Ahead of him the long narrow street was dark and deserted, the open-fronted shops shuttered and closed. Nearer the front there were lighted windows in the houses and once he passed a tea house and through the bamboo-slatted screen out over the front he glimpsed a number of soldiers sitting inside at long trestle tables.

As he turned onto the front he saw the *Gertrud Lüth* lying some way upstream, her deck-lights lighting the burnt out sheds and wharf. There were few lights along the front and the river

277

was black and running in the pilings of the wharf. A number of partly burnt rail wagons were parked clear of the end of the wharf and he stood into their shadow, watching the street he had just left. The girl was first to appear, walking a little way toward him, then stopping. Then almost immediately he saw the old man come around the corner, walking slowly, carefully keeping to the shadows.

He waited until he saw there was no one following, then stepped out to meet them. The girl was first to see him.

'Are you all right?' he asked when they were with him in the shadow of the wagons.

'We saw no one,' the old man said very quietly. Beside him, his daughter was silent and dark and lost in her wide-hooded cloak.

From the darkness they watched the mouth of the street they had left but no one came out onto the front and after a few minutes Müller turned his attention to the *Gertrud Lüth*. 'Wait here,' he told them. 'If I can get you on board it will be all right. If there's too many people about then I can't do anything.' He could feel them watching him but neither of them spoke.

He started along the front, coming up astern of the ship. The smell of her fires hung heavily across the wharf, damp and acrid and mingling with the smells of the gutted sheds. Huge sections of shed had collapsed and were down into the river where the wharf was built out across the water. Work had already started on the sheds toward the far end and two long, throbbing lines of white canvas hose pipes were strung out along the wharf to rise high over the forward well of the *Gertrud Lüth*. There were a number of people moving on the wharf and as he came up astern he saw they were coolies, baskets on their heads, carrying vegetables from a high-sided truck up on the far end of the wharf by the water storage tanks. Then watching from the deep shadow cast by the fantail, he saw them stack the baskets alongside the midship ladder. After a few moments he turned and went back along the wharf, careful of his footing in the darkness.

They had gone in under one of the wagons.

'Come on,' he said, helping them out. 'Now listen to me,' he said, the sweat beginning to run on his face and neck. 'Do exactly as I say. Understand?'

The old man silently moved his head, not trusting himself to speak now.

They started along the front to the wharf. It was very quiet and dark and the river ran against the pilings below them. Then Müller stopped below the fantail.

'See those baskets?' he asked. 'Next time those coolies start back to the truck I want you to get one of them on your head and follow me up the ladder. And whatever happens, keep walking.' All the while he was talking he was watching the coolies stack the baskets.

'Now,' he said.

The baskets nearest the ladder were filled with white cabbage. He quickly lightened the top two, took the small bundle from the girl then glanced overhead at the alleyway. Up the end of the wharf he saw the coolies start back.

'Hurry!' he urged, helping the old man with the wide basket.

The girl was right behind him as he started up the long ladder. Then as he stepped into the alleyway he heard someone call them from below.

'This way,' he told the girl and started aft to the well.

A sudden shout brought them to a halt as they neared the end of the alleyway and he quickly stepped aside and pushed the girl on toward the well, seeing Kamei as he stood outside of the screen door.

'It's the vegetables!' he called. 'They're bringing them on board now. I'll see to it.' He turned his back and went on out to the well without waiting for Kamei to reply.

The girl and her father were cowered flat against the casing by one of the engine-room fanlights. Quickly he thrust the bundle into the girl's hands then kicked both baskets under the tarpaulin covering Number Three donkey engine.

'Up there!' he said, pointing to the vertical ladder to the boat-deck.

Keeping close to the housing, he hurried them forward, the

port wing of the bridge dark and deserted. The boatdeck locker was already open.

'Inside!' he told them, thrusting the girl in first.

The locker was long and narrow, cluttered with spare boat gear and cordage. From beyond the steel inboard bulkhead came the steady low humming whine of electric motors in the Radio Office.

'You'll be all right here,' he said into the darkness. 'I'll lock the door after me. Now the money.'

He heard the old man move in the darkness and found the bag thrust into his hand. Closing the door, he pulled the clasps hard down across the stops and snapped on the heavy padlock. Then in the light of the after end of the boatdeck he rapidly transferred the money to the pockets of his tunic and tossed the empty bag below to the river.

The first of the coolies were already on board when he reached the after well and he led them across to the long wire cages inside the fantail tunnel.

'Müller!'

Looking overhead, he felt his stomach knot up tightly as he saw Schepke on the after end of the boatdeck.

'Müller! Is that you, Müller?'

'Yes?'

'All right,' Schepke told him. 'I didn't know you were back.'

'I've been seeing to the stores.'

'Stand by to let go as soon as we're through taking water. The pilots are already on board.'

Müller, standing in the glow of the overhead derrick-lights, watched him turn and walk back toward the cabin deck passage. It was a long way down-river and now he wished that he had never met the old man and his daughter, but six thousand American dollars was a lot of money.

'Come on!' he shouted at the coolies. 'Get the rest of those vegetables on board!'

THEY had made good time down-river during the night and as daylight began to come in a breeze came up out of the north-east and took the night clouds out to the ocean. It was a fine, clear morning with the early daylight, and the stars and the moon were low down and still bright above the low rolling south shore and the fishing craft working the banks still burned their stern flares and the small fishing villages were huddled closely together as if against the great rolling emptiness of the vast shores.

Then as the *Gertrud Lüth* came within sight of the forts at Woosung, Karl Schepke slowed her, letting the current take her down while he watched the pilot boat put out.

'We came down there in good time,' Hechler said as he came onto the bridge, pausing to take a deep breath of the cool morning air coming in through the dropped down windows.

'The old pilot told me it's worst above Nanking,' Schepke said.

'Well I don't want to be here when the floods come,' Hechler replied. 'Neither here nor above Nanking. There must be an easier life than this.'

'I know what you mean,' Schepke told him. 'Simple and uncomplicated. Like some woman you imagine but never find. I thought about it a long time ago.' While he spoke he watched the pilot boat begin to close. Below him he saw Kamei with the ladder out and the two pilots waiting by the bulwarks. Then turning, he saw Cheng waiting alongside Pulst on the wheel for the next order.

'Altmeyer told me there was an execution ashore,' Hechler said. 'Not that he said much about it.'

'I think it's changed his ideas some,' Schepke said. 'The bloom and wonder has begun to go. Maybe it's better for the disillusionment to come altogether than grow a little at a time. I wouldn't have wanted it a little at a time.'

281

'He's a good boy,' Hechler said.

'You should talk him into going home if von Pittkamer can fix anything.'

'I think he's still at the point where he wants to see the world,' Hechler said.

'The world can come later,' Schepke told him. 'Maybe it would be better if none of us ever saw it.' The pilot boat was abeam of them, coming around and downstream, closing the ladder. All that was taking the ship down now was the current, and Kamei had both pilots out ready on the ladder.

'All clear! Half ahead!' Schepke called as he saw the pilots drop cleanly onto the foredeck of the boat as it started to turn away.

'What about yourself?' Hechler asked. 'What are you going to do?'

'I don't like thinking about it. It just happens. I'm not Altmeyer. I've seen it all. There's no dreams.'

'I'd go home for a while, anyway,' Hechler persisted. 'Think about it.'

'Everything's something that happens,' Schepke told him. 'I don't want to know what's going to happen. Maybe if you knew what was going to happen you'd jump over the wall here and now.'

Hechler looked out across the river at the forts at Woosung, but remained silent. And anyway to the east the sun was rising and the rays were filling the bridge with its new light.

'Forget it,' Schepke said, suddenly. 'I don't know anything. I'm not one of the bright boys. But we've got one with us,' he said quietly, glancing at Cheng. 'I knew he was one of the bright boys first time I saw him. Müller's another, though he's not a thinker. But he's bright just the same. So's our Mr. Wang.'

'Well I hope he's bright enough to find another Chief,' Hechler said.

'Come on,' Schepke said, smiling. 'Let's go to breakfast.'

LATE in the evening of the second night out from Chingkiang the *Gertrud Lüth* was below the bleak Formosa Straits and headed south toward Hong Kong. Karl Schepke stood leaning on the ledge of the window, the night-glasses hanging by their strap around his neck. The ship moved slowly, lazily, the long smooth swell lifting in out of the vast China Sea. The night was bright with moonlight and there was no breeze and the ocean was black and silent and meeting the sky.

'Kapitän! Herr Kapitän!'

He turned as Altmeyer almost fell through the doorway.

'What is it?' he asked, and Altmeyer stood aside, and below in the passage he saw Kamei effortlessly holding the girl in his massive hands, her head tilted back, her hair almost touching the deck.

'Where the hell did she come from?' Schepke demanded as he went swiftly down the stairway.

'There is another one,' Kamei told him.

'He's on the boatdeck,' Altmeyer explained. 'They were in one of the lockers.'

'In here,' Schepke said, opening the door to the big cabin.

Kamei laid the girl carefully onto the bunk. 'I will bring the other one.'

'Altmeyer,' Schepke said. 'Get some water and a towel.' He was leaning over the girl, lifting her head to the pillow. She was still unconscious, her face pale and waxy-looking beneath her dark hair.

'Do you think she will be all right, Herr Kapitän?' Altmeyer asked, back with one of the galley bowls, broken ice floating in cubes on top of the water.

Schepke took the towel, wrung it out, then folded it across the girl's forehead. 'Who found them?'

283

'I did,' Altmeyer said. 'I went to switch on in the office and I heard a moaning sound on the other side of the bulkhead. I knew there was a locker there and when I went to get the key from the board I saw it wasn't there. I was on my way to tell you when I met the bosun. He broke the lock off.'

Just then Kamei came in with the old man and Schepke immediately stood up from the bunk. 'Good Christ! Him! I met him when we were in Shanghai.'

'I think somebody knows they are on board,' Kamei said. 'The door was locked and the clasps were down.'

Schepke touched the old man's head, fingering the long bruise down the left temple. 'They must have almost suffocated in there. You better get the bedding from my cabin,' he said, turning to Altmeyer.

Kamei nodded silently toward the bunk. Schepke turned to see the girl watching them with wide apprehensive eyes.

'Who brought you on board?' he asked her in English.

The girl cowered a little, looking at her father in Kamei's massive hands.

'Where will I put the bedding?' Altmeyer asked.

'Here by the bunk,' Schepke told him, then stood aside while Kamei laid the old man down.

The girl sat up suddenly. 'My father,' she said in English. 'He is all right?'

'He will be,' Schepke said, curtly. 'Who brought you on board?'

This time the girl looked away from him to her father. Schepke watched her, his mind moving rapidly over the movements of the day they had sailed from Chingkiang. The old man was moaning softly now as Altmeyer again applied the cold towel to his forehead.

'Stay with them,' Schepke told Kamei, and went out and pulled the door shut behind him. In his cabin he took the Walther he had bought in Flower Market Road from the wardrobe and put it into the pocket of his tunic.

Müller was asleep, the cabin lit only by the light coming in through the open scuttle from the boatdeck.

'Müller! —Müller!'

284

Müller stirred and opened his eyes, blinking against the brightness of the cabin lights.

'Get up!' Schepke said and levelled the Walther directly at his jaw.

Müller stiffened and slowly sat up, his face heavy with sleep but watching Schepke very carefully.

'Get dressed!'

While Müller pulled on his uniform Schepke went down through the drawers of the dressing-table, covering Müller all the while with the Walther. The money was in the bottom drawer, under some clothing.

'All right,' he told Müller, kicking the drawer shut behind him and motioning Müller out ahead of him into the passage.

The old man was sitting up when they entered, and Schepke put the Walther into his pocket, Kamei looking from one to the other, only his eyes moving.

'Go down to Müller's cabin and get the money from the bottom drawer of the dressing-table,' he told Altmeyer.

'That money belongs to me,' Müller said sullenly.

Schepke hit him suddenly on the mouth and he went back and down against the outboard bulkhead. He sat looking up dazedly at Schepke, licked his lips, then put up an arm and wiped his mouth with the back of his hand, seeing the blood. Again he licked his lips, then spat.

'I am afraid it is my fault entirely,' the old man said very quietly.

'Shut up,' Schepke told him. 'I don't want to hear it.' The anger had been slow but now welled suddenly.

'But I wish to—' the old man started to say.

'Shut up!' Schepke shouted, his face fierce and white under his high peaked cap.

The old man slowly dropped his head forward onto his chest. At the same time Müller dragged himself up and stood leaning his back against the bulkhead as Altmeyer came back with the money. Taking it, Schepke threw it at the old man's feet. 'Call Hong Kong and tell them we've got two stowaways on board.'

'Yes, sir,' Altmeyer said, and went out, glancing at the girl.

The girl had not looked at any of them since Schepke had knocked Müller down, and now she sat looking at her folded hands.

'Get out,' Schepke said turning to Müller. 'Kamei. Put a man outside the door and see nobody comes in here.'

'You are taking us to Hong Kong?' the girl asked, looking at him now, not quite knowing what to think, her voice sounding very small.

Karl Schepke looked at her for a moment, then turned suddenly and went out. There was something familiar about it all, something he knew, and he did not want any part of this thing and he did not want to think about any of it.

'Herr Kapitän! Kapitän, sir!'

He came quickly awake, sitting up and seeing Altmeyer by the bunk.

'This just came through, sir.' Altmeyer handed him the signal pad.

> *Already in receipt of direct notification from Shanghai re stowaways. Do not inform Immigration Authorities. Will meet ship.*
>
> *H. L. Wang.*

Schepke read it then looked at his wrist watch. It was just after four o'clock in the morning.

'All right,' he said, dismissing the boy, then lighting a cigarette and sitting on the edge of the bunk.

'—Sir.'

'What is it?'

'What will happen to them, sir?'

Schepke shrugged. 'I don't think they could ever have really got away.'

286

'She's very beautiful,' Altmeyer said, a little self-consciously.
'I know.'

'Well good night, sir.'

Karl Schepke, sitting on the edge of the bunk, did not answer.
Then when Altmeyer had gone he put his tunic on and went
aft to the galley.

Hechler, having just completed the middle watch, was pouring
coffee.

'It's close tonight.'

Schepke looked in at him. 'It's not much of a night for sleeping.'

Hechler poured another mug full of coffee, dripped milk from
a can into it, and stirred methodically. Sweat gleamed on his face
and neck and his overalls smelled sharply of drying sweat and
the clammy, oil and steam atmosphere of the engine-room.

Schepke took the coffee from him and led the way out onto
the boatdeck. High astern of them was the fantail, the housing
silvered with moonlight. The moon was away far to the south-
west, the bright silver riding the smooth lifting swell. The only
stirring of the humid air was that caused by the passage of the
ship through the black water. The coffee was hot and bitter and
smelled of the canned milk. Below them, the water washed and
hissed whitely, bubbling and foaming on the outward rush from
the ship's side. Far out the ocean was quiet and there were no
other lights in the early morning. Astern of them the wake stood
out long and straight and coral white in the vast lifting blackness of the ocean.

'Dorsch told me about the old man and the girl,' Hechler
said after a while.

'They might just have got away with it if they had been
ordinary Chinese.'

Hechler looked at him. 'What are they, some sort of celebri-
ties?'

'I met the old man that time in Shanghai. We were in the
park. It was quite accidentally.'

'Who is he?'

'He's some sort of artist. At least that's what he told me. The girl's his daughter. He talked about them being politically suspect or something. I didn't take it all in at the time. He was acting sort of strange. Like maybe he was expecting somebody to leap out of the trees.'

'They don't sound dangerous to me,' Hechler said. 'But how did they get from Shanghai to Chingkiang if they're political suspects. People like that don't get to move around as they want.'

'I never asked them. But it's since struck me as strange as well,' Schepke said, remembering the last time he had seen the old man was him crossing the roadway outside of the park.

'What about Chingkiang?' Hechler asked. 'Won't they be missed?'

'They've been missed. I just had a signal from Wang. I don't really think they could ever have made it. Anyway, I don't know the immigration procedure for landing anybody in Hong Kong.'

'The Limeys will have plenty of regulations for that. They've got regulations for everything. They thrive on them.' Hechler emptied his mug out over the wall. 'Well I'll leave you to it,' he said. 'I want to get some sleep before morning.'

Karl Schepke shook a cigarette out and lit it. It was quiet and peaceful on deck and there was nothing but the steady hum of below deck machinery and the sound of the ocean washing against the hull.

After a time he went inside and returned the mug to the galley before going forward. The old man was sitting at the table. He seemed a very meek and tired old man and he had a long livid bruise down his left temple. The girl was quietly asleep on the bunk, her face turned away from the lighting. Motioning the old man to be seated again, he joined him at the table.

'Hong Kong already knew about you,' he said. 'Shanghai had wirelessed the company.'

The old man sat and looked steadily at him but did not say anything.

'I don't think you could ever have made it,' Schepke told him. 'Ordinary coolies, maybe.'

'I see that now. Perhaps I saw it before but did not allow myself to think about it. It was thoughtless and selfish of me. I am profoundly sorry for the trouble I have caused you.' He looked directly at Schepke while he spoke. 'But it was not for myself,' he went on again quietly. 'My own time here is almost over. It is my daughter for whom I am saddened.' The sadness was in all of him, in his bearing, in his eyes, and in his voice. He had a pleasant old face, the flesh about the corners of his eyes deeply wrinkled, and his beard growing white and wispy.

'What will happen when they take you back?'

'I would rather not think,' the old man said very quietly. 'It will come soon enough.'

'What about your daughter?'

The old man looked at the table.

'Does she understand?'

'I think so. She is a very brave and sensible daughter. I am very proud of her.'

'I don't think there's much I can do.'

'She will manage well. The Chinese have many proverbs. One says: Fish swim at the bottom of the sea, yet the angler hooks them; birds fly high in the heavens, but the marksman brings them down; only the depths of the human heart cannot be fathomed.'

Karl Schepke rubbed his cigarette out. He wanted to change the subject now.

'Do you mind if I ask what you were doing in Chingkiang?'

'I am afraid we were arrested the evening of that day in Shanghai. I was sent to Chingkiang before going on to the penal colony north of the river. I am told there are large and secret factories to be worked in.'

'What did they arrest you for?'

The old man lightly shrugged. 'It was a certain Major Pao. He is of the Special Police. He did not explain why, but does anyone in China today bother to explain anything? There is nothing—'

'Father!' The girl had wakened suddenly and was watching them.

'Rest child,' her father said. 'We only talk. There is nothing to worry about.'

Karl Schepke, feeling suddenly awkward under her gaze, shook out another cigarette. She lay with her head on the pillow, watching his every movement.

'What are you called?' Schepke said, looking again to the old man.

'Chao Kang-nien,' the old man answered politely. 'My daughter is called Fu-chen.'

Karl Schepke felt himself becoming involved. He wanted to get up quickly and leave. And since the girl had wakened she had watched him continuously.

He rose from the table. 'I'm sorry I will not be able to help,' he said.

'No. Please do not feel sorrow,' the old man told him. 'In this world there are both wakers and dreamers. It is just that I am a dreamer.'

'Good night,' Schepke said. And he did not look again at the girl.

She watched the door close quietly behind him.

'I do not like him, Father.'

'My child,' her father said sadly. 'Where there are no scars there has been no battle.'

And the ship moved very smoothly through the dark, moonlit ocean.

KARL SCHEPKE swung the ship's head out through Lei U Mun Pass, putting the foremast directly in line with Whampoa Dock, and started the long easy run in past Shaukiwan, and Sai Wan Ho, and past Taikoo Dock and Quarry Bay, and on around North Point, putting Whampoa Dock astern on the starboard quarter, Kowloon spread out white and hot in the brilliant after-noon sunlight, all the water of the harbour flat and the deep blue of the sky, Sugar Loaf Peak and Big Hat Mountain cleanly outlined and high and sharp, looming above the foothills beyond the city. Across the harbour the high hills of Hong Kong stood up clean and fresh and green against the sky. Then as he brought the *Gertrud Lüth* around Tsim Sha Tsui he saw them gathered on the wharf by Peking Road, a tight little knot of people watching the ship swing around into view.

As he rang off the main engines he saw Mr. Wang and Mr. Sung start down the wharf. Pushing his cap back off his forehead, he turned and went below.

They were waiting for him in the passage.

'Well how did it happen?' Mr. Wang asked, annoyed.

'How did what happen?' Schepke asked him.

'These people! How did they get on board?'

'Don't talk to me like that,' Schepke told him, not thinking much of either of them.

'But this is a very serious situation,' Mr. Wang countered, but having lost some of his fire. 'Shanghai is extremely upset. These persons are enemies of the people.'

'They don't look much like radicals to me,' Schepke said, evenly.

Mr. Wang ignored him, looking at the man outside the big cabin. 'They are in there?'

Schepke nodded, and they both started for the door.

'They will have to be returned to China as soon as possible,' Mr. Wang said, considering the outcome beyond question. 'You will put them ashore as soon as it can be arranged. The police and immigration authorities know nothing as yet.'

'Not me,' Schepke told him. 'I don't put anybody ashore. That's an offence in itself.'

'Very well, Captain,' Mr. Wang said, smiling his superiority.

Mr. Sung had said nothing at all and now he followed them into the big cabin.

The girl and her father were waiting, standing close together, unsure of what to expect.

Mr. Wang set his brief-case on the table and regarded them coldly. The girl's eyes met his and her chin lifted slightly. She was wearing a severely-cut blue cheongsam and had her hair pinned high on her head. Then Mr. Wang turned again to the old man and sharply asked him something in Mandarin. The old man answered him very quietly, looking directly at him, then at Mr. Sung.

'What's happening?' Schepke asked.

'He tells me they came on board by themselves,' Mr. Wang said. 'Is that correct?'

'Do you think I had something to do with it?' Schepke asked.

Mr. Wang smiled politely. 'I had not thought about it,' he said. 'Now, Captain, if you would kindly leave us for a few minutes.'

Karl Schepke looked at the girl and her father. They stood very humbly across on the other side of the table. There was nothing he could do and he stepped quietly out into the passage and waited.

After a while Mr. Wang came out followed by Mr. Sung, both of them looking a little happier in themselves.

'Did you find out all you wanted?' Schepke asked them.

'I think so,' Mr. Wang said. 'I am just disappointed that this had to happen. You see, we also had information through Shanghai that you had previously been seen with the old man. However, I now believe that was purely coincidental. The old man swears he did not know that it was your ship until the night they were discovered.'

'You know a lot for somebody so far removed,' Schepke said.

'Let us just say that I look after our mutual interests,' Mr. Wang said, blandly. 'But rest assured, Captain, you are completely exonerated from the whole business. I am glad.'

'Think nothing of it,' Schepke told him.

'As I have already said, they will go ashore as soon as it is possible. However, I do not think it wise to move them at the moment and it may be late Sunday evening or Monday morning before we can do anything.'

'How are you going to get them back across the border?'

Mr. Wang smiled his superiority again. 'There should be no difficulty, Captain. As far as the girl and her father are concerned they believe they will be remaining on board until the ship returns later to Shanghai. But that is not for you to worry about. The *Gertrud Lüth* sails directly for Kobe this time. The *Fenching Liberator* arrives tonight from Canton with a cargo of oil and paint containers and electrical fittings. For the present you off-load everything except Number One hold. That, too, is for Kobe.'

'All right,' Schepke said. 'But the old man and the girl is your worry. You can land them any way you want.'

'Of course, Captain,' Mr. Wang said, smiling.

Karl Schepke went below with them. Out on deck, Cheng was already clearing away the after hatches. Schepke, leaning on the alleyway rail, watched the two of them walk back across the wharf to their car on the corner of Peking Road; the two of them, very confident, their oiled-down hair shining smoothly in the sunlight.

HE was in the messroom when Menzies came on board. Dinner was over and they were drinking coffee.

'This is a surprise,' he said rising, taking Menzies' hand.

'I thought it would be pleasant to see how you were,' Menzies said, glancing at Cheng and Altmeyer.

Karl Schepke led the way out onto the boatdeck, the clatter of winches carrying up loudly from the wells as the transfer of cargo began from the *Fenching Liberator* berthed on the starboard side.

'Is there something I can do for you?'

'I heard you have someone on board,' Menzies said, watching his face.

Karl Schepke leaned his foot on the port rail. 'Who told you?'

Menzies smiled. 'That sort of news travels fast.'

'It gets more complicated the more you know about it,' Schepke said. 'It's an old man and his daughter. They seem harmless enough. The old man's some sort of artist. I believe the girl was an actress. That's all I know.'

'I hear that Shanghai was upset,' Menzies said. 'That's what made me more inquisitive. Are you taking them back?'

'Listen,' Schepke said. 'What happens to anybody coming in through the New Territories?'

'Well most of them have been turned back lately.'

'What if these two had come in that way?'

Menzies shrugged. 'It depends on who they are. If it's anyone important enough, and with good grounds for asylum, they usually stay. As it is, you haven't landed them, and technically, they're still on foreign soil.'

'Is there any means of finding out what could happen to them?'

'You wouldn't be thinking of landing them, would you?' Menzies asked, watching his face closely again.

Karl Schepke looked back at him but made no reply.

'All right,' Menzies told him. 'Come across and see me tomorrow.' They walked toward the ladder to the after well. 'By the way, what's the old man's name?'

'Chao Kang-nien,' Schepke told him. 'At least that's what he told me.'

Menzies looked at his wrist watch. 'Then I'll see you tomorrow,' he said and started below.

Karl Schepke waited until he was ashore then turned back into the cabin passage.

The old man was sitting quietly at the table while the girl was looking out through one of the scuttles toward Victoria.

'You can go out on deck if you wish,' Schepke told her.

She did not look at him. The bright sunlight coming in through the scuttle fell on her hair and face.

'Believe me,' he told her.

This time she looked to her father.

'That is extremely kind of you,' the old man told him.

He walked out with them to the boatdeck. The hard afternoon sunlight reflected glaringly from the bleached decking, a cool, lightly-moving breeze gently ruffling the deeply-blue waters of the harbour. Across the harbour, below the dwelling-studded Peak, the tall, many-storied buildings of Central Victoria stood up brightly white and angular.

'What do you think of it?' he asked.

'It is very beautiful,' the girl said. 'There is so much to see. So much people and traffic.'

'It's better at night,' he told her.

'It is even more beautiful?' she said, this time looking up at his face shadowed under the peak of his cap.

'Well not altogether to me,' he said, smiling. He had not seen her smile yet and he wondered how it would be when she smiled.

'I'm sorry to interrupt.' It was Hechler, dressed ready to go ashore. 'I'm going across to see von Pittkamer now,' he said.

'I hope you'll be lucky,' Schepke told him, then introduced him to the old man and his daughter.

'I am pleased to have finally met you,' Hechler said.

They both politely bowed their acknowledgement.

'I just saw Wang coming across the dock,' he then said to Schepke.

'Please excuse us,' Schepke said.

They met Mr. Wang coming up the main stairway.

'Ah, there you are, Captain,' Mr. Wang said. 'And how are you, Chief?'

'Fine. Great,' Hechler said and walked past him and went on down the stairway without looking at him.

Mr. Wang shrugged, then turned again to Schepke. 'May I talk with you?'

'All right,' Schepke told him. 'Come on up to the bridge.'

'It is the old man and his daughter,' Mr. Wang said when they were on the bridge. 'Arrangements have been made to take them ashore early Monday morning. There will be someone here to collect them. Had the *Liberator* not been bound for Singapore there would have been no difficulty. But as it is we can still manage. Now when do you expect to complete off-loading?'

Karl Schepke looked at his wrist watch. 'There's only Number Two left. We should be through with it about six o'clock. We've already started the transfer to Three and Four.'

'Good. Good,' Mr. Wang said. 'All I ask you to do now is to see both are ready to go ashore when the time comes. You will do that?'

'Of course.'

'Thank you, Captain,' Mr. Wang said, smiling that smooth superior smile again. 'Now you must excuse me. I have other business.'

Karl Schepke, watching from the port wing, saw him go ashore. The old man and his daughter were still on the boatdeck. They, too, were watching Mr. Wang walk quickly up the wharf and across the dock toward Peking Road.

'Excuse me, Captain,' Cheng said as he entered the bridge. 'I thought you would like to know that we can finish Number Two hold in another two hours.'

'Good,' Schepke said, still looking out to the boatdeck from the after windows.

'Do we know yet what is to happen to them?' Cheng asked, looking at the old man and his daughter.

'It's got nothing to do with me,' Schepke told him. 'That's political.'

'She is a very beautiful woman,' Cheng said.

Karl Schepke looked back at him.

'I saw Mr. Wang leave a few minutes ago,' Cheng said, changing the subject.

'He was in a hurry,' Schepke said, crossing to the charthouse.

'What about Müller?' Cheng asked, hesitatingly.

'What about him?' Schepke said, stopping in the doorway.

Cheng shrugged. 'I just thought maybe you would have sent him ashore. After all, he started this business. He could have caused a great deal more trouble for us than he did.'

'What makes you think Müller had anything to do with it?' Schepke asked, watching him closely.

Cheng smiled. 'Please do not let us fool ourselves, Captain. Someone must have brought them on board and it was certainly not you or the boy. But no one saw Müller come back. He boarded the ship from the China Merchants Wharf.'

'You've thought about it all, haven't you? You're one of the bright boys, all right,' Schepke said, watching him. 'As far as you're concerned, Müller stays on board. I'd rather have somebody I know I can't trust than have somebody I don't know anything about.'

'Then I assume you do not altogether trust me, Captain,' Cheng said, watching his face.

'You can assume anything you want,' Schepke told him and went on into the charthouse. Leaning on the chart table, he listened to Cheng go below, and suddenly the beach seemed relatively simple.

They were still on the boatdeck when he went out, the old man pointing out some particular sight toward Green Island. The girl was very beautiful in the sunlight and the severely-cut cheongsam did not altogether hide her figure.

'What do you think of it?' he asked, nodding toward Victoria out there across the deeply blue water.

The girl looked to her father. 'There is much beauty,' he said, simply.

'How would you like to go ashore?' Schepke suddenly asked the girl.

She looked at him, then to her father.

'Well?' Schepke asked him.

'It is possible?'

'I assure you no harm will come to her.'

The old man turned and spoke something to his daughter, and she looked again at Schepke with dark, long-lashed eyes.

'My daughter will be delighted. Thank you,' the old man said.

Karl Schepke glanced at the girl but her face showed nothing.

'We—we can go now if you're ready,' he said, finally, feeling slightly awkward.

She said something to her father, and he smiled, and Karl Schepke led the way below.

As they started across the dock he glanced back and saw Cheng watching them from the forepeak.

'This way,' he told her and they went out onto Canton Road, not talking, the girl walking very quietly by his side, and when they reached Salisbury Road he saw there was a ferry at the pier and he hurried now across the wide expanse of shimmering tarmac to the ferry entrance, and they went in and down to the pier and up the long wooden ramp to the ferry. There were only a few people on board and the sunlight came in very brightly through the saloon windows, and the girl sat very quietly as the ferry started across the harbour, the sunlight on her fine skin and on her hair tied carefully up high on her head.

It was a long and uncomfortable silence across the harbour and Karl Schepke looked out past her to the busy front with the sunlight riding the deeply blue water, and he thought two or three times to say something but changed his mind. Then when the ferry docked he led the way up past the New City Hall to Connaught Road Central. The road was very busy and, when crossing, a taxi came close and he reached his hand to her arm and felt her recoil at the touch and he withdrew his hand immediately. She did not look at him but merely walked at his side in the manner of two pedestrians walking in a street in the same direction and by some accident walking at the same pace.

'Do you mind if I look for Hechler?' he asked when they had gone a little way.

She looked up at him momentarily but did not say anything, and he turned down the narrow side street that led toward the Viaduct Bar.

Hechler was at the counter when they went in and Schepke saw the surprise on his face when he saw the girl with him.

'I thought you might be here,' he said, then turned to the girl. 'What would you like to drink?'

She looked along the sparkling array of bottles on the mirrored shelves. 'I am afraid I do not know any of them,' she said, finally.

Schepke glanced at Hechler, and Hechler raised his brows, careful to put Schepke between him and the girl.

'Three gins,' he then told the waiting barman. 'Put limes in one of them.'

'Did you see von Pittkamer?'

'You'll never guess,' Hechler said. 'The *Kota Pinang* is due here in two weeks before going up to Yokohama. Von Pittkamer's

298

already been in touch with the company and she's going to pick us up on the way home. She'll take us all.'

'Then make sure Altmeyer goes with you.'

'I won't ask about you,' Hechler told him, then glanced at the girl. 'On the other hand I'd give a lot to know what's going through your mind now.'

'Forget it.'

Hechler pulled a long, knowing face. The girl was quietly watching the people in the bar, and Schepke saw her drink still untouched.

'Won't you try it?' he asked her.

She looked up at him, then slowly sipped her drink.

'Like it?'

She nodded lightly. She had tremendously long eyelashes that curled upward and reflected the light.

'Have another one. Please,' he said.

They each had another drink, then Hechler said: 'What have you two got in mind now?'

Karl Schepke shrugged. 'I just thought I would take her ashore.'

'You didn't bring the old man.'

Schepke just looked at him.

'Of course, that's entirely different,' Hechler said, grinning.

'What about you?' Schepke asked, changing the subject.

'There's a race meeting out at Happy Valley. I thought about going down there for an hour before going back to give Dorsch and Fraunheim the good tidings.'

'What about this trip?'

Hechler rubbed a hand across his jaw. 'I'll tell you when I've seen the others,' he said.

Schepke turned to see the girl watching them. 'I'm sorry we have to talk like this,' he said, apologizing. Then: 'Would you like to go to the races?'

She looked up at him, a shadow of a smile touching her mouth, and her lips were smooth and wet and mirroring the light. She was very beautiful and her eyes had a way of seeming bottomless.

Hechler asked the barman to call them a taxi, and they sat together and finished their drinks.

It was a long run down through Wanchai to Happy Valley and when they arrived there was only the last race to be ran. Karl Schepke bought the programmes as they made their way to the paddock. The horses were circling with their boys. There were nine horses. They went around the paddock one after the other, and there was one grey in the race. Then as they watched, the bell rang for saddling, and with the boys holding the horses by their heads the jockeys in brilliantly coloured silks swung up into the saddle and headed the horses out onto the course toward the start.

'Is there one you like?' Schepke asked the girl.

Hechler was watching the horses go out through the gate.

'That one,' the girl said, pointing to the grey as it left the paddock.

'What about you, Hans?'

Hechler grinned. 'They all look the same to me.'

Schepke took some money from the pocket of his tunic, counted it, then gave it to him. 'Put that on the grey,' he said. The grey was Number Four on the programme and was called Noon Express.

They waited for Hechler to return with the tickets then made their way up to the nearside of the winning post. They were eventually some way below the post and Schepke wondered if they would be able to tell which horse was first to go by. Then suddenly, there was an excited shout from further down the course and the horses came very fast in the five furlong sprint, split into two groups, the grey disputing the lead on the nearside, the jockey showing him the whip. They came very fast and the turf shuddered as they went past. As they went away it was difficult to see what was happening on the nearside and all the horses appeared to go past the post together.

'It was close,' he said to the girl. She had been watching him. Her eyes had taken on a new depth and suddenly she smiled, not widely, not merrily, but a simple little smile that showed her even white teeth. And she had a beautifully simple smile.

'It was second,' he heard Hechler say and he looked up to see the numbers in the frame and saw Number Seven had won, with Noon Express second, beaten a short head.

'It was very close,' he told the girl. She moved her eyes to meet his but she did not say anything this time.

'What about a beer?' Hechler asked.

They walked to the gate they had come in by. Everyone appeared to be walking for the same gate and the road outside was blocked by people and traffic. They stopped in the crowd outside a white stucco-fronted hotel on Morrison Hill Road. There was a large revolving door opening from the street to the air-conditioned lobby. As they crossed the lobby a young, evening-suited Chinese swiftly rose from the desk and smilingly stopped them.

'What is it?' Schepke asked him.

The young man coughed discreetly. 'The lady, sir,' he said so very humbly. 'I am afraid the hotel may be used by Europeans only, sir.'

'And you,' Schepke said, looking down at him. 'What about you?'

The Chinese drew himself up haughtily and looked past them to the door. Then as Schepke shifted his weight slightly he felt the girl gently touch his sleeve.

'Please,' she said. 'Do not make trouble because of me.'

'She's right,' Hechler said. 'Come on, let's get out of here.'

They went back outside and a taxi had stopped at the door and two English Navy officers were getting out. Schepke waited until they had paid off the driver then asked him to take them to the Kwangtung Hotel. He was still annoyed about the whole business and he stayed silent during the journey uptown. Then when they reached the Kwangtung, Pancho came out to meet them. There was no one else in the bar and they sat at a table close to the counter and Pancho brought the drinks.

'You have come here before?' the girl asked, making the conversation for the first time.

'I lived here for a time, Schepke told her. 'Before we went to China.'

'And before?'

'Before that I lived in Singapore.' She had been watching him since they entered the bar and now he could see Hechler feeling a little awkward.

Then when they finished their second drink Hechler rose and gathered his cap from the space under the table. 'I better get back now,' he said. 'I'll have to find out what we're going to do. Enjoy yourselves.'

They watched him walk out into the hallway.

'If I remember correctly, I think your father said you were an actress,' Schepke said when Hechler had left. 'Was that on films?'

'Sometimes,' she answered. 'Mostly in China one studies for the stage.'

'What made you want to escape? Film-making and acting must be more or less the same the world over.'

'Not today,' she said. 'Today there is nothing in China. Or at least there is little that is good. The ghosts have become landlords and the dragons capitalists. And even the Mayoral minutes can become a film now.'

'I wish it was possible for me to help.'

She smiled, sadly. 'I do not think it could ever have ended the way one dreams. I know that now. Perhaps I knew it all along. But you, you have been too kind.'

Karl Schepke now felt he wanted to get away hurriedly before the gloom settled again. 'Pancho,' he called to the boy. 'Do you know where we can have supper?'

The boy considered it carefully, his young face lifted to the ceiling.

'I know, he said, glancing smilingly sideways at the girl. 'You go to Aberdeen. Many big floating restaurants. Everything very beautiful.'

'Can you get us a taxi?'

They finished their drinks and went out to the doorway. Pancho was waiting with the taxi. Schepke tipped him and he grinned in the open window at them.

'You come back stay sometime?' he asked.

302

'Sometime,' Schepke told him, and the driver let the clutch in and they drove away leaving the boy looking after them. Light was fading as they swung onto Stubbs Road and began the long climb up out from the city to Repulse Bay before swinging back toward Aberdeen on the coast road on the other side of the island.

It was almost dark when they arrived at Aberdeen. The harbour was tightly packed with fishing junks and sampans in for the night and after paying off the taxi they walked down to the narrow jetties. A number of young men, touts for the restaurants moored out in the harbour, called to them from sampans as they went down the few steps to the water's edge. They settled on a moon-faced young man with long shiny hair. As they passed some of the floating restaurants the white-coated waiters and cooks called down to them, and then they came up astern of a high junk lit by acetylene lamps. Overhead on a long streamer between the masts was the name in English: The Restaurant of High Morals and Good Digestion.

'How about this one?' Schepke asked the young man.

'Very good,' the young man answered enthusiastically. 'Peking Duck speciality.'

One of the smiling, white-coated waiters helped the girl up onto the deck while Schepke paid the sampan. Then the waiter guided them to a table in the single well deck. A soft breeze came in off the channel. The acetylene lamps were slung in two lines directly overhead either side of the deck, and high on the fantail were the wire cages full of birds with snow white feathers and yellow beaks and feet. Beneath the fantail was the spit, the trough glowing red with fire.

Karl Schepke sat across the table from the girl. There were no other diners on board and it was early and the moon was not yet risen. The girl wore no make-up and the light from the overhead lamps highlighted her hair. She was beautiful and her skin was flawless and white almost to the point of transparency. Her eyes were shadowed under their long curling lashes and she smiled softly as they waited. But she did not smile with her eyes. Her eyes were shadowed, and deep and dark.

303

There had been no menu, nor any orders to a waiter, but now he brought them small bowls of duck's feet soup. The soup was grand and they sipped it while overhead the paper lanterns and acetylene lamps moved gently in the breeze from the channel.

'When does your ship sail again?' the girl asked while they ate.

'I'm not quite sure yet,' he lied, not wishing anything to change. Then: 'Were there many films that you made?' he asked, steering her away from the present.

'Yes, quite many,' she said. 'The first I ever played in was with my mother. I was very young and she was a wonderful actress. Many people knew her. Then she died suddenly. We lived in Peking in those days and after she died my father thought we should go away and we went to a place he had lived in at one time. It was far up the Great to Witches' Mountain Gorge. I liked it very much there as a child. The people lived simply and everywhere was this wild, fierce beauty of the river and the gorge. Those days were very happy.'

While they talked the waiter brought the duck's liver in a paste, with an almond sauce with soya and cayenne.

'Do you ever go to see films?' she asked suddenly, looking at him.

'When I was a boy,' he said. 'Now they've lost their appeal. Unfortunately, one usually knows how they will end before they have really begun.'

'You do not care for happy endings?' she asked, arching her brows slightly.

'What made you ask that?' he said.

'It is something I feel about you.' She was watching his face very carefully.

'I never knew anything that ended happily yet,' he said, then suddenly wished he had not said it.

She was looking at the small shallow bowl before her.

The waiter appeared at the table with a giblet dish with small side dishes with rice and bamboo shoots and tiny mushroom buttons.

The girl ate quietly, devoting herself only to the eating. Karl

Schepke wished he had thought more carefully about what he had said.

Then suddenly there appeared a tall man in white with a silver sword in his hand. 'The duck,' he said simply. And one of the cooks swept a brown and smoking duck on a silver dish onto the table. Meanwhile the waiter placed paper-thin pancakes on the plates and brought tiny cups of rice wine, then left immediately and returned with small shallow plates of brown sauce. The tall man shelled the duck of the smoking skin with one swift stroke of the sword, and the waiter hurried the brown, smoking crackling onto the plates. Karl Schepke waited for the girl. She rolled it in the white flour pancake, dipped it in the sauce, then put it in her mouth and followed it quickly by sipping the warm rice wine. Then she watched him eat the crackling as she had done, smiling softly again. Afterward they sat in the quiet of the warm night lit only by the lanterns and lamps, and Karl Schepke felt very grand in her company.

She had spoken very little but the soft smile was there again and after they had gone ashore he found a taxi and they drove back up the Aberdeen Road, the road climbing up around Mount Kellett, the moon now showing above the hills out beyond Tai Tam Bay, the moonlight lighting the whole island and reflecting on the reservoir far below them to the right. Out beyond East Lamma Channel were the brightly lit villages of Lamma Island, two of them close upon the shore of Picnic Bay, and beyond to the south was Mount Stenhouse, tall and darkly shadowed where the moonlight did not reach. Aberdeen was far below them now, brightly lit and the smooth dark ocean lit by the moon.

'The Tramway,' Karl Schepke told the driver.

It was not far to the Peak Tramway and after paying off the driver they crossed to the parapet on the other side of the roadway and looked down on the beautifully lit city. The city was strung out in a long straggling curve, the streets brightly lit and the coloured signs of the bars and hotels rapidly and splendidly changing colour high above the lighted buildings and roadways. Out on the harbour were the lights of the ships at the buoys and the black waters scored by the lingering fire-dragon wakes of the ferries and motor craft. Beyond the harbour were the many lights of Kowloon, and the hills outside of the city silvered by the moonlight.

'It is so very beautiful,' the girl said.

'Yes.' And he was looking at her in the cool darkness of the high Peak.

'It was so kind of you to take me ashore,' she said, turning to him. 'Thank you.' And she said it very simply.

'I'm afraid you will have to forgive me for being selfish,' he said. He was standing close to her and he could feel the warmth of her without them actually touching. The lights of the city below lighted the long smooth curve of her neck and the smooth roundness of her bare shoulders. She was very beautiful up there in the cool moonlight of the Peak and he wanted very much to touch her.

'You must be cold,' he said finally.

She smiled to him and they turned and walked to the tramway station. The tramway went very steeply down the side of the Peak, their ears popping gently with the loss of altitude. They came out from the station to Garden Road and walked down past the floodlit banks on the left, just off Lower Albert Road, then across Queens Road and on down Jackson Road to the ferry. It was pleasant walking in the warm lighted streets after the cool darkness of the Peak, and now she smiled softly up at him when he looked at her.

IT was early afternoon when Karl Schepke came down from the charthouse and met Cheng in the cabin passage with a letter.

'A messenger left it at the brow,' Cheng told him.

Schepke took the letter and saw the company name printed along the top left hand corner. 'All right,' he said.

The letter contained instructions for the loading of a late cargo of latex in the forepeak tank, then went on to state that the old man and his daughter would be taken from the ship shortly after midnight.

Müller was asleep in his cabin.

'Müller!'

Müller sat up and looked at him.

'There's a tanker due here early this evening with a cargo of latex,' Schepke went on. 'I want you to try and get her here this afternoon instead. It's important.'

'I—I thought maybe I was through here.'

'Forget what happened,' Schepke told him. 'I want you on board. Just don't let me down again. I'm trusting you to do this thing. All right?'

'What are you planning on doing?' Müller asked, still undecided.

'Never mind that. Just get that tanker here this afternoon.'

'Wait,' Müller said as he turned to leave. 'What did the old man tell Wang about them coming on board?'

'He didn't tell him anything.'

'Cheng knows. He found out.'

'Forget Cheng,' Schepke told him. 'Just do what I asked.'

'All right,' Müller said. 'But what's going to happen to them now?'

'Wang's taking them ashore tonight.'

Müller shook his head. 'I don't know what all this trouble is about. What can an old man and a girl do?'

Karl Schepke, watching him, did not say anything. Then Müller took his tunic from behind the door and put it on. 'There is one other thing,' he said. 'Can you do without me on the way back from Japan?'

'Do you really want to do that?'

Müller nodded. 'If it's all right with you.'

'Is something wrong?' Schepke asked, watching him carefully.

Müller hesitated. 'Not exactly,' he said, finally.

'All right,' Schepke told him as he stepped into the passage. 'Do what you want.'

'You won't say anything to Cheng?'

'Nobody,' Schepke assured him, and he knew now that something had Müller worried. Then as he went below he thought about Cheng.

The door to Kamei's cabin was locked.

'Kamei,' he said through the doorway.

The key clicked several times in the lock and the door opened.

'I forgot to tell you that you're going home,' Schepke told him when he went inside. 'We'll be sailing for Kobe sometime around midnight. Can you manage to get ashore there?'

Kamei grinned. 'There will be no trouble,' he said. 'Thank you.'

'Well you better stay below here until we start to move. Things might go wrong here before we get clear.' Outside Kamei's cabin he met Frauenheim on his way aft.

'Seen Hechler?'

'He's working with Dorsch on Number One winch,' Frauenheim told him.

Karl Schepke found them still working.

'Made your mind up yet?'

'We'll stay the trip,' Hechler told him, wiping grease from his face and hands. 'It's better than waiting around on shore.'

'Thanks,' Schepke told him, and glanced quickly around the well and lowered his voice. 'Stand by for coming away fast tonight. All right?'

'Are you expecting trouble?' Dorsch asked, his face serious.

'Maybe. I'll let you know more when I get back.' And while he was talking huge wooden crates and packing cases were swinging in from the *Fenching Liberator* to Number Two hold. 'If there's anything else I'll let you know,' he said, and as he turned to leave them Dorsch casually nodded toward the forepeak where Cheng was watching them.

'Keep your eye on him,' Schepke told them.

'You don't have to tell us,' Dorsch said.

Karl Schepke went on down to the wharf. It was almost three o'clock, and then he saw a hire motor boat put out from a Maersk Line freighter at the bottom of Haiphong Road, and he waved it across.

'Gloucester Road,' he told the boatman. 'Ferry Pier.'

He saw Cheng still watching him as they pulled away from the pilings and headed out across the harbour.

THEY docked almost directly outside Wanchai Police Station. The front was very quiet in the Sunday afternoon and there was not even the women about.

Menzies came to the desk himself and took him back to the office.

'Enjoy the races?' he asked when they were seated.

'You saw us?'

'Believe me, she is a most attractive girl,' Menzies said, smiling.

'She is,' Schepke agreed. '—And did you find out anything?'

'Well they are genuine people. Both of them are known here in Hong Kong. However, little or nothing has been heard of them for some years now.'

'What happens if they land?' Schepke asked, rather anxiously.

'That's a very difficult question,' Menzies told him. 'There hasn't been much time to get all the details, and even so it is entirely up to the immigration people. In this case it would very probably go to an even higher level. After all, these people are not ordinary working coolies defecting because they think they might get more to eat here. They may be allowed to stay, but on the other hand we could expect strong protests from Peking. They would have to be considered as well. In this case I wouldn't like to make any guess at the eventual outcome.'

Karl Schepke sat back in the chair and lit a cigarette. 'What about Japan?' he asked. 'What's the procedure there?'

'Is that where you're bound?' Menzies asked, watching him.

'We sail around midnight.'

'Well I wouldn't care to give an opinion on that either,'

Menzies told him. 'This is a difficult business. But tell me what you had in mind.'

Karl Schepke leaned forward, resting his forearm on the desk. 'I thought about taking them with me.'

'You're going to be very unpopular in certain quarters.'

'I've thought about that as well. Anyway, the rest of the men are going home on the *Kota Pinang*. It won't hurt them any.'

'And you?' Menzies asked. 'Or is that an unfair question?'

Schepke looked up at him across the desk. 'I don't think she's interested,' he said. 'Maybe I'll go down to Manila.'

'What's wrong with going home?'

'You know how it is,' Schepke told him. 'You only remember it as it was, never when it rains.'

'Yes, I know what you mean,' Menzies said and pushed a long, wide, stiff-covered book across the desk. 'It's some of the old man's work,' he explained.

The book had been published in America and contained about thirty beautifully coloured reproductions of the old man's paintings. Most of them were of animals, and fruit, and flowers. The last three plates were described as 'at the beginning of spring, Witches' Mountain Gorge, 1948'. There was nothing else of a later date.

'That's quite a collection.'

'I have it on good authority that there were few better than him.'

'And nobody can promise anything?'

Menzies shrugged resignedly. 'At this stage I'm afraid not,' he said.

'All right,' Schepke said, suddenly. 'I'll take them north. But I'll want your help.'

'Now wait a minute,' Menzies said. 'I can't get involved in anything like this.'

'I've said the same thing for as long as I can remember, but it never works. Take my word on that.'

'Well it depends on what you want me to do,' Menzies said, reluctantly.

Karl Schepke brought Wang's letter from his tunic pocket and passed it across the desk.

Menzies read it then looked up at him. 'I could have everyone arrested as soon as these people land them.'

'No,' Schepke told him. 'You said yourself they could still be sent back eventually. What I want you to do is put a guard on the ship after dark and stop everybody going on board. Wang expects us to sail about two o'clock. I can upset that by slipping earlier.'

'What about this ship alongside you, she's Communist,' Menzies said. 'Can't they transfer them to her?'

'They might have done but Wang tells me she's bound for Singapore.'

'And what happens if you do get them away?'

'I'll be all right once I clear the harbour.'

'They could get the Chinese to send a boat out and stop you in the Straits,' Menzies said. 'They're active enough up there.'

'I've thought about that as well,' Schepke told him. 'Once I clear Hong Kong I'll keep well to the south of Formosa.'

'You've thought about it all, haven't you,' Menzies said. 'But what about coming back down?'

'We'll leave her in Kobe. The others can pick up the *Kota Pinang* at Yokohama. That way nobody has anything to worry about.'

Menzies leaned forward onto the desk. 'You have a lot of nerve,' he said. 'I wouldn't want to do it. But I'll certainly put a guard on the wharf if that will help.'

'Thank you. If you can do that for me I can manage the rest,' Schepke told him, then looked at his wrist watch. 'Well, I would like to get back on board now,' he said, rising. 'There's a lot to be done before midnight.'

'Then I'll see you on the wharf sometime after dark,' Menzies said. 'I only hope this works out for you.'

KARL SCHEPKE looked up from the chart table to the bulkhead clock. It was almost eleven-thirty. Hechler had just left for the engine-room, and now he gathered his cap from the bunk and pulled it on down low and went out to the boatdeck. Cheng and Müller were below in the after well. The small latex tanker had slipped a little after ten o'clock and Müller had gone to hurry the loading.

'Müller!' he called into the well. 'How much longer?'

'About ten minutes!' Müller answered, glancing about the well.

Schepke turned and went forward to the big cabin. The girl and her father rose apprehensively from the table as he entered.

'They have come?' the old man asked, his voice very quiet.

'They?' Schepke said, puzzled.

'It was the one Cheng,' the girl said. 'He came here after supper and told us to ready ourselves for going ashore.'

He saw the two small bundles and the cloak spread across the back of the chair. 'Bring them with you.' he said going to the door. There was no one in the passage. 'Hurry,' he said, and led them below to the port inboard passage.

'Kamei,' he said and knocked on the door.

It opened almost immediately.

'Both of you stay here with Kamei until I come back. Understand?'

'We do not go ashore?' the girl asked, the anxiety and apprehension showing in her face and in her voice.

'You're going to Japan,' he told her. 'You'll be all right. — Kamei. Lock the door after me and don't let anybody in.' He waited until he heard the door locked then went on down to the wharf.

The Maersk Line freighter had put to sea during the afternoon and now the wharves were clear right the way across to Yaumati Shelter.

Menzies was waiting along with another officer by the ladder, the sound of running machinery carrying very loudly through the hull.

'What time do you expect to sail?' he asked.

'Not before twelve-thirty,' Schepke told him. 'We'll have to wait for the *Liberator* to get clear.'

'There's been no one about yet.'

'It shouldn't be long now. Have you somebody on the other end of the wharf? They might come by boat. That was how I thought they would probably do it. It would be easier than getting past the police on the dock gate.'

'There's five men down there,' Menzies told him. 'There's also some dock coolies in the watchman's hut ready to slip your moorings as soon as you give the word.'

'Thank you,' Schepke told him. 'Well I better get back on board. I'll be on the bridge. If I see anything headed in astern I'll flash you. And thanks again for all you've done.'

'There's nothing like going all the way,' Menzies said, smilingly. 'I only hope the Commissioners don't hear about this.'

Karl Schepke smiled with him in the darkness cast by the sheer wall above them.

'Good luck,' Menzies said.

Karl Schepke took his hand then turned and went back up the long ladder. They were through loading and Müller was having the after hatches battened down. Going on up to the bridge, he looked out along the port side of the *Liberator*. They were still not ready to slip. Then he saw one of her officers cross the well. He hailed him and saw him stop and squint up through the glare of lights.

'Get those moorings óff!'

The man went on squinting up at him through the lights.

'The moorings!' Schepke shouted. 'Get those moorings off!'

The man turned away toward the port alleyway and Schepke suddenly saw the powerful headlights of a car sweep in through the dock gate and swing across the end of the wharf. Then as he watched he saw someone get out from the car and start down the wharf. Snatching the engine-room receiver from its hook he spun the handle. Hechler was waiting.

'Stand by to come away,' Schepke told him. 'We'll let go as soon as I get rid of Wang.' Slamming the receiver back on its hook he hurried below to meet Wang in the passage. Cheng was with him.

'The police! What are the police doing on the wharf?' Mr. Wang asked excitedly. 'They even ask questions before allowing me on board my own ship!'

'I don't know anything about the police,' Schepke told him. 'There was nobody there ten minutes ago.'

Mr. Wang glanced along the passage toward the big cabin. 'They are ready?'

'Ready?' Schepke said, puzzled. 'They went ashore about twenty minutes ago.'

'Ashore!' Mr. Wang shouted, incredulously.

'I just told you,' Schepke said, evenly.

'Who came for them?' Mr. Wang demanded, his eyes appearing twice their normal size behind his thick-lensed spectacles.

'There was three of them. They went ashore together.'

'And the police?' Mr. Wang asked excitedly.

'There wasn't any police,' Schepke said. 'I went ashore to the wharf with them. They had a boat waiting.'

'You are certain of this?' Mr. Wang asked, not knowing what to think.

'Sure I'm sure,' Schepke said. 'What do you take me for? There was three of them.'

Cheng went and opened the door of the big cabin. 'There is no one here,' he told Mr. Wang.

'What were these people like?' Mr. Wang asked, quietened a little.

'They were Chink,' Schepke told him. 'They all look the same to me.'

Mr. Wang dabbed his forehead with a silk handkerchief. 'I do not understand this at all,' he said. 'They should not have arrived yet. And there were four of them. I just do not understand it.' Then to Cheng he suddenly said something in Mandarin, and Cheng shook his head.

'What is it now?' Schepke asked.

'It is nothing,' Mr. Wang said. 'You had better remain here. I will have to get in touch with Mr. Saito before allowing you to sail. I do not understand this at all. I was to be on board when our people arrived.'

Schepke watched him go below, then turned to Cheng. 'Take the forepeak. Be ready to slip when I give the order.'

'But Mr. Wang—'

'You heard me! To hell with Mr. Wang!'

Schepke watched him go reluctantly below. Then the ship gave a sudden lurch, vibrating heavily, something grating along her starboard side. Hurriedly he crossed to one of the scuttles in the big cabin and saw the *Fenching Liberator* drawing slowly astern. On the way to the bridge he met Altmeyer coming from the Radio Office.

'Come with me!' he told him.

Mr. Wang's car was still parked by the end of the wharf but there was no sign of him anywhere. The *Liberator* was out in the stream now, still drawing astern, headed into the Central Fairway. Then as he watched he saw the lights of a motor boat round her bows and angle in astern. As she closed, her lights went out and she was just a dark shape with a fading bone in her mouth. There was still no sign of Mr. Wang on the dock. He got the torch from the charthouse and flashed it slowly three times into the shadow cast by the port wall. Immediately Menzies and the other officer stepped into the light and hurried out along the wharf. The dark shape of the motor boat was still some way astern. Then he saw Müller on the boatdeck below him, watching the *Liberator*.

'Let go aft!' he told him through the open window, then went across to the front of the bridge and called to Cheng.

'Altmeyer! You take the wheel!'

'Are we in trouble, Herr Kapitän?' Altmeyer asked, running the wheel amidships.

'I thought you wanted excitement,' Schepke said, hearing

315

Müller give the all clear from the boatdeck. Out forward he could still see the spring. 'Forepeak! Hurry it up!' he called from the open window. Then: 'Slow astern!' he told Altmeyer. He heard him ring it on and almost immediately felt the deck come alive with the slow gathering pound of the engines. Out on the forepeak they were still working on the spring. The stern was already swinging clear of the wharf and there was no longer any sign of the motor boat.

'Half astern!' he told Altmeyer. 'Keep the wheel amidships!'

'They're still on the spring, sir!' Altmeyer shouted.

'Not for long!' Schepke said and reached for the siren lanyard, the great echoing blasts of noise and steam crashing out across the docks, startling and deafening.

'Full astern!' he shouted and heard the spring part and recoil viciously back across the forward well. Out on the forepeak he saw them all flat on the deck. Then he saw Mr. Wang running down the wharf, all arms and legs, bellowing something at the bridge. He leaned from the window and waved to him. It seemed to encourage him and he picked up speed. Then suddenly he tripped and went down full-length on his face. He was extremely surprised, Mr. Wang.

Then as the end of the wharf came in sight abeam of the bridge he saw Menzies and the others looking down into the water, the dock coolies joining them ahead of Mr. Wang. Then as the forward derrick arcs lit the swirling black water he saw the motor boat spinning around, hull upward, the heads of the swimmers bobbing around in the wash.

'Port fifteen!'

'Port fifteen!' Altmeyer replied. 'Fifteen port wheel on, sir!'

'Stop engines!' Schepke shouted almost immediately, watching the bows swing wide and clear now of the wharves. 'Half ahead!'

'Half ahead, sir!' Altmeyer shouted.

As the ship started to draw clear Schepke saw one of the policemen throw a line down into the water. There was no sign anywhere now of Mr. Wang.

316

Bahr and Pulst were both on the bridge before they cleared Tsim Sha Tsiu.

'You better take over, Bahr,' Schepke told him. 'Altmeyer. You know what to send.'

'Yes, sir,' Altmeyer said and started for the flying bridge.

"Midships.'

"Midships,' Bahr answered. 'Wheel amidships, sir.'

Below him he saw Cheng come down from the forepeak. 'Cheng! Get that port ladder inboard!'

The many sprawling lights of Wanchai and Causeway Bay slid slowly past in the darkness to starboard as the *Gertrud Lüth* put Hunghom on the port beam, the lights of Whampoa Dock showing just clear on the port bow, and right ahead the string of lights showing off Kai Tak runway. And overhead he heard Altmeyer clatter out on the starboard searchlight: S.S. Gertrud Lüth, *outward bound for Kobe.*

'Starboard five.'

'Starboard five. Five starboard wheel on, sir.'

They were out past North Point now, the string of runway lights on the port beam.

"Midships.'

"Midships. Wheel amidships, sir.'

Lei U Mun Pass was right ahead. It was a fine clear night with the moon showing high and silver between Devil's Peak and Black Hill, brilliantly lighting the smooth black water inside of the Pass. Leaning from the window, Karl Schepke looked out to starboard to the lights of Shaukiwan, seeing all along the entire length of Shaukiwan Main Street as the ship moved slowly into the Pass toward the ocean. Then suddenly it was quiet and with no more lights, and below, the moonlit water hissed and foamed gently back along the hull. He had that sure, high-singing feeling inside of him now as the Pass fell astern leaving Tathong Channel wide and open and leading to the ocean.

It was the third night and Karl Schepke watched it get dark and saw the moon begin its long slow climb from the horizon. The ocean was flat and black and lit only by the moon far out on the horizon, and there was no breeze and the only sound was the gentle foaming and hissing of the water far below. They were well to southward and everything had gone simply and easily, and now that it was dark he watched the moon climb and listened to the ocean on the hull.

After a while, when he went to the charthouse, he caught a glimpse of Altmeyer below in the passage.

'Heard anything?'

'Nothing, sir,' Altmeyer said, shaking his head. 'There's been no call of any sort.'

'All right.' He went on into the charthouse, a little puzzled and undecided. He was worried about Mr. Wang. Mr. Wang had not acted the way he had expected. Mr. Wang and Peking were big business.

When Müller arrived to take the first watch the moon had risen high into the starlit sky.

'What's Sam got for supper?'

'I haven't been,' Müller told him. 'I'm not hungry.'

Karl Schepke was watching him, thinking. He had seen Müller only once in the messroom since leaving Hong Kong, and that time Cheng had been on watch. But he did not pursue it. 'If you see any lights, ignore them,' he said.

Müller nodded and hung the night-glasses around his neck. Karl Schepke left him in the wing and went below.

'—It was particularly foolish to have done such a thing,' he heard Cheng say as he neared the messroom. 'There will be much trouble because of this.'

Cheng was sitting at the table with Hechler and Dorsch, gesturing with his fork.

'Something wrong?' he asked as he came in.

Cheng started to say something, then silently returned to his supper.

'You let me take care of the trouble,' Schepke told him. 'Any trouble on board this ship is my business. Understand?'

Cheng kept his eyes on his plate.

'Kapitän, sir.' It was Altmeyer. He made a slight movement with his head and stepped back into the passage.

'This just came through in company code.'

Schepke took the pad.

Confirmation received to effect both prisoners now held in civil custody in Hong Kong pending appeal for asylum. Regret Wang's interference.

Signed, K. I. Saito.

'Any reply, sir?'

Schepke tore the signal from the pad and handed it back. 'Not for the moment.'

Cheng rose from the table when he returned, then left. As he watched Cheng leave he saw Sam pass his supper through the hatchway to Kuang.

'No supper,' he told the boy.

'Something wrong?' Hechler asked, watching him pour some coffee.

He passed them the sheet of signal paper.

'What do you make of it?' Hechler asked, puzzled.

'I don't know yet.'

'How about this Menzies? Do you think he has something to do with it?'

'I've got a feeling it's more complicated than that,' Schepke said, thinking.

'I can't see what they can do now,' Dorsch said. 'Besides, they don't even know where we are.'

'I don't feel good about it just the same,' Schepke told them. 'We'll leave the ship at Kobe and you can pick up the *Kota Pinang* at Yokohama.'

'Do you think it's that bad?' Hechler asked.

'I've got a sure feeling about this one,' Schepke told him.

'Well it's all the same to me,' Dorsch said. 'I don't mind where I wait as long as I'm going home.'

'That reminds me,' Hechler said. 'I haven't heard Müller say anything about going home.'

'I think he's got other plans,' Schepke told them.

'Well he's nothing to me,' Dorsch said. 'Just as long as I get home that's all I'm worried about. I've had my fill of the Mystic East.'

Karl Schepke rose and took his cap from the bulkhead. 'I'll see you both later,' he told them.

The old man was sitting at the table with one of Emmermann's books.

'Have you had supper?' Schepke asked him.

'Yes. Thank you very much,' the old man said, rising politely from the table.

'Where's your daughter?'

'She has gone out for some air. It is so very hot in here tonight.'

'Is everything all right?'

'I think she is just a little tired and upset after all that has happened.'

'Of course,' Schepke said. 'I'll talk with you later.'

The old man gently bowed his head as Schepke left, closing the door behind him.

She was standing at the starboard rail, and she turned as she heard him come out from the passage.

'You're not feeling ill?' he asked.

'No. It was the stuffiness of the cabin. I feel well now,' she said, smiling softly. 'Perhaps it has also been the excitement of the past few days.'

'Don't worry about it now,' he told her. 'It's all over.'

She dropped her long eyelashes, then looked out at the ocean. 'It is a very beautiful night,' she said. In the moonlight her hair was that shiny bluish black of the raven.

'Yes, it's a fine night,' he said, and he was looking at her, at her mouth and the curve of her neck, at her eyes and at the smoothness and roundness of her shoulders.

Then she was watching him, her eyes deeply shadowed under the long, delicately curling lashes. And far below the ocean was black and silent and lit by the moon.

'There is something worries you,' she said, feeling sure about it.

'It's nothing,' he said.

'There will be much trouble because of what you have done,' she went on, quietly, and caring.

He did not look at her. The horizon was very faraway in the moonlight.

'You wished to say something?' she asked, after a little.

'What do you mean?' he said, looking at her now.

'I just felt perhaps you wished to say something,' she spoke very quietly, looking at him. She was very beautiful in the moonlight, and in the moonlight her shoulders were smooth and round and delicately bare.

'No. I wasn't thinking of anything,' he said, finally.

'What will happen when you return to Hong Kong?'

'We won't be going back,' he said.

'You will stay in Japan?' she asked, still watching him.

'Maybe I'll go down to Manila,' he said.

'That is a nice place, Manila?'

'I never thought about it like that,' he said.

'You are such a very strange man,' she said.

He was looking at the moon on the ocean, the ship moving very gently in the long smoothly lifting swell.

'We shall be eternally grateful to you for taking us away. You have sacrificed much because of our selfishness.'

'Do you think I would have done this if you had been fat and old and ugly?' he said.

'You are being unkind to yourself,' she said very softly.

'No. I was being very selfish about it.'

'Please do not say such things.'

He looked down at her face, their eyes holding in the moonlight. She was very beautiful and her arms and shoulders were smooth and round and delicately bare. Then he felt her fingers lightly touch his sleeve and he took her hand in his. She let him take it and hold it, and he bent and lightly kissed the corner of her mouth. Then he straightened, looking at her, and she turned slightly and was close to him, her face lifted to his. Now he kissed her mouth and her heart was beating against his chest and she was pressed tightly and warmly against him. Then her arms were around his neck and her head resting lightly against his chest.

'Please do not think that is only because of what you have done,' she said, her lips moving smally against his neck and her hair smooth and soft against his mouth.

He lifted her face to him and kissed her lightly on the mouth, and her lips were soft and moist and trembling. Then suddenly he felt very guilty and he did not know what to say or do next.

Then: 'I think someone calls you,' she said suddenly.

He heard Altmeyer the same moment as she spoke.

Altmeyer stepped out from the messroom as he entered from the boatdeck.

'Something wrong?'

Altmeyer handed him the signal pad. He read it through twice. 'No answer,' he said and went past the boy to Hechler's cabin. Hechler was reading in his bunk.

'Hans. You better come to the charthouse. We've just had another signal.'

Hechler was right behind him when he reached the bridge.

'Something wrong?' Müller asked, seeing them both.

'Maybe,' Schepke said, going into the charthouse, Müller crowding in behind them.

'What's it all about?' Hechler asked.

'Listen,' Schepke told them, and read from the pad:

'*Panamanian freighter* Hoboken *on voyage from Singapore to Yokohama suffered explosion and severe damage to engine-room. Unable to make General call until part of cargo has been transfered. Alter course at once to assistance. Ship under contract to company. Position—*'

He bent over the chart and made some rapid calculations.

322

'According to this she's about here,' he said, marking the estimated position on the chart. 'About sixty-five kilometres east-south-east of here.'

'We could reach her by about ten, ten-thirty,' Hechler said, looking carefully at his wrist watch.

'No,' Müller interrupted. 'There's something wrong. What's she carrying to Japan that stops her making a General call?'

'I agree,' Schepke said. 'And she can't be in any great danger of sinking because as far as Hong Kong is aware we're already through the Straits and from where we should be at present is a good fourteen hours steaming from here. Nobody knows we're this far south.'

'But what's she carrying?' Hechler asked.

'I say we ignore her,' Müller said.

'Get her in the register,' Schepke told him.

'What are you going to do?' Hechler asked.

'I'm not sure yet. Maybe Müller's right. Maybe we should ignore her.'

'Here she is,' Müller told them. '*Hoboken*. Twelve thousand tons. Steamship. Ex-American Liberty ship. Now owned and registered in Panama. Call sign RJFR.'

'What do you think?' Schepke asked him.

'Well,' Müller said, thoughtfully, 'she's only a little way south of the main run for Japan. It's the cargo I don't understand. Unless it's some sort of contraband.'

'I thought about that,' Schepke said. 'I'll tell you what,' he went on, looking at Hechler. 'Nobody knows we're this far south, and if we don't acknowledge the signal in some way we could start a Communist hunt for us. What I suggest is that we alter course and try and sight her. If she looks badly damaged we'll find out exactly what cargo she has before we do anything.'

'She's fitted with all radar aids,' Müller said, looking at the register. 'She'll pick us up long before we sight her.'

'But they aren't going to know it's us,' Schepke said. 'If there's anything suspicious about her and she calls us up we'll give her another name. We could be some blundering tramp bound for

Okinawa. Wang will probably have been in touch with her giving our ETA. She won't be expecting us before daylight.'

'What if she turns out to be a Communist gunboat?' Müller asked.

'No. I don't think they would try anything like that in International waters.'

'Sir,' Altmeyer said as he entered from the bridge. 'Another signal.'

Schepke took the pad from him.

Request information as to your intentions re previous signal.

Signed, K. I. Saito.

'Can the *Hoboken* get a fix on our position if we reply?' Schepke asked him.

'Only if they're keeping close radio watch. I'd say that's more than likely, sir.'

'All right, forget it. If anything else comes through let me know at once.'

'Yes, sir.' Altmeyer turned to leave.

'Wait,' Schepke called to him. 'Is there any traffic close by?'

'About three or four hours ago there was. I didn't pay much attention to it at the time. It was coded stuff.'

'All right,' he told him. Then: 'Bridge!' he called through the doorway. 'Steer one-one-five! Full ahead!' Then making the alterations to the chart, he could feel both Hechler and Müller watching him.

'I think we're making a mistake,' Müller told him.

'If there's anything suspicious we'll keep going,' Schepke said leaning up from the table. 'But for the moment just keep her going as she is. I'll be back.'

Hechler followed him below to the passage.

'How do you feel about it?' Schepke asked him.

'I'm not sure. But we might as well have a look at her. I'll be in the engine-room if you want me.'

Schepke went aft to the big cabin. The old man was asleep.

Quietly closing the door he went on out to the boatdeck. The girl was still there.

'The moon has moved,' she said, smiling.

'We're going further south,' he told her. 'There's another ship in difficulty. I think you ought to go to your cabin now.'

'You are expecting trouble?' she asked, her voice showing her concern.

Karl Schepke did not say anything. He did not know what to say and he did not wish to say anything that might upset her.

Her father was awake when they went inside.

'We're going to the assistance of another ship,' Schepke explained. 'I want you to stay here in the cabin until I tell you.' While he spoke he closed both scuttles and dropped the deadlights down over them. 'All the lights will go out soon but it's nothing to worry about.'

The old man was looking at him carefully but he did not say anything, and Schepke left them and went below to find Kamei and have him swing out all lifeboats ready for launching. He did not quite know what to think, and he did not like any of it, and he had the almost sure feeling of being on the brink of something happening that he was not expecting.

THE night was quiet and empty, and the ship, darkened except for her steaming lights, ran smoothly through the flat, moonlit ocean to the south-east. Both Cheng and Müller were on the bridge with him. From the starboard wing he could see Kamei and the watch on deck gathered below him in the forward well. Looking again at his wrist watch he saw it was almost twenty minutes to eleven o'clock. Then raising the night-glasses he began another close-searching sweep of the horizon, beginning abaft the port bow and working back across the bows to stop suddenly a few points abaft the starboard bow. She was long and high-looking, darkly-shadowed and without lights, but too distant to make clear any of her details.

'Müller! Call Hechler and tell him we've sighted the Panamanian.'

Cheng moved aside to let Müller reach the telephones, his own night-glasses focused on the darkened *Hoboken*.

'Cheng!' Schepke said across the bridge. 'Get Altmeyer up here.' Then: 'Kamei!' he called to the forward well. 'Have the crew stand by Number Three lifeboat!'

He put the glasses back on the Panamanian. She was taking shape now, completely blacked out and seemingly deserted.

Cheng came back closely followed by Altmeyer and Hechler.

'Stand by the starboard searchlight,' Schepke told the boy.

'See anything of her?' Hechler asked.

'She's blacked out,' Schepke told him, not moving the glasses. 'She's down at the stern. I can't see much more. The angle's still bad. We'll have to close her some more.' All the while he was watching the upper deck of the Panamanian for any sign of movement or light. She was drifting, and the *Gertrud Lüth* keeping her course, bore in on her port bow.

Watching her, he decided to pass on her port side.

'Steer one-two-zero,' he called. Then as he kept the glasses firmly on the Panamanian he felt the bows slowly come around onto the new course, slightly widening the angle of vision.

'She's down at the stern, all right,' he heard Müller say.

She was down at the stern and there was no wash around where her counter now met the ocean. Through the glasses, the moonlight casting the deeply black shadow of her bridge onto the forward well, he made out a tarpaulined deck-cargo set out forward of her high, wide-winged bridge.

'Half ahead,' he called, crossing the bridge to join Cheng and Müller on the port wing. Again he raised the glasses. The after end of the Panamanian's boat and cabin decks caught his attention. 'There's been a big fire,' he said. 'See that wreckage?'

'Why doesn't she call us?' Hechler said.

'She's probably trying to figure out who we are,' Müller told him.

326

As Müller spoke several streams of water spouted whitely out high over her port wall.

'They are using the hand pumps,' Cheng said.

'There must have been an explosion with the fire,' Schepke said. 'Those derricks on the after housing are thrown out of line.'

As the *Gertrud Lüth* closed the Panamanian they saw the fire hoses festooned across the break from the boatdeck to the after well.

'Why the hell don't they call us?' Hechler demanded.

Karl Schepke was studying her closely as they drew abeam. Then suddenly her port searchlight flashed out across the moon-lit ocean.

S.S. Hoboken, *effecting engine-room repairs. Request recognition.*

'Kapitän, sir!' Altmeyer called through the open hatchway to the bridge.

'All right,' Schepke told him. 'I saw it.'

'She looks in a bad way,' Hechler said. 'That's been a big explosion aft.'

'Are you going in?' Müller asked.

'She looks genuine,' Schepke told them, then turned to the open hatchway. 'Altmeyer! Tell them who we are!'

Altmeyer had just finished clattering out the message when the first of the lights began to come on in the Panamanian's bridge.

'Those are hurricane lamps,' Hechler said. 'Her dynamos are out of action.'

'Port ten!'

'Port ten,' repeated Bahr. 'Ten port wheel on, sir.'

'Slow ahead.' Then as the ship's head began to ease around Schepke saw the Panamanian's searchlight come into action.

'I better get back below,' Hechler told them. 'Let me know what happens.'

'Kapitän, sir!' Altmeyer called into the bridge. '*Hoboken* asks you to go on board. They're sending a boat.'

'All right,' Schepke told him. 'Cheng! Tell Kamei to get a rope

327

ladder out starboard side. Müller! Take over up here. Stand her off until you hear from me.'

'Wheel amidships!' Müller ordered.

They had made the slow easy turn and were coming up astern of the Panamanian on her port side. A motor cutter was already in the water. The big, high ex-Liberty ship was sitting with a slight list to port and with her counter well into the ocean and her hand pumps pouring water out over her walls. In the bright moonlight Schepke saw the crewmen manning the pumps watch them come up astern.

'Don't do anything until you hear from me,' he said from the doorway.

'I understand,' Müller told him.

The engines set the deck shuddering as Hechler threw them astern to bring the *Gertrud Lüth* to a stop. Kamei and Cheng, and a number of seamen were gathered in the starboard alleyway where they were watching the Panamanian about three hundred metres away on the beam.

Glancing across the wall, Karl Schepke saw the long open cutter headed in close astern.

'Kamei,' he called, and gripped the wooden rung of the ladder and went swiftly down almost to the water, the ladder swaying and bumping against the wall as Kamei followed him down.

THE stale, washed-out smell of the fire hung raw and pungently over the steeply-walled Panamanian.

'Welcome on board, Captain.' There were three of them, two of them officers. 'I am First Officer Sekularac,' the taller of the two continued, addressing him in English. 'The Captain waits for you on the bridge.'

Schepke turned to see Kamei drop noiselessly in over the bulwarks. Then in the light of the hurricane lamp the seaman held he saw them all stare incredulously at the massive, barefooted Kamei.

'All right,' he told the taller of the two.

The inside of the ship had a dingy, almost prefabricated appearance, the close shipboard air heavy with the smell of the fire and hot oil.

The Captain was waiting at the head of the bridge stairway. 'This is very much a surprise indeed, Captain,' he said, addressing Schepke in English. 'We had not expected you until morning at least.' He was Polish like the others, and old, with a heavy build, and with a heavy, bushily eyebrowed face. The bridge was lit by three hurricane lamps and the air was foul with smoky paraffin fumes and the harsh-smelling smoke of pasteboard-tipped cigarettes.

'How bad is the trouble?' Schepke asked him.

'Very bad indeed. We have five already dead. We suffered a heavy explosion in the boiler room yesterday afternoon.'

'Why didn't you put out a Mayday?'

The Captain smiled. 'I am afraid it was not so easy as that,' he said. 'I wish clear of this cargo on the forward well first.'

'What is it you have?' Schepke asked.

Again the Captain smiled. 'I am not altogether certain myself,' he said. 'I believe, however, it is some sort of machinery. You will have to be careful with it. Lyebedev will explain to you,' he paused, looking beyond Schepke and Kamei to the rear of the bridge.

The three of them had come in from below.

'Lieutenant Lyebedev,' the Captain said.

The Lieutenant came across the bridge, the others remaining by the open doorway. He was a big man with a wide face and closely cropped sunburned hair.

'Pleased to meet you, Captain—' he said, pausing.

'Schepke.'

'Pleased to meet you, Captain Schepke,' Lyebedev continued. 'You are German?'

Karl Schepke nodded, experiencing a deep revolving feeling of uncertainty begin in the pit of his stomach.

'We were not expecting you until morning,'

'Yes,' the Captain said, looking at Schepke. 'We were not certain just who you were at first. We had been watching you for some time. According to Hong Kong you should have been far to the north.'

'I changed my mind about going through the Straits,' Schepke calmly said.

'You expected trouble?' Lyebedev asked.

'We had some with the Nationalists. I thought it better to stay clear.'

'Quite understandably,' Lyebedev agreed. 'One can never quite trust the Americans and their friends.'

'What about the cargo?' Schepke asked, a little impatient now.

'Machinery,' Lyebedev explained. 'For Chingkiang.'

It took Schepke unexpectedly.

'Something is wrong, Captain?' Lyebedev asked, watching his face.

'I'm afraid there's some misunderstanding,' Schepke said, his voice changed. 'My ship's bound for Kobe.'

'There is no misunderstanding, Captain,' Lyebedev said evenly. 'Now it is arranged you go to Chingkiang.'

'I'm sorry,' Schepke said. 'It's Kobe.'

'Chingkiang,' Lyebedev corrected, then glanced meaningfully toward the doorway. 'You see, Captain. It would be unwise to argue.'

'No!' Schepke shouted as he sensed Kamei begin his move.

Kamei slowly straightened, glaring at the two men standing just inside the doorway with drawn pistols.

'Thank you, Captain,' Lyebedev said, smiling thinly. 'Now please ask your ship alongside. This way,' he went on, leading Schepke out to the port wing and handing him a hailer.

Back amidships the Captain was already shouting orders to the forward well.

'Please,' Lyebedev prompted. 'We wish to get this done with as soon as possible.'

Schepke looked toward the *Gertrud Lüth*. '*Lüth* ahoy!' he called, his magnified voice echoing across the flat moonlit water.

'Müller here!' came the shouted answer.

'Bring her along port side!'

Lyebedev waited with him until the *Gertrud Lüth* began to draw slowly astern. 'Thank you, Captain,' he said, and motioned Schepke back across the bridge. 'We wait here now until the cargo has been transferred. Afterward we all go on board together. There will be six of us. Let us just say that we wish to make certain everything arrives safely at Chingkiang.'

TOGETHER with Lyebedev and the Captain, Karl Schepke watched the transfer of the deck-cargo from the bridge of the *Hoboken*. There had been sixteen cases, all of them carefully handled as they were winched on board the *Gertrud Lüth*.

'After you, Captain,' Lyebedev said when the transfer was completed.

The three others were waiting for them in the port alleyway, two of them carrying automatic rifles. They boarded the *Gertrud Lüth* together, Lyebedev covering Schepke with a squat, heavy-barrelled revolver.

'We go straight to the bridge,' he said, motioning Kamei on ahead of them. 'Tell him I want the inboard lights on. All of them.'

'Put the lights on,' Schepke told Kamei when they reached the cabin deck.

'What's going on?' Müller said when they all came in through the doorway, the two with the automatic rifles immediately covering him and Cheng.

'Everything is secure?' Lyebedev asked, looking first at Müller then at Cheng.

Müller glanced uncertainly at Schepke, then nodded.

'Take her away, Captain,' Lyebedev said, turning to Schepke.

Schepke looked at the revolver.

331

Lyebedev smiled. 'Please. You are free to carry on,' he said, glancing significantly at the seamen spaced out along the rear of the bridge. 'You see, we are in complete control here. We understand this?' he asked, looking now at Cheng and Müller.

Karl Schepke went to the starboard wing and called the orders below for taking them clear. Then: 'Half ahead,' he ordered. 'Steer due North.'

Müller glanced across the bridge at him. 'That's course for the Yangtze!'

'I am afraid there has been a slight alteration to your plans, gentlemen,' Lyebedev said, carefully watching them as Pulst brought the ship around onto her new course. 'Your immediate destination is now Chingkiang.'

Karl Schepke stood watching the *Hoboken* from the after windows. She was right astern, once more completely blacked out and drifting on the empty ocean in the moonlight.

'Before we go further,' Lyebedev told them. 'Let me make it clear that no harm will come to anyone as long as he does as ordered. I have no wish to take control of the whole ship. The bridge will be sufficient. Everyone here at the moment will remain so until we arrive at Chingkiang. We understand?'

No one said anything, and now Lyebedev put the revolver back into the pocket of his reefer coat. The seamen with him remained spaced out along the rear of the bridge, the two with the automatic rifles covering the bridge and Lyebedev careful not to put himself in any line of fire. Then going out to the starboard wing, he looked astern, then at his wrist watch. 'Full ahead, helmsman,' he ordered, then turned to Schepke. 'We can expect to be in the river a little after daylight, yes?'

'About that,' Schepke said, thinking now about the girl and her father.

'What about the *Hoboken*?' Müller asked.

'She will wireless a Mayday come daylight,' Lyebedev told him. 'By that time we shall be clear. And your radio operator. Where is he?'

'He's below somewhere,' Schepke told him.

'Then please get him up here.'

Schepke hesitated, then went to the doorway. 'Altmeyer!' he called below.

'Yes, sir?' They could hear Altmeyer answer from somewhere aft.

'Come on up here!'

Altmeyer entered the bridge, then suddenly saw the men and guns.

'Easy,' Schepke told him.

'You are the only radio operator on board?' Lyebedev asked.

Altmeyer swallowed, then nodded. No one had ever pointed a gun at him before.

'Then you remain here,' Lyebedev told him. 'Get over there by the big one,' he added, motioning at the expressionless Kamei standing out in the port wing.

'Bridge!' It was Hechler, below somewhere in the passage.

Lyebedev motioned for Schepke to remain silent.

'Bridge!' Hechler called again.

One of the men with an automatic moved quietly in behind the bridge door as Hechler started upstairs.

'Karl. What—' And he saw Lyebedev and felt the muzzle of the automatic in the small of his back.

'I take it you are our Chief Engineer?' Lyebedev said.

Hechler looked from him to Schepke.

'We're headed in for Chingkiang,' Schepke told him.

'I think you better return below,' Lyebedev said. 'But before you go I wish you to understand that should any attempt be made to make trouble below the outcome will not be as you expect.' Then he spoke across Hechler's shoulder to the man with the automatic, and to one of the others on the starboard wing. 'These two will accompany you,' he said again to Hechler. 'Remember, no trouble. You make trouble and your Captain shall be first to suffer.'

Hechler looked at Schepke again, then turned silently and went below with the two seamen.

Lyebedev looked at them, smiling. 'Perhaps everything will go smoothly now,' he said.

Karl Schepke turned and leaned onto the ledge of the open

window. Out ahead of the bows the ocean was black and empty and lit only by the moon. It was very quiet and there was a dew falling now in the cool night air, and he was thinking about the girl and her father, and what would happen at Chingkiang.

THE *Gertrud Lüth* entered the Yangtze a little after daybreak. It was a dull overcast morning and there was thick fog covering the lower reaches of the river. The pilots came out from Woosung in a navy launch, accompanied by a naval officer and eight seamen. The seamen carried rifles slung over their shoulders and Karl Schepke watched them come on board from the port wing.

'It will be over soon,' Lyebedev said joining him at the window.

Karl Schepke looked at him but did not say anything.

'You know. Captain,' Lyebedev went on. 'I am profoundly sorry that this should happen. Had it not been for that unfortunate accident on board the *Hoboken* you would now be well on your way to Kobe.'

Again Schepke remained silent.

'Yes. I, too, would be angry,' Lyebedev said.

Schepke looked down at the tarpaulined cases on the forward well. Then he heard the two pilots and the naval officer arrive on the bridge.

'Let them take her,' he said turning to Pulst.

Pulst left the wheel to the youngest of the two pilots and joined Altmeyer and Kamei on the port wing. They were both sitting on the deck and Cheng and Müller sitting by the door to the charthouse.

Schepke watched the pilot ring the engines on and saw them opened up Full Ahead. Then as they drove on up above Woosung the fog thinned then passed astern, leaving the river ahead of them wide and yellow and fast-flowing. Two of the Chinese naval seamen were on the bridge with their officer, and the officer was talking now with Lyebedev. After a few minutes he left Lyebedev and crossed the bridge to Schepke.

'I am sorry there is so much haste, Captain,' he said, politely. 'However, we have orders to proceed up-river with all possible speed. Your ship will be in no danger. The pilots are of the most accomplished on the river.'

'I'll take your word for it,' Schepke told him.

The Chinese politely bowed and smiled.

'Why all the guns?' Schepke asked, glancing at his two seamen.

Again he smiled. 'I merely carry out my orders, Captain. I do not question them.'

'Captain.' It was Lyebedev. Sam was standing in the open doorway, staring wide-eyed at all the guns.

'What is it?'

Sam nervously cleared his throat, his face pale beneath the yellow. 'Someone take key to meat store,' he said, finally. 'Not able get any meat.'

Schepke looked at Lyebedev, and the Russian shrugged. 'We are in the river now,' he said. 'You may go below if you wish.'

Schepke followed Sam down into the cabin passage, then aft to the galley.

'Girl very sick,' Sam said when they were in the galley. 'Sick all morning! I not able tell you before! Too much guns!'

Schepke glanced out along the the passage to the bridge and saw Lyebedev standing with his back to the open doorway. Grabbing Sam by the arm, they went quickly back along the passage to the big cabin.

The girl was lying in the bunk, her father leaning over her. 'What happened?'

'She has been ill since early morning,' the old man told him. 'Since before daylight.'

She was lying very quietly on the bunk, her eyes closed. He felt the light flutter of her pulse.

'Fu-chen,' he called very softly to her.

She moved her head slightly on the pillow and looked up at him.

335

'How do you feel?' he asked. 'Tell me how you feel? Is there any pain?'

'She has been sick,' her father said.

'It is nothing,' she said very quietly.

'I couldn't get down before,' he said.

'It is nothing,' she said. 'It will go soon.' The shadow of a smile touched her mouth. 'I am sorry to be ill,' she went on, then closed her eyes again, her breathing very light.

'There's not much we can do,' he told her father. 'It could be almost anything. Even the strain of the past few days.'

'I had thought about that too,' her father said.

'We'll get some ventilation,' Schepke said crossing to the scuttles and lifting the deadlights and swinging the heavy scuttles open. The breeze came in very coolly and smelling of the shore and the river.

'What happens above?' the old man asked. 'When we stopped I saw we were in the Great.'

'We're going to Chingkiang.'

The old man looked at him again but did not say anything.

'Sam. Get some iced water. Give her plenty to drink. There's nothing else we can do just now.'

The old man moved his fingers very gently across his daughter's forehead. He had not said anything about Chingkiang.

'Let me know if she gets worse,' Schepke told him. 'Tell Sam.'

'—I did not know you had passengers on board, Captain,' Lyebedev said from the doorway.

Schepke turned on him angrily. 'It's none of your business!'

'My apologies,' Lyebedev politely said, at the same time entering the cabin and quietly closing the door. 'How long has she been ill?' he asked, looking at the girl.

'Since morning,' Schepke said, not looking at him, but gently touching the girl's forehead. Her skin was cool and there seemed no trace of fever.

'It is hot in here,' Lyebedev said. 'It may be the heat.'

'She complained about the heat last evening,' the old man said.

336

'It may be a slight form of heat exhaustion,' Lyebedev said. 'Beyond that I would not offer an opinion.'

At that moment Sam returned with the iced water.

'Give her anything she asks,' Schepke told him. 'I'll be back when I can.'

'They are friends of yours?' Lyebedev asked when they were in the passage.

'Yes. They're friends of mine,' Schepke told him.

'I am sorry I should bring you all this trouble.'

'So you already said.' He was feeling bitter now. Nothing ever seemed to go good once it began to happen.

'I said I am sorry,' Lyebedev persisted.

Schepke went on up to the bridge, Lyebedev following. The Chinese officer stared at them for a brief moment then turned back to the pilots. Karl Schepke leaned on one of the open windows and looked out at the river. The river was narrowing slightly now and a number of junks, their great spreads of straw matting sails catching the damp breeze, headed in on Kiang Yin. And then he was thinking again about the girl, and what would happen at Chingkiang.

WITH the coming of darkness the pilots dropped speed.

'What time do you expect to arrive?' Schepke asked.

'Two hours,' the officer said, smiling. 'In two hours we will have reached Chingkiang.' He was extremely pleased with his accomplishment.

'I'll want the bosun now,' Schepke said turning to Lyebedev. 'I'll have to ready for anchoring or going alongside.'

'As you wish,' Lyebedev told him.

Kamei followed Schepke down into the passage to the big cabin.

'How is she?' he asked the old man.

'She has been sick again this evening.'

'I couldn't get down before,' Schepke told him. 'There were too many of them on the bridge.'

The girl was lying very quietly on the bunk, her eyes closed against the light.

'Has she complained of pain?'

'No,' her father answered him. 'She has said nothing about there being pain.'

'Maybe it would be better if there was,' Schepke said. 'At least we might know what was wrong.' While he spoke the girl stretched out on the bunk, moaning gently as she moved. 'Fu-chen,' he said very quietly to her.

'She has begun to get restless this past hour,' her father told him.

'Fu-chen. Do you hear me?' Schepke said again.

She moved her head very lightly on the pillow but did not open her eyes. A thin film of perspiration showed on her forehead but yet her skin was cool to touch. Her face was grey now and tired-looking, and her breathing was very light.

'We are far up the river,' the old man said glancing to the lights of a village on the north bank.

'We'll be at Chingkiang soon,' Schepke said rising from the bunk.

The old man turned back from the scuttle and took his daughter's hand very gently in his.

'Everything's not over yet,' Schepke told him. He had not been able to think of a place for them to hide if the ship was searched, but now he saw a possibility. 'Please,' he said, motioning the old man away from the bunk then sliding the top drawer all the way out. It was a full-length drawer and it went about half the way in under the bunk to the after bulkhead.

'I think it just possible,' Kamei said, kneeling by him as he swiftly slid the remaining drawers from their spaces.

'What about the carpenter?'

'He will say nothing if questioned,' Kamei said, very sure about it.

'Get him up here. And you better stay with him. I'll see to

the deck.' He stood up and quickly lifted part of the mattress and saw the solid wooden floor of the bunk. 'Get him to take this up and make the bed on open boards. They will want plenty of air. Get him to take the drawers off then fit the faces. Sam can make up some bedding inside.'

'I know,' Kamei said, then slipped silently out into the passage.

'You think it will work?' the old man asked.

'There's nothing else,' Schepke told him. 'It's your daughter I'm worried about. They'll probably search the ship at Chingkiang and it's going to be difficult to stay in there for very long.'

The old man moved his head sadly. 'I have been very foolish.'

'There's nothing you can do now,' Schepke told him as Kamei came in with the Chinese carpenter. 'Tell him what to do. I'm going below now.'

Both watches were on deck and up on the forepeak he saw Dorsch with the rest of the cable party.

'We won't be at Chingkiang for some time yet.'

'I didn't mind coming up,' Dorsch told him. 'I've had a gun in my back all day.' He stopped and glanced up at the darkness of the bridge. 'I thought the days of piracy were over. And what about all this yellow stuff with guns?' he said looking at the Chinese navy men in the well.

'I know about as much as you,' Schepke told him.

Dorsch glanced below at the well again. 'Who's this one?'

Schepke turned to see Lyebedev, bulky-looking in his reefer coat as he passed under the glow of the overhead floods.

'Russian,' Schepke said, and went below, leaving Dorsch at the rail.

Lyebedev had stopped by the tarpaulined cases and was lighting one of his pasteboard-tipped cigarettes.

'I do not think there is anything to worry about, Captain,' he said as Schepke approached. 'All they do now is off-load the cases. It is possible you will be on your way down-river again before daylight.'

Schepke declined his offer of a cigarette but lit one of his own, arcing the lighted match out across the wall.

'The girl. She is some better?'

339

'Not yet,' Schepke told him, drawing on his cigarette, the glow lighting his face under the high peaked cap.

'She is very beautiful,' Lyebedev said very quietly.

Schepke looked at him in the glow of the overhead floods. 'Yes. She is a very beautiful girl.'

Lyebedev looked now at his wrist watch. 'In another hour,' he said.

Karl Schepke was wondering how things were going in the big cabin.

'A Dutchman sighted the *Hoboken* just before daylight,' Lyebedev went on. 'She is headed for Taipeh. The Chinese officer told me. She alerted Shanghai for us. That was why the military were waiting.'

Karl Schepke wondered now if he had mentioned the girl and her father to the officer. Then he wondered if Major Pao would be waiting. Then suddenly he did not wish to think about any of it.

'This deck-cargo must be very important,' he said instead.

Lyebedev shrugged. 'Personally I do not know why we give anything to China,' he said. 'She is not to be trusted. One day everyone will realize that, probably when it is too late.'

'What I don't understand is why the *Hoboken* was so far south when she was supposed to be from Singapore. Besides, you're Russian.'

'I am afraid there are complications,' Lyebedev told him. 'But then I suppose most things are complicated when one examines them. As it is, we were transferred to the *Hoboken* in the South Atlantic. We were returning home after being diverted from Cuba when ordered to deliver part of the cargo to China. The *Hoboken* did not call at a single port on the way north. It has been a long voyage.'

Karl Schepke drew on his cigarette then arced it out across the wall. 'I'll have to get back to the bridge now. We'll be in Silver Island Pass soon.'

It was quiet and dark on the river and he crossed the welldeck to the starboard alleyway, Lyebedev watching him from where he stood by the tarpaulined cases.

There was no one in the cabin passage and, above him, some-one had closed the bridge door. The carpenter had finished with the drawer facings and was working on the floor of the bunk, the old man watching him from where his daughter now lay with the rest of the bedding by the table.

'How is she?'

The old man slowly shook his head. 'She wakened once,' he said. 'But there is no improvement.'

'Have you seen anybody ill like this before?'

'There are many fevers of similar nature at this stage,' the old man told him.

He had already thought about fevers but said nothing further.

'Inside there is plenty room,' Kamei told him.

Schepke joined them as the carpenter removed the last of the bunk flooring. Without the drawers there was a long empty space the complete length of the bunk. 'Just fix enough spars to hold the bedding,' he told the carpenter. 'They'll want all the air they can get.' Then he turned to the old man again as Kamei spread the bedding out inside. 'We can only try this,' he said. 'Either that or you can go ashore.'

The old man glanced at his daughter. 'We will remain,' he said very quietly. 'I only wish we had not burdened you so.'

Schepke looked down at the girl. Her face was grey and waxy-looking against the smooth shining blackness of her hair. 'I'll have to get back to the bridge now,' he said. 'Kamei will help you both inside when we go through the Pass. I'll do all I can.'

The old man politely bowed his head as Schepke turned again to Kamei and the carpenter.

'You know what to do. Get them inside when we go through the Pass. Then fix the spars and replace the bedding. The rest you'll have to leave to me.' He paused, closely examining the face of the bunk. The carpenter had done a good job and unless someone tried to open the drawers they would never know. 'Get Sam to clear up,' he told Kamei. 'Put everything over the wall.' Then he stopped in the doorway and looked back at the girl. He started to say something and saw the old man watching him, and instead he went on out into the passage.

341

THE night was dark when they entered Silver Island Pass and there was no moon showing and the high perpendicular cliff on the south shore was a solid mass of blackness, the temples on the island lost in the darkness. Then once they were through the Pass there was suddenly the long straggling mass of lights that was Chingkiang.

'I'll want all officers at anchor stations now.'

The Chinese officer looked across the bridge from where he stood by the wheel. 'Of course, Captain. Please carry on.'

'You know what to do,' Schepke said looking at Müller and Cheng. 'Altmeyer. Stand by on the flying bridge.'

'The signal station is calling now, Captain,' the Chinese said.

'Forepeak!' Schepke called from the open window. 'Stand by in case we go alongside!'

'Bridge!' Altmeyer shouted in through the open hatchway. 'Message reads: *Proceed to Number Three Anchorage Area.*'

'Stand by to come to anchor!' Schepke called to the forepeak.

As they came to anchor he saw the boat come up astern of them in the glow of shipboard lights. It was an old steam picket boat and there were soldiers gathered on the foredeck, their upturned faces reflecting the yellow glow of light as they stared at the deck above them.

'Main engines rung off, Captain,' the Chinese officer reported.

'Boat alongside, Herr Kapitän!' Altmeyer called below.

'Good!' Schepke crossed to the forward windows. 'Müller! Stand by on the bridge!'

He saw Müller leave the forepeak and hurry across the well, and when he turned from the window he saw there was only Bahr and Pulst and the Chinese officer still with him. 'Stay here with Müller,' he told them then followed the officer below.

Both Kamei and Cheng were waiting in the port alleyway by

the ladder, the soldiers already gathered forward by the well, and the steam picket boat now lying about one hundred metres off the beam, her tall spindly funnel belching thick grey smoke as she kept her head into the stream.

'Captain Schepke.' He turned to find Major Pao behind him in the alleyway. Major Pao was wearing the full uniform of a major in the Chinese People's Army. Lieutenant Lyebedev was standing a little way behind him with his men, the two with the automatic rifles carrying them slung over their shoulders.

'This is such an unexpected meeting, Captain.'

'And the soldiers?' Schepke said. 'What do they want?'

Major Pao withdrew his hand and smiled. 'Please do not worry about the soldiers.'

'When can you get this cargo off-loaded?'

'But you have only just arrived, Captain.'

'You're a bright boy, Major.'

'I am afraid we can do nothing until morning,' the Major said, an edge of authority coming into his voice. 'Unfortunately we are still unable to have shipping alongside the wharf. However, there will be lighters out first thing in the morning.'

'All right,' Schepke said. 'Have it your way.'

'Splendid. Then we will have the cargo off-loaded at daylight. Meanwhile—' he paused, smiling.

'Meanwhile what?' Schepke said, watching him carefully.

'Your passengers. I wish them to accompany me ashore.'

'I don't know what you mean.'

'Come now, Captain,' Major Pao said, smiling thinly.

'They were taken ashore before we left Hong Kong,' Schepke told him. 'They're in civil custody. We have a company signal to that effect. I'm afraid you've been misinformed, Major.'

'No. It is you who has been misinformed, Captain. That signal was sent to you purposefully so you might go to the aid of the *Hoboken*. This cargo was extremely important, too, Captain. Peking is under no illusions. Now perhaps I may have your passengers.'

'I told you,' Schepke said, coldly. 'They're in Hong Kong.'

The Major Pao stared impassively at him for a moment then

turned to Lyebedev. 'What about you, Lieutenant? Have you seen the old man and girl?'

Lyebedev glanced briefly at Schepke. 'I have seen no one,' he said. 'Certainly not a girl.'

'Then I will search the ship!' Major Pao said whirling again on Schepke, shouting orders to the soldiers.

The soldiers spread out aft along the alleyway, their rifles clattering against the metal casing.

'One moment, Major,' Lyebedev interrupted. 'Myself and my men wish to be taken ashore as soon as possible. The cargo is no longer our responsibility.'

'You will be taken ashore when I am ready!'

'Then if you are to be any time at all I wish a boat sent from shore,' Lyebedev told him.

The Major Pao started to say something then turned abruptly, shouting at the soldiers already searching the after well and fantail.

Lyebedev saw Schepke looking at him and he smiled, shrugging his shoulders.

'Thank you,' Schepke told him.

'I hope she is well soon. She is a very beautiful girl.'

HE was waiting in his cabin passage when Major Pao and the three soldiers came in from the boatdeck.

'I told you there was nobody on board,' he said when they had searched Hechler's cabin.

'What is in there?' Major Pao asked, pointing to the door in under the bridge stairway.

'The Radio Office. Go ahead.'

One of the soldiers went forward and opened the door.

'And here?' Major Pao said, stopping outside the big cabin.

'Nobody uses that,' Schepke told him.

344

Major Pao swung the door open and glanced around the cabin.

'You're wasting your time, Major. They were taken ashore before we left Hong Kong.'

'No, Captain! They are somewhere on board this ship! Major Pao said, his anger mounting again. 'I want them!'

'That's up to you,' Schepke said.

Major Pao stepped back into the passage and saw the soldier come out from the Radio Office.

'Captain!'

Schepke turned to see Cheng come in from the boatdeck. 'What is it?'

'The Lieutenant Lyebedev wishes to know how long it is before the Major is ready to go ashore.'

Major Pao started to say something then stopped himself.

'—Tell him I will be now!'

Cheng hesitated for a moment, glancing at Schepke, then turned abruptly and left.

Major Pao turned again to Schepke. 'Since you refuse to hand these people to me now you must accept the full consequences of your actions. You can consider yourself and ship under immediate arrest. I suggest you have these people ready to land when I return at daylight. Otherwise—'

Lyebedev and his men were waiting by the ladder.

'We are ready?' he asked.

Major Pao ignored him, raising his arm instead and signalling the picket boat. Then looking forward to the well he called something to the soldiers and seamen searching the forepeak tunnel lockers.

They were all amidships when the picket boat came alongside.

'Think carefully about what I have said, Captain. I shall return at daylight.'

Schepke watched him go down the ladder.

'Goodbye, Captain,' Lyebedev said.

Schepke watched him follow Major Pao below, then saw the four soldiers still in the alleyway.

'Pao!' he called over the wall. 'What about these?'

Major Pao stood looking up at him from the deck of the boat. 'A guard boat will be here soon!' he called. 'Good night!' He sounded extremely confident.

Schepke watched the boat pull slowly clear of the wall, the acrid fumes and funnel smoke filling the alleyway.

'Kamei!' He motioned with his head toward the screen door, then saw Cheng watching them. 'What are you waiting for?' he asked, as Kamei went on up to the big cabin. 'You better get turned in. I want you on deck early tomorrow.'

'Karl!' It was Hechler. He had just come from below, wiping oil and coal dust from his face and hands with a sweat-rag. 'What's all this?' he asked, glancing at the soldiers.

'Pao was here. I'll tell you about it later.'

The door of the big cabin was locked.

'Kamei,' he said, listening.

Kamei opened the door and he saw the girl on the bunk bedding on the deck, her father kneeling by her side. She was breathing very heavily through her mouth, the perspiration dampening her hair and showing on her forehead and cheeks.

'She has just been sick,' her father said.

'Has she ever had malaria?'

'Never.'

'Is there any rash?' Schepke asked, kneeling and touching her face. 'She's cold,' he said. 'Kamei. Get Sam to get more blankets.'

'What of the soldiers?' the old man asked as they waited.

'Don't worry about them.' He took the blankets now from Kamei and carefully covered the girl. 'I'm sorry I can't stay. I have to go on deck now. Lock the door when we leave.'

Kamei followed him out into the passage and then waited until they heard the door locked.

'She is very sick,' Kamei said.

'There's nothing we can do without a doctor.'

'There is only Chingkiang,' Kamei said.

'See there's a watch on the anchor,' Schepke told him and went on up to the bridge.

Both quartermasters and Müller were out in the starboard

346

wing. A large, well-lighted motor-ship was almost abeam of them. headed down-river.

'What's happening?' Müller asked.

'There's a guard boat coming out.'

'What about the old man and girl?'

'They didn't find them. They'll be out again at daylight.'

'I wouldn't mind any being on her going out of here,' Bahr said, watching the motor-ship put Chiao Shan on her starboard beam.

Schepke looked at him suddenly then hurried to the after windows. The motor-ship was stern-on to them now as she went in through the Pass on the north side. Quickly he crossed the bridge to the charthouse and leaned over the chart used coming up-river. It was a long way to the ocean, even on paper.

'Kapitän. sir!' Pulst shouted. 'Guard boat coming alongside!'

'Good. Tell Altmeyer I want him.'

He was still at the table when Altmeyer entered.

'Close the door,' he told him; then waited. 'What was she? The motor-ship.'

'Oh, she was Dutch,' Altmeyer said. 'The *Jacob Droonkart*.'

Schepke looked again at the chart. 'What river-lights was she using?'

'Yellow over red,' Altmeyer said.

'All right. Go on back to the bridge. Note everything that moves on the river. Everything. Understand?'

He followed the boy out and went straight to the telephones.

'Engine-room. Frauenheim here,' the voice the other end said.

'Listen carefully. Give me five minutes then cut the dynamos. Got that?'

'Five minutes then cut the dynamos,' Frauenheim repeated. 'What about the—'

'Just cut the dynamos,' Schepke told him and hung the receiver back on its hook.

'What do you want to do that for?' Müller asked.

'I'll tell you when I come back. Just watch the river.'

He found Hechler in the galley.

'I've just told Frauenheim to cut the dynamos.'

'—You did what?'

'The lights are going to fade any minute now,' Schepke told him. 'Come on up to the bridge. I just thought about something and I want to hear how everybody feels about it.'

They arrived on the bridge just as the lights suddenly flickered and faded, leaving the ship strangely quiet.

'Müller. Call the engine-room and ask Dorsch and Frauenheim up here right away.'

'Bridge!' It was Kamei, abreast of Number Two hatch. 'The guard boat asks what has happened to our lights!'

'Tell them the dynamos have broken down! Tell them we're trying to repair them now!' As he turned from the window he saw Frauenheim and Dorsch come in.

'Altmeyer!' he called through the open hatchway.

He waited for the boy to come in down the ladder.

'Now that we're all here I won't waste any more time,' he told them. 'As you know we still have the girl and her father on board. Major Pao will be out again at daylight and this time he won't leave until he finds them. I know these two people probably mean nothing to you and before I tell you what I had in mind I want you to understand that going through with it is entirely up to yourselves. I don't want to—'

'You want to go down-river,' Hechler told him.

Schepke looked back at him in the gloom. 'It would be dangerous. We might not even get far.'

It was suddenly quiet and the only sounds were those of the river carrying in through the open windows.

'As you say, it would be dangerous,' Hechler said, noncommittally.

'The river's high,' Schepke offered. 'We should have plenty of depth for the tricky parts.'

'It's a long way from here to the ocean,' Dorsch said.

'It's up to you,' Schepke told them. 'Don't think you're being forced into anything. We abide by the majority.'

'I'll go,' Altmeyer said, not hiding his excitement.

'There's a lot of artillery on the river,' Müller told them. 'I've seen it. We could be dead before we reached Rose Island.'

'What about you, Gerhard?' Hechler said.

Frauenheim sighed. 'I guess it's a way of getting our own back.'

'You can count on me any way you want,' Dorsch said.

'That's three of us and Altmeyer,' Hechler said.

'Anybody else?' Schepke asked, looking in turn at Müller, Bahr, and Pulst.

'I don't know why, but I'll go,' Bahr said.

Pulst nodded. 'Same here.'

'What about you, Müller?' Schepke asked, waiting.

'What about the guard boat?'

'I've already thought about her,' Schepke told him.

'How are we going to get away?' Dorsch asked. 'Even if you can handle the guard boat they will still see us from the shore.'

'You'll have to leave that to me. The difficult part will be getting down and around Rose Island, then Kiang Yin.'

'What about daylight?' Müller asked. 'Even if we got clear we wouldn't be past the forts at Woosung by daylight.'

'You saw the river this morning. Fog like that lasts for days. Even now there's no moon and the cloud's low. It would be difficult to see anything moving on the river tonight.'

'That counts both ways,' Müller argued. 'I don't like it.'

'Well if we're going we'll have to start soon,' Hechler said, impatient now.

'We're risking our lives for nothing,' Müller continued to argue.

'You're forgetting something,' Schepke told him. 'It was you brought them on board. What do you want to do now, sell them back?'

Müller started to say something then changed his mind.

'Well when do we start?' Hechler asked, considering everything settled.

Schepke looked carefully at his wrist watch. 'It'll take some time to arrange,' he said, then turned to Altmeyer. 'Use the Aldis and make the following: *Dynamos failed. Spares required to effect necessary repairs. Engineer officer will land at daylight.*'

Altmeyer collected the Aldis from the charthouse and hurried above to the flying bridge.

'You better close up all watches,' Schepke told Hechler. 'Stand by as soon as you go below. First of all I'll try and get below Chiao Shan on the other side of the Pass. Dorsch can close up on the forepeak. I want him to start running the capstans. Give the impression we're having trouble with the anchors dragging. All right?'

'Leave it to me,' Dorsch said.

'We're going to be pressed for time,' Frauenheim told them, thinking about daylight now as Müller had done.

'We should make good time on the way down,' Schepke said. 'There'll be a five, six knot current behind us.'

'You're going down all out?' Dorsch asked, slightly shocked at the thought.

'I want to be at maximum before we reach Kiang Yin. After that we don't stop.' He paused, looking at Müller. 'What about you?'

'There's nothing I can do about it,' Müller said, sullenly.

'Then rig out a few huricane lamps. Put out some steaming lights first, but keep the bridge and foredeck dark.

'Bridge!' Altmeyer called below. 'Message acknowledged, sir!'

'Good!'

'It's going to be dark on the river,' Bahr said.

'Just carry out the orders as I give them. Once the river begins to widen it won't be so difficult. I'll be back in a few minutes.'

He found Kamei in the port alleyway. Two of the soldiers from the guard boat were standing in the screen doorway and in the gloom he saw one of them wore the insignia of an officer. He was tall and wore a sword at his side.

'I'm sorry about the lights,' Schepke told them in English. 'Perhaps Major Pao will help in the morning.'

'I am certain he will,' the officer said perfectly in English, then looked quickly forward as the sudden harsh steel clatter of the capstans carried down from the forepeak.

'We're also having some trouble with the anchors,' Schepke explained. 'They're dragging with the current.'

'It is impossible to go alongside, Captain. The wharf is still in the process of being rebuilt.'

350

'We may have to drop below Chiao Shan,' Schepke said, casually. 'We would be in lee of the island then.'

'You would first have to seek permission,' the officer said. 'No one is allowed to move on the river without permission.'

'Of course,' Schepke agreed. Then as he turned forward he motioned Kamei to follow him. Once on the forward well they stopped and looked back along the alleyway. Both the soldiers had gone below to the guard boat.

'Are they all down there?'

Kamei nodded. 'Those two came on board when the lights failed.'

'How many are there?'

'Six with the boat and the other four.'

'We'll have to do something about them,' Schepke told him. 'We're going down-river.'

Kamei looked at him closely in the darkness of the forward well. 'It is a difficult river in darkness,' he said.

'I think we can manage. What I want you to do now is get some light on the forepeak. I want it to look as though we're having trouble holding against the current. Afterward stay here in the well where I can reach you.'

Going back along the alleyway he stopped and looked over the wall. The guard boat was still tied up to the ladder and a light in under the canopy showed the soldiers sitting around in the cockpit talking and smoking cigarettes.

Pulst was waiting for him on the bridge stairway. 'There's another ship on the way down, sir. Altmeyer reported it just after you went below.'

Schepke crossed to the open windows and saw the lights some way up above Chingkiang. Reaching for the engine-room telephone, he spun the handle. It was Hechler who answered.

'Listen carefully, Hans,' Schepke told him. 'I'm going to manoeuvre a while here at anchor. Let them think we're having trouble with the current. Have somebody stay close to the telephone from now on.' When he replaced the receiver he saw them with lamps on the forepeak now and steam blowing back across the rails in the breeze.

351

'Ring on main engines,' he told Pulst. 'Bahr. Bring her up on the cables, stop her, then let her drift astern again. Do that three or four times. I'll be overhead with Altmeyer.'

'Yes, sir.'

'Slow ahead.'

'Slow ahead, sir,' Pulst answered, ringing the telegraph on. Schepke went on up to the flying bridge as the ship began to move slowly ahead. 'What is she?' he asked, looking at the lights approaching from upstream.

'She looks like cargo passenger,' Altmeyer told him.

Schepke heard the telegraph bell repeat as the engines died, and then they were beginning to drift and Dorsch was running both capstans in neutral and with the steam cocks open.

'Bring her ahead again!' he called into the bridge. Then: 'Stand by with the Aldis,' he told Altmeyer.

Altmeyer went out onto the port wing and Schepke waited until they had drifted astern again.

'Make: *Anchors dragging. Seek permission to proceed to anchorage in lee of Chiao Shan.*'

The ship coming down-river was close upon them now. She was high and wide and with her cabin deck brightly lit. Putting the glasses on her bow he saw she was the *Kaptjan Frederiksen*. Keeping the glasses on her he watched her draw abeam, passing close along the starboard side. There were several of the crew and passengers gathered at the near rails as she passed.

'She's Danish,' Altmeyer said, watching her pass astern.

Schepke was watching the shore now, seeing the lights of the signal tower to the north of the wharf.

'Still no reply, sir.'

Pulst and Bahr had brought the ship ahead again and now she was beginning to drift.

'There looks like a boat coming out from shore, sir.'

Schepke was already watching her lights as she drew away from the shore, fighting hard against the fast current. Astern of them the *Kaptjan Frederiksen* was putting Chiao Shan between them.

'She looks like a motor patrol boat, sir.'

352

Schepke watched the lights get brighter and now he saw her turn away to port and take up station ahead of them on the port bow, her engines running full ahead and the noise carrying loudly in the night.

'Message beginning now, sir!' Altmeyer shouted.

From S/T Chingkiang to S.S. Gertrud Lüth. Permission granted to proceed to anchorage lower side Chiao Shan.

Karl Schepke read it himself, then stepped onto the ladder to the bridge. 'From now on watch the river closely,' he told Altmeyer. 'If that boat follows us downstream keep it in sight.'

THE *Gertrud Lüth* moved slowly in under the lee of Chiao Shan, the lights of Chingkiang hidden now beyond the Pass and all that showed in the darkness over the island was the shadowy blackness of the temples above the shore. Astern was the small tight cluster of lights that was the village of Yin-kin-chow on the larger island of Ta-sha on the bend of the river. Then below them, on the south shore, showed the lights of Chin-chia-shan and Tan-ta-chen, both villages to the west of the entrance to the Grand Canal to Soochow.

'Altmeyer!' Schepke called above. 'Where's the patrol boat?'

'Directly astern. About six hundred metres away. She's between us and those lights on Ta-sha.'

Schepke swore. He was worried now about the time. 'Kamei!' he called into the well. 'Come on up here! Then: 'Forepeak! Douse those lamps!'

With the engines shut down it was very quiet in under the lee of Chiao Shan.

'Pulst. Go down and tell Sam to make supper for the soldiers. Tell him to hurry.' Then as he turned to the wing he saw Kamei

353

come in. 'I'll want you to help,' he told him. 'But first I want that patrol boat to move. We can't do anything with her lying astern.'

'It is something special you want?' Kamei asked.

'If that boat moves I want as many soldiers as possible to come on board for supper. If we can get them in the messroom it should be easy. It's the ones who will still be in the boat I'm worried about.'

'Leave to Kamei. I fix good. No trouble,' Kamei said, very confident.

'Bridge!' It was Altmeyer. 'Patrol boat moving to starboard. I think she's headed into the Pass.'

'Good!' Schepke told him, feeling a sudden lightness of excitement in his chest.

'Sam's busy on it now, sir,' Pulst said as he came in.

Schepke turned to Kamei again. 'I'll send Sam down to the boat when he's ready. Give them time to start eating.'

Kamei nodded, his great bulk adding to the gloom in the bridge.

'Kapitän, sir!' Altmeyer called below. 'She's just entering the Pass now.'

Sam was in the galley with Kuang.

'Ready now, sir,' Sam told him.

'Go down and tell them. Tell them what you have even if we haven't got it. Tell them anything. Get as many on board as you can.' He took one of the galley lamps and went forward to the big cabin as Sam went below.

The old man opened the door, blinking against the brightness of the light.

'How is she?' Schepke asked him, closing the door.

'She is asleep now.'

He set the lamp onto the table. The girl's face was pinched and grey, although now her breathing sounded more regular and even.

'Let her sleep,' he said. 'This could be the turning point. It seems like some sort of fever.' He stood up, taking the lamp from the table.

'We have come below in the river,' the old man said.

Schepke nodded. 'We'll be moving again soon. We're going—' he stopped suddenly, listening to the sound of movement in the passage. 'We're going down-river,' he went on again quietly. 'Stay in the cabin whatever happens.'

'I hope there will not be further trouble for you,' the old man said. 'Perhaps in the morning it would be better if we went ashore. We have already over-burdened you with troubles.'

'It's too late now. You're going down-river.' He did not wish to say more. They would be sitting down to eat. Then he stopped at the door and looked back at the girl. She was lying on the bedding on the deck, her face pinched and grey-looking in the yellow light of the hurricane lamp.

'Stay here in the cabin. If there's any shooting lie flat on the deck and cover yourselves with the spare bedding. It might help.'

He went out into the passage and waited for the old man to lock the door. Then as he started aft, Sam put his head out from the galley and looked both ways along the passage.

'How many?'

'Seven,' Sam whispered, nervous now, the sweat beading on his forehead.

Schepke handed him the lantern then unbuttoned the right hand pocket of his tunic and felt the smooth, cool heaviness of the Walther. With it still in his pocket he slipped the catch off and entered the doorway of the messroom. The officer was sitting at the table with his back to the hatchway, his sword resting on the worn carpeting. The rifles were stacked against the outboard bulkhead, and all six of the private soldiers busy eating. Kuang was on the far side of the table when he saw Schepke motion him away.

Then the first of the soldiers saw him and the officer turned and Schepke stepped quickly behind him and put the muzzle of the Walther against the back of his neck.

'Don't move! Tell them to keep their hands on the table!'

The soldiers sat dumbly watching him, not moving.

'Tell them to keep sitting and don't move.'

The soldiers sat watching him, only their eyes moving in their wide cheekboned faces.

'Sam! You and Kuang take those rifles out.' He waited until they had carried the rifles out into the passage then stepped smoothly away from the back of the chair. 'All right,' he told the officer. 'On your feet.'

The officer stood quietly to his feet, moving the chair away with his legs, his hands raised shoulder-high. Schepke withdrew the sword from its scabbard and threw it across by the doorway, then did the same with the holstered revolver.

'Now get back against the forward bulkhead. Take it slowly.' He held the Walther pointed the length of the table now, none of the the soldiers eager to move. They sat quietly, their eyes fixed on the heavy Walther. The officer now had his back against the forward bulkhead. Then somewhere a sudden solitary gunshot broke the quiet, and one of the soldiers jumped automatically to his feet.

'Sit down!' Schepke shouted, levelling the Walther.

The soldier looked directly into the muzzle and sat slowly onto his chair.

'Schepke!' Müller was somewhere out in the passage.

'Here!' Sam shouted from the doorway. 'Captain here!'

Schepke kept the Walther on the soldiers. 'Get a rifle,' he told Müller as he came in.

Müller came back with one of the rifles, snicking the bolt up and over then levelling it the length of the table.

'What happened outside?'

'It came from the boat,' Müller told him.

'All right,' Schepke told the soldiers. 'One at a time.' He beckoned the nearest to his feet and motioned him back against the forward bulkhead. He watched them line up carefully against the bulkhead, their hands raised shoulder-high, none of them anxious to make any sudden movement.

'Keep them like that until I come back,' he told Müller and turned and hurried to the boatdeck.

'Kamei!' he called into the darkness. 'Kamei!'

'I am here.'

He turned to see Kamei loom massively out from the darkness above the after ladder.

'Are you all right?'

'I fix,' Kamei said.

'What was the shooting?'

'It was a rifle,' Kamei explained unconcernedly.

'Where are they?'

Kamei looked back at him in the darkness. 'They are in the boat.'

'All right. Get a rifle and help Müller put the others below to that empty storeroom on the port side. The rifles are in the passage.'

The soldiers were still lined up apprehensively against the bulkhead.

'Kamei will help you put them below,' he told Müller. 'When you've finished come up on the bridge.'

On the way forward he met Cheng coming from his cabin. 'What was the shooting? I heard shooting.'

'Get back in your cabin!' Schepke told him as he pushed past.

Bahr and Pulst were waiting for him.

'Pulst! Douse those steaming lights! —Altmeyer!' he called into the hatchway. 'Anything moving out there?'

'Only some junks to the north toward Hsin-chow! There's nothing moving this side!'

'Forepeak!' he shouted through the open window. 'Slip both!'

He waited, hearing the pins being knocked from the cables simultaneously, then hearing the heavy rumbling of the parted cables in the hawse-pipes and the splashes coming quickly upon each other.

'Full ahead!'

'Full ahead!' Bahr shouted.

'Starboard twenty-five!'

'Starboard twenty-five!' Bahr shouted, this time running the wheel full around.

The sound of voices carried up from the forward well as the bows began to come swiftly around, first the distant lights of

Hsin-chow showing, a background for the black bat-like shapes of some junks headed in toward the northern canal, then quite suddenly there showed the nearer lights of Yin-kin-chow in the midst of the blackness that was Ta-sha. With full wheel on and with the aid of the current, the *Gertrud Lüth* made her turn in her own length.

''Midships!'

''Midships!' Bahr shouted, pounding the wheel around. 'Wheel amidships, sir!'

'Meet her!'

'Meet her!'

'Steaming lights out, sir!' Pulst shouted as he came in.

'Stand by the telegraphs!' Schepke told him, feeling the sweat beginning to run between his shoulders. Then: 'Port five!' he called to Bahr.

They were close in to the south shore of Ta-sha, using the blackness of the island to shield them from anyone watching the river from the south shore below Chao Shan.

'Altmeyer!' he called into the hatchway. 'Bring the Aldis!' Then turning back to the open windows he lifted the heavy night-glasses from his chest and waited for the boy. 'Leave the Aldis here and go around the ship and make sure there's no lights showing,' he told him.

Far ahead of them, somewhere toward Hsiao-ho Creek, he saw the distant lights of the *Kaptjan Frederiksen*. To the south, on the low rolling shore, showed the nearby lights of Chin-chia-shan, and Tan-ta-chen, and the cluster of lights around the entrance to the Grand Canal.

''Midships! —Steady!'

The south shore of Ta-sha seemed close enough to touch from the port bulwarks, but all of it in darkness and nothing showing on the river.

'That's them all locked up,' Müller said as he came onto the bridge with Kamei.

'Get some glasses and take the south shore,' Schepke told him. 'Kamei.' Kamei joined him at the open window. 'Move the girl and her father across to my cabin. If there's any shooting it'll probably come from the south shore. When you've done that, stand by the main lighting box. We might want to use everything in a hurry.'

'We're completely blacked out, sir,' Altmeyer said as he came in past Kamei.

'Good. Now take the starboard wing and keep watch astern.'

'The starboard ladder's still out, sir. And the guard boat's with it.'

'Forget about it.'

It was almost solid darkness ahead and then he raised the glasses and saw the shadowy shapes of two junks right ahead.

'Starboard ten!'

The ship heeled a little as she swung out toward midstream, and then they were past the junks, close on the port side, ghostly-like, no lights showing, and seemingly deserted.

''Midships!'

''Midships!' Bahr answered. 'Wheel amidships, sir!'

'Port five!' He was bringing the ship close in to the shore again away from the approaching lights of the south shore villages.

'Anything astern?' he called to the wing.

'Not a thing, sir,' Altmeyer shouted.

Out ahead of them the lights of the *Kaptjan Frederiksen* were lost now, the Dane having cleared Rose Island and turned down toward Kiang Yin.

Now the *Gertrud Lüth* was past the entrance to the Grand Canal, and past Ma-chia-shaw, and Chen-pi, and Chen-kou, the lights of the latter showing almost on top of each other. Then they were past Pu-shun-wei on the main north bank, leaving the island of Ta-sha astern of them in the darkness.

'Lights starboard bow!' Müller shouted. 'It looks like something putting out from Hsiao-ho Creek.'

Schepke put the glasses on her. 'She's a steamer of some sort. Too large for river-craft.'

'She's beginning her turn downstream now,' Müller said, his eyes jammed to the heavy night-glasses.

Karl Schepke watched her as she turned downstream ahead

of them, and then they were in Tan-tu Reach, gradually over-hauling her.

'Anything astern?'

'Nothing, sir!' Altmeyer shouted.

The steady pounding of the engines vibrated throughout the ship, their way setting up a cool breeze that came in the open windows of the bridge.

Now they were abeam of Hsiao-ho Creek, gaining fast on the vessel ahead.

'Half ahead!'

'Half ahead!' Pulst shouted, ringing the telegraph all the way back and up again.

'We'll stay astern of her until we're around Rose Island,' Schepke told them. 'Müller. Rig river-lights both sides of the boatdeck. Yellow over red.' As Müller left he put the glasses back on the vessel ahead. She was a small coastal steamer in ballast and now she was beginning to make her turn around Rose Island.

'Port ten!' he called, bringing them close to the north bank again, away from the lights on Rose Island.

'Port ten! Ten port wheel on, sir!'

''Midships!'

''Midships! Wheel amidships, sir!'

Suddenly a red Very light arced lazily out across the river to hang suspended above the steamer already rounding the north bank of the island. Schepke waited for the steamer then saw her shoot a yellow flare in reply.

'Altmeyer! Stand by with a yellow flare! Pulst! Tell the engine-room to stand by lighting dynamos!'

'River-lights rigged both sides boatdeck!' Müller shouted.

'Port ten!'

'Port ten! Ten port wheel on, sir!'

They were hugging the shore lights of San-chiang-ying now.

''Midships!'

''Midships! Wheel amidships, sir!'

Abeam of San-chiang-ying, they could see clearly the lights on the shore and the roadway and the yellow lights in the win-dows of the stone-walled houses.

'Starboard five!' he shouted as they came into the bend.

Suddenly a searchlight came on ahead, wavered, then swung slowly back upstream to touch the forepeak before settling on the bridge, blindingly brilliant and dazzling.

'Full ahead!' Schepke yelled. 'Shoot, Altmeyer! Shoot!' At the same time he grabbed the siren lanyard and a great roaring blast of steam and noise thundered the night apart.

'Keep shooting, Altmeyer! Shoot anything!'

They had picked up way again, still carrying starboard wheel and rounding the bend on the river now beyond Rose Island. Then above all the noise and confusion came the sudden rolling rattle of small-arms fire and somewhere on the bridge glass shattered and flew off the windows in the brilliantly dazzling light. But they were already drawing away, the searchlight falling further astern and shining in now only from the after windows of the starboard wing.

Schepke's eyes probed the darkness ahead, trying for a glimpse of the north bank.

"Midships!' he shouted, and another burst of firing was followed by a red flare exploding then settling lazily in the sky ahead. Then he saw the steamer some way ahead, well in to midstream, riding high in ballast.

'Follow ship ahead!' he shouted to Bahr.

A long flighted stream of red and green tracer suddenly arced and lifted across the bows without warning, the lighted shells spraying the solid darkness away to port. Now the *Gertrud Lüth* was lit only by the rapidly fading brilliance of the searchlight astern.

The first of the heavy shells landed about two hundred metres ahead, a little to port. Then three more landed almost together, fountaining great geysers of white water high into the night. On the bridge they could hear the rapid double crack of the guns somewhere astern and then the whirling cloth-ripping rush followed by the fountains of white water geysering high out of the river.

'Ship ahead hove to!' Bahr shouted.

They were rapidly coming up astern of her, her searchlights

working full speed as she flashed ashore on both sides.
'Port ten!' Schepke shouted, putting the steamer between
them and the south shore.

Then as they drew abeam of her a shell hit the river close
alongside, showering the bridge with white-hot shrapnel and
fountaining water.

The firing stopped as abruptly as it started, and they were
down into the blackness of the river again and astern of them
the steamer was hove to, slewing with the current, all her cabin
and deck-lights ablaze.

'Anybody hurt?'

'That last one was close,' Müller said. 'The only time they hit
us was with that first burst.'

'Well they know now,' Schepke told him. 'Keep a close watch
both sides. The whole river will have been alerted.'

'I thought for a moment we were going to make it without
them seeing us,' Pulst said.

'It was the lights at San-chiang-ying that gave us away,'
Schepke said. 'We were silhouetted as we came into the bend.'

'No hits astern,' Kamei said from the doorway.

'Anybody hurt?'

'No one.'

'Searchlights ahead!' Müller yelled.

They were on the south shore, their beams sweeping the
breadth of the river.

'Tell Hechler to start the dynamos! Altmeyer! Stand by with
the Aldis! Kamei! You stay with the lights!' At that moment the
lights flickered, faded, then came on brightly, the steady hum of
the dynamos carrying throughout the ship.

'Are those river-lights working?'

'They're all right!' Müller shouted from the wing.

The first of the searchlights found them, settling on the bridge.

'Altmeyer! Tell them—' he stopped with the whirling cloth-
ripping rush of the first shell. It hit the river almost abeam,
sending water high across the fantail. '—Tell them: *Kaptjan
Frederiksen* bound Shanghai! Keep on sending it!'

Again there carried the oncoming rush of a shell, its locomotive roar quickly following as it went on over into the darkness of the north bank. Altmeyer flinched, waiting for the explosion, then quickly re-sighting the Aldis as it failed to come.

Schepke counted five more hits on the river around them before the shooting finally stopped.

'Keep sending,' he told Altmeyer.

The searchlights continued to hold them, everyone on the bridge hoping they were too far out toward the north bank for the name along the bows to show clear.

Still the guns remained silent and the *Gertrud Lüth* drove on at full speed, the searchlights holding her as she passed.

Then suddenly when they were below the lights the shells came again, two of them hitting the river close ahead, the water coming down heavily across the forepeak, the spray blanketing the bridge as the ship heeled in the wild undercurrents of the shell bursts.

'Port ten!'

Bahr spun the wheel around, his reply lost in the crashing explosions of shells bursting on the river around them.

''Midships!' Schepke yelled after letting the ship run in toward midstream.

''Midships! Wheel amidships!'

Out ahead two more shells exploded to starboard, everyone crouching below window-level as steel fragments sung through the outside darkness.

'Cut the lights!' Schepke yelled.

Almost immediately the ship plunged into darkness.

'Müller! Take the flying bridge! Keep a sharp look out ahead for any more lights!'

It was Kiang Yin that worried him now. There would be patrol boats out ahead and below Kiang Yin. Once they were past Kiang Yin there would be only the forts at Woosung. It would be daylight when they reached the forts. But he did not want to think yet about Woosung.

Astern he could still hear the double booming crack of the guns, the echoes crashing back off the north bank, filling the blackness of the river with a steady unrelenting thunder. The shooting was wild, the shells splaying the river, and then one fell directly ahead, quickly followed by a sudden roaring crash somewhere aft and the ship shuddering violently, heeling to port, the stern swinging toward the north bank.

'Starboard ten!' he yelled, and suddenly all the shipboard lights came on, those in the bridge momentarily blinding him. 'Pulst!' he yelled. 'See what the hell's happening below! Get those lights out!'

'—Stand where you are! Everyone!'

He wheeled to find Cheng with his back against the bulkhead, standing a little way to the right of the bridge doorway, covering them with a blunt-nosed revolver.

'Put your hands up. Slowly.'

Schepke obeyed, carefully watching Cheng's face.

'You! Pulst. Both of you out to the wing. Hurry!'

Bahr, still on the wheel, was nervously watching both Cheng and the river.

'Stop engines,' Cheng told him.

Bahr rang the telegraph all the way back then up to Stop, the repeater bell sounding immediately.

'Wheel amidships.'

Bahr glanced at Schepke then swung the wheel over amidships. Out astern of them the guns were still firing. Then as the engines died Müller suddenly appeared on the bridge ladder, then stopped suddenly, seeing Cheng below him.

'Down, Müller!' Cheng shouted.

Müller hesitated momentarily, then flung himself upward on the ladder. Cheng shot him as he went through the hatchway, then Schepke, shooting from his pocket, fired and missed and fired again and shot Cheng high in the chest. Then as Cheng slewed against the bulkhead Schepke shot him twice more. Cheng's mouth came open and he was looking at him, and then he toppled to his knees and went down slowly, the red stains rapidly widening across his tunic.

In almost the same moment Schepke grabbed the telegraph and slammed it all the way over to Full Ahead.

'Kamei!' he shouted. 'Cut the lights! Cut all lights!'

The engine-room had still not repeated the Full Ahead order and he grabbed the telegraph and slammed it all the way back, then up. This time the repeater bell sounded along with it.

'Take the wheel,' he shouted to Bahr. 'Altmeyer! See what's happened to Kamei. Throw all the switches.'

The engines were gathering momentum again.

'Starboard ten!'

'Starboard ten!' Bahr shouted as he rammed the heavy wheel around.

Suddenly all the lights went out as the ship started her swing to starboard. Schepke put his glasses on the river ahead but saw almost nothing after the brightness of the lights.

''Midships!'

They were well below the searchlights and the shooting seemed to have stopped.

'Kamei's unconscious,' Altmeyer shouted as he came in.

'The shooting's stopped,' Pulst said.

Schepke listened for the sound of the guns above the engines but heard nothing.

'Müller's still alive, sir!'

Schepke glanced around to see the blurred outline of Altmeyer kneeling by the ladder.

'Here!' he told the boy. 'Take the glasses. Keep us to as near midstream as you can.'

Müller was lying on his back by the ladder, his head out toward the starboard wing. There was a light bubbling sound deep in his chest when he breathed and then he went into a long, half-smothered bout of coughing.

'Müller.' Schepke touched him and felt his hand warmly wet and sticky where Cheng had shot him high in the chest under his right arm.

'Cheng. —Cheng.'

'He's dead,' Schepke told him.

'—Other two,' Müller said, his voice sounding very faint. 'The fantail. Somebody signalling—' he paused, coughing, the blood sucking noisily in his throat. 'It was only money,' he went on. 'Wang. —Listen—'

'Go on,' Schepke said, waiting.

'—Cheng blew the *Somerville*. The other two—' he started coughing again, talking through blood now.

'What other two?' Schepke asked, his face bent close to Müller's mouth. 'Müller, listen to me! What other two?'

Müller was unconscious now.

'Keep her in midstream!' he shouted to Altmeyer as he felt his way out onto the stairway.

'Captain?' someone said in the darkness of the passage.

'Is that you, Kamei?'

'Yes,' Kamei said in the darkness.

'Are you all right?'

'Someone hit me.'

'It was Cheng. He's dead.' He started toward the boatdeck, Kamei following him. 'Müller says somebody was signalling from the fantail,' he said across his shoulder. 'That could be why the shooting started again.'

'We were hit aft,' Kamei said as they crossed the boatdeck. Then: 'Look!' For a brief moment a light showed in one of the scuttles on the starboard side of the fantail housing.

'Come on,' Schepke told him.

There were several small fires in under the after end of the boatdeck. The shell had hit the casing by the end of the port alleyway, and as they crossed the after well they saw several bodies lying around on the smouldering deck, and one of the bodies was burning. The whole of the after well smelled of burnt cordite and burning flesh.

'Take the port ladder,' he told Kamei, and saw that blood covered the whole of one side of his face from a wound high on his head.

He took the starboard ladder, and climbing quietly, reached the shelter of the after steering position. The light still flashed, the probing beam directed toward the south shore. Glancing shoreward he saw it was quiet and dark and only astern of them were there any lights.

'You will have to go by the door,' Kamei whispered, watching the flashing light reflect on the brass ring of the open scuttle.

366

Schepke dropped into a crouch and ducked below the scuttle as he went around to the after doorway. He remembered the three doors on the outboard side of the passage and he quietly felt for the first two in the darkness. There was nothing to be heard but the terrific pounding and vibration of the engines far below, and moving cautiously, he found the third door almost at the end of the narrow passage where it joined the messroom. It was locked. Readying the Walther, he put his back firmly to the inboard bulkhead, then kicked. The lock splintered the wood as it held, and he kicked again and dropped in the same movement as the door flew open. A violent orange-red explosion framed the doorway before him and something screamed wildly off the bulkhead above him. He fired blindly, three times, both guns firing together, the noise deafeningly loud in the enclosed space. And with the shooting still in his ears, someone went down heavily in the doorway. Throwing himself sideways, he fired once more.

'Hallo! Hallo!' someone called in the sudden quiet.

'It's over!' he shouted along the passage, and touched the body with his foot as Kamei joined him. 'See who it is.'

Kamei reached down and felt for the body then dragged it out onto the deck.

'It is the one Tah Gu Tze,' he said, looking closely at the body in the gloom of the river.

'Müller said there were two.'

'I know the one,' Kamei told him. 'These are the ones I talked with you about before. After Taipeh.'

'The other one could be anywhere. We'll look for him later. Come on.'

In the well the body was smouldering now, and they went forward into the port alleyway, climbing across the debris. Below them he saw the guard boat still lashed to the ladder, towing crabwise in the side wash.

'Get those soldiers out! Hurry!'

Kamei disappeared into the inboard passage and a few moments later the first of the soldiers stepped hesitantly out through the screen door to the alleyway.

'The boat!' Schepke shouted into his face, jabbing the Walther in his side, pushing him out onto the ladder. They came out quickly after the first one and he herded them onto the ladder without giving them time to look around. The officer was the last one out and Schepke grabbed him and shoved him onto the ladder. 'The boat!' he shouted. 'Go on!'

They had to leap for the boat and someone was already hacking at the painter when they grabbed their officer on board. When the painter finally parted they had him half across the gunwale and the bows rose, slewing the boat sideways, shipping water, almost over-turning as she was caught in the wake and backwash. Then she was lost suddenly in the darkness before they had reached the boatdeck.

'Lights showing ahead, sir!' Altmeyer shouted as they came in off the stairway.

Schepke took the glasses from him. It was the *Kaptjan Frederiksen*. Then carefully searching the shore to the south he picked up the sky-glow that was the lights of Kiang Yin.

'Down twenty!' he told Pulst. 'We'll let her go through ahead of us.' Then putting the glasses on the north bank, he searched the shore. 'Port five!'

'Port five!' Bahr shouted. 'Five port wheel on, sir!'

Schepke watched the north bank carefully as they closed it. ''Midships!'

''Midships! Wheel amidships, sir!'

'Pulst! You take the wheel for a spell.' Then crossing to the ladder to the flying bridge he knelt by Müller. He was dead, and as he rose his hand knocked against something solid and bulky in the pocket of Müller's tunic. It was a gun, and bringing it out, he saw it was Emmermann's Mauser.

'Lights of Kiang Yin showing, sir!' Altmeyer called to him.

He put the Mauser into the other pocket of his tunic and crossed to the windows. They were still gaining on the *Kaptjan Frederiksen*. She was well into midstream, steaming quite steadily, all her lights ablaze.

'Kamei! Stand by those lights again.'

The first Very light went up just outside of Kiang Yin. It

368

came from somewhere on the river, close to the south shore.

He watched the Dane ahead then saw the sudden rush of green flame as she shot a flare skywards towards the south shore.

'They've changed the procedure,' he told Altmeyer. 'Stand by with a green. But don't shoot unless I tell you.'

The Dane's flare was drifting slowly in toward the south shore as it began to fall. He put the glasses carefully onto that part of the river from where the Very light had been shot, but against the solid blackness of the land he could see nothing. Then as they ran on past that part of the river, nothing happened, and then they were beginning to come into the first of the lights of Kiang Yin.

'Up twenty!'

'Up twenty, sir!' Bahr shouted as he spun the revolutions onto the telegraph.

'Port five!'

'Port five,' Pulst answered. 'Five port wheel on, sir!'

The lights of Kiang Yin stretched out along the starboard side, the *Kaptjan Frederiksen* still ahead of them and in toward midstream.

"Midships!' Schepke shouted, switching the glasses to the north bank as it loomed menacingly on the port side. Out in midstream the *Kaptjan Frederiksen* began to ease her speed, the *Gertrud Lüth* now rapidly overhauling her, putting the Dane between her and the south shore.

'There's a change of lights on the *Kaptjan Frederiksen*!' Altmeyer called below from the flying bridge. 'River-lights now showing red over green!'

'Kamei!' Schepke shouted into the bridge doorway. 'River-lights red over green. Hurry! And don't use them unless I tell you!'

They were almost abeam of the Dane now.

'We're going through,' Bahr shouted.

'Two points to starboard!'

'Two points starboard!' Pulst answered.

'—'Midships!' Schepke put the glasses on the Dane as they began to draw ahead.

369

'Lights dead ahead!' Altmeyer shouted below from the flying bridge.

Schepke swivelled the glasses. The lights were those of a large junk or river-boat.

'Starboard five!' he shouted and suddenly the darkness was filled with red and green tracer shells weaving erratically around the bridge.

'Get down!' he yelled, grabbing the wheel from Pulst and spinning it savagely around to port. Overhead was a great hammering noise and the steady pumping bark of guns right ahead.

Quickly he spun the wheel again, driving the *Gertrud Lüth* on toward the lights and gun-flashes. Then she appeared very suddenly out of the darkness and he rammed the wheel to starboard and there was a heavy jolt on the port side that heeled them, and the long screaming of rending metal; and then the *Gertrud Lüth* was past, racing in toward midstream.

'Flares and gun-flashes from the south shore!' Altmeyer was shouting, and the river lit up suddenly very brightly around them and the first of the shells hit the water about thirty metres off the starboard bow, and before the sound of the explosion had died a tremendous grinding crash came from somewhere amidships and the *Gertrud Lüth* lurched and halted momentarily before regaining speed and balance.

'We're hit!' Pulst shouted, his voice almost lost in the blast of hot air and cordite fumes that concussed through the bridge doorway.

'Take a look!' Schepke yelled, and as he turned back to the open windows the first of the yellow-burning flares drifted into the river. Then the darkness ahead brightened again and the rapid double boom of the guns sounded and two more shells hit the river just short of the starboard side of the forepeak.

'We took it in the big cabin!' Pulst yelled above the locomotive rush of shells passing closely overhead of the bridge.

'My cabin! See my cabin!'

'They're all right! I was in!' Pulst was almost across the bridge when the next one hit.

Schepke clung to the wheel, the dazzling flash of orange

flame blinding him, the noise deafening, and the explosion closely followed by two more that staggered the *Gertrud Lüth* from stem to stern, slewing her across the river.

The first thing he was conscious of was the sound of the engines still pounding them ahead. Wrenching the wheel hard around to starboard, he began to bring their head back toward midstream.

'What happened?' Pulst yelled. 'I thought they hit the foredeck!'

Schepke studied the foredeck in the eerie glow of the overhead flares. 'It must have been close by!' he shouted. 'Here! Take the wheel!'

Stumbling below to the passage he saw the big cabin was on fire and Kamei and a number of seamen hosing the flames.

'There are two more fires on the boatdeck and after well!' Kamei shouted to him.

'Try and hurry it! They'll see us all the way down!' And as he spoke another heavy explosion staggered the *Gertrud Lüth* and heeled her savagely to port.

As he turned he saw the old man with the door open and the cabin inside lit by a hurricane lamp. 'Are you all right?'

'We are hit many times!' the old man said.

Schepke saw the girl was awake, watching them in the doorway. 'How are you?' he asked, stooping over the bunk, gently touching his hand to her cheek.

'You do all this for us?' she said, her voice sounding very small and tired.

'You're going to be fine now,' he told her. 'Don't worry about the noise. We'll be out of the river soon.'

'You will come back?'

'I'll come back,' he said, then turned to her father. 'Keep the door locked and don't let anybody in.'

Across the passage the fire was almost out, and stumbling across the smouldering debris, he hurried forward to the bridge.

'Bridge!' Altmeyer shouted in from above. 'Flares falling well astern now!'

'You better come below,' Schepke told him as he crossed to

the starboard wing. Far back on the river the flares still lighted the low cloud while the searchlights continued to probe the down-river darkness. They were still shooting but it was scattered now that the gunners had lost them.

Out ahead there were no lights showing and everything was dark and deserted, and now it was beginning to rain. It was a fine, thinly falling rain that hung in the night, and with this rain would come the fog on the lower reaches of the river.

'The shooting's stopped now,' Altmeyer said, close beside him.

'There's a long way to go yet,' Schepke told him. 'How are the fires?'

'They're working on the one in the after well. The others are already out.'

'I can't see any damage below but we were hit twice forward,' Schepke said.

'It was happening so fast,' Altmeyer said, a little dry-mouthed. 'We lost Number Two lifeboat right after the big cabin was hit.'

'This time there's the luck,' Schepke said looking at him in the darkness.

'What about Woosung?'

Schepke ignored him. 'Port five!'

'Port five!' Pulst answered. 'Five port wheel on, sir!'

'Are we going back across the river?' Altmeyer asked.

'If that fire's still burning they'll be watching us. I want to make sure they see us on the north side,' Schepke said, searching the stretch of solid blackness that was the north bank. '—'Midships!'

''Midships! Wheel amidships, sir!'

'Meet her!' He turned to Altmeyer. 'Tell me when that fire's out.'

Again he searched the river, and everything was dark and quiet and the fine rain fell damply through the open windows. Then as he searched back down the river he saw the faint glow of lights reflecting in the night somewhere far ahead.

'All the fires are out, sir,' Altmeyer said as he came in.

'Listen,' Schepke told him. 'Go on up above and see if you can make out those lights up ahead.'

'THERE'S a lot of water here now,' Dorsch shouted above the tremendous pound and whine of the engines.

'That was plenty of stuff landed close by,' Hechler told him. 'There's plates sprung almost everywhere.'

'How many times do you think we've been hit?'

'Four times. Maybe more,' Hechler shouted.

'There's been nothing landed close by for a while. Think we're clear?'

'Go on up and take a look,' Hechler told him.

He watched Dorsch start up the steel ladders to the overhead catwalk. Then he looked back at the array of gauges before him, sweat running down his face and neck, his overalls clinging damply to his massive bulk. Wiping the sweat from his eyes, he glanced back around the engine-room, seeing Frauenheim working in the tunnel. Then hearing the clatter of an overhead hatch, he saw Dorsch start down the long series of ladders.

'Everything black as hell. The after well's been hit a couple of times. They've just put the fire out.'

'What about overhead?'

'I couldn't see anything.'

'I thought we were hit a couple of times forward somewhere,' Hechler shouted.

'I couldn't see anything.'

'We must be well down the river,' Hechler shouted, glancing at the clock on the manoeuvring platform. 'That shooting must have been Kiang Yin.'

'It was like years back.'

'It's going to be light soon.'

Dorsch wiped his face with a dirty sweat-rag, the lights of the engine-room shimmering in the terrific humid heat.

'It's started to rain.'

'Heavy?'

Dorsch shook his head. 'No. With this sort there's fog.'

'You better take another look at the stokeholds. We're going to have to watch this water.'

'What's happening?' Frauenheim asked as he came out from the tunnel.

'We're past Kian Yin,' Hechler told him.

Frauenheim straightened his stooped shoulders and carefully looked at his wrist watch. 'There's a long way to go yet!' he said.

'THERE's a plane somewhere around!' Altmeyer shouted in through the open hatchway.

'Starboard ten!'

'Starboard ten! Ten starboard wheel on, sir!'

'How about those lights?' Schepke called into the hatchway. 'I think they're on the river.'

'Keep watch for that plane.'

The *Gertrud Lüth* was angling fast across the river, Schepke keeping his glasses on the south shore.

'Plane astern!' Altmeyer shouted. 'I can see her lights!'

'Port ten!' Schepke shouted as he crossed to the port wing. 'Midships! —Steady!'

The red and green and yellow-blinking belly lights of the aeroplane showed clearly astern in the darkness. She was coming very low and throttled back, flying to port of them, close above the north bank. He watched it quickly overhaul them, draw abeam, then pass down-river, the powerful roar of motors hammering the night apart. Then as he watched the navigation lights recede he saw the thinly falling stream of fire slow then float before suddenly and brilliantly exploding into a glaring brightness that lit the whole of the north bank.

Back amidships, he put the glasses to the south shore.

'If she had dropped that flare sooner she would have caught us,' Bahr said.

Schepke watched the parachuted flare go out suddenly in the blackness of the river. 'She'll be back,' he said. 'Port ten!'

'Port ten!' Pulst answered. 'Ten port wheel—' The shot cut his words off in mid-sentence, the framework of the window shattering above his head. The second shot came in through the window a little way to his left, ricocheting from somewhere off the rear of the bridge. Altmeyer dropped bodily in through the open hatchway to land heavily in the darkness as the others dropped below window-level.

'Altmeyer!' Schepke shouted.

'It came from the forepeak!' the boy told him. 'I saw the flash of the second shot!'

'Müller said there were two!'

Just then Pulst raised his head above the wheel and the bullet came in very close, splintering the woodwork of the bridge door-way.

Schepke grabbed the lower spokes of the wheel from him and eased it amidships. They were somewhere out across the river now and he put the wheel a little way to starboard to meet their way, then raised his head to glimpse the solid blackness of the north bank showing close in.

'Take it easy and ring back Slow Ahead,' he told Bahr.

Keeping low, Bahr reached up and brought the handle of the telegraph all the way back, then ahead, the repeater bell sounding immediately.

'What is happening?' Kamei asked from somewhere at the rear of the bridge.

'Keep down!' Schepke told him. 'There's somebody on the forepeak with a gun.'

'I know this one,' Kamei said.

'Kamei!' Schepke called after him. Kamei went on down into the passage and as Schepke turned back to the wheel the bridge was lit suddenly by the pale reflected light of a flare dropped some way down-river.

'The plane's coming back!' Altmeyer shouted to them.

Schepke raised his head and took a quick look at the north

bank, then put the wheel two points to starboard before meeting her again.

'Here!' He brought the Mauser from his pocket and slid it along the deck in Altmeyer's direction. 'Never mind what you shoot at, just shoot!' He turned and moved a little way toward the port wing. 'Pulst! Hold us just as we are,' he shouted, and after reloading the heavy Walther, raised his head as the flare went out leaving the river in darkness.

Nothing moved on the foredeck and he turned his attention to the forepeak. Everything was quiet and dark and the sounds of the river carried in above the ceaseless pounding of the engines. Then he raised the Walther and deliberately squeezed off a shot at the shadow of the port ventilator. The answering shot splintered the woodwork of the window next to him. This time he saw the gun-flash in the mouth of the forepeak tunnel. Quickly he squeezed two more shots off and moved further out to the wing. This time the answering shot ricocheted off a light channel somewhere toward the rear of the bridge. Altmeyer was shooting blindly, still crouched below window level, and now the answering gun-flash showed on the port side rigging.

Altmeyer's Mauser was already empty and as Schepke knelt to reload, the down-river darkness was brightly lit again, the sudden brightness quickly followed by the hammering roar of aeroplane motors as it passed close on the starboard side.

The flare was still some way downstream, suspended directly above the south shore, the gunman silhouetted against it as he appeared on the derrick platform.

Schepke shot twice, seeing the man drop flat to the platform. This time the answering shot sent wooden splinters whirring across the bridge. Then as he raised his head he saw Kamei on the starboard side rigging.

'Wait!' he shouted, shooting twice, hurriedly toward the platform. '—Kamei!'

The gunman had already seen him and started shooting, slowly, deliberately, shooting through the open grid-work of the platform, not showing himself to the bridge.

Kamei staggered with the second shot, then went on again.

376

The fourth shot stopped him and he clung to the rigging. Schepke shot twice at the platform, the single answering shot smashing one of the extreme port wing windows. Moving hurriedly amidships, he saw Kamei now close to the platform, moving slowly upward on the rigging. The gunman was kneeling and Schepke shot once and saw him turn and shoot point-blankly at Kamei as he hauled himself up onto the platform. Kamei stopped, almost overbalanced, then moved ponderously forward again. They fell against the after safety rail and the flare went out suddenly on the shore and they saw a vivid gun-flash against the two bodies and then something toppled outward from the rail, the long rising scream cut suddenly with the hollow thud of a body hitting somewhere in the darkness of the deck.

'Keep her as she is!' Schepke shouted.

Kamei lay under the starboard side bulwarks where he had struggled below from the platform, shot three or four times high in the chest and shoulders.

'Kamei. Kamei, can you hear me?'

'—I knew the one,' Kamei said, his eyes open wide and searching for Schepke's face in the darkness.

'You should have waited.'

'It is nothing to lose. This way—' he paused, coughing, the sound beginning deep in his chest. 'This way it is easy.'

'Don't talk,' Schepke told him. 'We'll get you up above.'

Kamei swallowed noisily, the blood wheezing in his throat and lungs. 'There is—time only for talk,' he said. Then: 'Listen,' he said. 'The girl. A man—a man is owed one thing valuable.'

'Sure. Sure,' Schepke said, his face bent close to Kamei's.

'One thing valuable,' Kamei said very quietly. '—One thing.' He died very quickly.

'Ship ahead!' Altmeyer called from the bridge.

Schepke looked forward across the bulwarks. She was still some way ahead, anchored close to the south shore in a creek of the river, all her lights ablaze and floods rigged on the bridge so as to light the flags unfurled across her walls.

He hurried for the alleyway, the decks already beginning to

377

run with the rain, and the rain was falling more heavily now, rainbowing the lights ahead.

'She's a Limey,' Altmeyer said, his glasses on her.

'They must have stopped all traffic on the river,' Schepke said. 'She was probably bound for Nanking.' And he put his own glasses on her and there was nobody about on deck, and there were rainbowed haloes around her lights as the rain fell heavily through them.

'Do you think she'll see us?' Altmeyer asked.

'We'll keep slow ahead and chance slipping past. She's some way off.' He dropped the glasses onto his chest and took the wheel from Pulst. Putting it around to port, he took them in closer to the solid darkness of the north bank. It was quiet on the bridge now and everyone was watching the Englishman, and overhead the rain was running in the scuppers of the flying bridge.

'There's an anchor watch below the forepeak,' Altmeyer said.

Schepke steadied the wheel amidships as they drew abeam. Then the Englishman was astern and he could no longer see her from the wheel.

'They haven't seen us,' Altmeyer said from the after windows.

'Full ahead!' Schepke said. 'Pulst! You take the wheel.'

The pounding and shuddering of the engines grew again as Bahr slammed the telegraph over.

'What about Kamei?' Altmeyer asked when the lights of the Englishman were dropped far enough astern.

'He's dead.'

No one said anything, and now the rain falling in through the open windows of the bridge, running on the decking.

'Starboard ten!' Schepke said.

'It's getting light,' Altmeyer told him.

Schepke glanced at the sky to the east and saw the very faint and pale greyness showing in the darkness above the land.

''Midships!' he said leaning on the ledge of the window, feeling the rain coolly and wetly on his face.

Now the *Gertrud Lüth* drove down-river almost in midstream.

'There's fog down there,' he said. 'You can feel it.'

Altmeyer joined him at the window, noting the change in the air and in the rain, smelling the ocean now above the smells of the river and the land.

Then one of the telephones rang.

'Bridge! Schepke here!'

'Hechler speaking,' Hechler said, shouting above the pound and high-powered whine of the engines. 'We're shipping water everywhere and all pumps working.'

'Can't you cope?' Schepke asked anxiously.

'We're doing all we can. It's already lapping the footplates.'

'Try and hold on to it. We'll be off Woosung soon. If we get out we'll rig the hand-pumps.'

'You'll never make Kobe,' Hechler told him.

'We'll go back through the Straits,' Schepke said, holding the receiver a moment, thinking, and Hechler did not say anything further, and Schepke slowly hung the receiver back on its hook.

'The fog's closing in,' he heard Altmeyer say.

Daylight was coming in quickly now, the dirty waters beginning to grey a little in the rain and fog.

'See if you can pick up anything on the wireless.' And after Altmeyer left he stayed at the window and watched the morning get light. It was a grey, solemn and overcast morning and the fog was closing in thickly over the river. Then he heard Altmeyer come in from below, hurrying up the stairway.

'There's so much stuff up ahead it's impossible to pin-point anything on RDF.'

'All right. Forget it. Close down and come back here.' He crossed the bridge to the charthouse and brought out a chart of the lower river.

'Starboard five!'

'Starboard five!' Pulst answered. 'Five starboard wheel on, sir!'

'Bahr! See if you can get some blankets and cover those bodies on the well.' Then raising the glasses he peered out into the fog and rain, searching across the bows, the river widened tremendously now so that the shores were lost far out in the fog. ''Midships!'

''Midships! Wheel amidships, sir!'

'Steer one-four-five!'

'Steer one-four-five, sir!'

'Don't you want to keep to the north bank, sir?' Altmeyer asked, a little surprised.

'I hope that's what they'll think,' Schepke told him. 'I'm counting on most of the patrol vessels being between Tsungming and the north bank. We'll try south of the island, keeping just far enough off Paoshan and Woosung so as they can't pick us up from the shore.'

Altmeyer turned quietly away and stared out at the fog swirling in across the bows. He did not want to think about any of it now. If they got through, he would remember it. And below him he saw someone had covered Kamei with a blanket, and the grey blanket was darkening now with the rain.

'Altmeyer! Call Hechler and tell him we'll be off Paoshan anytime now. And ask him about the water-level.' Then as Altmeyer reached the engine-room receiver off the hook he turned to Pulst. 'Steer one-five-zero!' he said.

The bows edged slightly around onto the new course and suddenly the high black sails of a river junk appeared out of the fog and passed close down the port side.

'If anything like that comes up ahead again you just keep going,' he called to Pulst as he brought the wheel around amidships, 'we don't stop for anything now.'

'Hechler says he'll want the pumps rigged the moment we're out,' Altmeyer said.

'Listen!' Pulst suddenly shouted.

It came again, long and bleating and muffled-sounding through the fog.

'That's Tsungming Island,' Schepke told them, hearing the siren again, lost somewhere in the fog and rain on the port beam. Then he looked carefully at his wrist watch. 'We'll be abeam of Paoshan soon. Keep her steady. The rest of you watch the river.'

The *Gertrud Lüth* drove blindly on through the fog and rain, her wake threshing and pounding apart the yellow muddy waters

380

of the Yangtze. Then twice more they passed close to the ghostly-like shapes of junks in full sail; junks that seemed to appear out of nowhere.

Then again he looked carefully at his wrist watch. The *Gertrud Lüth* was past Paoshan now.

'Steer one-six-eight!'

'Steer one-six-eight, sir!' Pulst answered.

The ship eased smoothly onto her new course, paralleling the south shore as it widened toward the great mouth of the river.

'Course one-six-eight, sir!'

'Good.'

It was quiet now on the bridge and the only sounds were those of the engines and the river and the rain falling through the fog.

Raising the glasses, he peered out beyond the bows before returning to the rain-sodden chart folded into the ledge of the window.

'Woosung should be abeam now,' he told them.

'—Ship ahead!' Altmeyer screamed.

Schepke saw her, shadowy and indistinct, the bows closing fast. Grabbing the wheel he flung it hard around to starboard, conscious at the same time of a great hammering sound and red and green tracer shells passing all around the bridge. Then in the next minute the *Gertrud Lüth* had smothered the fire in her port side superstructure as she heeled and drove on down-river.

Astern of them there was still the sound of firing and tracer shells arced through the fog on the port side as they continued to heel. Then as the tracer fell astern Schepke quickly brought them around on to course, away from the hidden shore.

'She's still firing!' Altmeyer shouted from the wing.

'She was moored!' Schepke told him. 'They'll take time to get the hooks up.' Then: 'Bahr!' he shouted. 'Take the wheel.'

Bahr quickly took over from him, the ship shuddering in every joint and plate as she drove headlong into the mouth of the river.

'Port ten!'

'Port ten! Ten port wheel on, sir!'

381

Schepke let her run, watching the minutes, taking them further out into the mouth of the river.

"Midships!'

"Midships! Wheel amidships, sir!'

'Steady!'

'Steady on one-three-two, sir!'

'Steer one-three-five!'

'—Course one-three-five, sir!'

He watched the fog swirl in damply across the lifting forepeak. They were far out into the mouth of the river and now the ship was settled into the long lifting motion of the ocean.

'Do you think they'll come out after us?' Altmeyer asked.

'We'll be into the Straits tonight.'

'What about Foochow and Amoy? They'll be watching the Straits.'

'We'll think about that later,' Schepke told him, and he did not want to think more about the luck now. 'Go down and tell the old man and girl that we're out.' And while he spoke he took the engine-room receiver from its hook and spun the handle.

'Hans! We're out!' he shouted into the mouthpiece. 'I think we'll get clear all right if this fog holds! —How are things below?'

'We're still taking water!' Hechler told him, his words almost lost amid the tremendous pound and whine of the engines. 'We've got all pumps working flat out!'

'I'll get the hand-pumps rigged as soon as possible! We'll be altering course again soon and cutting back in toward the mainland! I don't think they'll be expecting that!'

'Well I hope it works all right!'

Schepke hung the receiver back on its hook and turned to the window. The fog was swirling in thick and damp across the lifting forepeak, rain streaming from the scuppers. Out on the foredeck the body of the dead Chinese lay sprawled across the tarpaulined cases below the foremast, the blood washing away now in the cold grey rain.

'Kapitän, sir,' Altmeyer said as he came in. 'The old man asks if you can talk with him. His daughter is unconscious again.'

'All right.' Stay here until I come back. Keep her just as she is. If you see or hear anything, shout!'

The old man stood away from the bunk as he came in. The girl's breathing was so light there was hardly any movement. Leaning across the bunk, Schepke touched her face and felt the skin cool and clammy.

'When did she get like this again?'

'A little while before it came light,' the old man quietly answered.

'Was there anything else? Any pain?'

'She did not complain of anything. At first I thought she was asleep. Then a little while ago she seemed to be taken with cramp. I have not been able to wake her.'

Schepke bent over the bunk again. The girl's face was pale and drawn and her breathing very light and irregular.

'Did you see any rash?'

The old man quietly moved his head. 'There is nothing showing outwardly,' he said.

Schepke looked at the girl again. 'It's just possible we could try for Taipeh,' he said. 'But I don't promise anything. They'll be watching the Straits for us now they know we're out. I think all we can do now is keep her warm. It's the only thing I know.'

'Thank you. You go back now. I will manage.' He was very tired and the weariness showed in all of him.

As Schepke stepped out into the passage he saw Sam come in from the boatdeck, his eyes big and round at the sight of all the wreckage and debris littering the passage.

'I thought maybe you went with the big cabin.'

Sam shook his head indignantly. 'Sam not go with cabin,' he said. 'Kamei tell Kuang and I to hide in his cabin.'

'See if you can find any hot-water bottles for the girl.'

'Yes, sir,' Sam said. 'Afterward I make coffee for everyone.'

'Sure. You do that, Sam.'

Altmeyer was out on the starboard wing.

'See anything?'

'Not a thing, sir.'

Schepke glanced at his wrist watch then looked at the overhead compass. They were well out to the ocean now.

'Starboard ten!'

'Starboard ten! Ten starboard wheel on, sir!' Bahr answered.

He let the *Gertrud Lüth* come around in the thick swirling fog, rain water streaming from her port scuppers with the tilting deck.

'Meet her!'

'Meet her!' Bahr answered, swinging the wheel around to port and meeting the ship's head. '—Steady on two-two-three, sir!'

'Steer two-two-zero!'

'Steer two-two-zero!' Bahr answered. '—Course two-two-zero, sir!'

'Good.' —Altmeyer! Get all hands on rigging the pumps. Then get somebody to sew up the dead. Pulst! You give him a hand to take Müller and Cheng below.' He turned to Altmeyer again. 'When you're through on deck go back to the Radio Office and stay there. Don't break silence unless I tell you. If you do have to send anything, use flash procedure. We're on the high seas now and any attempt to stop us is an act of piracy. —Got that?'

Altmeyer nodded. 'Yes, sir.'

'And if there's any trouble getting those pumps rigged, let me know.'

'Yes, sir.' And Altmeyer was looking at the stiffening bodies of Müller and Cheng.

'All right. Leave them,' Schepke told him. 'Get somebody from deck. Pulst! You go below with him and see to the pumps.'

As they left he returned to the windows. The rain was falling in heavily through the windows and the fog was damp and swirling thickly in across the port side.

And above it all the *Gertrud Lüth* smelled of death and burnt cordite.

It was dark when they buried the bodies. The canvas-wrapped shapes slid silently over the wall without any slackening of speed, and now the *Gertrud Lüth*, black and looming in the darkness of the ocean, drove down into the Straits of Formosa. With the coming of darkness the fog had partially lifted and the ocean was dark and empty and lost in the heavily falling rain. Karl Schepke looked closely at the luminous dial of his wrist watch then raised the night-glasses, searching the darkness beyond the bows. They were still closely off the mainland but in the darkness there was no hint of the rugged coast to starboard.

'Keep her as she is,' he told Pulst.

The old man was sitting by the bunk, the hurricane lamp turned down so low that it barely burned.

'How is she?'

'There is no change,' the old man told him.

The girl lay very still and quiet. Her face had a grey and drawn look now and she breathed very light and flutteringly through her mouth.

'We'll have to get a doctor. I'll try and make for Taipeh. But understand,' he said looking at the old man, 'I don't promise anything. We might have to go on.'

Stepping into the sudden blackness of the passage, he felt his way forward to the Radio Office.

'Heard anything?'

Altmeyer pushed the headphones from his ears and swivelled the chart around on the bench. 'There's heavy traffic on the Formosa side,' he said. 'Here. Here, and possibly here.' He indicated the areas already marked in pencil.

Schepke studied the marked areas, all three of them spaced out along the Formosa coast. 'What about these two?' he asked, pointing at the two other pencilled areas directly ahead of them.

385

'I'd say they were shore stations,' Altmeyer said. 'They're all using intermediate. There's some other stuff too. Very faint. It could be some sort of light craft patrolling the north and south lanes. That's the best I can do with our RDF.'

Schepke looked again at the chart. To port was the most northerly of the pencilled areas, directly between them and Taipeh.

'We'll have to go on. We don't stand a chance of making Taipeh.'

'What about these two ahead of us?'

'If they're shore stations we'll ease southward when passing them. What about other traffic? Anything?'

'There's a couple of Limeys about midway through the Straits. They're both headed northward. They've been talking on and off since darkness.'

'Let me know if you hear anything else.'

He went out and back along the passage to the big cabin.

The girl had not moved.

'I'm sorry. We'll have to go on. They're waiting for us off Taipeh.'

The old man did not say anything. He was looking very much older and tired and there were dark pouches under his eyes.

Karl Schepke closed the door quietly and went forward again to the bridge. The night was suddenly cold and lonely and the rain drummed noisily on the flying bridge overhead and streamed down the unbroken windows of the bridge. Then, dropping one of the windows down, he lifted the heavy night-glasses out beyond the bows. Nothing showed in the rain-filled darkness, and he ran the window up and saw Pulst peering at his wrist-watch.

'It's all right,' he told him. 'We're staying this side. They're waiting for us off Formosa.'

And it was quiet now on the bridge.

At four o'clock in the morning they were well to southward, the rain still falling heavily and the ocean lifting in a short uneasy swell as it was caught up in the tide race through the Straits. Out on the starboard wing Karl Schepke dropped one of the after windows down and carefully searched astern. There was nothing but the quiet and the darkness, and the ghostly white of the wake showing dimly through the falling rain.

'Kapitän, sir!'

'Yes?' Schepke shouted through the doorway.

'That ship to the south is closing rapidly!'

'How long do you give her?'

'An hour,' Altmeyer said, 'maybe less.'

'Anything else in the vicinity?'

'No movement anywhere else, sir.'

'All right. Stand by in case we want the wireless. No matter what I tell you, send it. Understand? Stay right by the phone.'

'Yes, sir!'

He crossed the bridge and grabbed the engine-room receiver from its hook.

'—Engine-room! Hechler here!'

'Start the lighting dynamos. We're going to have to bluff our way through. If there's any shooting give her all you can and cut the dynamos.'

'How long have we got?'

'An hour. Maybe less,' Schepke told him. 'How are things below?'

'We're keeping the water down. I've just trimmed her again. With any luck she should see us to Hong Kong.'

'I'll let you know what's happening.' He put the receiver back on its hook and dropped the nearest window down. It was still raining heavily, hissing in the blackness of the ocean and running

387

in the scuppers with the lifting of the ship in the short uneasy swell. The breeze had eased some and was now shifted to the port quarter, drumming the rain against the after windows of the wings.

'Pulst! Go down and put the lights on. Everything except the deck and fantail.' He leaned back onto the window and watched the lights come on, their glow reflecting gloomily on the rain-wet foredeck.

'Captain, sir.'

He turned to see Sam come in with the coffee. 'Thanks, Sam.'

Sam took the coffee to Bahr then handed Pulst the third mug as he came in.

'That's all lights except deck and fantail, sir.'

'Good.'

Sam was waiting in the doorway.

'What is it, Sam?'

Sam hesitated. 'We dock Hong Kong all right, sir?' he said, finally.

'Sure. Sure, we'll dock Hong Kong all right, Sam,' Schepke told him then turned back to the open window, looking toward the south. Everywhere it was dark and only the rain falling gloomily through the pale glow of shipboard lights.

He looked at his wrist watch again then went to the charthouse and took his storm-coat from the door before finding the Lloyd's Register of Shipping.

'Lights showing three points abaft the port bow!'

Bahr's shout brought him hurriedly to the bridge. The ship was still some way distant, her lights showing thinly through the falling rain.

'Keep her as she is.' He told them as he threw the hatch open to the flying bridge.

She had already begun her message, the Aldis beam brightly probing the darkness.

—*requests immediate recognition.*

Swinging the port searchlight around, he rapidly hammered

the lever, the steel shutters clattering noisily and the reflected beam brilliantly lighting the ocean.

United States Transport Canoga Park *outward bound from Okinawa to Hong Kong.*

He waited, the rain streaming from his storm-coat and the high peak of his cap. There was no immediate reply and while he waited the *Gertrud Lüth* drew rapidly ahead.

Then shortly afterward the Aldis came on again.

Request Canoga Park *stop immediately.*

He waited a moment, seeing her lights swing as she came about. 'Pulst!' he yelled through the open hatchway. 'Tell Altmeyer send: *United States Transport* Canoga Park *intercepted on high seas by unidentified gunboat!* Give our position!' Then swinging the searchlight astern, he began a repeat of his previous signal as the gunboat gathered way ahead. Part of the way through a vivid flash showed astern and an orange star shell exploded high overhead of the bridge.

Grabbing the rail, he swung himself in through the hatchway. Pulst still had the telephone.

'—Altmeyer! Send: Canoga Park *under fire!*' Thrusting the receiver at Pulst he hurried out to the port wing. Dropping the window down, he saw the lights of the gunboat off the port quarter. Then the star shell went out suddenly and everything was darkness again.

'Pulst! Tell Altmeyer: *Request immediate assistance!* Canoga Park *under heavy fire from Communist gunboat!*'

The gunboat was still gaining on them, her course about seven or eight hundred metres abeam. She was still gaining on them when suddenly she slackened speed and began to drop astern. Immediately he put the glasses back on her. The superstructure was lost in the darkness and only her steaming lights showed through the rain.

'Pulst! Watch her until I come back!'

Altmeyer was still busy with the key when he went below.

'What's happening?'

'I think they ordered her to break off! The air's jammed! Every ship and shore station within a thousand kilometres must be on the air!'

'All right! Make nothing further unless I tell you!'

'She's just about lost, sir!' Pulst shouted as Schepke entered from below.

Schepke looked at his wrist watch. In little over an hour it would begin to get light. Then glancing at the compass, he crossed to the wing and took the glasses from Pulst. The lights were far astern now and he watched them until they were finally lost, and then there was only the darkness and rain and the sound of the vast ocean. With daylight would come the fog. He could smell it now in the night.

Running the window up, he crossed to the telephones.

'Engine-room! Frauenheim speaking!'

'Is Hechler there?'

'He's just left for topside.'

'I think we're through,' Schepke told him. 'You can cut the dynamos now. We don't want to risk anything picking us up again. Tell Dorsch next stop Hong Kong!' He replaced the receiver and dropped the nearest window down. Outside everything was wet and dark and smelling of the coming fog.

'Karl.'

He turned to see Hechler come in just as the lights flickered briefly and went out.

'We're through,' he told him.

'Good. I was beginning to wonder if we would ever make it.' Hechler removed his cap and wiped the sweat from his face and forehead with the sleeve of his overalls.

'Captain! Captain, sir!' Sam shouted from below. 'Girl very sick!'

Hechler followed them aft to the cabin.

The girl was unconscious, her face contorting with pain as spasms of cramp gripped her body. Schepke looked up from the bunk to Hechler.

'I think now it is cholera,' he heard the old man say.

Hechler nodded but did not say anything.

Schepke stood quietly by the bunk looking down at the girl. 'Maybe I should have known,' he said. 'There was something wrong that time at Chingkiang when you came on board. I should have remembered Pao and the ambulances.'

'It is not for you to condemn yourself,' the old man said. 'It was I who should have known. Only it did not begin as I have seen it before. With the usual symptoms it generally occurs within the fifth day of infection.'

'We might be wrong,' Schepke suggested, but without hope.

Again Hechler looked at him briefly. Then the old man sat by the bunk and smoothed the hair back from his daughter's forehead.

'There's some cramp mixture below,' Hechler said. 'I'll get Frauenheim to send it up.'

'Sam,' Schepke said turning away from the bunk. 'You better stay here now that you've been with them. Kuang will have to do what he can himself. If you want to sleep you better take Müller's cabin. You'll probably be all right but it's better to keep away from the food.'

'There is nothing we can do?' Sam asked.

Schepke looked at the girl again, her face looking white and pinched as though having come in from the cold. 'Apart from the cramp mixture we can only keep her warm. She's at the stage of collapse. It could last anywhere between two and twenty-four hours.' He paused, looking at his wrist watch. 'I'll have to go back to the bridge now,' he said to the old man. 'Hechler will be here with the medicine soon.'

The girl was moaning again, her face contorting with the sudden fierceness of the cramp. She was very deeply unconscious, and it was very probable that she would die. He suddenly did not wish to be present when she died.

Then Hechler came in with the large bottle of cramp mixture from the firemen's locker.

'Give it to the old man,' Schepke told him, and went out, and Hechler followed him out into the passage after giving the old man the instructions for the medicine.

'What do you think?'

'I wouldn't like to say,' Hechler told him.

'They can come out of it,' Schepke said.

'She's very ill.'

'Kuang!' Schepke called toward the gloomily lighted doorway of the galley.

'Yes, sir?' Kuang said stepping out into the passage.

'Put some coffee in the cabin. Make it sweet and hot. Then give Sam hot water to change the bottles.'

'Yes, sir,' the boy said.

Schepke glanced up at the bridge and saw the pale patch of greyness showing outside of the rain-washed windows.

'I better get back. I want to be away from the coast before it gets too light.' He left Hechler outside the cabin and went forward to the Radio Office. Altmeyer was still at the bench.

'Anything new?'

'The Straits are busy. There's a lot of ship to shore stuff on intermediate.'

'What about up ahead?'

'There's some stuff to the south-west. Nothing else.'

'All right. You can close down. Go and get some sleep. I might want you to take a watch later.'

When he came out from the office he looked back along the darkness of the passage to the cabin, then turned and hurried overhead to the bridge. He did not want to think about any of it now.

THE rain had continued all day but now with the coming of darkness it had turned to a fine, thinly falling rain that hung in the fog swirling damply in across the high blunt bows as the ship lifted in the long swell rolling in out of the vast China Sea toward the mainland. Karl Schepke stood alone on the bridge, the windows forward of the wheel dropped down and the fine, thinly falling rain coming in through the window spaces as it eddied in the breeze across the flying bridge from astern. Then he looked at his wrist watch and saw it had stopped at a little after one o'clock. Easing the wheel to starboard, he shivered in the raw night air, then drew the high collar of the storm-coat closer around his neck.

Some time later he heard someone on the stairway and turned to see Altmeyer. Outside the rain ran suddenly from the forward scuppers of the flying bridge as the *Gertrud Lüth* slid her bows into the swell.

'We're still making top speed,' Altmeyer said, speaking very quietly as though afraid to raise his voice against the quietness of the night.

'She'll never do it again,' Schepke told him. 'Everything's gone inside of her now. You can feel it.'

Altmeyer shivered in the rain and fog eddying in through the window spaces, and it was very quiet and only the sound of the ocean and the rain running in the scuppers disturbed the night.

'What time do you expect us to make Hong Kong?'

'Somewhere about mid-morning,' Schepke said probing the darkness ahead. 'Maybe a little after.'

Again it was quiet and even now the rain had not washed clean the smell of death that hung over the ship.

'Is there any change in the girl yet?' Altmeyer asked, after a time.

Schepke moved his head, his eyes lost in the deep shadow of his high peaked cap.

'I'll take the wheel for a while,' the boy offered.

'What time do you make it?'

'Just after four o'clock.'

'You better wake Bahr first. He's in the charthouse.'

After a few moments Altmeyer came out onto the bridge with Bahr pulling on his storm-coat.

'I'm going below now,' Schepke told him. 'Hold her as she is and keep a sharp watch ahead. We're steaming close to the lane.'

The old man had dozed and now he woke suddenly as Schepke

393

came in. The girl was still unconscious, her strength seeming almost to have gone.

'I do not think she will suffer much longer.' Her father spoke very quietly, sadly.

'I think you should try and rest a little,' Schepke told him. 'I can stay a while.'

The old man looked up at him, avoiding his eyes. 'Maybe I should remain with her now,' he said very simply.

Schepke looked at the girl again, the tightness in his throat and chest almost choking him, and he knew he did not truly wish to be present when it came. There was already enough to remember and he did not wish to remember her always when it came.

He put his hand silently on the old man's shoulder, feeling the frailty of him through the thin black coat. Then as he turned to the doorway the sudden, lifting, booming explosion threw them to the deck, showering them with loose fittings and drawers scattered from the dressing-table.

He lay momentarily stunned, then scrambling dazedly to his feet, threw himself out into the passage. The *Gertrud Lüth* was wallowing in the long lifting swell, all way completely off her but the engines still turning. The wall of flame had already lit the bridge bright as day, and when he reached the forward windows he saw the whole deck forward of the mast alive with flame and heavy black smoke. Then scrambling across Bahr, he reached the engine-room receiver as it swung from its hook.

'Hechler! Bridge here!' he yelled into the mouthpiece.

'—What the hell's happening?' Hechler was yelling, his voice almost lost amid all the noise and confusion.

'The foretank's blown! Number One's forward bulkhead's gone with it! The whole deck forward's on fire!'

'We're taking water fast down here!' Hechler yelled.

'I'm going below!' Schepke dropped the receiver and went out and down into the forward well, the terrific heat meeting him as soon as he made the open deck. Solid black smoke was funnelling high across the bows above the flames, the breeze carrying it out ahead. Shielding his face with his arms he found the starboard bulwarks abreast of Number Two hold, and leaning outboard, saw a whole mass of buckled plates and girders hanging free above the waterline, blazing latex streaming into the ocean and burning on the water.

'What happened?' Hechler shouted as he followed Dorsch out from the alleyway.

'I think we took a couple of shells forward when we passed Kiang Yin! The wool cargo must have smouldered!'

'What are we going to do?'

'The wind's astern!' Schepke shouted above the noise of the fire. 'What water are we making?'

'There's still three watertight bulkheads between here and the boiler room!' Hechler told him. 'Maybe we can hold it yet!'

'What about that deck-cargo!' Dorsch shouted. 'Is it safe?'

'Get a fire-axe from the alleyway!' Schepke told him, and immediately started ripping the tarpaulin from the cases stacked aft of Number Two hold.

Dorsch splintered the first two cases and Schepke and Hechler tore the packing aside.

'It's some sort of complicated motor system!' Hechler shouted as he peered at the carefully packed and oiled machinery.

'We'll chance there's nothing that can blow!' Schepke told them. 'See what water we're taking before we do anything else!'

Dorsch started aft at a run as Schepke and Hechler went back to the bulwarks.

'Most of it seems above the waterline!' Hechler shouted.

Schepke turned at the sudden loud commotion and burst of shouting overhead on the boatdeck. The forward lifeboat was already moving in its davits. Running aft, pulling the heavy Walther from his pocket, he fired twice, the second shot ricocheting wildly off the forward davit, sending the Chinese flat on the deck, the lifeboat swinging suddenly free in its falls and pitching bow down into the ocean.

He went on aft to the well and hauled himself up the vertical ladder to the boatdeck.

'On your feet!' he screamed. 'Come on! Up! On your feet!' He grabbed the first Chinese and hurled him toward the ladder.

'Man those pumps! Come on! On your feet!' He swung the heavy Walther on the others and sent them scrambling for the ladders. Then waiting, he watched them man the pumps again. 'I shoot the first man to leave those pumps!' he shouted below, the Walther levelled through the rails.

'Boatdeck!'

Looking to port, he saw Hechler by the bulwarks.

'Keep her going!' Hechler shouted through his cupped hands. 'We'll do all we can to keep the water down!'

'All right! Start her up! Make what you can!' He turned and hurried forward and met Altmeyer by the galley.

'Here!' he thrust the heavy Walther into the boy's hand. 'Stay on the boatdeck. If anybody leaves those pumps put a bullet in him!'

'What about the fire?' Altmeyer called after him. 'Don't you want me to call Hong Kong?'

'I'll tell you when,' Schepke told him, then stopped, meeting Sam and the old man outside the cabin. 'Sam! Get a stretcher for the girl. Keep her in the cabin until I tell you.'

Bahr was at the wheel with Pulst when he entered.

'Put her back on course,' he told them.

'I can't see anything ahead,' Bahr shouted.

'Just keep her on course. Anything ahead will see us fifty kilometres away!'

All the windows had gone with the explosion and the air was filled with the acrid fumes of blazing latex and wool, the terrific heat reflecting off the rear of the bridge.

'You! Pulst! Go aft and clear away those floats on the fantail. On the way back see the girl is properly buckled into a stretcher.'

'What about the other lifeboats?'

'Just do what I told you, Bahr! How's she answering?'

'The helm's all right but she's dead underneath.'

'All right,' Schepke said standing close to him. 'Now listen! If we abandon ship you stay with me. I want to make sure the girl and her father get clear. Number Three lifeboat's gone as well now and the other two won't float for long. So if we go, try for one of the floats or take something over the wall with you. This is shark water!'

The *Gertrud Lüth* was now sitting her bow low in the water, blazing latex clinging to her hull and trailing in her wake, the smoke and flames from her forward deck carrying out ahead of her in the raw breeze.

'Starboard five!'

'Starboard five! Five starboard wheel on, sir!'

'We'll go further in toward the shore,' Schepke shouted to him. 'If she gives us time when she goes we might be able to put her ashore somewhere.'

Now the *Gertrud Lüth* leaned wearily over as even those few points of wheel edged her slowly around toward the hidden shore. Already she was far down by the head and developing a list to port, and edging slowly around to starboard she loomed wearily through the fire-reddened fog, the fine, thinly falling rain hanging in the breeze above her ghostly white wake.

JUST before noon the fog began to ease.

'What are we making?' Schepke called from the starboard wing.

'Just on five knots,' Pulst answered, sweat streaming down his face and neck with the terrific heat reflected by the fire.

'I wish to hell this fog would clear,' Schepke cursed as he made his way across the angled deck to the bridge doorway. 'Altmeyer!' he called below to the passage. '—Altmeyer!'

Altmeyer appeared in the passage at a run, still carrying the heavy Walther.

'Go on up to the flying bridge,' Schepke said taking the gun from him. 'Keep watch for Tathong Light. Keep a watch for anything.'

He waited a few moments then went to the hatchway. 'See anything?'

'There's a fog bank between us and the shore,' Altmeyer called down to him.

'You should see something soon. I'll take her further inshore. —Starboard five!' he called to Pulst.

'Starboard five! Five—' The tremendous crash and shower of burning debris blasted into the bridge, the whole ship reeling under the impact.

'The foremast's down!' Pulst shouted, rising to his feet as Bahr grabbed the wheel.

'Altmeyer!' Schepke shouted.

Altmeyer's white face peered in through the open hatchway. '—I just saw it in time,' he said. 'It hit the port wing before going over the side.

'Telephone!' Bahr shouted.

Schepke grabbed the receiver where the button glowed. 'Bridge!'

'Hechler here!' the voice the other end shouted. 'The water's just taken the fires of One and Four boilers.'

'How long do you give us?'

'It depends on the forward bulkheads. There's only those empty drums keeping her head up now.'

'What about the water?'

'The list has taken it clear of Three and Six boilers. I'll give Two and Five another hour at the most. —That's as long as the bulkheads hold! At the moment we're knee-deep in sludge!'

'I'll call you back!' Schepke told him. 'We shouldn't be far off now.' He slammed the receiver back on the hook. ''Midships!' he called to Bahr. '—Meet her!' He started up the ladder to the flying bridge.

'Steady on two-seven-three!' Bahr shouted.

'Steer two-seven-five!' Schepke called after him.

'There! Look!' Altmeyer shouted. 'There's three hills showing!'

Schepke put the glasses on the mist- and fog-shrouded hills

on the starboard bow. 'They're just beyond Tolo Channel,' he told the boy. 'That one nearest inshore is Mount Hallowes. Sharp Peak to seaward, and Tai Mun Shan a little beyond.'

'Do you want me to call Hong Kong now?'

'Wait until we sight Tathong. If they know too soon they might order us to stay outside just in case we go down in the channel.'

'You could still put her ashore in Tolo or the Port Shelter,' Altmeyer offered.

'We're going inside,' Schepke told him. 'We're going in even if I have to hold her guts together with bare hands.'

Altmeyer turned toward the hills as Schepke looked anxiously below at the foredeck. Everything forward of Number Two hold was a mass of flame and acrid black smoke, the flame roaring from the mouth of the tunnel like a massive blow-torch. Then he looked with Altmeyer at the distant hills.

'Let me know when you sight Tathong Light,' he said and swung himself in through the hatchway.

'Engine-room!' Hechler sounded as though he had been waiting.

'We're just off Tolo,' Schepke told him. 'Once we make the harbour get everybody on deck. I'm going to try and put her ashore on Stonecutters. I don't want anybody below when we hit the beach. Those bulkheads are going to come down.' He slammed the receiver onto its hook without waiting. '—Pulst! See if that port ladder's safe. Bahr! You stay on the wheel from now on.'

The three hills were spaced out evenly abeam now.

'Steer two-eight-five!' he called from the starboard wing.

'Steer two-eight-five, sir!' Bahr answered, again edging the bows to starboard as Schepke brought them around Tai Long Wan and started the run in toward the Nine Pin Group and Tathong Light.

'Making out Tathong Light now, sir!' Altmeyer shouted below.

'Good. Stand by the Aldis.'

Out ahead of them the raw breeze was carrying the acrid

black smoke low across the grey ocean in a thickly swirling cloud that hung in the thinly falling rain.

Now the *Gertrud Lüth* was close in on the Nine Pin Group, the islands bunched tightly to starboard.

'Steer two-nine-five!'

'Steer two-nine-five, sir!'

'The port side ladder will hold all right,' Pulst shouted as he came in from below.

'Get Sam to help you take the girl and her father below to the alleyway. There'll probably be a boat coming out.' Then he turned to Bahr again. 'I'll be on the flying bridge now. Listen for the orders.'

Altmeyer had the Aldis sighted on Tathong Light, the long, lifting swell of the grey ocean breaking sharply white on the rocks below Whitewash Corner.

'Starboard five!' Schepke shouted below, the ship now beginning the long starboard turn into Tathong Channel. 'All right, Altmeyer. Make: S.S. Gertrud Lüth *badly damaged. Require immediate medical assistance.*'

They came slowly around Tung Lung Island, the raw breeze carrying the acrid black smoke across Big Wave Bay, Cape Collinson now easing to port as they entered the channel.

'Tathong Light acknowledging, sir,' Altmeyer reported.

"Midships!' Schepke shouted below.

One of the salt-encrusted telephones in under the forward screen suddenly buzzed and Altmeyer answered. '—Engine-room, sir!' he said.

Schepke grabbed the receiver from him. 'Schepke here!'

'We've just lost the fires of Three and Five boilers,' Hechler told him. 'Water's increasing rapidly now.'

Schepke looked ahead at the wide mouth of Junk Bay on the starboard side, then changed his mind. 'We're in the Pass,' he said. 'Get everybody you're not using up on deck.' He thrust the receiver at Altmeyer and turned to the hatchway. 'Port five!'

The bows eased sluggishly around into Lei U Mun Pass as

the *Gertrud Lüth* slowly answered the helm. Sai Wan was astern now, and Devil's Peak directly abeam on the starboard side as they entered the Pass, watched by a crowd of villagers at Sam Ka Tsuen.

'Midships!'

As they came out into the harbour he saw the fire-float *Alexander Grantham* turning abreast of Channel Rock as she prepared to meet them.

'Tathong Light didn't waste much time,' Altmeyer shouted.

'Tell her: *Latex explosion forepeak tank*!' Then: 'Port five!' he called into the bridge.

A great deal of smoke was carrying astern with the alteration of course, and now the heavily listing ship began the long run in past Shaukiwan, and Sai Wan Ho, and past Taikoo Dock and Quarry Bay, the *Alexander Grantham* keeping close on the starboard side, her hoses pumping a steady stream of foam into the blazing foredeck.

'Boat showing port side!' Altmeyer shouted.

Schepke glanced outboard and saw the long white launch heeling far over as she raced around in a tight turn to come in astern on the port ladder.

'Midships!'

They were around North Point, Whampoa Dock astern on the starboard quarter, and out ahead Victoria City was barely showing through the smoke and flame.

'Tsim Sha Tsui asking what we're doing, sir!' Altmeyer shouted from the wing.

'Tell them I'm putting her ashore on Stonecutters!' Schepke shouted, then grabbed the engine-room telephone as it started buzzing.

'Two and Five fires just gone!' Hechler yelled. 'All pumps stopped! Water gaining fast!'

'All right! Get everybody out!' Schepke slammed the receiver down. 'Starboard five!' he called into the bridge.

The *Gertrud Lüth* cut close in on Tsim Sha Tsui as Schepke swung her into the Northern Fairway. Ahead of him he could see nothing but flame and smoke. Then he grabbed the siren lanyard, the great dull-throated blast of noise and steam crashing out across the docks and harbour.

"Midships!'

'The boat's on its way inshore, sir.'

Schepke glanced to port and saw the long white launch with her bow raised clear of the water as she raced full out for Victoria, her cockpit crammed with people and the stretcher showing in her stern.

They were in the Northern Fairway, now, the *Alexander Grantham* still with them, foam pumping into the blaze.

Then again the engine-room telephone buzzed.

'All fires gone!' Hechler yelled. 'Everything shut down! She's beginning to go now!'

'Throw her Full Ahead and get out!' Schepke shouted, and when he turned he saw Menzies come out through the hatchway.

'You better get aft,' he told him, 'she's going fast.'

'What about you? You're almost on your own,' Menzies shouted as he pointed astern.

Schepke turned and saw the crew going in over the starboard wall, making the long drop into the grey harbour, the floats still high on the fantail.

'The girl's on her way. We had a doctor with us.'

Schepke nodded and someone on board the *Alexander Grantham* shouted something through a loud hailer and suddenly she began dropping rapidly astern.

The *Gertrud Lüth* hit Stonecutters beach long and smoothly, followed swiftly by a tremendous explosion that lifted her foredeck high in the water then turned her on her port side, settling her quickly with two further explosions deep inside.

Schepke was first on his feet. 'Bahr!'

Bahr was already on the ladder and he grabbed him out onto the flying bridge. The whole ship forward was hugely on fire, smoke and flame swirling around the bridge.

'The boatdeck!' Schepke shouted. 'Hurry!'

They went over the rear of the flying bridge, dropping quickly to the steeply angled boatdeck, the after decks awash and the starboard wall now high out of the water.

Clinging to the rails, Schepke glanced below to the after well and saw Hechler and Dorsch mount the fantail. Frauenheim some way ahead of them. For a brief moment they saw each other then Hechler raised his arm and went in over the stern behind the others, hitting the water solidly.

'See her?' Schepke shouted to the others.

Looking outboard, they saw the *Alexander Grantham* lying off the starboard quarter, her crew lining the deck and pulling swimmers from the water.

'Go on!'

Altmeyer went over first, quickly followed by Bahr.

Menzies looked at Schepke, then at the water, then went quickly out over the wall.

Schepke took one last look around the ship, glanced below, then leapt out away from the rails.

THE launch drove in fast toward the Vehicular Ferry Pier on Connaught Road Central.

'There's a car waiting,' Menzies shouted as he peered ahead through the spray-lashed windscreen.

Karl Schepke stared silently out at the city. All the city showed grey and bleak in the thinly falling rain, and beyond, shadowed by the dark and towering Peak.

'I don't understand why you didn't radio,' Menzies said.

'They might have ordered us to stay outside,' Schepke told him, his mind on the girl now.

Menzies turned and looked astern at the blazing hulk of the *Gertrud Lüth*, the smoke hanging in a giant black pall above the western end of the harbour.

'The old man told us it was cholera,' he said.

'How was she?'

'Unconscious,' Menzies said, avoiding his eyes. 'They were taking her to the Peak.'

The roar of the engine cut suddenly and slowed as the launch swept in toward the pier.

'I can get you a change of clothes.'

Schepke looked at the waiting police car. 'I thought maybe I would go right up,' he said.

Menzies nodded. 'Yes. They'll take care of you there.'

They crossed the pier to the waiting car and Menzies spoke to the driver then climbed in beside Schepke. 'I'll go with you,' he said.

The car started along the front then turned on to Pottinger Street, then through Chung Wan on Hollywood Road to Glenealy, and then onto Peak Road. They drove rapidly up the winding road above the city to the Peak, the sky beginning to darken now with the coming of night and the lights of the city coming on below in a long straggling mass.

'It's going to be a long night,' Menzies said.

Karl Schepke sat and looked out of the window and did not say anything.

'They'll do all they can.'

Schepke looked at him. 'I'm sure they will,' he said.

The hospital was close to the summit, on the right of the winding roadway, the north wall dropping far below to the foundations.

The car stopped in the wide courtyard and Schepke climbed out into the thinly falling rain.

'I hope everything will be all right.'

'Thank you,' he said into the car.

'I'll be at Wanchai if you want me.'

He watched the car's headlights sweep around the wide courtyard in the growing darkness as it swung onto the roadway.

Inside in the hallway there was a young woman at a desk.

'I came about the girl from the ship,' he told her.

'One moment, please,' she said, and called and spoke into one of the telephones behind the glass screen.

After a few minutes a white-coated English doctor arrived.

'I'm from the *Gertrud Lüth*. Kapitän Schepke,' Schepke told him.

'Of course,' the English doctor said. 'Will you please come this way, Captain.'

His office was near the end of the long hallway, the long window overlooking Wanchai and the high hills beyond Lei U Mun Pass. It was almost dark now and everywhere below were the lights of the city in the thinly falling rain.

'The fog seems to have cleared now,' the doctor said as he drew the curtains on the darkness.

'She is going to be well?' Schepke asked him in English.

The doctor sat into his chair, looking at him across the desk. 'I'm afraid it is really too soon to give an opinion, Captain. She is extremely ill. Fortunately the stage of collapse had passed its crisis before she arrived. We must wait for the reaction to set in now.'

'That's all we can do, wait?'

'At the moment she is undergoing the very latest treatment,' the doctor told him. 'I assure you that it has already been tried highly successful. The treatment consists of frequent oral administrations of a solution of salt, glucose, streptomycin potassium and soda bicarbonate. That may not seem significant to you, but I like to think we have every hope.'

'When will it be possible to know?'

'Tomorrow. Sometime tomorrow,' the doctor told him.

'And it will be possible for me to wait?'

'Yes, you must. We will want to see everyone from the ship for precautionary measures.' He rose from the desk now. 'Perhaps we should find you a change of clothing,' he said. 'If you will come with me I will show you to a room. You can have the one next to the girl's father.'

Karl Schepke followed him out into the hallway. The air in the long hallway was close and heavy with the clinical smells of hospital.

'Her father believes that she contracted the disease in Chingkiang,' the doctor said as they walked.

'There was something wrong ashore when they came on board,' Schepke told him. 'I just wondered why it didn't show itself before it did.'

'I'm afraid these things do not always go exactly by the book. If they did then I should have a far easier time.' They stopped outside one of the rooms and the doctor opened the door. 'If you will change from those wet clothes. I will have someone attend to them,' he said. 'There is a shower through at the back and I think you will find a dressing-gown in the closet.'

'Thank you.'

'I will let you know just as soon as there is any news.'

Karl Schepke watched him close the door, then went to the window. Far below the *Gertrud Lüth* was blazing fiercely, lighting the darkness above the harbour and casting an eerie red glow far across the low cloud.

When he came out from the shower his clothing had gone. Crossing to the window he looked once more below at the harbour, then drew the curtains. Just then there was a light knock on the door and a nurse came in carrying a napkin-covered tray.

'I thought you might care for supper,' she said. She was an English nurse and she set the tray carefully onto the bedside table.

'I don't suppose there is any news yet,' he said.

She smiled softly. 'I'm afraid not,' she told him. 'The doctors are doing everything they can.'

'I know. Thank you.'

'Is there anything else I can do?'

'If it is possible to have some cigarettes,' he told her.

'Of course.'

'There's some money there on the table. I'm afraid it's wet.'

She smiled. 'We saw you come into the harbour,' she said. 'It was very spectacular.'

He was finished eating when she returned with the cigarettes.

'Thank you,' he said.

She covered the tray again with the napkin and opened the door.

'Which room is the old man in?'

She stopped in the doorway. 'Next door,' she told him. 'On the right.'

He closed the door after her and lit a cigarette. He was thinking now about the old man and he went out into the corridor and knocked lightly on the door. It was dark inside the room and the curtains were open on the window and on the doors opening to the veranda.

'It is you, Captain,' the old man said turning away from the doors.

'It's getting late,' Schepke told him.

'Yes.' The old man's voice was very quiet in the near-darkness.

Schepke joined him by the glass doors. 'It's stopped raining now,' he said, looking below him to the lighted city.

The old man opened the doors and they went outside to the veranda. Below them on the steep slope were the gardens of the hospital and the dark trees and bushes, and it was very mild after the rain and everything smelled of the rain and the wet earth and the night scent of the bushes and flowers, and there were cicadas out after the rain and fireflies flitting around the tall trees on the slope.

'The ship is still burning,' the old man said very quietly.

'She might burn for weeks,' Schepke said.

'She did much for us.'

'She had little luck,' Schepke said. 'The luck left her a long time ago.' He arced the cigarette over the veranda and watched it go out in the darkness of the garden. It was very mild after the rain and the clouds were moving swiftly across the Peak to the south. The clouds were very low and sometimes they came down over the Peak and the darkness of the summit was lost in them. Below in the garden, some way to the left, was a smaller building and a number of the lighted windows opened to the garden.

'It is very quiet and beautiful up here in the night,' the old man said, then started to say something more but stopped, listening.

Somewhere in the building to the left there was the quiet sound of music and it carrying softly across the darkness of the garden. Schepke listened with him, hearing the strangely haunting tune.

'Many years ago Fu-chen used to play and sing that same music,' the old man said. 'It brings back memories of many years ago.'

'It's very beautiful,' Schepke said.

'It is Japanese,' the old man said. 'It is called *Moon on the Ruined Castle*.'

'You should try and rest a little,' Schepke told him. 'I'll stay here.'

The old man looked at him in the darkness. 'Perhaps you are right,' he said.

'I'll wake you if there's anything.'

'I will rest only for a little while.'

Karl Schepke remained on the veranda, the hulk of the *Gertrud Lüth* lighting the whole sky to the west, the eerie light of the fire reflecting on the underside of the low clouds.

Then after a time he went inside and saw the old man was asleep. Taking a chair to the doorway of the veranda, he lit a cigarette and watched the clouds pass in the sky. The breeze was high up and the clouds were moving swiftly away to the south, and it was very mild now and the night smelled clean and fresh, and the strangely haunting music still carried softly across the garden. The music was on record and across in the nurses' or doctors' quarters someone was playing it over and over again. It was a very haunting piece of music and he hoped that whoever was playing it would soon go to bed. He was tired now and he had the feeling as though it had always been night, and he did not know whether she would die or not. He did not want her to die. And suddenly the night was empty even with the music carrying across the darkened garden.

The cloud was going to clear. Already the low cloud had gone and the faint flickering of lightning was playing amongst the towering columns of cloud high in the sky above the New Territories. The sky was clearing very rapidly with the breeze and he could see patches of clear darkness and stars showing and the towering clouds now lit by the hidden moon. Below him the city was very quiet and the ferries now running at longer intervals. The ferries moved very slowly across the dark waters of the harbour, their fire-dragon wakes standing out in long phosphorescent tails. He did not look again at the *Gertrud Lüth* but went inside and sat in the chair. The night was very empty and lonely and he did not want to think about anything now.

WHEN he woke the sky had cleared and the moon was away somewhere far to the south beyond the island, and now the sky was beginning to grey a little in the east. He rose and went out to the veranda and below him in the garden the tall trees and bushes were taking shape in the first false light of the morning, their fronds and leaves shiny with wetness. It would be a fine morning and the city was quiet and the harbour was quiet and the air smelled clean and fresh and of the wet earth and the faint early smokiness that comes in a city, and everything was very quiet, and nothing moved.

The old man was awake, watching him.

'It will be light soon,' Schepke told him.

The old man turned his head toward the doorway.

'There's been nothing yet,' Schepke said, and went out to the veranda again while the old man rose. There was a certain coolness with the early morning and far out beyond High Junk Peak the sky was beginning to redden faintly with the rising of the sun. Then he heard someone come into the room and saw the English nurse from the previous evening. With her she carried a tray with coffee and had his clothes folded across her arm.

'I brought your clothes with me,' she told him.

'Thank you.'

'The doctor may be here shortly,' she said. 'I hope that everything will be well.'

The old man sat silently on the bed and looked at the coffee. Karl Schepke dressed quickly and as he pulled on his tunic there was a knock on the door and the tall English doctor came in and looked at him, then at the old man.

'I thought you would like to know as soon as possible,' he said still looking at the old man. 'Your daughter has improved during the night. She is awake now.'

The old man sat back onto the bed. '—Thank you,' he said, the words coming with great difficulty.

'Is it possible to see her?' Schepke asked.

The doctor looked at him, hesitating. 'Well, perhaps so,' he said, finally. 'But it can be only for a moment you understand.'

Schepke looked to the old man.

'No. You go ahead, my son,' he said, smiling faintly. 'I must have a few moments.'

Karl Schepke followed the doctor out along the corridor. There were closed doors all along the corridor and the doctor stopped outside one of them and turned to him. 'Remember. Only for a moment.'

'Are you sure she is going to be all right?'

The doctor nodded. 'I would not have told you so otherwise,' he said. 'Only we must be very careful that such complications as pneumonia, pleurisy, or nephritis do not occur.'

'Is that possible?'

'Anything is possible. But unlikely with the proper care.'

She looked up at him when he went in. She was very pale and tired-looking, but with still a certain loveliness about her. He did not think that he had ever seen anyone before so beautiful.

'I came to see you,' he said standing close to the bed. 'Your father is here as well.'

She smiled up to him, smiling with her mouth and her eyes, and he felt very large and awkward.

410

'You're going to be fine,' he said. 'The doctor told me.'

She went on looking at him.

'We're in Hong Kong,' he said, not knowing really what to say and embarrassed by it all.

'Thank you,' she said very softly, finding his hand, lightly touching his fingers. Standing very close to the bed, he took her hand in his.

'Look,' she said. 'Outside it is a new day.'

He looked with her at the windows and the scarlet rays of the rising sun had filled the whole sky in the east.

'Yesterday I would have said they were all new days, once,' he said.

Her fingers moved very smally in his hand.

'I—' he said; then waited and said, 'I thought—'

'Yes?' she said, her fingers moving very smally in his hand.

He hesitated. Then: 'I love you,' he said.

'You would say something more?' she said very softly.

'Perhaps you would not have me ask,' he said.

Again he felt her hand move inside of his.

'Once I could have chosen a man who was a poet,' she said. 'Now I choose a man whose heart is too full to speak.'

He bent and very lightly touched his mouth to her cheek.

And outside the sun was rising.